BECOMING BOONE

ANDY LAPLANTE

For All The Cats
Wild and Domestic
Past—Present—Future

1

LARGER THAN LIFE

Nathan Boone gripped the door handle of Eve Hart's ancient Volkswagen Caravan as they barreled south down Interstate 91, leaving Strafford, Vermont—the only place he'd ever called home, a place he didn't think he'd ever see again.

He didn't want to leave. He wanted to be locked in his room, tucked under the eaves, with nowhere to be and nothing to worry about. It was the only place that could offer the kind of quiet escape that pushed away the outside world.

He'd only been gone an hour and a half, and he was already homesick. He closed his eyes, and imagined himself back there. On nights like this, when the weather was particularly angry, he'd be locked in his room, with his laptop resting warmly against his legs as he typed furiously. The words would flow out of him, just like they always did.

There, he didn't have to hide. He didn't have to brace himself for the next awful thing waiting around the corner to come and turn his world upside down.

There—he could just be.

Even before they backed out of Eve's driveway, he'd been sure of one thing—moving to college was the worst decision of his life.

Now, as they rattled down the highway in a VW deathtrap, with four bald tires, toward a future he never really wanted, he knew there was no going back.

Frozen rain hammered the windshield in sharp bursts, causing the worn wipers to screech uselessly across the glass. Then, as if the storm itself had a hand on the wheel, a gust of wind slammed into them, making them fishtail wildly before finding traction again.

"Jesus, Eve! Can you please just slow down a little?" he pleaded, his voice cracking mid-sentence. "It feels like we're sliding all over the place!"

She barely reacted. She just blew out a lazy stream of smoke and flicked the ash from her joint out the cracked window.

"Relax, dude," she replied, "I've driven in way worse. I'm a New England girl, remember? I'm made for this shit."

Then, as if offering a peace treaty, she held what was left of her roach toward him.

"Here, take a hit. It might help."

He shook his head, refusing the offer. "No, thanks. You know that stuff just makes me paranoid."

"Suit yourself," she replied with a shrug, before tossing what was left out into the cold air, then rolling up her window, cutting off the freezing wind with a final rush.

Just as she settled back in her seat and adjusted the van's heat, they hit a deep puddle of slush, dragging them dangerously close to the snowbank lining the highway.

He slammed his hands against the dashboard, bracing himself as Eve fought to regain control.

"Are you sure your van can handle this?" he snapped. "It sounds like it's about to fall apart."

He let out a short laugh, shaking her head like he was being dramatic.

"Yeah, don't worry. We're fine, I promise." She patted the dashboard like it was a beloved pet. "This old girl's as tough as they come. She might be stubborn, moody, and a bit loud, but she hasn't let me down—not once."

He shot her a desperate look, silently begging her to take him seriously.

But she was lost in her own world—humming along to the radio and drumming her fingers on the wheel like they weren't hurtling down an icy highway in a rusted-out deathtrap held together by peeling paint and a patchwork of bumper stickers preaching peace, love, and the kind of existential wisdom that only made sense at 2 a.m. after one too many bong hits.

What Nathan felt wasn't new.

Fear had lived inside him for as long as he could remember. He had practically grown up in doctors' offices, bathed in sterile white light, surrounded by the hum of monitors and the hushed murmur of concern.

His mother had always assured him that nothing was wrong. That he was fine. But he knew better. He knew that one day, they'd find out the truth. One day, he wouldn't be fine.

He'd met Eve during one of his endless hospital visits when they were both eight years old. He'd watched from across the room as she was wheeled in post-op, and groggy from anesthesia. For a moment, he was convinced that whatever she had was contagious, and he'd be next in line for surgery.

It wasn't—she was only there for a routine appendectomy.

Nothing serious. Not like his problems.

By the next morning, she was already cracking jokes with the nurses, like she hadn't just had surgery. Nathan watched from across the room, quietly stunned by how fast she had bounced back, like being sliced open and having doctors root around in her guts was no big deal at all.

That was the thing about Eve. She moved through the world like nothing bad could ever touch her. Like life wasn't something to be afraid of. She took things as they came and shrugged off the stuff that would have kept him up at night.

While Nathan braced for the worst, Eve made it seem like there was never anything to worry about in the first place.

Another gust of wind slammed into the van, causing him to gasp again.

"Are you sure we're okay?" His voice shook. "Because that one felt like we were about to fly off the highway."

She kept her eyes on the road. "Yeah, man, we're good. You just gotta trust me." Her voice was pure Eve—calm and laid-back as always, like nothing could possibly go wrong.

The thing was, he did trust her. More than anyone in the world, but in this moment, he trusted physics more.

She must have caught the sheer terror radiating off him because, for the first time, her tone lost its usual teasing edge.

"Look, Nathan, I know you—probably better than anyone at this point. You're not really worried about my driving, are you?"

She jerked the wheel suddenly to avoid another patch of ice, and Nathan tensed up like a coiled spring.

"Well, maybe a little," he admitted through clenched teeth.

Eve let out a short breath, shaking her head.

"Okay, I'll admit, that one was close. But seriously," she continued, "you're freaked out about moving away, right? Look, I get it. I know this is a big deal for you."

"A big deal?" Nathan scoffed. "That's the understatement of the year."

Eve rolled her eyes.

"Listen, you need to relax, dude. You're going to college; it's not like you're getting shipped off to war or something," she scoffed. "Come on, Boone—talk to me. Maybe you'll feel better if you get it all off your chest. How've you been feeling?"

He exhaled sharply.

"It's been bad, Eve. I mean, I can't sleep... I've been getting these insane headaches lately, and then there are the dizzy spells—oh, and now there's this fun new thing where I randomly can't breathe at all. That one's my new favorite."

He let out a short, humorless laugh, like maybe if he said it the right way, it wouldn't sound so terrifying.

She shot him a sideways glance.

"So—par for the course, then?" Her tone was teasing but not unkind.

"Yeah, pretty much," he sighed.

She smiled, glancing at him for just a second.

"Sometimes," she said lightly, "you just gotta let go."

"That's easier said than done," he scoffed. "You know, letting go isn't really my thing."

She smiled again, keeping her eyes steady on the road.

"I know it's not, but maybe it should be. I think it's time for you to stop fighting everything all the time, and only worry about what you can control. You know—just let whatever is going to happen... happen."

He wanted to take her advice. He wished he could just absorb some of the easy, breezy confidence she always had and wrap himself up in it until it felt real. But the truth was, she had always lived without fear, while he had lived with nothing else.

To Nathan, the idea of relaxing and giving up control felt impossible.

Desperate for a distraction, he pulled out his phone and started scrolling aimlessly, letting the endless feed blur into white noise—until something made him stop.

His thumb froze mid-swipe at the sight of an ad for the MIND chip flashing on his screen.

The *Medically Integrated Neural Device* had been everywhere since its release in the late 2000s. Everywhere he looked, it was plastered across television, billboards, and endless social media feeds.

It was impossible to ignore, and every time he saw one of the ads for it, something twisted inside him.

The annoyingly loud, neon headline screamed at him:

Upgrade Your Life: The Future of Wellness is Now,

Beneath it was a lineup of perfect models, each one was more flawless than the last, with clear skin, chiseled bodies, and hair that looked like it was made for a shampoo commercial—thick, glossy, and somehow always perfectly in place. They looked untouchable, like they belonged to another world entirely.

The entire ad was drenched in nostalgic 90s vibes, selling a picture-perfect future he wasn't entirely convinced was real.

The MIND chip had started out as a groundbreaking healthcare device, but now it was something else entirely. It promised perfection, offering the ability to rewrite yourself completely. You could change your appearance, erase every flaw, and become exactly who you'd always wanted to be. It guaranteed immunity from any illness, and a mind that stayed sharp and confident, no matter what life threw your way.

For someone like Nathan, who'd spent his entire life battling anxiety and fear, it sounded like freedom.

It sounded like an escape—maybe his only real chance to break free from the endless cycle of doctors, dread, and the constant fear that his body might betray him at any moment.

On the screen, the tiny device sparkled like something from an old sci-fi movie. The microscopic implant could scan every cell in the body, instantly fixing imperfections at a genetic level.

His eyes locked onto the ad. Becoming Enhanced meant freedom—no more sleepless nights, no more endless doctor visits, no more fear of the unknown.

The MIND chip could erase all of that. It could finally make him feel normal.

His finger hovered over the ad, the perfect faces cycling across the screen, looping endlessly with flawless smiles.

The Future of Wellness is Now.

The words blinked, practically daring him to tap for more.

It was everything he'd ever wanted.

The wipers screeched again, pulling Nathan back from his biotechnical fantasy.

"Earth to Nathan," Eve said, shooting him a sideways glance. "Where'd you go just now? You totally spaced out on me."

Nathan shifted uneasily in his seat.

"Oh, I was just—" he mumbled, angling his phone away, but Eve had always been annoyingly good at reading him.

She raised an eyebrow, waiting.

He sighed and tilted his phone back toward her.

"It's just... this," he said quietly, the ad still glowing brightly on his screen, casting a soft light across her face.

When she looked down at it, her expression hardened instantly.

"Oh God, not that thing again. I swear, if I hear one more person talk about how the MIND chip will magically fix all the problems in their life, I'm going to lose my shit."

He blinked, startled by the sharpness in her voice.

"Wait, I mean—it does some good, right? The ads say—"

She cut him off.

"Nathan, those ads exist to make you feel like you're broken. It's not just about health anymore—it's about turning you into some fake, impossible version of perfection. All it does is give people these manufactured bodies, and perfect faces. And don't get me started on all those expensive upgrades nobody actually needs."

She let out a frustrated breath. "It all makes me so sick."

He turned away, staring out the window as her words sank in. He didn't say anything, but her anger echoed loudly in his mind, shaking his uncertainty loose.

"I'm telling you, Nathan," she continued, her voice softer but still firm, "you don't need some stupid chip to fix you. You're not broken. You're just... you."

She paused, letting the words sink in before adding, "Honestly? I think your quirks are what make you such a good writer. You see the world differently, and that's exactly what makes you who you are."

Nathan let her words settle, doing his best to push away the fantasy of feeling normal again.

He was just starting to relax when an eighteen-wheeler thundered past them, sending a wave of icy water crashing against the van and rocking it hard.

He shot his hands out to brace himself against the dashboard.

"I swear," he muttered under his breath. "There's no way we're making it to campus in one piece."

Eve chuckled softly beside him, completely unfazed.

"We're almost there. I promise—I'll get us there in one piece." Her voice was warm, effortlessly relaxed, like she didn't have a care in the world.

He let out a shaky breath and sank back into his seat. There was something about Eve—the way she could handle everything that came her way, no matter how chaotic life got—that made him feel a little safer. She was the only person who could quiet the storm in his head, the only one who made the world feel less overwhelming.

But even as he focused on her calming presence, the thought of the MIND chip wouldn't leave him. It wasn't the idea of perfection that drew him in—it was the promise of security, the reassurance that everything would be okay.

"What are they like, Eve?" Nathan asked suddenly, unable to stop himself. "You know—the Enhanced? I know you hate the tech and all, but I've never actually met someone with a MIND chip. I guess I just wanna be prepared."

She chewed the corner of her lip as she thought it over. Finally, she shrugged and glanced at him, her expression shifting into mild disdain.

"Well, most of them keep to themselves," she said, her tone casual but laced with annoyance. "I don't know if it's a cliquey thing or if they think they're above us, *Orgos*." She made air quotes with one hand, her voice dripping with mockery.

He couldn't help but crack a small smile at her use of the word Orgos. He'd never heard it said out loud like that before, and the way she said it made it sound ridiculous.

"I mean, I guess they're not all jerks," she said, softening a bit. "But— they're definitely different. Most of them act like they're better than everyone else. Honestly, it's pretty annoying."

"Different how?" he asked as he stared out the rain-smeared window.

"Well, they don't deal with the stuff we do," Eve said, tapping the steering wheel. "You know, like getting sick, or getting older. They don't freak out over every random ache or weird pain either." She shot him a side-eye. "Their chips keep them in perfect shape. If they catch so much as a sniffle, they can just delete it from their genetic code or whatever."

"That sounds pretty good to me," Nathan sighed.

She scoffed. "There's nothing good about it. It's cheating, Boone. It's like they don't even have to try."

She gave a dry laugh.

"Everything's easy for them, and when life's that easy, it stops feeling real. It's no wonder they get bored and act like they're better than the rest of us."

Nathan frowned.

"Still—That doesn't mean they have to be jerks about it."

She gave him a half-smile, keeping her eyes on the road.

"Maybe not, but it's hard to stay grounded when you never have to worry about anything."

"Not worrying... that's all I want," Nathan said quietly.

Eve glanced at him, her expression softening.

"Look, I get it," she replied. "But here's the thing—life's not supposed to be easy. If everything was all sunny days and good vibes all the time, you wouldn't appreciate any of it. It's the rainy days—the shitty times— that make the good ones feel worth something. So yeah. If you never had it hard, you'd never even notice when things finally go your way."

She kept her eyes on the road.

"Life is supposed to be hard, you know? You're supposed to struggle. That's the whole point."

He stayed quiet, letting her words settle. He understood where she was coming from, but that didn't make the constant fear and uncertainty that lived inside him any easier to carry.

She smiled softly, like she knew he was still wrestling with it.

"But hey, that's just me. To each their own, I guess," she said, her tone lighter now. "They can keep their perfect lives. I like my mess, thank you very much."

"So that's it? They're just high-tech snobby assholes?"

"Well, there is one super weird thing that they don't talk about in all those fancy ads," she said, her tone suddenly conspiratorial. "It's actually pretty bizarre."

He let his curiosity momentarily distract him from the weight in his chest.

"Weird how? Like, I mean, what kind of bizarre are we talking about here?"

Eve chuckled, her eyes gleaming.

"Well, it's not like secret-society-cult weird or anything." She giggled to herself. "It's just—Well, they're just totally obsessed with old stuff, and I'm not talking about in a cool, vintage-chic way. I'm talking like, they exclusively love the worst stuff our parents grew up on. Neon colors, acid- wash jeans, horrible throwback TV shows, and bubblegum pop."

She mock-gagged, rolling her eyes.

"Oh God, the boy bands! They're the worst, you'll see."

He blinked, intrigued despite himself.

"Wait, seriously?"

"Yeah, totally—I guess it's got something to do with how that old junk makes them feel. It's like anything that came out before the chip's release in the late 2000s feels real to them. But anything after? If it's stored on their neuro-network or whatever they call it, it doesn't hit them the same way the old stuff does. I guess to them, it doesn't feel real."

"That's wild," he said after a beat. "I mean, I love that old stuff too, but don't they ever get tired of it? They've gotta be running out of ways to keep themselves entertained."

"Exactly. That's the problem," she said, leaning slightly to the side as she kept her eyes on the road. "They've seen it all. All that retro junk— they love it, but there's nothing new for them. That's why—"

His eyes widened as the realization hit him.

"That's why organic art is booming."

She snapped her fingers, her eyes lighting up.

"Exactly—people like you—organic artists, writers, musicians who don't have enhancements—you're all priceless. Why do you think NCSU is giving you a full ride? They want what's in that brilliant mind of yours."

He froze, caught off guard.

"Wait, they're gonna milk me for all I'm worth, aren't they?"

She laughed, nudging him playfully.

"Oh, there's no doubt about that. But hey, a place to live with an unlimited meal plan and a degree? It could be worse."

He forced a smile back. For Nathan, writing was personal. He didn't do it for anyone else—it was how he made sense of things. The idea of someone reading his work, judging his choices, and potentially hating it was enough to keep it locked away forever.

Sensing he was about to spiral into a wave of panic, Eve decided to shift the conversation.

"So, do you know anything about your roommate?" she asked, keeping her eyes focused on the road ahead.

"Yeah, I looked him up last night. Some guy named Gabe Kowalski," he said, scrolling through the apps on his phone, pulling up his roommate assignment from the housing portal.

At the mention of Gabe's name, Eve just shook her head. "Oh man, you are in for a wild semester, that's for sure."

Nathan's heart skipped a beat.

"Wait, what's that supposed to mean?"

"Well, I've seen Gabe around at a few parties," she chuckled, glancing at Nathan from the corner of her eye. "Let's just say he's larger than life—in more ways than one."

Nathan's mind raced, trying to make sense of what Eve was trying to tell him.

"Eve, what the hell does 'larger than life' even mean?" Nathan's voice cracked, more desperate than he'd meant it to sound.

Eve just smiled, a familiar sparkle of mischief in her eyes—like she knew something he didn't.

"Oh, you'll see. Just relax. You're going to be fine."

2

NCSU

Northern Connecticut State University wasn't exactly a school that prospective students were throwing themselves at. With a campus nestled in a part of New England that most people didn't even know existed, in a town that was nothing more than a pit stop between Massachusetts and New York City, it wasn't exactly what you'd call a "dream school."

Overall, the university was, well—fine when compared to the massive campus of UConn or the prestige of Yale. While those schools were regularly on the national stage for athletics or academics, NCSU was smaller, quieter, and much easier to overlook.

It was the kind of place you drove through on your way to somewhere better, barely noticing the exit sign—a place you didn't visit unless you absolutely had to.

Back in the day, NCSU had built its reputation as a solid liberal arts college, mainly for its programs in Education, Criminal Justice, and Mass Communications. If you wanted to be a teacher, a cop, or, as the campus joke went, unemployed, NCSU was the place to be. But reputations don't last forever. While the world around it evolved with new tech and flashy programs, NCSU was left stuck in the past, just like the town it called home.

By the year 2000, NCSU was on life support. No one was exactly lining up to attend a school where the programs felt like relics from another century.

An explosion of unimaginable technology, particularly the MIND chip, had reshaped the world. Education, careers, and even the concept of human longevity evolved. People were living longer, healthier lives, and with that came a shift in priorities. Automation had swallowed whole industries, and while people once feared the worst, new doors opened.

Those who chose to live enhanced lives finally had the freedom to pursue the things they once only dreamed of. Some uncovered new passions, took up hobbies, and created art.

The Enhanced, with their biotech implants monitoring every molecule in their bodies, suddenly found themselves with nothing but time to chase meaning.

The irony was, even with every advantage and all that perfection, what they created was missing something important—the organic touch.

That's where NCSU saw its opening. They weren't on the cutting edge of tech, but they could tap into the growing demand for something technology couldn't replicate—real, raw, human art.

The kind that was messy, flawed, and full of imperfections, the Enhanced population craved but could never produce.

So, the school got creative. They revamped their curriculum, adding the Organic Arts Initiative, a program designed for students who worked without the crutches of technology. It was tailor made for people who created art the old way—with their hands, with their unenhanced brains. These Orgos, as they were called by some, were suddenly in high demand.

Nathan had never seen himself as a commodity. He was just a nervous guy who spent his time scribbling stories no one ever read, all while trying to keep himself hidden at a small community college. But everything changed after his mom passed away.

Maybe it was the grief, or maybe it was the full-ride scholarship NCSU dangled in front of him, promising a fresh start in their Organic Writing Program—and a place to live. Either way, after weeks of resisting, he found himself saying yes.

Not because he thought he was the next great writer, but because he needed something—anything—to keep him from sinking into the anxiety that chewed him up every day.

So, he said yes to the program. He said yes to NCSU's whole "we foster raw talent" pitch. And now he was here, standing in front of Shaker Hall—a dorm built on the bones of a long-dead shopping mall.

The university had done its best to cover up its past life, slapping on tall columns and a fancy brick façade, but you could still feel the ghosts of what it used to be.

The remnants of its retail past clung to the place like a bad haircut—an awkward mix of old shops and desperate attempts at being a legitimate university.

If you knew where to look, you could still see the outlines of what used to be there. The faded imprint of store signs long since removed, the imprints of tile beneath layers of polished flooring,the unmistakable shape of what had once been an escalator, that now lead nowhere. And if you squinted, you could almost make out the outline of the old Macy's entrance, its grand glass doors now transformed into a campus entryway that never quite matched the rest of the school.

It was a space caught between what it had been and what it was trying to be.

Much like everything else at NCSU, no matter how much polish the university applied, it couldn't erase its past. The campus, much like the town it was built in, carried the weight of what it used to be—an echo of something else, caught between what it was and what it wanted to become.

For Nathan, though, this wasn't just another stop along the way. It wasn't a stepping stone or a temporary detour. This was it—NCSU was his new home, whether he liked it or not.

3

PIGGING OUT

Nathan packed light—only two duffel bags and an old, beat-up footlocker. They weren't just luggage, they were his whole life: his entire wardrobe, years' worth of journals, a few favorite novels, and a laptop that had been outdated since he got it as a gift for graduating high school. Growing up, there was never enough money to collect more than the basics, and after his mom died, hanging on to anything beyond necessity felt pointless anyway.

The freezing rain had slowed to a drizzle by the time Nathan and Eve started unloading his stuff from her van and headed toward Shaker Hall.

Eve was calm as always, her free-spirited energy undimmed even in the damp chill. She slung one of Nathan's bags over her shoulder with an ease that didn't make sense, considering how small she was. She moved gracefully—almost like a dancer, though Nathan was pretty sure she'd never taken a class in her life.

As they stepped inside the dorm, he took in how hard the building was trying to look modern and impressive, but it still felt weirdly like an old department store. If he squinted, he could almost see the outline of what it used to be beneath the shiny floors and fresh paint.

They stepped into the elevator, and Eve leaned back against the wall, completely at ease. Typical Eve, he thought. He wished he could borrow even half of her chill. She had always been this way, ever since they were kids—effortlessly calm, even when he could barely breathe. Then again, she wasn't the one transferring mid-year, walking into a dorm full of strangers, with zero clue what came next.

Everything about her looked natural, earthy, and free—like she belonged barefoot at a music festival, spinning in the grass. She wore her usual boho-chic layers: flowy patterned pants, a simple white tank, and a worn suede jacket that was definitely vegan. Her dirty-blonde hair, which was always sun-kissed no matter the season, hung loose around her shoulders like she'd just finished road-tripping through the desert with the windows down. Her style wasn't a trend; it was who she was, and somehow, she made it work.

She was all he had left. His mom was gone, and his entire life was stuffed into a footlocker. The only thing familiar about this moment was the girl standing beside him, carrying one of his bags loaded with books as if it weighed nothing.

Sensing his nerves, she shot him a sideways look.

"You gonna make it, Boone?" she asked with a sliver of concern.

"Yeah," he muttered, knowing she wasn't fooled. "I'm just... nervous, I guess."

"I told you, you'll be fine," she replied with a steady voice. "Just breathe, you can do this."

He nodded and swallowed hard. Maybe she was right. Maybe she wasn't. Either way, this was happening.

When the elevator doors slid open, Room 365 was just a few steps down the hall. Somehow, the walk felt longer than it should have. His shoes scuffed quietly against the worn floor, each step heavier than the last.

He stopped in front of the door and adjusted the strap of his duffel, though it felt heavier than it should. His hand shook as he fumbled with the keycard, nearly dropping it.

He scanned the lock and waited for the soft click, then pushed the door open before he could think twice.

He plopped his bag on the bed, then turned toward the window. Everyone said this place was just a flashy shell slapped over an old retail skeleton. But from up here? The view wasn't half bad. Streetlights glowed against the wet pavement below, and the trees shimmered with ice like they'd been dusted in crystals. It wasn't perfect, but it was better than he'd expected—enough to quiet the worst-case scenarios he'd been playing in his head since leaving Vermont.

Beyond the campus parking lot, the ground sloped up into dark athletic fields. Above them, a decent-sized mountain rose into the night sky, and the moon hung just off-center from its peak. Its glow painted soft silver streaks across patches of melting snow. The whole scene looked like it belonged on a postcard—frozen in time, and perfectly still, as if the world outside wasn't on the verge of changing completely.

When he turned back, whatever peace he'd just managed to find was immediately crushed.

One-half of the room—his side—was practically empty.

The other half was a total shitshow.

Soda cans littered the floor—some crushed flat, others still half-full and leaking sticky soda in random puddles. Snack wrappers crunched under his feet. A collection of neon-colored shirts were tossed across the bed and desk like someone had fired them out of a leaf blower. And then, in the corner, was the laundry—a massive pile, at least five feet high, that was one deep breath away from toppling over. Some clothes were definitely dirty, others might have been clean— it was hard to tell the difference. All of it was mashed together into one giant heap that completely blocked the closet door.

As if that wasn't enough, muffled music—some weird, electronic beat —thumped from deep inside the pile, like the laundry was hosting an underground rave.

"So... this is what larger than life means?" he asked as he waved a hand at the disaster zone. "Dude's a total slob. Look at this place—it's a straight-up pigsty."

She chuckled, eyes scanning the mess like she was trying to make sense of it. "Yeah, well—all I said was he's larger than life. I never said he was a neat freak."

She crouched, holding a pair of neon gym shorts between two fingers like the fabric might bite her. "Remember when I said I liked my mess? Yeah, this is not what I meant."

He let out a quiet laugh, the sound slipping out before he could stop it. "How do people live like this? This is insane."

She let the shorts fall back into the heap, then glanced his way with a dry kind of amusement. "Some people are just wired differently."

Her tone softened as she turned toward him. "Look on the bright side. At least he's not here yet. You've got time to settle in before you have to deal with—" She motioned toward the chaos like she was revealing a magic trick gone wrong.

"—whatever this is."

The humor helped, but deep down, it wasn't the mess that was freaking him out. It was everything else—the unknown, the weight of change that pressed in on him from every direction. The fear that had been building since they left home.

He looked back at the window. The mountain glowed silver under the clouds, quiet and distant. "Well... I guess I can't complain about the view."

She stepped beside him, joining him in the quiet for a beat before turning in close. Rising onto the balls of her feet, she wrapped her arms around him and didn't let go right away.

He let himself sink into it. Just for a moment. Just long enough to feel his heart find something steady.

"You got this, kid," she said, drawing back slowly. "And if you don't? You know where to find me."

"Thanks," he replied. "I'll try to keep it together."

"No, you won't." She gave him a wink. "But when you do fall apart, you've got me to help pick up the pieces."

She gave him one last look, then turned, grabbed her purse, and walked out, leaving him in the middle of the room, alone, surrounded by someone else's mess and the kind of silence that made it real.

As Nathan unpacked, folding clothes neatly into the dresser, the mess on Gabe's side somehow seemed bigger now that he was alone. A sliver of dread crept in as he thought about his new roommate.

Larger than life.

What exactly did Eve mean by that?

Just as he was about to finish, a noise broke the silence—low, quick, and undeniably a snort.

He froze. Then scanned the room.

Another snort.

"What the hell?" he whispered, stepping back like the air had shifted.

Then, from somewhere beneath the pile of laundry, a voice rose like a nursery rhyme sung through a cracked baby monitor—too sweet to sound safe.

"Piggy... piggy."

Another snort followed, louder this time. "Piggy—welcome to my pigsty. Snort—snort."

Nathan's pulse surged. "What the hell?" he whispered again.

The pile of clothes giggled.

The mountain trembled, and another snort rose from beneath the layers. "Piiiiiggeee," the voice drawled, every syllable stretched like a lullaby gone wrong.

Something shifted under the laundry.

Nathan looked around the room for something he could defend himself with. He spotted a broom propped near the closet door, its price tag still dangling from the handle.

He grabbed it.

The heap rustled again, but the voice kept humming. "Piggy, snort snort, piggy..."

Nathan drove the broom into the pile like he was trying to exorcise it.

"OW!"

The mound erupted like a possessed jack-in-the-box, Nathan's new roommate launched upright, limbs flailing in every direction. Socks flung into the air. One clung to his shoulder. Another dropped from his head as he blinked around like someone waking from cryo-sleep. He wore cargo shorts that hadn't been fashionable since middle school and a pink-and-blue Hawaiian shirt that looked stolen from a party store discount bin.

Nathan stood frozen with the broom still raised in his hands, and his brain too scrambled to process what he was looking at.

The guy rubbed his stomach in slow, dramatic circles, then pouted like a cartoon baby who'd missed nap time.

"You hurt my widdle belly," he whined, drawing out the syllables like he was auditioning for a stage play.

Nathan stayed frozen. He couldn't speak. He couldn't breathe. He couldn't decide if this was a prank, a breakdown, or the start of something much worse.

The crying reached a crescendo—and then, like someone had flipped a switch, it stopped.

"Oh! Sorry," the guy said, suddenly cheerful. He stuck out his hand like they were mid-introductions. "Gabe Kowalski, at your service. You must be Matt Larson, my new roommate."

Nathan lowered the broom just a little. "Uh... no, I'm Nathan."

Gabe snapped his hand back and gasped like he'd been betrayed. "Nathan, eh? Well, if you're not Matt and you're Nathan, then..." His grin widened, and without warning, he launched into a perfect Chris Farley impression.

"You're not my roommate—you're my brother! And brothers don't shake hands—brothers gotta hug!"

Nathan barely had time to react before Gabe lunged at him, wrapping him in a bear hug so intense it felt like being crushed by a human-sized golden retriever with his favorite chew toy.

"Put me down!" Nathan gasped, limbs flailing. "Put me down!"

Gabe let out a theatrical growl, shaking Nathan like a ragdoll before finally releasing him with a hearty slap on the back.

"Sorry, dude," he said, completely unbothered. "Just wanted to make a proper first impression."

Nathan stumbled, still gripping the broom, trying to recalibrate reality.

"Uh, yeah... can I just finish unpacking? It's been a long drive, and I'm kinda beat."

"Of course, of course! *Mi casa, su casa*," Gabe said, arms flung wide like he was welcoming him to a palace.

"I gotta make a call to my old roommate anyway. I need to let him know his bed's been reassigned. He is not gonna like this, no, not one bit."

Before Nathan could ask what that meant, Gabe raised his hand to his ear and mimed a phone.

"Yeah, get Matty Larson on the phone!" he barked, deep and official. Then, instantly, he shifted into a high-pitched wail.

"Matty, buddy! How are ya? Look, we gotta talk." He paused, placing a hand to his chest with a gasp. "You and me, we've been through hell and back, and you know I love you, but..."

He broke into motion, pacing the room like a rejected contestant on a dating show. "Oh no—please don't cry, Matty! You know I can't handle it when you cry."

Nathan just stared, his brain short-circuiting.

"Listen, Matty, it's not me, it's you," Gabe said, his voice dripping with tragedy. He turned dramatically, as if being watched by a fake camera crew. "Plus, I have to tell you something—there's someone else."

Nathan blinked.

"Yes, Matty, it's true. Someone else will be sleeping in your bed." He paused, searching for the drama. "His name is Nathan... and he smells like cheese."

Nathan blinked again. "What the actual fuck?"

Gabe barely missed a beat. "That's right, I said cheese, and you know how much I love cheese." His eyes glazed over with mock longing.

"Anyway, I need to start my new life now—with Big Nate Cheeseman here."

Nathan didn't respond. Couldn't. His brain had stopped keeping up.

Gabe pressed on. "Well, it's been real, Matty, but I've gotta run. *Toodles!*" He dropped the imaginary phone with a flourish and turned to Nathan with an oddly sincere expression.

"Whoa, jeez. I'm really sorry you had to hear that," he said, still fully in character. "It got pretty ugly there for a second. Real messy stuff."

Nathan managed a reply, though his voice felt distant. "Uh-yeah. It sounded... intense."

"Nothing like a little drama to kick off your stay at *Casa Kowalski,* huh?" Gabe winked. "You're gonna love it here."

Nathan wasn't so sure about that, but he was too stunned to argue. If this was day one, he could only imagine what the rest of the school year had in store.

4

———————

THE SECRET STASH

Nathan huddled in the dorm stairwell with his back pressed against the cold cement wall. His hands shook as he fumbled for his phone, barely managing to pull up his contact list.

It only took two rings before Eve's voice, light and amused as ever—answered.

"Nathan Boone, please tell me you're not freaking out already. I know I said I'd help pick you up when you fell apart, but come on, man—you've only been here for, what… like ten minutes?"

"You're damn right I'm freaking out," he hissed, gripping his phone as if it might steady him. "Eve, you have no idea. It's Gabe—he's insane."

She let out a long, theatrical sigh. "What'd he do? Spill soda on your bed or something?"

"No. It's worse than that—way worse," he snapped, launching straight into it as he paced in the cramped stairwell.

"Okay, so I'm unpacking, minding my own business. You know that mountain of laundry in the corner? Just dirty clothes, right? Wrong. Eve, nothing about it was normal."

He barely heard her soft laugh over the pounding in his ears. "Oh, come on, Boone, stop being so dramatic."

"I am not being dramatic, I swear—it was pure insanity." his breathing grew heavier. "At first, I heard something. Like, a noise from the pile."

He paused, trying to pull himself together.

"And then—this voice starts coming out of it. Singing. *Piggy—piggy*—like, straight-up horror movie stuff. Eve, I'm telling you, it was creepy as hell."

"And?" Eve asked, her voice cracking with barely contained laughter.

He inhaled sharply. "And then I panicked. So I'm frantically looking around the room for something—anything—to defend myself with, and that's when I spot it."

He let out a breath, shaking his head. "A broom. Just sitting there in the corner. It had never been touched. The tags were still on it and everything."

"And?" she prompted again, her amusement bubbling over.

"And—I stabbed that pile of nonsense as hard as I could!" His voice bounced off the stairwell walls.

"Oh—my—God," she wheezed, barely able to speak.

"Don't laugh, Eve! Seriously—what was I supposed to do? Just stand there and wait for the Laundry Demon to eat me alive?"

He didn't wait for her to respond.

"So I jabbed it again—and he shot up like Jason freaking Voorhees. It nearly scared me half to death. Oh God—some of that stuff definitely wasn't clean."

She cackled on the other end. "Oh, man, I wish I could've seen your face."

"And then he makes a phony breakup call. To his old roommate. Using his hand as a phone. It was madness, Eve."

Laughter exploded through the line, and Nathan could practically feel his soul leave his body.

"What do I do? Do I file a restraining order? Because this guy is off the charts—I mean, he's full-on batshit crazy."

She gasped between laughs.

"Please—Nathan—stop—I'm gonna die—"

He let himself slide down the wall until he was sitting on the floor, staring at the ceiling like it might offer answers. "I can't believe this is my life now."

Through a hiccup of laughter, she finally managed a full sentence.

"Nathan, listen to me. I've seen Gabe around. He's a performing arts major—comedy's his thing. He did that exact bit at a party before winter break. The pig thing, the fake call, all of it. It killed. It's his act. He's not actually crazy. Well—maybe he is, a little, but in a good way."

"You knew about him?" he groaned.

"I thought it'd be funnier if you met him cold."

He let out a half-defeated breath. "Eve, I can't do this. There's no way I can live with a human cartoon character for a whole semester."

"Yeah, you can." She didn't even pause. "Just—give it a chance, okay? He's harmless. He's just, like I said, larger than life."

He tipped his head back against the wall. "You keep saying that like it means something."

"It does," she replied, and this time her voice steadied. "Honestly? I think having Gabe as your roommate might be good for you."

He let out a dry laugh that didn't carry much warmth. "What, you think my constant anxiety could use a certifiable madman as a copilot?"

"Honestly?" she said, too quickly to take back. "Yeah, I do. Look, I know Gabe's a lot, but he's a super positive person. I think you need that in your life. Everybody does, really."

He didn't answer right away. He let the silence carry the weight of everything he didn't want to say. "Eve, I swear—"

She didn't let him finish. "Nathan, you literally just got here—it's not time to give up. Just give it a chance. Please, for me... just promise me you'll try."

He hated that she was right. What he hated even more was that she knew it.

"Fine," he muttered. "You win. I'll try."

"That's the spirit," she replied, her smile practically jumping through the phone. She knew she'd worn him down. "You'll survive. But if he does that Piggy act again? You'd better send me a video. Man, I love that bit," she added with a laugh. "It's pure gold."

Nathan let out a tired laugh of his own. "I hate you."

"No, you don't." Her voice was quiet now, steady in a way that didn't need to perform sincerity. "Just finish getting settled in, and I'll see you bright and early for breakfast."

She hung up, leaving him staring at his phone, still processing the last half hour of insanity. He took a slow breath, rolled his shoulders, and forced himself to his feet.

Maybe Gabe wasn't so bad. Maybe he was. Or maybe he was just some unpredictable tornado of chaos that didn't fit any usual definition.

Either way, Nathan had no idea what to make of him. But for now, he'd agreed to give him a shot.

～

When he got back to his room, he was half-expecting another surprise, but Gabe was sprawled on his bed, glued to a handheld video game. He didn't even look up as Nathan walked in, the soft clicking of buttons the only sound in the room.

Once all his things were put neatly in their place, Nathan sat cross-legged on his bed, finally giving himself a moment to breathe. He powered up his laptop and pulled up his latest work, hoping it would calm him. Classes started in two days, and he needed to get his mind right—or at least as close to right as it ever got for him.

The screen lit up, and Nathan's world shifted. With the press of a key, he dove into his latest story. That was the beauty of writing—it was the only place where everything made sense to him.

When he was deep in it, everything else disappeared. The noise, the anxiety, the chaos of the real world—all of it faded away, leaving only the words in front of him.

His fingers danced over the keys as the story took shape on the screen. The characters spoke in voices that felt more real than anything he'd experienced in days. The setting came alive, vivid and comforting in ways the room he was in would never be. In his writing, he could get lost in the worlds he created—worlds where he felt safe.

For a moment, his thoughts cleared, and all that existed was the story.

For once, his brain wasn't working against him—it was working with him.

Across the room, Gabe was oblivious to the sanctuary Nathan had found in his head. And for that, Nathan was grateful.

Until Gabe's voice sliced through the silence.

"Hey, man," Gabe said casually, still not looking up from his game. "You hungry? I know I am."

Nathan blinked, the words pulling him out of his flow. He glanced over at Gabe, still sprawled on his bed, completely at ease. It was such a simple question, but after everything earlier, it felt like a setup.

"Uh—yeah, I guess I could eat," Nathan replied, shaking off the momentary disorientation.

"Perfect," Gabe said, hopping up from his bed with surprising athleticism for someone his size. "What's your pleasure?" He turned to the corner of the room, where the massive pile of laundry still blocked the closet door.

With one quick shove, Gabe effortlessly moved the heap aside, revealing the closet before looking at Nathan with a mischievous glint in his eye.

"Raise your right hand," Gabe demanded.

Nathan hesitated.

"Come on, dude, just do it." Gabe's eyes twinkled with mischief.

With a reluctant sigh, Nathan raised his hand.

"Now repeat after me," Gabe said solemnly. "I, Nathan Cheeseman—"

"That's not my name," he deadpanned.

"Just say it!" Gabe pleaded, tossing his arms up.

Nathan rolled his eyes. "Fine. I, Nathan Cheeseman."

"Do totally swear," Gabe continued, barely containing a grin.

"Do totally swear," Nathan echoed, his tone flat.

"To never tell anyone about what I'm about to show you," Gabe added, leaning in with theatrical seriousness.

Nathan's face didn't move. "Look, if something jumps out of there, I'm gone."

"Just promise!" Gabe was practically vibrating with excitement now.

"Okay, fine," Nathan said. "I swear, whatever's in there, I won't tell anyone."

"Not even that cute hippie chick you showed up with earlier," Gabe teased, "I mean, seriously—hubba hubba."

Nathan narrowed his eyes. "Wait—what? Who? Eve? No way. I mean —fine. No one will ever know, I promise."

"Excellent," Gabe said, straightening up with a look like he was about to pull off the greatest magic trick of his life.

"Now, I present to you—" He paused, dragging it out as he slowly opened the closet. "My secret stash."

The door creaked open, revealing a full-sized fridge tucked neatly inside the closet. Surrounding it were shelves stacked high with every snack imaginable—chips, candy bars of every kind, including some from Japan, Hostess treats in all varieties, and an assortment of energy drinks with names Nathan didn't even recognize.

Most of the stuff Gabe had, you couldn't even get anymore, not since junk food had been practically outlawed.

The real kicker was what was inside the fridge. An arsenal of drinks— cans of Mountain Dew and Dr Pepper lined the shelves surrounding a seemingly endless supply of Gatorade. Beyond the sodas, tucked into every available space, was beer. Loads of it. Bottles of cheap lagers were stacked alongside craft brews and a few suspiciously homemade-looking bottles that Nathan didn't even want to think about.

"Dude, this is insane," Nathan said, shaking his head.

Gabe beamed, clearly proud of his treasure trove. "This, my friend, is how you survive college. 24/7 snacks and booze, right at your fingertips. No dining hall lines, no overpriced vending machines."

He patted the fridge fondly. "I've got everything a growing boy like you could ever want. Chips? Got 'em. Candy bars? You bet. Energy drinks to keep you up for three straight days? Absolutely. And, of course, we have beer. Lots and lots of beer."

Nathan just stared, still trying to wrap his head around the sheer absurdity of it all.

"So," Gabe said, tossing Nathan a bag of Cheetos, "what's it gonna be? We've got time before the cafeteria closes, but trust me, you'll end up here sooner or later." He shot Nathan a wink.

Nathan caught the bag, shaking his head in disbelief. "I don't even know what to say."

"Don't say anything, Cheeseman—just eat," Gabe replied as he grabbed a box of Entenmann's and a pair of Cokes from the fridge before dropping down beside Nathan, making the bed creak like it might give out at any second.

"Look, man," Gabe began as he tore open the box of donuts and shoved one into his mouth without missing a beat. "Peace offering." He said as he held out one of the Cokes to Nathan.

"I think I might've overdone it with the intro." Gabe glanced at him, his tone softening just a little. "I do that sometimes."

Then, as if on cue, he launched back into his Chris Farley routine, smacking himself squarely on the forehead. "I'm so stupid sometimes?" The impact of his hand against his skull echoed around the room as he winced dramatically. "I just can't help it!"

Nathan stared at him as a mix of confusion and disbelief flooded his brain.

"Listen, I'm really sorry. I didn't mean to freak you out, really," Gabe said, looking a little more serious now—but still with that gleam of mischief in his eye.

"Honestly, I'm glad to have a roommate again. My last one—" He dragged his thumb slowly across his throat in a mock execution move.

"Let's just say, he didn't make it."

Nathan's mouth fell open, and a half-chewed Cheeto tumbled out, rolling off his lap and onto the floor.

Gabe nudged him, nearly knocking him over. "I'm just messing with you, man!" he burst into laughter again, rocking the bed even more.

"But seriously, I'll try to tone it down a bit. You know, ease you into it. Fair?"

Nathan was still caught in the whirlwind that was Gabe Kowalski. "Uh-yeah. That's fair."

Gabe tossed him a donut. "So, I saw you working on something earlier. What was it? You know, classes don't even start until Monday—are you some kind of overachiever or something?"

Nathan wasn't used to talking about his writing with anyone, let alone this larger-than-life character, but for some reason, he found himself answering.

"Uh, no—I'm a writer," he admitted, the words felt awkward as they tumbled out. Sharing this part of himself felt like stepping into unfamiliar territory.

"I mean—I write stories. I'm here on a scholarship in the Organic Arts program."

Gabe's eyes widened, and to Nathan's surprise, his response was genuinely enthusiastic. "Really? You're a writer?" He sat up straighter, clearly impressed. "What kind of stuff do you write?"

Nathan shrugged, feeling the weight of Gabe's excitement crash into him. "I don't know, man. Fiction, I guess. Mostly short stories—just stuff I never show anyone."

Suddenly, as if a thousand-watt lightbulb lit up in Gabe's head, he snapped his fingers. "You know what would be awesome? You could write some stuff for me. You know—for my act. I could use new material. The pig routine and the fake phone call bits still kill, but they're getting old. I need something fresh for the next off-campus party."

Nathan chuckled nervously, "I don't know. I'm not really a—"

Gabe cut in, his eyes sparkling with excitement. "You're a writer, right? Maybe there's something in your work that I could use. You know, something fresh, something unexpected. You and me—we could make magic happen!"

Nathan bit his lip. The idea of letting someone into his writing world felt wrong, but Gabe's enthusiasm was impossible to ignore. It was like a spark, lighting something in him he didn't know was there.

Before he could talk himself out of it, he found himself nodding. "I guess I could think about it."

"What's there to think about?" Gabe shot back, bouncing on the edge of the bed until it groaned like it might collapse.

"There's no better time than now, man. Come on—show me what you've got."

Nathan hesitated, unsure of what to say.

Gabe's energy was impossible to resist—like a game show host on a caffeine bender.

As Gabe shoved another donut into his mouth, he looked up at Nathan, eyes wide with excitement.

"Come on, man," Gabe said through a mouthful of food. "We've got snacks for days. We can pull an all-nighter. It'll be great. We'll have a marathon comedy writing session—just you and me. We'll crank out some killer stuff."

Nathan's reluctance began to fade as the absurdity of it all slowly disarmed him, making it impossible to say no.

"Alright," Nathan finally sighed. "Fine. Let's do it."

Gabe leapt off the bed with surprising agility, the springs creaking but holding steady. In one fluid motion, he snagged another donut from the now half-empty box and downed nearly the rest of his Coke.

"This is gonna be epic!" he said, bouncing on his toes. "We're gonna make comedy gold. You'll see—We're gonna be campus legends!"

As Gabe stuffed his face and rambled off wild ideas, Nathan couldn't help but feel a strange sense of comfort.

His new roommate's personal snack empire, the ridiculous energy, all felt surprisingly comfortable. For the first time all day, he wasn't thinking about his anxiety or the mountain of unknowns waiting for him.

Right now, he was just here—and for once, that felt okay.

5

SUGARBOMB HANGOVER

Nathan's head pounded like a jackhammer. Every throb was a painful reminder of the chaos from the night before. He cracked his eyes open, only to wince as sunlight poured through the dorm window.

This wasn't just exhaustion—it was the aftermath of his first college all-nighter, fueled by way too much sugar, an overdose of caffeine, and nowhere near enough sleep.

His mouth was dry, his tongue felt like sandpaper—like he'd eaten an entire sleeve of saltines in his sleep. His legs felt like lead as he lay in a heap on his bed, surrounded by a collection of empty soda cans and snack wrappers.

A sudden, sharp pounding on the door sent pain ricocheting through his skull. He groaned, barely able to lift his head from the pillow.

"Nathan? You in there?" Eve called from the other side of the door, way too chipper to deal with.

"Yeah, hold on—" he croaked, through a voice that was as rough as gravel.

Slowly, he sat up and took in the wreckage of the previous night. Gabe's half of the room was as messy as ever, but now Nathan's once-neatly organized side had been swallowed up by the disaster zone. It looked like a battlefield where the only casualties were self-respect and basic nutrition.

Gabe was nowhere in sight. That should've been a relief, but somehow, it just made him more suspicious.

The room tilted, and his head spun like a broken carnival ride. He squeezed his eyes shut, fighting the urge to puke as he gripped the bed like it was his last lifeline.

His body was rebelling against last night's reckless choices, his entire system was staging a full-blown protest. If his stomach had legal rights, it'd be filing for eviction over the mess of junk barely hanging on in his guts.

He felt sluggish and heavy, like somebody had swapped out his organs for wet cement. Everything inside him churned from the overload of sugar, caffeine, and whatever mystery ingredients had been crammed into that energy drink Gabe gave him.

He tried to erase the memory of the adorable cat printed on the can. It was way too sugary sweet, with little diamond eyes that probably should've been a warning.

He still had no clue what was actually in that thing. All he knew was that when Gabe handed him one, he took it without asking questions and pounded the entire thing like an idiot.

He had learned a very valuable lesson: don't trust anything with a label you can't read—especially not one with a cute mascot secretly plotting to take over the world, one unsuspecting liver at a time.

As he stumbled toward the door, his eyes landed on the mountain of laundry, now back in its rightful place, barricading the closet. Just knowing what was behind it almost made him lose his hard-fought battle to keep everything in his stomach.

He stared the pile down as he cautiously grabbed the broom from the corner and gave it a careful poke.

Nothing.

"Just checking," he mumbled, as he tossed the broom back in the corner, where it could stay until the next time he had to defend himself from enormous flying pigs.

The insufferably cheerful voice outside the door rang out again.

"Nathan Boone! Rise and shine, time for breakfast!"

He sighed as he pulled on the same T-shirt he'd worn the day before, the fabric still creased from where he'd left it crumpled on the chair.

"Alright already, I'm coming," he called, swaying a little as he yanked it open.

And there she was—Eve, practically glowing, her usual breezy energy turned up to eleven. She wore a faded denim jacket over a loose graphic tee, paired with worn-in combat boots that made her look like she could either start a revolution or sell healing crystals at a farmers' market.

"Good morning, sunshine," she sang as she stepped into the room and took in the carnage—like a detective arriving at a crime scene where self-control had died a messy death and the body was still warm.

Then, turning back to him, she took in her first real look at him.

"Jesus, Nathan," she said, eyebrows shooting up. "You look like you got flattened by a Mack truck."

Nathan groaned, rubbing his temples with both hands. "More like a snack truck," he muttered.

As soon as the words left his mouth, a spark lit in his brain. He grabbed his notebook off the bed and scribbled fast.

Mack truck… snack truck…

"Oh, that's good," he mumbled to himself. "There's definitely something there."

She raised an eyebrow and folded her arms over her chest. "Um, excuse me, who are you, and what have you done with my best friend?"

He didn't even look up— he just kept scribbling. "Huh?"

"I mean, this." She gestured to the mess, to the notebook, to him. "This isn't the Nathan Boone *I* know. The one I know would be freaking out over how messy this room is. He'd be spiraling into an existential crisis, and he definitely wouldn't be trying to come up with jokes about getting hit by a runaway snack truck."

Her expression softened—just slightly. "Last time we talked, you had one foot out the door. What changed?"

He hesitated. "I dunno. I guess Gabe surprised me. I didn't expect it, but I think he actually gets me."

She raised her eyebrows, suspicious. "Is that so? He gets what it's like to be a neurotic hypochondriac who's afraid of his own shadow?"

He chuckled. "Honestly— I think he kinda does. I told him about all that stuff—you know, my problems and everything. And he listened. Like, really listened, Eve. He didn't brush it off. He got it."

She opened her mouth like she had something to say, but paused to find the right words. When she finally found the words, her voice sounded more grounded.

"What, you don't think I believe you?"

He rubbed his thumb against his jeans, as if the motion might help him find the words.

"No, it's not that. I know you look out for me. It's just… sometimes it feels like you've heard it all before, so it's not a big deal anymore."

His eyes followed the seam in the floor to the wall, like it held an answer.

"With Gabe, it just felt different."

She leaned against the edge of the desk, arms crossed, like she needed something solid under her before she answered.

"Listen, I never meant to make you feel like that, Nathan. But maybe you're right. Maybe I've gotten used to you always being, well… you."

He didn't try to shrug it off. He just met her eyes.

"I know you don't mean to brush me off on purpose, Eve. I just think —I needed to talk to someone who didn't already know all my baggage. You know, someone new."

"Well, I'm glad you guys hit it off," she said. "I kept my phone's ringer on all night, waiting for your next freakout call—so thanks for letting me get a good night's sleep. I finally passed out around midnight, so I guess I should be thanking you for that. —And hey, I'm glad you decided to stick it out and not hop on the first train back to Vermont."

"Oh, I almost did," he replied as he sat down to pull on his sneakers. "But you were right—Gabe isn't so bad. I mean, he is intense—super intense—but I think I can handle it."

"I'm almost too afraid to ask, but what exactly went down here last night?" she laughed, kicking an empty cookie box, sending it skidding across the floor and under Nathan's bed.

He shook his head, still half in disbelief as he looked over the mess around them. "I'm not even sure—it's all kind of… hazy."

"Hazy, huh?" she replied, brushing another box out of her way with her boot. "Looks like you two hosted the Snackpocalypse."

She scanned the wreckage, then looked back at him, one eyebrow raised. "I think we need to get some real food in you. You know, something with actual nutrients. Maybe something that doesn't come with a barcode."

"Yeah, I should probably eat something with ingredients you don't need a chemistry degree to pronounce," he said as he shrugged on his jacket and followed her out into the hall.

The weather had done a complete 180-degree turn from the day before. The sky stretched out in a deep, cloudless blue, and the air carried an unnatural warmth for January in New England.

Steam rose from mounds of snow still piled high after the storm that blasted through over winter break. Something about it felt off—like the universe was setting them up for something worse.

Nathan and Eve walked side by side as their footsteps crunched over gritty salt scattered across the concrete. Even with winter hanging on, the day carried that fake promise of spring—like the world was holding its breath, ready to snap back into a deep freeze at any moment.

Puddles caught the sunlight, and the air smelled fresh and almost earthy. It felt like the seasons were fighting it out, with neither ready to give in.

"I can't believe how warm it is," Nathan muttered, shifting uncomfortably in his jacket. "It feels wrong."

She smiled, her breath visible in the cool air. "Yeah, it's like Mother Nature's messing with us. My dad always says New England doesn't have weather; it has moods. Guess it's a good mood day. Whatever it is, I'll take it."

"Yeah, but you know it won't last," he replied. "She's probably just waiting for us to get comfortable before she dumps another blizzard on our heads."

The world was stuck in that annoying in-between, where it was too warm for a winter jacket and too cold for just a hoodie. Nathan was just starting to enjoy the rare break from the bitter cold when—right on cue—the universe reminded him not to get too comfortable by sending a fully tuned cobalt blue Subaru WRX whipping around the corner from the lower parking lot, its engine screaming as it tore down the hill straight toward them.

Nathan barely had time to register what was happening before the car sped past, hitting a massive puddle and launching a tidal wave of filthy road slush directly at them.

The impact was instant, sending dirty water splashing up his jeans, soaking his jacket, and—worst of all—flooding into his sneakers, where it sank into his socks, guaranteeing a soggy, miserable day ahead.

Eve screamed at the car as it sped away, her voice cutting through the cold air. "You bitch!"

In a final act of defiance, a single arm shot out of the driver's side window, middle finger raised high. The nails were painted a glossy black that caught the sunlight, and rings crowded every knuckle. A few dangling metal bracelets clattered against the sleeve of a worn leather coat as the car roared off, leaving them drenched in its wake.

Nathan flapped his arms uselessly, trying to get rid of the icy slush clinging to his jacket, but it was no use. The damage was done.

Eve sighed as she wiped a blob of filthy slush off her cheek with an annoyed grimace.

"Well, there you have it, my friend," she said, her tone dripping with sarcasm. "You've just met your first full-on chiphead. Valerie Reynolds—Queen Bitch of NCSU."

"Chiphead?" he echoed, shaking the slush from his sleeves as they started walking again.

"Yeah. Remember on the drive down when I told you some of the Enhanced crowd hang in cliques? Well, Val's crew is the biggest—and the worst."

She scoffed. "Her, that awful sidekick of hers, Simon Wu, the whole group, all of them. They're just rich, entitled assholes—and easily the meanest people on campus. I hate to admit it, but they pretty much run this place.

He shivered as the cold slush bit into his skin. "So, she's just—"

"Vanity, Nathan—total vanity," she cut in, her voice edged with disgust. "I know I've made it pretty clear how I feel about enhancement. It's not for me."

She paused, taking a breath.

"But Val and her gang? They're exactly what happens when people have too much money and too much tech. It's all such a waste."

Her face hardened, her usual carefree vibe replaced by frustration.

"Her and Wu, they're not just the worst of the Enhanced. They're the worst of all people. They're just mean for no reason. It's exhausting."

Nathan rubbed at his sleeves, trying to shake off both the chill and the uneasy feeling creeping up his spine.

"Great. Sounds like I've made a fantastic first impression," he muttered. "I was kind of hoping to stay off their radar, at least for a little while."

She gave a weak chuckle. "Yeah—about that. There's something I haven't told you yet, and you are not gonna like it."

His gut twisted anxiety flared up inside him. "Oh God, what is it now? Just tell me."

She took a deep breath. "Nathan, it's Dante—he's here, at NCSU."

His mind went blank. The name hit him like a sucker punch, knocking the wind out of him. "No—no way. He can't be."

"I'm serious," she said, her voice hesitant. "He's here, and he's Enhanced now."

The words sank in, and everything around Nathan blurred.

Dante Edwards, the guy who'd tormented him for years, was here—at the same school—and now, he had a MIND chip. A heavy dread settled in his chest like a stone sinking deeper with every second. He stopped walking, the weight of it all too much to process.

"This is exactly why I didn't want to come here," he said, his voice trembling. "I don't belong here. I knew this was a mistake—every part of me has been screaming it since we left Vermont. I should've listened."

He froze in place, too overwhelmed to keep moving.

"This is bad, Eve. I mean, like… really bad." He fought to get the words out as all the awful memories slammed into him.

The teasing, the relentless bullying—it had all started in elementary school, but middle school had been worse. That was when Dante started the rumor. The one that stuck.

After a long stretch of hospital visits and inconclusive tests that made Nathan miss a few weeks of school, Dante told everyone he'd had a heart transplant—from a baboon. After that, the nickname BaBoone was born, and it followed him all the way through high school.

Dante had made Nathan's life a living hell. He could still hear the animal noises kids made whenever he walked by. The fake heart transplant rumor—and all the freak jokes that came with it—had haunted him for years. There was no escaping it, and Dante had loved every second.

Eve's voice cut through his spiraling thoughts.

"I know. I should've told you sooner, but I didn't want to freak you out." She paused. "But it's true. Dante's here, and he's part of Val's clique. I'm really sorry, Nathan. I didn't mean to keep this from you."

He let out a sharp, bitter laugh. "Do you even know what he did to me, Eve? All that *'BaBoone'* crap? It stuck. For years, I was the freak with the monkey heart. And it was all because of him."

"And you're telling me he's Enhanced now?" He scoffed. "Of course he is. He was already the guy everyone loved—the jock, the golden boy. Now he's basically unstoppable."

He shook his head, the question hanging heavier than he meant it to.

"What am I even doing here?"

She reached out and grabbed his arm, trying to ground him.

"You're here to become who you know you can be. You're here for your future—it's time to let go of the past."

He waved off her words, frustration tight in his voice.

"And now it's gonna be even worse. He's got a whole new crew of superhuman Enhanced kids to mess with me. I can already hear the new jokes they'll come up with."

She tightened her grip on him. "Look, I know this is a lot, but I'm here with you. You don't have to go through this alone."

He wanted to believe her, but the fear inside was starting to suffocate him.

"I don't think you get it, Eve," he said, his voice strained. "Dante isn't just some jerk from my past. He's the reason I am the way I am—the anxiety, the fear—it's all because of him."

The world closed in on him. The idea of possibly having to see Dante again, and hearing that stupid nickname—it was all too much.

"I can't stay here—I have to leave."

Eve didn't flinch. "No, Nathan. You're not running away this time. You just got here—you're staying."

His breaths came fast and uneven. "I can't do it, Eve! You don't know what it was like. He destroyed me then, and he'll do it again."

She stood firm. "This is supposed to be a fresh start for you, Nathan. It's time for a new version of you to step up. It's time for you to become the kind of person who doesn't let some asshole from your past control you."

He wanted to believe her, but the thought of facing Dante again was unbearable.

"Please, Nathan. Don't give up. Don't let him win again. You've got me, and you've got Gabe now. Don't let Dante ruin this for you."

He just stared at the ground, silent.

"Look, before your mom died, she made me promise something." She lifted his chin gently, meeting his eyes. "She made me swear I'd make sure you stuck this out. So I can't let her down, Nathan. Not her."

He felt the weight of Eve's words press deep. He didn't want to disappoint anyone, especially not the memory of his mother.

She stepped closer, her grip firm on his arm. "You always bail, Nathan. Whenever things get tough, you shut down, you run and hide."

"That's not true," he shot back.

She didn't budge. "It is *so* true, and you know it."

"You almost did it last night when Gabe pulled his act. You were ready to run. You called me, freaking out. And look what happened."

He didn't say anything, unsure of how to respond.

"You made a new friend," she said. "Do you know the last time that happened? I do—Third grade, in the hospital—me."

"Yeah, but…" Nathan started.

"No 'yeah buts,'" she cut in. "You've doubled your friends in the last 24 hours, shared your writing with someone you barely know, and had an all-nighter doing God knows what."

He winced. "It was just junk food, okay?"

"You sure about that? None of this?" she said, pinching her thumb and forefinger together and bringing them to her lips.

"No, none of that—you know I don't do that stuff." He chuckled despite himself.

"See? I got you laughing," she said with a grin. "It's not all doom and gloom. So what if Dante's here? It's a big campus. You may never see him. Even if you do—who cares?"

"If he tries to start with that 'BaBoone' crap again," she said, "just look him dead in the eye and ask him if he's feeling alright. You know, act like his chip is glitching or something."

He raised an eyebrow. "You're kidding, right?"

"Nope," she replied. "I bet it'll totally work. He's just looking for a reaction out of you—don't give him one."

He wanted to believe he could face Dante, but he couldn't see how he ever would.

"You've got this, Boone," she said, looping her arm through his and tugging him down the sidewalk.

He wasn't sure he believed her, but he'd make sure it looked like he did.

It was the only way he knew how to survive.

6

CHOCOLATE TIDAL WAVE

As soon as Nathan stepped into the cafeteria, his whole body screamed to turn back. The noise was so intense that he felt like he had just been hit in the face with a shovel. Trays clattered, chairs scraped across the tile, and conversations overlapped into a constant blur of nonsense.

Laughter exploded like fireworks, and shouts rang out like thunder. The energy pulsed through the space like a hungry animal, swallowing him whole. All he could do was stand there, frozen, and blink against the assault on his senses that was coming at him from every direction.

He scanned the room, taking in the scene as it unfolded in front of him. People filed through the serving lines, their trays piled high with every breakfast food imaginable. The smell of bacon, syrup, and fresh bread wafted through the air, causing his stomach to rumble in response.

As good as everything looked, the idea of eating real food for the first time since arriving on campus couldn't stop the creeping anxiety that was crawling up his spine. It was too loud, too bright—too everything.

Eve's eyes lit up as she leaned in and pointed toward the various food stations.

"Alright, check it out," she said, her eyes sparkling at the sight. "They've got everything you could ever want—omelets, bacon, pancakes, the works."

She kept going. "And that's just brunch. Dinner's even better. I'm talking gourmet burgers, wood-fired pizza..."

She wrinkled her nose with a laugh. "Not that I eat the burgers, but honestly, they smell so good it almost makes me rethink the whole vegetarian thing. And Wednesday nights? Oh man," she sighed, "that's sushi night. It's incredible. I'm telling you, Boone, you've never eaten this good in your life."

Her excitement came through loud and clear, but he could barely focus on what she was saying. His mind was already racing, jumping between the noise around him and the haunting thought of Dante.

Eve was still going on about the endless options the caf had to offer, her voice was as enthusiastic as ever, yet it sounded distant—like she was speaking through a tunnel.

All he could hear was the pounding of his own heart. The air felt thick and heavy, like it was pressing down on him.

What if Dante saw him first? What if the taunting started again?

The cafeteria sounds twisted in his head, warping into memories of Dante's taunts.

He tried to focus. He tried to listen to Eve's voice and use it as an anchor, but the memories kept pulling him under, dragging him back to those awful days he thought he'd left behind.

Sensing he was checking out, Eve gave him a soft nudge against the arm. "Nathan, hello? Anyone home?"

He blinked as her voice cut through the fog in his mind.

"Yeah, I'm just, uh, taking it all in, I guess," he said, forcing a nod. He adjusted the strap of his backpack, like that tiny motion might make everything feel normal again.

She studied him for a second, like she was deciding whether to press or let it go after the bomb she'd dropped on the walk over.

"This place is pretty great, huh?"

He forced a smile, but anxiety clawed at him. "Yeah, it's definitely something."

"Come on, let's find somewhere to sit," she said, her tone light but laced with just enough concern that told him she was keeping an eye on him.

She took the lead, scanning for seats, letting Nathan follow. His eyes darted from table to table, searching for a face he didn't want to find.

Please, God. Don't let Dante be here.

The thought looped in his head, steady and sharp, until it drowned out everything else.

And then, like the universe decided to cut him a break, he found Gabe.

Buried behind a monstrous stack of pancakes so ridiculously tall it looked like he was trying to set a world record was Gabe, devouring them like a man on a mission. On one side of him sat a plate of scrambled eggs, on the other, a mountain of breakfast sausage, and in the middle of it all, a pool of syrup that looked ready to spill over the edge of the table at any second.

Totally astonished by the scene, Nathan leaned toward Eve as they both took it in.

"How is it even humanly possible for one person to eat that much?"

She looked in Gabe's direction with a mixture of amusement and disbelief. "I think the better question is, why would anybody want to?"

As if sensing their eyes on him, Gabe looked up mid-chew, his cheeks stuffed like a chipmunk hoarding food for winter. His eyes lit up the moment he saw them, and without missing a beat, he waved them over with syrup-covered fingers, completely unaware of the sticky mess dripping down his hand, causing Eve to laugh out loud—her voice rising above the rumbling cafeteria crowd.

"Well, looks like we've found our seats," she said, steering them toward Gabe's table, clearly amused as they made their way over to the syrup-drenched spectacle.

Nathan, despite everything racing through his mind, couldn't help but crack a genuine smile. There was just something about Gabe that instantly put him at ease. He couldn't explain it, but the natural connection between them instantly calmed his nerves.

As they sat down, Gabe greeted them, oblivious to the stray drip of syrup hanging from his chin.

"Welcome to The Caf, Cheeseman. Pretty great, huh?"

"My lady," he continued, looking up at Eve as a genuine blush crept up his cheeks. "I don't believe we've formally been introduced."

When he started to get up from his seat, planning to offer a grand bow or some other over-the-top gesture, his elbow caught the edge of his monster-sized chocolate milk and sent it toppling. The drink tipped in slow motion, then spilled across the table like a sugary tidal wave.

His eyes widened in exaggerated horror as the chocolate milk spread across the table.

"OH NO!" he shouted, slamming his hands down on the table like a dramatic actor mid-scene. "My breakfast! This is a disaster!"

He then cupped his hands around his mouth, mimicking an intercom announcement. "Bob, cleanup on aisle four!" he called out, pretending to be a frantic supermarket manager.

Without missing a beat, he dashed off to grab something to clean up the mess, leaving Nathan and Eve chuckling at his over-the-top disaster management.

Nathan was unable to hold back a smile. Gabe's absurd energy had completely taken over, and for once, he wasn't stuck in his head.

"That guy is something else," Eve said, shaking her head in disbelief.

"He sure is," Nathan chuckled, glancing at her. "I don't know why, but he always seems to make me feel better. It's kind of weird." He shrugged, still smiling, feeling lighter than he had in a long time.

In a flash, Gabe returned with his arms overloaded by a mess of paper towels he'd somehow charmed out of the kitchen staff. He hummed cheerfully as he launched into the sticky battlefield of chocolate milk, syrup, and scattered crumbs, scrubbing with the energy of a game show host.

"Clean up, clean up, everybody everywhere—" he sang in an exaggerated, booming tone, his voice carrying across the cafeteria like a kindergarten teacher rallying toddlers for chore time.

Nathan and Eve exchanged amused glances as they watched Gabe wipe down the table with theatrical dedication, dramatically wringing out imaginary water from dry napkins, and tossing used ones behind him like a chef discarding failed dishes. He even swiped at the air above the table for good measure, as if cleansing it of negative breakfast energy.

Eve shook her head. "I swear, he has the energy of a five-year-old who just mainlined a gallon of Mountain Dew."

Nathan chuckled, unable to deny that his roommate's antics had fully taken over the moment. His usual nervous tension had been replaced by something lighter, something dangerously close to amusement.

With one final flourish, Gabe gathered the balled-up mess of soaked paper towels, spun on his heel, and lobbed them across the room toward a trashcan near the drink station.

"From downtown!" he bellowed as the wad soared in a perfect arc and landed smoothly in the bin. He threw his arms up in celebration, like he'd just drained a game-winning three-pointer in the March Madness finals and the crowd was losing its mind behind him.

"And the crowd goes wild!" he shouted, before cupping his hands over his mouth to mimic the roar of the stadium.

Nathan shook his head. "You're ridiculous."

"Ridiculously talented," Gabe corrected, flashing a triumphant smile.

With the table finally back to normal, Gabe flopped into his seat, and his eyes sparkled with barely contained excitement as he launched into another one of his bits.

"Welcome to the Gabe Show! Tonight's guests: Nathan Cheeseman…" Gabe declared with a grand, sweeping gesture, his voice booming across the room. Nathan's eyes widened as he shifted uncomfortably, caught off guard by the sudden spotlight. Gabe, loving every second of it, leaned in with exaggerated flair. "And the love of his life… uh, Steve, was it?"

Eve giggled, her shoulders shaking as she watched Nathan squirm, while Gabe soaked in the awkward tension like a true showman.

Catching on instantly, Eve giggled. "Yes, Steve. But my enemies call me Stevie."

"Well, Stevie, it is, then." Gabe nodded as he leaned in like a talk show host. "So, tell me, how long has our boy here been your main cheese?"

Nathan's face turned red, clearly flustered. "Wait, we're not—" he began, but Eve jumped in, playing right along with Gabe's act.

"Oh, we were high school sweethearts, of course," she said with an exaggerated sigh. "He swept me off my feet in tenth grade. It was love at first sight—the way he tripped and spilled his lunch all over the cafeteria. It was adorable."

Gabe pretended to swoon. "Ah, yes, a true meet-cute!"

Eve continued, "And the poetry—it was so romantic. Oh, and then there was the time he serenaded me in front of the whole school. He has a voice like an angel, you know." She giggled, continuing to play along with Gabe's pretend talk show bit.

"Cheeseman, you dog! I never had you pegged for a ladies' man. It's always the quiet ones!" Gabe teased, laying on the dramatic shock.

Nathan stammered, "But she's not my—"

Before he could get another word out, the cafeteria door swung open. A sharp blast of cold air cut through the noise, silencing the room for half a second.

Gabe leaned forward in his seat, his eyes locked on her. "Hold that thought, Cheese—my wife just walked in."

7

CAFETERIA GIRLFRIEND

Nathan turned to look, and when he did, he instantly regretted it.

There she was—Valerie Reynolds, undeniably striking and equally fierce. She didn't walk through the cafeteria, she cut through it. Every step was smooth and purposeful, like she owned the place and knew everyone was lucky just to watch her move. Her skirt drifted around her legs like it was following orders. Her short bob was sleek and sharp enough to draw blood, without a single strand out of place.

He watched as she peeled off her coat, revealing the tattoos that wrapped around her arms and twisted up to her collarbone. They weren't like anything Nathan had ever seen. They shimmered faintly under the cafeteria lights, shifting just enough to make his pulse stutter. For a moment, it almost looked like they moved along her skin, as if they had a heartbeat of their own.

The room felt like it leaned toward her. Conversations dulled for half a second. Heads turned without meaning to. Even the background noise seemed to pause before remembering to start up again.

She didn't have just presence. She had power.

"Isn't she breathtaking?" Gabe muttered, sounding as if he was watching a goddess glide by, rather than a girl in designer heels with a superiority complex.

Eve didn't answer at first. Her eyes were locked on Val with a

43

sharpness Nathan hadn't seen before. When she did speak, her voice was pure ice.

"Great," she groaned. "Just what we need—The Queen of the Chip Heads."

Gabe, still in his own world, sighed dreamily, his eyes locked on Val. "What? You don't like her?" He let out another wistful sigh, pausing to bask in her presence. "I think she's—perfect."

Nathan watched as Val commanded the room with an energy that sent chills up his spine. He wasn't a stranger to fear—he knew that emotion intimately—but what he felt in that moment was different. It was pure, instinctual self-preservation.

His brain went into full red-alert mode, screaming one thing: *avoid Valerie Reynolds at all costs.*

"I hate her. I hate everything about her," Eve grumbled, her voice barely above a whisper.

"Oh, come on, she's not so bad." Gabe turned to her, eyebrows raised, smirking like he already knew the answer. "What's your problem with her? You don't like six-foot-tall, world-dominating types?"

Eve shot him a look of pure disbelief. "Have you ever actually spoken to her?"

"Oh god, no," Gabe replied, his face suddenly serious—more serious than Nathan had ever seen him. "I couldn't. That would ruin everything. Our relationship is too perfect to do something stupid like talk to each other."

Nathan stared at him, convinced this had to be a joke. It wasn't. Gabe looked completely serious, like he'd just described the meaning of life.

"Wait, what?" He shook his head. "What do you mean, your relationship? You two are dating, and you don't talk to each other? That doesn't make any sense. How does that even work?"

"It works perfectly, my good man," Gabe replied with absolute confidence, his tone as casual as if this were the most normal thing in the world.

Eve's eyes rolled, clearly not buying it. "Yeah, no thanks... If this is another wacky Gabe game or performance, I don't get it, and I definitely don't want any part of it."

"Oh, it's not a game. I am totally and completely serious," Gabe said, his tone flat like he meant every word. "She's my Caf Girlfriend—and the best one I've ever had."

Nathan frowned. "Your Caf Girlfriend?"

Gabe sat back, folding his arms as if he'd just made the grandest revelation of all time.

"Yup. The rules are simple. I admire her from a distance; she never acknowledges me, and we live in perfect harmony."

Nathan pressed his fingers to his temple. "That doesn't sound like a real relationship."

Gabe gasped, looking utterly scandalized.

"Excuse me? It is *absolutely* a real relationship. Matter of fact, it's the perfect relationship, if you ask me. No drama, no fighting, just pure, untainted admiration."

Eve shook her head, letting out an incredulous laugh. "I've known you for what—like ten minutes? And you've already clinched the title of 'Weirdest Person I've Ever Met.' Impressive."

"Oh, Eve, that is one of the sweetest things anyone has ever said to me," Gabe chuckled.

"Alright, let me explain," he continued, leaning back in his seat.

"A Caf Girlfriend—or Caf Boyfriend, I guess," he added, throwing a glance at Eve, "is kind of like a crush, but with boundaries. You pick someone, admire them from a distance, and never actually talk to them. If you do, it's over."

"Ms. Reynolds and I? We've been *Caf dating* since the spring semester of my freshman year," he explained proudly. "And there hasn't been a single word between us. It's been perfect."

He sighed, his eyes glazing over in a daydream. "At this rate, I'll Caf propose in the spring, and by graduation, I figure we'll be Dining Common Law Married."

Nathan rubbed his forehead, trying to keep up with whatever bizarre logic Gabe was laying out. "Okay, let me get this straight. You've been— *Caf dating*—without ever talking to her?" Nathan repeated slowly, as if saying it out loud would somehow make it make sense—It didn't.

"Yup!" Gabe confirmed proudly. "My old roommate came up with it. That Matty—he sure was something else. Rest in peace, good buddy," He chuckled, patting his chest solemnly and kissing his hand before placing it in the air.

Nathan shook his head, still utterly baffled by the entire concept. "You're unbelievable."

Gabe beamed. "I know, right?"

"Look, man, we're in college. We're gonna do all kinds of stupid stuff. I just try to make sure I do the stupidest stuff possible, you know?"

Nathan raised an eyebrow, still trying to comprehend how they went from a fake late-night talk show to cafeteria dating so quickly.

Gabe, clearly on a roll now, swept his arm across the cafeteria like it was his personal kingdom.

"Come on, Roomie, what do you say? Let's get you your first Caf Girlfriend. It's an NCSU rite of passage. All the cool kids are doing it."

He shot Nathan a convincing look. "Just choose wisely—no easy outs. Eve's already off the table. I'd bet she's some nerd's Caf Girlfriend and doesn't even know it."

He flashed her a goofy face, eyes wide, lips puckered. "No offense," he added, throwing up an *okay* hand gesture as he did his best Rodney Dangerfield impression.

"Wow, thanks, Gabe. I'll try not to cry myself to sleep over it," she scoffed, pretending to be offended.

Gabe shrugged, turning his attention back to Nathan, his eyes lighting up with enthusiasm. "But you, my friend, you've got options. Pick someone, anyone—but aim high. No one's out of your league."

Nathan's face twisted in disbelief as he glanced around the cafeteria, trying to gauge if Gabe was serious. "No way, man," he said, shaking his head. "I'm not just going to pick someone. This whole thing seems super creepy."

"Creepy?" Eve echoed, raising an eyebrow. "That's the understatement of the year. He's basically setting you up to pick some poor girl to ogle until she tells you to stop." She groaned. "And to think, Gabe, I was just starting to become a fan..." She trailed off, shaking her head in disappointment.

"No, no, it's not like that at all," Gabe said, pointing at Eve like he was trying to win an argument he wasn't sure he understood. "She doesn't get it, Cheese. Guys like us don't have any game. This is just... practice, you know?"

Eve groaned and dropped her head into her hands. "Typical college guy behavior," she muttered. "Seriously, Boone, you're better than this."

With a sigh that could win an Oscar, Gabe pleaded with her.

"Come on, Eve. Don't yuck my yum." His voice dropped a little, the usual theatrics fading just enough to show some sincerity. "Just let us have this. Let Nathan have it."

Nathan caught it—a brief flash of something real behind the act. It reminded him of the night before when Gabe had just listened while

Nathan talked about his fears, his anxiety, and how the weight of everything pressed down on him.

He didn't judge him for having issues, he just asked questions because he wanted to understand. Now, even with all this Caf Girlfriend nonsense, there was still something there. Like, Gabe was trying to give Nathan an easy way to fit in.

"Look, it's totally harmless," Gabe continued, pushing forward with renewed energy. "It's not like we're gonna sit here and gawk at some poor unsuspecting girl. I mean, take my choice for a Caf relationship." He subtly gestured toward Val, lowering his voice. "You think for a second that I'd say so much as a peep to Ms. Reynolds over there? If you do, you're crazy. Seriously, that chick is terrifying. If anything, I'm a total wimp for picking her of all people."

Nathan shook his head. "I dunno, man. This whole thing seems pointless. I'm not doing it."

"Oh, you are definitely doing it," Gabe replied with complete confidence. "I'm telling you, Cheese, it's the perfect distraction from the college grind. Like I said, it's totally innocent, and hey, you never know—maybe it'll give you some great material for your writing."

Nathan stared at him, deadpan. "Yeah, right, college guy picks a random girl and avoids her at all costs. That's truly riveting stuff."

Gabe pointed at Nathan dramatically, "You mock me, Cheese, but this is prime observational content. It's about the human experience! The tension, the unspoken connection, the—"

Nathan held up a hand. "Oh god, please stop, don't make this any weirder than it has to be."

Gabe scoffed. "Okay, fine, I'll shut up if you stop stalling and just pick someone already."

"Alright, I'll do it," Nathan sighed, finally caving. "So let me get this straight: all I have to do is pick someone to be my Caf Girlfriend, avoid them at all costs, and that's it?"

Gabe nodded enthusiastically. "Well, technically, there are a few rules to make it official. First, you find someone you're drawn to—not just anyone, but someone who catches your attention. Then, you go up to them and stay within six feet for ninety seconds without saying a word. But here's the real test—you've gotta make eye contact. That's the move right there. If you can pull that off, you're essentially asking her to be your Caf Girlfriend without actually asking. Easy enough, right?"

Nathan blinked, already regretting everything. "I just go over there, stand near her for a minute and a half, make eye contact, and say nothing—that's it?"

Gabe nodded. "Yup."

"This is the dumbest thing ever," Eve cut in, shaking her head, her voice laced with exhausted disbelief. "I mean, like, all-time, Guinness Book of World Records-level dumb. Please tell me you're not actually considering this, Nathan."

He hesitated, torn between Gabe's relentless enthusiasm and Eve's barely restrained contempt. His brain screamed at him to back out, but instead, he heard himself say— "I mean, he does have a point, it could be research."

Gabe slapped the table triumphantly, laughing. "That's the spirit! See, Eve? This guy gets it. Alright, Cheese, let's find you a Caf Girlfriend!"

Nathan rubbed his temple. "Tell me again why I am doing this?"

"Because you're a good sport," Gabe answered before Nathan could spiral.

"Screw it," Nathan muttered, throwing his hands up and leaning back in his chair, and letting his eyes sweep across the cafeteria.

Eve groaned, crossing her arms. "Guys like you two are the reason why girls have trust issues."

Nathan let out a breath, scanning the room. If he was going to do this ridiculous thing, he might as well rip the Band-Aid off.

Gabe leaned in close, dropping his voice to a hushed whisper, adopting the serious, quiet tone of a golf announcer.

"And here we have it, folks. Young Nathan Cheeseman is setting his sights on the fairway. He's got his eyes locked on the course ahead, scanning each table like a pro. Will he find his target or be forced to settle for a mulligan?" Gabe paused, stroking his chin, clearly enjoying himself.

"The cafeteria goes quiet, the pressure's on—can he keep it together?" His voice dropped to a whisper, dragging out the suspense. "The tension is real, the stakes are high—let's see what he's got."

"Shut up, dude, you're making this way worse than it already is," Nathan mumbled, second-guessing his decision to play along.

He was just about to back out when he saw her, and in that split second, it felt like his soul left his body.

She wasn't just pretty—She wasn't someone to admire from a distance—She was perfect. He'd never seen anyone like her in his life, and for a moment, it was like he couldn't catch up to the world around him.

"Oooh, I think we've got something, folks!" Gabe whispered, noticing Nathan's sudden stillness.

"What do we have here?" he asked, barely containing his excitement.

Nathan swallowed hard. Oh god, she's incredible. The thought struck him like lightning. In that moment, he knew—he was in deep trouble.

She was tall, moving through the salad bar with an effortless grace that seemed to slow everything else around her. Her skin was fair, glowing softly under the cafeteria lights, but it was her hair that caught his attention—straight, parted down the middle, and a soft gray that shimmered like silver in the light. It wasn't the kind of color you'd expect on a college-aged student, yet somehow, it made her look even younger. It suited her in a way that felt almost unreal.

Her blue eyes, which Nathan could barely make out from across the room, held a sharp intensity like they were hiding some unspoken secret.

She was dressed in classic preppy style: a soft cashmere sweater resting just above the ribbon belt of her neatly pressed khaki skirt, the whole outfit looked like it had been pulled straight from an early '90s Abercrombie & Fitch ad.

"Whoa, whoa, whoa! Look at Cheeseman over here!" Gabe exclaimed, shooting up an eyebrow. "I think he's got something! Ladies and gentlemen, Ooh, looks like he's been struck by Cupid's salad fork! What a shot!"

Nathan's brain short-circuited as he tried to process what he was seeing. He couldn't take his eyes off her. His heart pounded, but not with his usual anxious tremor. This was something different, something more electric.

"Who is she?" Nathan muttered, his voice barely above a breath.

"No idea," Eve replied. "I've never seen her before, but I'd say she's definitely out of your league, and by the looks of it, totally Enhanced. There's no two ways about that."

Nathan blinked, still caught in a trance. "Yeah, totally—Enhanced," he whispered, the word slipping out as if it meant nothing at all.

Eve snapped, clearly unimpressed. "Ugh, look at her. No one has hair like that unless they've been optimized. She's definitely got a chip. I can practically smell the artificial perfection from here."

Gabe, ever the romantic, leaned back in his chair, arms behind his head. "Hey, Enhanced people need love too, you know?" he said, pretending to be offended. "So what if she's had a little help? That doesn't mean he can't go for it."

"She's on a whole other level, man," Nathan said, keeping his eyes locked on her.

Eve shrugged. "I'm just saying, people like her usually stick to their own kind. You might as well aim for someone a little more—oh, I don't know—real."

"Hold up," Gabe interjected, holding up his hand. "Let's not be hasty. This is a Caf Relationship we're talking about here. This is perfect! There won't be any rejection, no awkward moments. There's really no downside here."

There was confidence in his voice, like he knew something no one else did. "I think she's a winner. You never know, Cheeseman here and that silver fox over there might just have a real Caf future together."

Nathan tried to laugh, but it came out weak, his mind still spinning. He couldn't shake the thought of what it would be like to talk to her, to step out of his comfort zone and leave his insecurities behind.

Eve rolled her eyes. "This is seriously so dumb, Gabe. You're really setting him up."

Gabe shrugged, unfazed. "Look, we all know you don't approve of this, but it's all in good fun. Besides, you never know. Maybe she's got a thing for anxious writers."

Nathan forced a smile, but his heart was still racing. He couldn't figure out why this girl had shaken him so much. There was something about her that felt untouchable—perfect in a way he knew he could never be. Maybe that was what fascinated him the most: how someone like her could exist in the same world as he did.

It's now or never, he told himself, as he tried to summon every ounce of courage left. This was it—the moment where he either stepped forward or let fear win.

He swallowed hard, eyes locked on her as she moved through the salad bar like she had all the time in the world. His nerves were on fire; his whole body buzzed with that restless, shaky energy he hated.

He took a breath, squared his shoulders, and forced himself to get up. His brain was screaming at him to back out before he embarrassed himself. And yet, somehow, the pull toward her was stronger.

Gabe gave him a thumbs-up behind his back. "You got this, Cheeseman!"

As Nathan headed toward the mystery girl, Eve and Gabe went quiet, watching like he was creeping into the final scene of a thriller, where everything could either work out...or go horribly wrong.

"You know how much I hate this, right?" Eve said, her eyes still fixed on Nathan.

Gabe nodded, his usual comedic energy fading. "Yeah, I know—totally. You've made it abundantly clear how you feel about this whole thing." He paused, watching as Nathan, who was scared of everything under the sun, walked toward a girl who was leagues above him.

For once, Gabe's voice sounded genuine, like this wasn't just about roping his roommate into some dumb game that, up until now, Eve had figured was just a pointless form of hazing.

"But look at our boy," Gabe said quietly. "He's scared of everything… and he's actually doing it."

Eve glanced at him, catching the shift. It wasn't his usual act—this wasn't a bit. This was the real Gabe.

"Look, Eve, I think he needs this," Gabe continued, his eyes still locked on Nathan. He grabbed his drink, taking a slow sip like he was making a calculated move in a poker game. "He told me about all of his issues last night. That's some really sad stuff. I guess I figured he could use a little push. You know, something to prove to himself that he can come out of his shell."

Then, shifting his posture, Gabe leaned back, stretching his arms behind his head with a dramatic sigh.

"Plus, do you have any idea how hard it is to find a decent roommate these days? I mean, one minute you think you've lucked out with a totally normal guy, and before you know it, he's clipping locks of your hair while you sleep. Let's just say, I've seen things, man—things that make you rethink dorm life altogether."

He paused, shaking his head like a war veteran reminiscing about battles best left unspoken, before giving a quick shiver to snap himself out of the pretend haze. "But seriously, Nathan is a good dude. I promise—I won't let him get hurt."

At that moment, Eve saw Gabe in a new light. Beneath all the sitcom-level antics and dumb jokes, there was an actual person—and maybe even a good one at that. She finally understood why he was pushing Nathan, and she appreciated him for it.

A wave of guilt hit her. She'd spent years brushing off Nathan's issues, acting like it was just who he was. She'd always chalked it up to Nathan being, well, just Nathan.

But Gabe had seen through it. And now he was doing something about it, trying to help Nathan figure himself out in a way she never tried to do.

"I can't believe you got him to do this," she said softly, a hint of pride in her voice. "You know, I appreciate you looking out for him."

Gabe quickly held a finger to his lips, eyes locked on Nathan. "Shh. Watch—he's almost there.

As Nathan stepped up next to her, his eyes shifted nervously between the salad bar and her graceful figure. Up close, she was even more beautiful. A subtle scent of plumeria drifted from her—sweet but not overpowering—and for a moment, a sense of calm washed over him, battling against the nervous flutter in his chest.

Not knowing what else to do with his hands, he grabbed a tray, like it would somehow solve everything. Before he knew it, he was standing way too close, pretending to care about salad options. He picked up the tongs, awkwardly stabbing at some spinach, then dropped a few cherry tomatoes onto the tray—no plate, just letting them roll around like that was totally normal.

Gabe's rules replayed in his head: six feet, ninety seconds, eye contact. *Is this six feet? Am I close enough?*

He wasn't sure, but it was too late to second-guess.

He shuffled a little closer, pretending to be interested in the fresh fruit as his mind raced to keep count. Ninety seconds. All he had to do was stay there, just close enough, for ninety seconds.

Ticking down the seconds in his head, Nathan felt the pressure mount. Thirty seconds—then sixty. He tried to keep count. Then he remembered —eye contact. That was the final piece of the puzzle. But how was he supposed to make eye contact without looking like a total weirdo?

Just as he was working up the nerve, she shifted. Her shoulder brushed against his, and she let out a soft, "Oop" that was barely more than a whisper. It was enough to make him freeze.

Their eyes met. Then she smiled. It wasn't big or flashy, just this small, easy curve of her lips that lit up her whole face.

For someone Eve was convinced had to be Enhanced, there was something completely natural about her. Like she wasn't trying too hard. Like she didn't have to.

Nathan felt warmth rise in his chest, slow and steady, settling in a way that surprised him. He'd expected the usual rush of panic, but instead, there was only calm. He felt like this moment had always been waiting for him to catch up.

Everything else in the room faded away. It was just her, standing close enough to feel real, and him, wondering how long they'd been locked in place like this. She was about to say something—he could tell. Her lips parted slightly, and for one reckless second, he thought about staying. He thought about waiting to hear what she had to say and letting it be enough to close the space between them.

But then the goal snapped back into focus: *ninety seconds, eye contact, say nothing.*

Panic surged through him, and before he could stop himself, Nathan spun on his heel and power-walked back to his seat.

His heart pounded, but this time, it was for a whole new reason.

He collapsed into his chair, slamming his tray of mixed greens and rogue tomatoes onto the table like they were the last thing he wanted to deal with. Gabe and Eve just stared at him, wide-eyed, like they were waiting for a performance.

Gabe looked at Nathan, his face full of genuine pride. "Congrats, buddy—looks like you've officially got your first Cafeteria Girlfriend. Now don't blow it. Remember, you can't speak to her—not even a word—not ever. If you do, it's cafeteria splitsville."

Nathan leaned back in his seat as a strange mix of emotions swirled inside him. He glanced over his shoulder, searching for his new Cafeteria Girlfriend.

He spotted her easily as she walked away from the salad bar, her tray balanced with an assortment of greens, veggies, and a Diet Coke perched perfectly beside them. Every step she took was flawless—elegant, poised —like she had everything under control.

All the usual noise in his head quieted. There was no anxiety, no fear of facing his childhood bully. Even Gabe's exaggerated snickering faded into the background.

As he watched her search for her seat, Nathan knew one thing—his part in the Cafeteria Girlfriend game had been doomed from the start.

There was no way he could stick to the rules. He had to figure out a way to talk to her. He couldn't just settle for fleeting eye contact or some distant, silent fantasy. He needed to hear her voice. He needed to know what she sounded like, to see if there was something real behind that smile.

She might have been way out of his league—and maybe even Enhanced—but none of that mattered.

At that moment, he made a promise to himself. One way or another, he was going to know her.

For a second, everything felt clear. He could see it all—walking up to her, striking up a conversation. Maybe it would be awkward, but maybe he'd find a way to be charming. Maybe he'd even get her to laugh.

But then, as he watched her find her seat, his entire fantasy crumbled.

Gabe, Eve, and Nathan watched in silent horror as she took her place at a table already occupied.

The group she joined: Valerie Reynolds, Simon Wu—and Dante Edwards.

8

CRACKS IN THE ICE

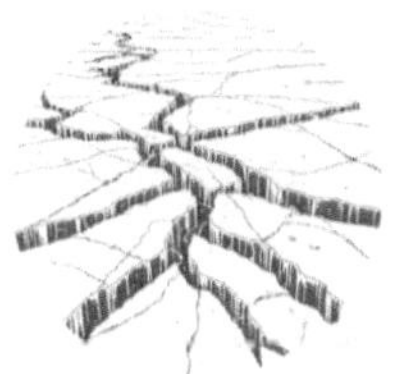

The world didn't just blur—it shattered. Everything slipped away, dissolving like someone had dragged a wet brush across reality, smearing it into a twisted, incomprehensible mess.

Colors bled together, leaking from every corner—warping, twisting—until nothing made sense. The blue of Eve's scarf, the dull green of the lunch trays, even the beige walls—faded, then vanished, leaving only white.

Not the soft, comforting white of snow, but the harsh, blinding kind—an endless sheet of ice stretching beyond the horizon, reflecting too much light, too much nothing. It burned through his skull, erasing everything familiar.

A vacuum swallowed the cafeteria whole. Voices, the scrape of chairs, the hum of conversation—all silenced, like someone had pulled the plug on the world. The only sound left was the relentless thud of his heart, echoing louder, rattling through his bones like his chest was hollow. The rhythm surged and crashed—unsteady, violent—like waves battering a frozen shore, threatening to break through.

He tried to breathe, but his lungs rebelled. Each inhale came shallow, clipped, like trying to suck air through a straw. No oxygen. Only a hollow ache pressing against his ribs, crushing him from the inside out.

His bones splintered under the pressure. His body screamed to escape, but his legs were locked in place.

The ice crept into every sense. Fractures spiderwebbed beneath his feet, the frozen lake under too much pressure. Each heartbeat split the surface wider, warning him that one wrong move would send him under.

Dread started deep—a cold knot twisting in his gut—then climbed his spine, wrapping tight around his ribs. His muscles seized. His limbs turned to stone, dragging him down.

Inside his head, everything exploded. Thoughts shattered into jagged shards, slicing through him. Images of his deepest fears collided in a frenzy, tangled like a film reel caught in overdrive.

Just breathe. Just breathe. The voice clawed through the panic. *You're okay. You're okay.*

But he wasn't. The rational part of his brain tried to scream for help, but no sound came.

His vision narrowed. The air thickened. The cracks widened—sharp, chaotic veins racing beneath the ice.

He was slipping. The surface groaned beneath him. There was nowhere left to stand.

He needed something to anchor him. Anything. But his mind was an ocean now, and he was drowning.

Every fear, every doubt, every buried truth surged up and slammed into him.

His heart pounded, wild. Sweat chilled his skin. His fingers tingled, numb.

The panic was a storm. Violent. Unforgiving. It tore through him. Devoured him. He was falling.

The cracks split open. The surface gave way. He plunged.

He couldn't move. Couldn't speak. His body trembled from a cold that wasn't real and the terror that was.

And then—before he knew it—he was on the floor.

9

THE ULTIMATE COMBO

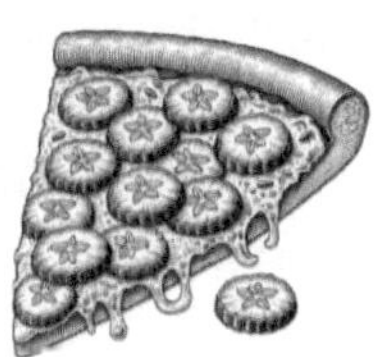

Gabe's voice was the first to cut through the haze. "Come on, Cheese, wake up!"

"My name's not Cheese," Nathan mumbled, his voice barely scraping past his lips. "It's Nathan."

Eve's voice, heavy with concern, followed. "Nathan Boone. Can you hear me? Snap out of it."

He tried to open his eyes, but it felt like they were glued shut—like something was holding them closed on purpose, keeping him trapped in the dark no matter how hard he fought. Sounds started to come back, but everything was muffled, like he was underwater. He wanted to move, to sit up, but his body felt heavy, like gravity had doubled just for him.

Then came another voice—new and unfamiliar, but calm and compassionate.

"Give him some space," the voice gently instructed.

He felt the pressure on his chest lift slightly. The vice squeezing around his lungs loosened, and the heaviness holding down his eyelids grew lighter.

He started to breathe again—shallow, but steady—syncing with the rhythm of the hand resting firmly on his shoulder.

"Hey," the voice soothed. "It's okay. Take your time. You're alright. Can you tell me your name?"

He struggled to find the words as his thoughts scrambled to catch up. "Um... my name is Nathan... Nathan Boone."

"Hi, Nathan," the voice said softly. "My name is Mia—Mia Bennet. It's nice to meet you. Can you open your eyes for me?"

He let the calm in her voice wash over him, and as he did, his panic started to fade, and he slowly opened his eyes.

Leaning over him was her—the girl from the salad bar. The one who had, just minutes ago, made his heart leap out of his chest. Her lips curved slightly with a small smile of reassurance.

"Do you think you can get up?" she asked, her voice a steady anchor in the storm of his thoughts.

As his focus returned, he noticed a small crowd had gathered around him, with Eve and Gabe at the front—their faces etched with the kind of worry he'd come to know too well.

Gabe leaned down and extended a hand. "Come on, Cheeseman. Let me help you up."

Nathan groaned, "I told you, that's not my name," he replied, reaching for Gabe's hand anyway.

With one solid pull, Gabe yanked him back to his feet. The ground still felt unsteady beneath him, and his body remained sluggish, like he'd just woken up from a dream he couldn't shake.

"What... happened?" Nathan rasped, already knowing full well what had triggered the episode, but the words fell out anyway.

"Well, buddy," Gabe whispered, leaning in as if sharing a secret, "you just broke up with your very first Cafeteria Girlfriend."

He glanced over at Eve, who was looking at him the way she always did after a panic attack. She had that expression like she was relieved, but bracing herself for the next one.

"That was a big one, huh?" she asked softly. "You alright?"

"Yeah, I'm okay," he whispered, feeling the weight of the words.

His eyes darted back to where Dante had been sitting, half-expecting to see him still there, watching with that smug, cruel look Nathan dreaded most, but he wasn't in his seat anymore. Only Val and Wu were left, and neither of them seemed bothered enough to acknowledge what had just happened.

"Hey, um... thanks," he said as he turned back to Mia.

The words felt too small for the moment, but it was all he had.

"I just... I have these panic attacks sometimes."

She tilted her head slightly, her silver hair catching the light as she studied him, her expression soft yet thoughtful.

"I get those too sometimes," she said, surprising him. "They're rough—You feel like you're drowning in your head, right?"

The admission caught him off guard. "Yeah," he replied. "Something like that."

She studied him for a second, her expression thoughtful, but not in that pitying, fake way he was used to. It wasn't the kind of look people gave when they didn't get it, but they felt like they were supposed to say something anyway.

"You're okay now, though. That's all that matters," she said, her voice calm. Then she paused and added, "Do you need anything? I can walk you over to the health center if you want. I have a work-study there—I'm pre-med."

Pre-med? Nathan thought, the words catching him off guard. That's usually an organic study track. Most of the Enhanced students didn't bother with it—they didn't need to.

Their implants handled everything for them.

If she was Enhanced, why would she be studying medicine?

His mind started unraveling the mystery of Mia Bennet before he could stop himself, curiosity growing like an itch he couldn't scratch.

Who was she, really? He thought.

Before he let himself spiral too far into speculation, Nathan straightened up.

"No, I'm good, really," he said, forcing a smile that felt just convincing enough. "I probably just need to eat something."

"Yeah, real food," Eve said, stepping up beside him, her tone light but her eyes locked on Mia, watching her carefully.

Mia let her eyes linger on Nathan, searching for confirmation that he was okay.

"Alright, well, if you change your mind, I'm around. I hope you feel better, Nathan. It was nice meeting you." Her voice was warm, but not overly sweet.

Nathan watched as she turned and walked away. As she faded into the crowd, he realized that for the first time in a long while, he wasn't just hoping to avoid his usual fears. He was hoping for something more.

A moment of silence stretched between him and Eve, but not an easy one. When he finally turned back to her, the expression on her face said it all.

"What?" Nathan asked, already regretting it.

Eve let out a sharp breath, shaking her head like she couldn't believe what she was seeing. "I saw the way you were looking at her," she said, giving him a playful nudge with her elbow. "You've got a major league crush on that girl, don't you?"

She sighed, her tone shifting just a little. "I'm telling you, Boone—stay away. The Enhanced are bad news bears."

Nathan frowned. "You don't know that she's Enhanced," he replied quickly, too quickly.

Eve shot him a look.

"Oh, come on, dude. That hair? Those eyes? Even if she isn't a full-on chiphead, she's definitely got some kind of optimization. Plus, she hangs with Val and her crew. It's not hard to connect the dots."

Nathan hesitated, chewing on the inside of his cheek. "I dunno, maybe she is, but she seems—different."

"Different?" Eve echoed, rolling her eyes. "Right... that's exactly how they get you. They make you think that they're different, that maybe they don't see the world the same way the others do, but at the end of the day, they still look down on us, Nathan."

Nathan glanced back toward where Mia had disappeared, his thoughts tangled and restless.

Maybe Eve was right. Maybe Mia was just another Enhanced girl pretending to be normal. But the way she had looked at him, it didn't feel like pity. It felt sincere—like she was someone who might understand him.

"Dude," Gabe's voice cut through Nathan's swirling thoughts, yanking him completely out of the panic spiral he'd just fallen into. "That was easily the fastest cafeteria relationship of all time. Tough break, man. But hey, you know what they say—plenty of fish in the caf. Well, at least there is on sushi night."

Clearly not thrilled about the Caf Girlfriend bit making a comeback, Eve shot Gabe a look that could've frozen boiling water.

"Gabe," she said, her voice low but sharp enough to cut glass. "Your roommate just passed out in the middle of a crowded cafeteria. Maybe hold off on the jokes for, like, five seconds."

Gabe blinked at her like she'd missed the point entirely. "Hey! I *am* just checking on him," he said, completely serious. "We need to make sure he's still got a sense of humor—you know?"

The wave of positivity pouring out of Gabe soaked into Nathan, dragging a reluctant smile out of him.

"It's fine, Eve. I'm good. Honest." His voice was still a little shaky, but he managed to get the words out.

"Oh, there it is... I saw that smile!" Gabe pointed like it was a rare wildlife sighting. "Look at him! He's coming back!"

Then, slipping effortlessly into the most ridiculous baby-talk voice imaginable, he leaned in a little closer. "That's it, little Cheese... come back to the light," he sing-songed. "It's warm here... search for it... find the light."

She rolled her eyes and let out a sharp breath through her nose. "You are such a jackass."

His face lit up like he'd just won an award. "Thanks. I do my best."

She shook her head. "You're always on, aren't you?"

Gabe shrugged like it was a basic truth. "Hey, being this awesome is a full-time job."

She groaned, shooting Nathan a look full of sympathy. "Ignore him. Gabe has the emotional depth of a ham sandwich with googly eyes."

"How rude!" He pulled a mock-offended face. "I was just trying to be a good friend, offer emotional support, and—"

Mid-sentence, his focus snapped toward the pizza line like he'd just spotted buried treasure.

"Speaking of distractions, looks like they just fired up the pizza ovens." Gabe nudged Nathan like he was sharing a secret. "Maybe I can work my magic and get them to make me a Gabe Special—extra cheese with pickles. It's the ultimate combo."

Still feeling the echoes of his panic attack, Nathan stared at him. Somehow, the nonsense was working. It chipped away at the fog.

"Pickles? On pizza? That's gross." Eve cringed, giving Gabe a look like he'd offended the food gods.

"Hey, don't knock it till you've tried it. Culinary genius is often misunderstood." His tone was light, but it shifted. "Seriously, man. You good?"

Nathan let out a breath, slower this time. "Yeah. I think so."

"See, Eve? He's fine." Gabe gave him a playful punch. "Just needed a little Gabe therapy. That, and maybe some carbs." He pointed toward the pizza line. "Want me to grab you a slice? A slice of pickle pie will change your life."

Eve stood, brushing invisible crumbs off her jeans. "Nathan, please don't listen to him. Let's get you some real food. Something that's a little less disgusting."

She held out her hand. He took it, and just that small gesture anchored him more than anything else had all day.

"Fine, but you're missing out," Gabe called over his shoulder as he headed off. "And don't come crawling over when you're stuck eating some boring sandwich. This is a one-time offer!"

With an exaggerated battle cry—somewhere between a yell and a howl—he dove into the crowd like a man on a mission.

Eve and Nathan shared a look.

"That guy is something else," she muttered, eyes tracking him as he disappeared behind a soda fountain.

"Yeah." A laugh started to push its way into Nathan's voice. "I don't know what it is about him, but he always makes me feel better."

"I get that." She lingered on the pizza line for a moment longer, her voice warm. "He's definitely a ball of positive energy. I told you he'd be good for you."

Then she turned back to him. Her expression softened. "Hey… I saw him too. Dante, I mean." A pause. "Are you sure you're okay?"

Nathan glanced at the table. "Not really. Just seeing him... it felt like I was back in high school. Everyone laughing. I couldn't move, couldn't breathe. All the years of shit he gave me just exploded in my head all over again."

Her hand rested on his arm. "I know that was rough. But I was watching him when you went down—he didn't even look over. If he was still the same jerk, he would've been front and center, loving every second of it. But he wasn't."

She squeezed gently. "I don't think you're even on his radar, Nathan. And honestly? I don't think he should be on yours either."

He let the words settle between them. "Maybe you're right," he said after a beat, though it didn't feel like enough.

"I know I'm right." Her no-nonsense tone kicked back in. "He's just another arrogant jock wrapped up in his own perfect world. I've been keeping an eye on him—trust me. He's not plotting anything. He just hangs with his perfect crowd and does their dumb Enhanced shit. Honestly, this is one of the few times I've even seen him since freshman year."

Nathan nodded, trying to take it in. But the memories were still loud.

10

————————————

RENT FREE

Nathan and Eve scanned all the options as they shuffled through the cafeteria line. The smell of grilled vegetables and spices drifted from one of the stations, and her eyes instantly lit up.

"Ooh, organic veggie wrap with truffle fries? Yes, please."

She gave him a playful look. "What about you? Which of these ultra-healthy options are calling your name?"

He looked over the spread. Everything was annoyingly nutritious—kale chips, quinoa bowls, tofu stir-fry. It was like the whole menu had been designed by people who chanted personal mantras to their plants under a full moon. None of it looked remotely appealing.

He needed something safe—something that wouldn't leave him flattened by a rogue snack truck or, worse, inspire him to ditch everything and join the Peace Corps—if that was even still a thing.

"Uh, this is great and all, but—" His tray hovered in indecision. "Don't they have anything normal? Like sandwiches or something? I think that I need something halfway between your intense veggie cult menu and, you know, whatever the hell it is that Gabe calls food."

"What, you can't handle all this earthy goodness?" she teased, nudging him toward the far end of the serving lines. "There's a deli bar over there —pretty sure they've got whatever your meat-eating heart desires."

He cracked a small smile. "Alright, sounds good."

As he turned to head for the deli, she called after him, "Oh, and if you

63

see your roommate and he tries to offer you a slice of pizza with pickles on it? Just say no."

~

The sandwich station looked like Subway on steroids. It had endless bread options, and more meats than any normal person needed. Nathan hovered in front of the counter, torn between turkey and roast beef, his brain lagging behind his hunger. And the cheese—sharp cheddar, provolone, swiss, pepper jack—it was impossible to pick.

He was still trying to make up his mind when someone shoved him hard from behind, sending him stumbling forward into the glass.

"Excuse me, my man. Let me just sneak in real quick."

Before Nathan could react, the guy who cut him in line barked out his order like he owned the place.

"I need an extra-large steak and cheese with double meat—I mean stack that shit high, with extra cheese, make it American, salt and pepper, and lots of mayo. And make it quick, I've got places to be."

When Nathan looked over to find out what kind of asshole could be ordering such a monstrous sandwich, his stomach dropped like a malfunctioning elevator plummeting into the ninth circle of hell.

Dante just stood there, eyes glued to his phone like Nathan wasn't even there.

"Thanks for letting me cut in, man," he muttered, not bothered enough to look up from whatever feed he was scrolling. "I'm starving."

BaBoone.

The name echoed in his head. The bully who had spent years making his life hell was now cutting him in line, and worse, he was acting like he didn't even exist.

He gripped the edges of his tray, preparing himself for another spiral, but the fear he expected never came. Instead, something darker slithered up his spine.

Dante finally glanced up from his phone, his enhanced golden eyes looking down at Nathan.

"Oh, hey, man," he said flatly. "I saw what just happened out there. You good?"

His voice was empty, as if he couldn't care less. He didn't wait for a reply—just went back to scrolling through his feed, clearly more interested in whatever was on the screen than anything Nathan might have to say.

Nathan just stared at him, waiting for some tiny crumb of recognition —anything—but nothing came. Just Dante, treating him like he wasn't even a person.

He knew right away this wasn't the same cocky high school Dante who spread rumors and laughed about it. This version was way worse.

Everything about him was flawless in the most obnoxious way. He had muscles stacked on top of muscles, like some scientist had designed him in a lab just to intimidate people, both on and off the football field.

The worst part was that he had no idea he was standing next to the kid whose life he had systematically dismantled for the better part of their shared childhood, leaving wreckage in his wake without a second thought.

Nathan's soul screamed.

Back in high school, if he so much as heard Dante was in the same wing of the building, his first instinct was to run as fast and as far as he could without looking back. It was the only way he'd ever known how to survive.

Now, though, something in him had shifted. His blood didn't chill anymore; it boiled.

Fear wasn't forcing him to run this time. Instead, rage was telling him to fight, and this new rage, real and intense, made his hands curl into fists without even thinking.

He wanted to hit him—not just one punch, but a relentless flurry of them. He allowed himself to get swept up in the violent fantasy. Each swing he would throw would be harder than the last, landing with the kind of force that would finally make Dante truly see him—see what he had done to him.

He needed to make Dante remember everything. Not in some distant, guilty flashback—he wanted him to feel it deep in his bones.

As angry as he was, and as much as he wanted to finally teach Dante a lesson, Nathan knew the truth. Physically, he was no match—and without a chip, he never would be.

But that didn't stop the daydream. What he really wanted was simple: to rip Dante's perfect face clean off.

Nathan imagined himself moving so fast that Dante wouldn't have a chance to react. He'd grab him by his too-perfect collar, yank him forward, and slam his head against the counter—hard enough to silence the entire tray line.

He'd pull him up by the back of the neck before unleashing a rhythmic pummeling on his former bully's face. Every rage-filled blow would land with precision and force, smashing into that flawless façade over and over —until his jawbone splintered beneath Nathan's knuckles. By the time he stopped, Dante's store-bought features would be unrecognizable, and the sandwich line would look more like a crime scene than a lunch rush. Nathan would revel in it—the moment the guy who'd ruled his life with fear finally realized he wasn't untouchable anymore. The bill for a decade of pain had finally come due.

The fantasy crumbled as the woman behind the counter slid Dante's sandwich to him like it was some kind of VIP order. Then she turned to Nathan, looking at him expectantly, waiting for his order, like his entire world hadn't just gone sideways.

Nathan trembled as Dante grabbed his sandwich and shot him a smug look.

"Alright, man. Be good. And hey—eat something. You're too skinny."

And just like that, the root of all Nathan's fears walked off—a steak and cheese in one hand, phone in the other, fully absorbed in his own world, as if Nathan had never existed.

When he got back to the table, Nathan sat down hard and dropped his tray with a dull thud. His fingers tore at the wrapper of his sandwich without thinking. It was the only thing he could do with all the nervous energy still rattling inside him. Any shred of appetite he'd had was long gone.

Eve slid into the seat across from him, her tray forgotten as her eyes locked on his face.

She immediately knew something was up.

"Nathan?" she asked, her voice low and steady. "What's wrong? You look like you're about to go sideways again."

"I just saw Dante," he said, letting out a slow breath.

She cracked open her bottle of kombucha, the hiss cutting through the noise between them. She looked straight at him, eyes scanning his face with one brow arched.

"Oh? I see. Did he mess with you?"

"That's the thing." He said, shaking his head. "He didn't do anything. He acted like he didn't even remember me."

"And that's a bad thing?" she asked as she sprinkled parmesan onto her truffle fries, shaking a little extra across the top before picking one up and snapping it in half, her gaze never leaving his face.

"I guess not—" He shrugged as he peeled the paper back from his sandwich, unfolding the edges with slow, distracted fingers, not even sure if he wanted to eat it.

"He hasn't changed though. He's still the same jerk he's always been. He cut me in line like he's the crowned prince of everything."

She casually fished another fry from the pile and popped it into her mouth.

"See? I told you—he's a self-absorbed asshole. He didn't remember you? That's a good thing."

He stared at the tray in front of him, as the anger brewing inside him began to rise again, pushing toward the surface like pressure under glass.

"I don't know. It's just that he was this huge thing in my life, you know? And now seeing him act like none of it ever happened... I guess it just somehow makes it worse."

She reached across the table and let her fingers rest lightly on his wrist, steady and present, like a tether pulling him back to the surface.

"That's because it never mattered to him," she said gently. "Look, when I told you he was here, what were you worried about the most?"

Nathan let out a long sigh as he tried to push the lingering new rage out before it could fully take hold of him.

"I guess... I was afraid all the same shit would start up again. That I'd have to live life like I did in high school all over."

"Right." She gave his wrist a gentle squeeze. "And now you've seen him, and none of that happened. So why are you upset?"

He didn't answer.

She leaned in a little, her tone soft but steady. "Listen to me, Nathan. Dante Edwards does not own you anymore. He's part of your past, not your present, and definitely not your future. Like I said, he's in his own little bubble. Too self-absorbed to see anything beyond himself. Let him rot there, where he belongs."

"I don't know, Eve. It was just... strange. I mean, I hear you. I hear what you're saying, and I know you're right. I wish I could just let it all go. But I can't."

She sat back slightly, the sharpness in her tone cutting through the comfort. "Look, Nathan, none of this is healthy for you. You've gotta stop letting him live in your head rent-free. He's not worth the space you're giving him—especially when he clearly has no interest in giving you any of his."

"I hate him," he muttered. "I wanted to rip his face off. I wanted to show him—"

He stopped short and drew in a breath, trying to swallow down the burn in his chest, like keeping it buried might stop everything else from spilling out with it.

"I don't know. I think I'm finally losing it—for real."

"You're not losing it, Nathan." Her voice didn't waver. "You've had a ton of crap thrown at you these last few months, and you're surviving. And soon, you'll be thriving. Don't let Dante drag you back down. He's not worth it."

He sat with her words, but the heat under his skin refused to fade. It wasn't the icy panic he'd known his whole life.

This was something else—something new.

Something alive and dangerous. And he had no idea what to do with it.

11

CHASING GHOSTS

Later that night, in the quiet of his dorm room, Nathan sat hunched over his laptop, Aside from the occasional beep from Gabe's handheld video game, the only sound was the steady click of his keyboard. It was the one sound that made sense. The one that felt almost like home.

The first full day on campus had been a mess, and Nathan was just glad to be somewhere that felt safe, at least, he hoped it was. He was looking forward to an easy night before the start of classes the next day.

Across the room, Gabe was flopped on his bed, tapping his fingers furiously on his handheld's buttons. He let out a loud sigh and tossed the device onto his comforter.

"Hey, Cheese," Gabe said, still staring at his screen. "Can I ask you something?"

"Yeah, I guess," Nathan mumbled, barely looking up from his laptop.

"What happened earlier—you know, in The Caf?" Gabe asked, propping himself up on one elbow. "You went down pretty hard. It looked intense. I mean, do I need to start following you around with a crash mat?" He chuckled, trying to keep it light.

"Nah, it's nothing to stress about," Nathan replied, waving it off with his focus locked on his laptop screen.

"I just get these panic attacks sometimes," he admitted. "Today was worse than usual."

"Panic attacks, huh? That sounds rough," Gabe said. "What made today so bad?"

Nathan let out a breath. "It turns out this guy—someone I knew from back home—goes here. Let's just say, he made my life hell all through high school, and I wasn't prepared to ever see him again."

Gabe sat up and pressed his fist into his palm with a solid smack. "Give me a name, Cheese. I've got no problem handing out a free beatdown to some bully who's got one coming."

Nathan gave a weak laugh and shook his head. "I appreciate the offer, but I don't think that'll help." He tried—and failed- to not picture Gabe standing toe-to-toe with Dante, the uber chiphead himself.

"His name's Dante. I guess he's part of your girl Val's crew now. I was hoping to avoid him, but he was in the Caf today. I guess seeing him again messed with my head, and I just—sort of spiraled."

"Ah, Dante Edwards." Gabe exhaled, shaking his head. "Yeah, I'm not a fan either."

Nathan raised an eyebrow. "Wait—you know him?"

Gabe shrugged. "Yeah, he was my freshman-year roommate. Believe it or not, I came here on an athletic scholarship. They stuck me and Dante together since we were both part of the so-called prestigious NCSU Orange Wave."

Nathan looked up. "Hold on. You were a jock? I don't believe it."

"Believe it, Roomie," Gabe said, patting his belly with pride. "Under all this top-tier junk food storage is a former all-conference linebacker." He flexed dramatically before laughing.

"There's no way. I can't see it," Nathan replied, shaking his head.

"It's totally true. But I found out pretty quickly that being screamed at by grown men in khakis just isn't for me. I took Intro to Theater as a fluff elective, and it turns out performing arts was a way better fit. Apparently, I'm a natural-born performer."

Nathan scoffed. "So what—you just bailed on him and moved in here?"

Gabe shook his head. "No, I've only ever lived in this room. Honestly? That used to be Dante's bed," he said, motioning to where Nathan was sitting.

Sharing the same space Dante had once slept in made Nathan's skin crawl. He didn't want to think about it.

"The day I told him I was hanging up my pads for good, he sat with me for hours, trying to talk me out of it. He begged me to stay, and to be honest, he almost convinced me. But I just couldn't do the gridiron grind anymore. My heart just wasn't in it anymore."

"So, what happened?" Nathan asked.

Gabe's expression faltered. "When I wouldn't budge, he totally flipped out on me. Said some really awful stuff that I won't repeat. A few days later, he moved out, and after that, he acted like he didn't even know me."

"Well, you're lucky you only had to deal with him for a little while," Nathan muttered."I had to deal with his crap for years, He started this rumor that I had a baboon's heart because I was always in and out of the hospital. And it stuck. Pretty soon, the whole school was calling me Baboone."

He gave a bitter laugh.

"They'd pound their chests and make monkey noises every time I walked into a room. Some of them would scratch under their arms or pick at their ears like they were in on some joke I never agreed to. And it didn't stop when I tried to ignore them either. One time, someone even put a stuffed monkey in my locker with a little plastic heart taped to its chest. You know, real creative stuff."

Gabe tossed his handheld onto the bed and shifted, edging closer so he was facing Nathan. "Wow—That's messed up, man. No wonder you freaked out at breakfast. I'm sorry you had to deal with all that."

"Yeah, it was pretty brutal," Nathan said, looking back at his laptop.

Gabe leaned in, letting go of the performance for once.

"Look, man, I can't even imagine how bad that must've sucked. I'm sure it's still tough to shake. But you made it through all that—and now you're here. That counts for something. You've got more strength in you than you think."

"I don't know about that," Nathan shrugged, keeping his head in his work.

"I'm serious," Gabe said. "I don't know what it is, but I think there's something in you—something just waiting to be unlocked. It's just a vibe I get. You're a good dude, Cheese, and for what it's worth, I'll always have your back—I promise."

Nathan gave a small nod. "Thanks, man. I appreciate that."

Before he could say anything else, Gabe clapped his hands together. "Alright, that's enough about Dickhead Dante. On to more pressing matters," he said with a chuckle. "Like your first campus heartbreak."

Nathan furrowed his brow. "What do you mean—campus heartbreak?"

Gabe shot him a flat look. "Oh, come on, man. I'm talking about your caf girlfriend—what was her name again—Mia? You're telling me you didn't feel even a spark? Not even a little?"

Nathan chuckled, shaking his head. "I don't know, maybe."

He avoided admitting how he felt when he saw her. "You and I both know there's no way a girl like her would ever be into me."

Gabe scooted back on his bed, crossing his arms as he leaned into the wall and nodded sagely. "Don't sell yourself short like that. I'm telling you, Cheese, that girl likes you. I can feel it."

"Whatever, man," Nathan sighed and closed his laptop. "She doesn't even know me, and even if she did, she's, I dunno—"

"What—Out of your league?" Gabe cut in, lifting an eyebrow.

"Look, man, if there's one thing I've figured out, it's that girls love a fixer-upper. Seriously. Think about it—if you were her, would you go for some asshole jock like Dante, or would you pick the guy who's a full-on project? You know… like you."

He gave Nathan a look of mock desperation before slipping back into his Rodney Dangerfield impression. "No offense!"

Nathan rolled his eyes. "Whatever, dude. Speaking of leagues—what's with you and Val? That's next-level crazy, even for you."

Gabe burst out laughing. "I guess she's *my* reclamation project. A little challenge for the sake of the greater good." He threw his hands up dramatically. "I mean, someone's gotta tame that shrew, right? If not for me, then for the good of the entire campus."

Nathan raised an eyebrow. "I don't know, man, that girl is bad news. She's not someone I'd ever want to be in the same room with if I could avoid it. There's just something about her that screams danger."

Gabe dropped his voice into a terrible James Bond impression. "Well, lucky for me, Danger is my mother's maiden name."

"You're a mess," Nathan snorted.

"Ah, Cheese, you're sweet for saying that. But seriously, the whole Cafeteria Girlfriend thing is just a goofy guy thing. Val isn't my type—like, at all."

"Oh yeah? So what is your type, then?" Nathan asked, raising an eyebrow.

A faint blush crept into Gabe's cheeks. "The Flower Child."

Nathan blinked. "Wait—Eve? Like *Eve*-Eve?"

"Hell yeah, man," Gabe replied, still blushing. "That girl's got style. Now, she is my type."

Nathan nearly choked. "Yeah, good luck with that, man. I mean, she's my best friend and all, and I love her, but she's tough. She might look like she's all sunshine and rainbows, but I swear—she's got thorns."

Gabe raised an eyebrow, intrigued. "Thorns, huh?"

"I'm just saying, man, you're not the first one to be into her," Nathan warned. "Her last boyfriend was crazy about her. He was a solid guy, too, treated her great and everything. I thought for sure they were gonna last. Then, out of nowhere, she dumped him. He couldn't handle it—dude went full-on rom-com, stood outside her window blasting some old '80s song, thinking it'd win her back."

Gabe's eyes widened. "Oh man, he pulled the *Say Anything* move?"

Nathan nodded. "Yup, He sure did. Went full Lloyd Dobbler, boombox and everything. Honestly, when I heard about it, I respected his effort."

Gabe laughed. "And she loved it, right?"

"Oh no, she hated it," Nathan said. "She called the cops on him. The whole thing turned into a disaster. So yeah, man, if you wanna go after Eve, be my guest. But just know—it's your funeral."

Gabe stared off into space for a second, clearly mulling it over.

"I dunno, man. What you're saying just makes me like her even more."

Nathan groaned. "You know you're asking for trouble, right? Just don't do anything that's gonna mess up all of us being able to be friends."

"Oh, don't worry, Cheese," he replied like it was no big deal. "I'll be super chill about it—I promise."

Nathan gave him a look. "Yeah, I'm sure you will. It's not you I'm worried about." He pointed at Gabe, half serious. "Just don't say I didn't warn you. I'm telling you, man—thorns. Sharp ones."

Gabe chuckled. "Well, that sounds perfect to me—" His eyes lit up with that usual spark of trouble. "You know my mother's maiden name, right?"

Nathan groaned. "Oh god, not this again. Please."

Gabe laughed. "Hey, I can't help it if I come from a bloodline full of Dangers.

Speaking of danger, it's the last night before classes. Let's do something to honor my mother's name."

Nathan looked at him, puzzled. "Like what? I don't think I'm up for raiding your snack stash again. I'm still trying to recover from last night."

Gabe waved dismissively, standing up like he'd been struck by divine inspiration. "No, no. I'm in the mood for something far more adventurous. Just get our favorite Hippie Chick on the phone. Tell her to meet us on the quad in fifteen minutes.

Tonight, my friend, we chase ghosts."

12

RETAIL GRAVEYARD

Nathan shoved his hands deeper into his pockets as the cold settled into his skin. His fingers had gone numb minutes ago, and every breath he took sent a sharp chill through his lungs. He resisted the urge to complain, but the way he shivered made it clear—he was miserable.

Gabe, meanwhile, was a whole different story. He paced in tight circles, radiating energy like a transformer ready to blow. Every distant sound had him whipping his head toward the path that cut across the quad.

"Dude, are you sure she's coming?" he asked, his voice jittery with anticipation.

Nathan rocked slightly on his heels. "Yeah, she'll be here. She just messaged me—she's on her way."

"Excellent!" Gabe rubbed his hands together in mock villainy, his excitement ramping up. "I need a full audience for this."

Nathan shot him a sideways glance, suspicion creeping into his voice. "Alright, spill it. What are we doing out here? Is this really a ghost hunt, or is it just another one of your stupid games? If it's either—tell me now."

Gabe stopped and turned to Nathan, looking way too pleased with himself. "Oh, this isn't a game, Cheese. Just call it a history lesson." He let that hang for a beat, then dropped his voice. "But I won't lie—there'll be ghosts. Lots of them."

Nathan groaned. "Gabe, after the day I've had, I'm not sure I'm up for whatever nonsense you have planned."

Gabe grabbed his shoulder, giving him a shake. "Relax, Cheese, this will be fun. I promise. You just need to trust me. I swear, you're gonna love it."

Before Nathan could press him further, the soft scrape of corduroy against frozen pavement cut through the night. He didn't have to turn to know who was approaching.

She emerged from the shadows, wrapped in a heavy wool coat built for the kind of cold only a New England winter could deliver. Her hands disappeared into deep pockets, and her shoulders hunched against the wind. A deep-green cable-knit hat, complete with a fluffy white pompom, held her sandy blonde hair in place. It slouched just enough to look effortless, but hugged tight enough to keep out the cold. A thick scarf looped around her neck, its ends draped over her chest.

Eve wore her winter armor like everything else—pulled together with the kind of ease that made it impossible to tell if she cared too much or not at all.

"Alright, what's this all about?" She called out as she approached, her breath visible in the cold air.

Gabe turned to face her with a dramatic flair, already turning on the charm. "Ah, the lady of the hour has arrived!" he declared, bowing slightly in mock reverence.

"You are about to embark on a night of history, adventure, and—dare I say—a little mischief."

Eve cocked an eyebrow, her expression hovering between intrigue and exhaustion. "Mischief? Just what kind of mischief are we talking about here?"

Gabe beamed. "The super-secret kind. Like I was just saying to Cheese here—you're gonna need to trust me."

Nathan gave a subtle shrug nod, his breath curling into the night air like smoke.

Eve looked at him, searching for an explanation, but he had none. He lifted his hands helplessly.

"I swear, Eve—I'm just as clueless as you are."

He shot her a look that said *save me*, but they both knew by now that once Gabe Kowalski got going, there was no stopping him.

Eve sighed, giving in. "Alright, Big Guy, you need to start making this interesting really quickly. Let's start with what's in that bag of yours."

"I thought you'd never ask," he said, with a triumphant gleam in his eye. "Here's a little taste of what's to come."

He reached into his backpack and pulled out what looked like an ancient map, yellowed from age. The corners were frayed, and the ink had faded, but the bold letters at the top were still clear enough to read.

Northern Connecticut State University: Proposed Campus Plan.

Eve was clearly unimpressed. "A map? Seriously?"

"I was barely up for chasing ghosts—now we're treasure hunting too? Come on, guys, I have better things to do than freeze my ass off out here playing Indiana Jones with you two.

Nathan held up a hand. "Hang on, Eve—this is pretty cool."

He stepped closer and narrowed his eyes at the map as he flicked on his phone's flashlight.

"Holy shit... this is a campus map of what the school looked like in the '90s."

"Bingo!" Gabe lit up. "This is what the town used to look like back when NCSU was just your average liberal arts college. Before all the fancy dorms and upgrades, this place was nothing but miles of C-grade retail. I'm talking dead malls, big-box stores, and the kind of fast-food joints you'd see off every highway exit."

She raised a brow, interest creeping into her voice. "You're telling me the campus used to be a mall?"

"Not just one mall." He leaned in, pointing at the map. "This whole place was a retail wasteland. At one point, there were seven McDonald's within a five-mile radius. Seven. You couldn't swing a dead cat without hitting a Walmart, Target, or some sad, half-empty strip mall. Fast food joints used to line both sides of this very road. That was back when fast food was still around, of course."

Nathan arched a brow. "Seven McDonald's? That's insane. How many Big Macs can one town eat?"

"I could've kept 'em all in business," Gabe replied with mock pride. "A Big Mac attack was a serious condition back in the day. Oh, what I wouldn't do for just one of those delicious burgers."

He closed his eyes and began to sing. "Two all-beef patties, special sauce, lettuce, cheese, pickles, onions on a sesame seed bun." With a slow nod, he let the nostalgia wash over him. "Such a classic."

Eve clapped her hands in front of his face, sharply. "Alright, focus. What happened to all of it? I mean, I know fast food has been dead for a decade—thank god—but what happened to everything else? All the stores, and everything?"

"I'm glad you asked," Gabe said, eyes widening. "I was starting to think you were too busy planning your early retirement from this conversation to appreciate the history lesson." He gave her a playful look. "Anyway, it all went down around the same time as the biotech boom in the early 2000s. That's when everything started to change. That's when fast food died practically overnight. One day it was Supersize Me this and Extra Value Meal that, and the next it was all gone."

"Okay, I get it. Everyone knows why fast food died—none of that stuff was good for anybody anyway. But what about everything else?" She traced her finger over the map. "People still liked going out to shop back then, right?"

Her voice softened.

"I mean… I wish we still could. You know? Go to an actual store and try things on. People used to make a whole day out of it." She let out a breath. "I hate online shopping. That's why I stick to thrift shops. They're the only places where you can walk into a real store and see what works for you."

"Oh, come on, online shopping is the best," Gabe said, flinging open his jacket to reveal another hideous Hawaiian shirt. "I mean, just look at this masterpiece. I ordered five of these quality garments before the semester started—each one louder and more offensive to the human eye than the last. I got free shipping, too. That, my friends, is modern convenience at its finest."

Nathan ignored his roommate's theatrics, still staring at the map.

"Okay, so everything shut down. But then what? The town just sat here, empty?"

Gabe leaned in like he was about to drop the biggest bombshell yet.

"For a while, yeah—it did. The town had no clue what to do with all the abandoned property. No one could agree on a real solution, and in the meantime? People left, businesses shut down, neighborhoods emptied, and before long, this place was a ghost town."

He inspected the map, trying to piece things together.

"But why the school? If everything else shut down, why was this the one thing that stuck? What made them think a college would survive when nothing else did?"

"That's the thing—I've been trying to figure it out, but all I've got are rumors."

Gabe let out a breath of steam into the cold night air.

"Some people say the town was desperate, and the university was their last hope. Others say that there was this super secret investor with really deep pockets that swooped in to save the day, but no one knows the full story. All I know is that whoever funded this whole thing moved fast. The entire town was turned over in less than a year. Construction crews came in masses and got it all done in record time."

Nathan kicked at a loose chunk of ice, watching it skitter away.

"That must've been insane to watch. One day, this place was a wasteland—the next, a full-blown construction takeover."

"Totally," Gabe replied, nodding.

"You know, that's how NCSU's mascot got its name."

He said it like it was common knowledge, but their blank faces made it clear they had no idea what he was talking about.

"Really, it's true," he continued.

"Back when the school was in full-on expansion mode, the few people who still lived here weren't exactly thrilled about their town being torn apart. So, to smooth things over, the town was allowed to choose the school's new mascot. People always said the transformation happened so fast, it was like a wave of orange construction vests swallowed the place overnight. And just like that, the Orange Wave was born."

Eve, now fully invested, tilted her head.

"I've always thought our mascot was weird, but I never really questioned it—now I get it."

She gave him a playful smile.

"Guess that makes you my personal guide to all things historic and ridiculous."

Gabe shot finger guns her way, a slight flush creeping up his neck.

"Well then, I'm glad I could educate you. That's why I'm here—to teach and, of course, entertain."

He smiled back sweetly, just enough to blur the line between teasing and something else.

Nathan was still trying to piece it all together.

"Still, that's pretty crazy. All that money to expand a college that no one even wanted to attend?"

Gabe shrugged.

"I guess some people saw an opportunity and thought the school had the chance to compete with the big schools, if they got a little push.

Back then, tech was moving so fast that everybody's head was spinning. Nobody knew what the future held; things were changing every day. The moment some cutting-edge tech dropped, you'd blink, and it was outdated.

One second, everyone was raving about their brand-new CD players—the next thing you knew, they were fossils. Streaming took over in a matter of months.

I mean, shit, we went from dial-up to broadband WiFi in what, a year and a half? It was insane."

"I know. I remember what it was like when I was little," Eve added.

"My dad would bring home some new gadget every week. Half the time, I barely figured out how to use it before it got recycled and replaced by the next big thing."

She shook her head, her expression darkening.

"It wasn't just the gadgets, though. It was the way everything felt—disposable. Nothing lasted. One day, my dad was obsessed with whatever new device he brought home—a week later, it would be collecting dust in a drawer, replaced by the next so-called upgrade.

I hated it—all of it. I hated how people would chase after the newest, shiniest lifesaver they could get their hands on, acting like it would solve all of their problems. I learned pretty quickly that all that nonsense wasn't for me. I'm perfectly happy living a life free from chasing *the next big thing.*"

Gabe nodded.

"It was the same way at my house, too. But here, in this town—and everywhere else, really—no one cared about what was being left behind. It was all about moving forward, faster and faster, until the past didn't even matter anymore."

He exhaled, stuffing his hands into his pockets.

"Somebody looked at this place, this abandoned wasteland, and decided it was worth something—and turned it into the place that we now call home."

After a beat, his trademark smile returned, but there was something different this time, like he was holding onto the joke just to keep things light.

"So yeah, our school was built on the bones of a retail graveyard. And lucky for us, I know exactly where the ghosts love to haunt the most."

Eve exhaled sharply, rubbing her temple.

"Fine, I'll bite. But if this turns into another one of your stupid games, Gabe, I swear, I will make you regret it."

"No games, I promise," he offered.

"But if all goes as planned?" He spread his arms. "You two will both be dying before the night is through."

13

THE LAUGH LAB

When she realized where they were heading, any interest Eve had in participating in Gabe's night-before-classes adventure vanished.

"Seriously, this is where you're taking us?" she said, shooting Gabe a look as they stopped in front of the building. "I had plans, you know. My playlist was ready, a bowl packed, and I was really looking forward to a chill night before classes tomorrow."

Gabe didn't flinch. "Hold your horses, tiny stoner," he teased, grinning. "You'll still have time for your pre-class ritual."

"My point is," she huffed, stomping her foot for emphasis, "you dragged me out here just to end up back at my dorm? I don't care if it used to be a Macy's or whatever."

"Nah, Macy's was where Shaker is now," Gabe replied like it was obvious. "That was the old west end of the mall. Winston Hall is down by where Sears used to be. But that's not why we're here."

"Then why are we here?" She tightened her scarf with a quick tug, the cold already wearing on her patience. "Make it interesting fast, or I'm going back upstairs."

"Okay, fine," Gabe said, his voice dropping into a slow, hunting tone that sent a chill up Nathan's spine. "We're not here to talk about what used to be in this building. We're here to check out what's under it."

"Wait—what's under it? There's not, like, a bunch of dead bodies or anything, is there?" Nathan asked, instantly regretting it.

"Relax, Cheese. Just—walk this way," he said as he hunched over dramatically and shuffled ahead like an underpaid extra in a late-night monster movie.

He led them around to the back of the dorm and stopped at a rusty, unmarked door. There was no sign, no handle—just the kind of door that looked like it shouldn't be opened.

With a little flourish, he swiped his digital wallet across the card reader. The device let out a soft beep, followed by a green light and the quiet click of the lock releasing.

Eve narrowed her eyes. "Wait—How do you even have a key for this?"

"I have a work-study with the facilities department," Gabe said. "It's a pretty sweet gig. Basically, I just sweep up the academic buildings, take out trash, and try to look useful."

Nathan shifted uneasily. "Can we even go down there? I mean... I don't want to get in trouble in my first week on campus."

"Yeah, it's fine," Gabe replied, waving it off as he creaked the door open. "My boss doesn't care what I do."

The door groaned on its hinges, revealing nothing but darkness ahead. Gabe turned back to them with a grin.

"What's down there?" Eve asked, eyeing the stairwell suspiciously. "I'm not going if there are rats or anything. Are you sure we're allowed? I mean, is it even safe?"

Gabe shot them a convincing look as he held the door open.

"Yup, totally safe. These tunnels used to be service corridors when the campus was still a mall. Abandoned for years. No cameras, no foot traffic —just history." He grinned. "Trust me. You're gonna love this."

They moved through the tunnels in near silence, their footsteps swallowed by the dark. Gabe led the way until he stopped in front of a solid, unmarked door.

It looked like it hadn't been touched in years. He glanced back at them once, gave a sly smile, and pushed it open.

What was on the other side wasn't anything they could've imagined.

"Welcome to my world, folks," he said, like he was finally sharing a secret he'd been sitting on for years. "This is where all the magic happens."

As they stepped through the doorway, it felt like they'd slipped decades into the past.

In front of them stretched a perfectly preserved movie theater, hidden like a time capsule under the campus. Rows of red velvet seats stood in neat lines, like they'd been frozen in time. Movie posters from the late 90s —*Titanic, Good Will Hunting, The Matrix*—lined the walls. The edges were curled and faded, but they still clung on, waiting for someone to notice them again.

"Whoa. This is amazing," Nathan breathed.

Eve's jaw dropped. "What is this place?"

"Told you you'd love it," Gabe said, grinning as he soaked in their reactions. He strolled down the aisle like he was unveiling a grand prize. "My secret hideout. My escape from campus—away from everything."

Nathan stepped farther in, sweeping his eyes across the rows. He ran his hand along one of the seats, half expecting dust, but the fabric was surprisingly soft. This place hadn't been forgotten. It had been waiting.

He cleared his throat. "How is this even here?"

Gabe chuckled. "Before the campus expansion, this was a six-theater cineplex. Four were above ground, and two were underground. They shut the bottom ones down in the late '90s, and when the mall closed, the university bulldozed everything—except these two. They just sealed them up and built right over." He gestured toward the blank screen like it was sacred. "I found it thanks to my work-study. No one else knows it's here."

Eve shook her head slowly, still processing. "This is insane. How have you kept it a secret?"

Gabe dropped into one of the seats, folding his hands behind his head. "I never had anyone to share it with." He nodded at Nathan. "Cheese is the first roommate I trust."

Then he glanced at Eve, a little more shy. "You get in by association."

She leaned against a seat. "I'm honored," she replied, deadpan. A small smile tugged at her mouth. There was something different in Gabe's energy—a quiet edge that softened her without her even realizing it.

He unzipped his backpack and pulled out two cold beers. The glass caught what little light there was as he tossed one to Nathan, who barely caught it, and handed the other to Eve.

"Now it's a party," he declared, hopping onto the little stage like he was about to perform for a packed crowd. "Welcome to my comedy club."

Nathan took a sip of beer, shaking his head. "Your comedy club?"

Gabe nodded. "Yup. I call it The Laugh Lab. It's where I work on my stuff. The world's not ready for my genius—yet."

Eve dropped into a seat, kicking her feet up on the chair in front of her. "I'll admit—this is pretty cool. So you just... perform here, by yourself?"

Gabe spread his arms wide like he was unveiling a miracle. "Exactly. The other theater is totally bombed out—but this one? This one's mine."

"It's perfect," he said, his voice echoing across the space. "I get to work out all my bits here, and the crowd in my head is always sold out. The cheers, the laughter—even the pretend heckles—they all keep me sharp."

Eve cracked open her beer, took a long pull, and rested it on her knee. "So," she said, eyeing Gabe, "do we get to see your show? From the look of your bag, you've got our two-drink minimum covered. Bob Marley and the rest of my night before classes start ritual can wait if we're getting front-row seats to a private set."

He stopped center stage and gave a little bow. "Of course, that's why we're down here. I'm gonna give you two the full VIP experience. So just sit back and enjoy the show."

Nathan settled in beside her, not sure what to expect next as he watched his roommate take center stage like he was about to work a sold-out room at the Comedy Store on the Sunset Strip.

"All right," he said. "Let's get the obvious out of the way. I'm a big guy —I mean, like, *real big.*"

He stopped center stage and dropped his head in mock shame. "Chairs hate me. I don't sit down—I negotiate."

He turned to an invisible chair. "Look, buddy. I don't want to be here any more than you do. But it's happening. If you hold up your end, I promise to go easy."

Eve let out a short, surprised laugh—more reflex than reaction—then covered her mouth, as if unsure whether she was supposed to be enjoying this.

"You guys ever hear a chair groan? Because I have," Gabe said. "And not one of those little polite squeaks either. I mean a full-on existential why me that rattles the floorboards and makes every other chair in the room go quiet. I sat in one last week that let out a noise so tragic, I almost apologized to it. I swear I heard it whisper, 'I had plans, man.'"

Eve stifled another laugh, her hand still hovering near her mouth like she wasn't sure whether to encourage him or stay guarded.

Gabe picked up on her reaction and ran with it. "Oh god, last week in my history lecture—which, by the way, is a whole different kind of awful —I dropped my bag and went to sit at the same desk I've been using all semester. I swear to you, the chair begged for its life. Like, full panic mode:

No, please! I have a wife and two little footstools at home! I just want to see them grow up and live their dream... become barstools."

He held the beat, then added, "Not just any barstools, either. Those kids had ambition. I'm talking real dive bar dreams. They wanted to be drenched in neon light, drenched with spilled whiskey, and honored with the lifelong duty of holding up a guy named Tank after his eighth IPA. They knew what was coming—beer farts, back sweat, and regret—and they were ready."

Eve lost it, clapping once before doubling over.

After looking into that furniture family's future, I couldn't go through with it. I dropped my bag and plopped my big ass right on the floor—not before giving that poor bastard a full military salute for his service.

Gabe stood still for a beat, then raised two fingers to his temple and gave a solemn, slow-motion salute toward the invisible chair. He followed it with a dramatic, backward step and bowed his head as if honoring a fallen comrade. "Gone, but not forgotten," he whispered.

"You're insane." Eve wheezed, finally breaking. Her laughter spilled out, uncontrolled, as she curled into the chair like she needed it to hold her together.

Gabe gave a theatrical wink. "I see I've got you now. Let's keep going." He dropped his voice to a confessional tone.

"Don't even get me started on the showers in Shaker Hall. Those things are an absolute crime against all the tall and fat." He struck a pose of exaggerated shame—hands on hips, head down. "I mean, I can get in fine. Now, getting out? That's a horse of a different color."

He slipped into his mimed phone bit. "Yeah, hi, it's Big Gabe again. Yup— same stall as last time. Yes, I brought my phone into the shower. No, obviously I didn't learn my lesson." He paused, squinting like he was listening to the imaginary voice on the other end.

He shifted his weight, leaned slightly forward, and nodded like he was being put on hold. Then, with a long-suffering breath, he launched back in.

"Yeah, of course I'm still here. Clearly, I'm not going anywhere." He paused, pretending to listen.

"Look, it's bad. You're gonna want to bring the crowbar." He gave a theatrical mime of struggling in place. "And a tub of butter." He held still, then slowly turned his head as if he couldn't believe what he was hearing —equal parts insulted and amazed by the absurdity of the question.

"No, I don't care if it's salted. Why do you always ask that?" He threw up his free hand in exasperation. "Whatever—just get here before I end up on the local news."

Eve howled, wiping tears from her eyes.

Without missing a beat, Gabe shifted into a flawless '90s anchor voice. "Breaking news—student tragically trapped in dorm shower. Rescue efforts are underway. More at eleven."

Gabe had the rhythm and energy of a seasoned pro. If he didn't know better, Nathan would've sworn his roommate was performing to an actual packed house. And maybe, in Gabe's mind, he was.

"Oh—and flying's no better," Gabe continued. "Have you ever purchased two seats and somehow still ended up stuck in the middle?"

Eve nearly spit out her beer.

"I mean, all I need is a triple-length seatbelt extender... is that too much to ask? So I ask for one, and the flight attendant looks at me like I just requested a spare engine. Look, I get it—they're busy slinging peanuts, handling toddlers with motion sickness, and managing a full-blown meltdown by some dad gone mad in row twelve. They didn't sign up to airlift me out of seat 19B at the end of the flight like I'm Shamu's long-lost son being helicoptered back to SeaWorld."

He scanned the imaginary crowd with mock seriousness. "And listen, if you're ever wondering how to make a six-hour flight feel eternal, ask someone else."

He took a beat and let the silence hang.

"Over winter break, I had to visit my grandparents in Daytona, and I made the mistake of eating one of those airport Cinnabons right before boarding. That was a bad idea, to say the least. I ended up sitting with my thighs suction-sealed to a vinyl seat while praying for the guy next to me to shut up about starting a podcast."

He glanced upward as if reliving the trauma, then turned back to the crowd. "I didn't even know a man could explain Bitcoin for that long without taking a breath."

He held up a hand like he was blessing the room. "I don't need heaven. I just want one flight where I don't leave with a bruise shaped like the armrest and a deep distrust of humanity."

Eve had lost her mind, wheezing, shaking, doubled over, laughing so hard no sound was coming out.

He bowed, arms wide. "That's my time, folks! You've been incredible! I'll be here all week—unless I finally get stuck in a shower stall for good.

Remember to tip your bartenders, salute your chairs, and for the love of humanity—never eat airport pastry."

Eve leaned back, still laughing, as she wiped tears from under her eyes with the back of her hand.

"Okay, seriously," she said, catching her breath. "That was amazing. I don't know whether to high-five you or ask for an encore—but you might have just made my whole semester."

She smiled at him, her eyes holding on a moment longer than she probably realized.

Nathan forced a chuckle. "You're really leaning into that, huh?"

Gabe raised an eyebrow. "Leaning into what?"

Nathan shrugged, swirling his beer. "All the jokes about—you know, your size and everything."

Gabe's smile didn't budge. "Oh, sure. The way I see it, if you can't laugh at yourself, what's the point?" He shrugged, totally unbothered. "And hey, I know I'm a big target—literally." He chuckled like it was no big deal.

Eve looked at Gabe, offering her perspective. "I admire the way you own your size. That takes guts. Plus, the way that you don't take yourself too seriously is hilarious."

Gabe hopped down from the edge of the stage and grabbed a beer from his bag, cracking it open with a practiced twist before taking a slow sip.

"You really want to know why I do all the fat guy stuff?" he asked, his voice quieter, steadier than before. He looked over at Nathan, holding his stare for a second longer like he was weighing whether to keep going. "Because people like to laugh at someone they think they're better than."

He took another sip, then shrugged. "And if they're gonna laugh, I want to be the one deciding where the joke lands."

Nathan peeled the label off his beer, shredding it into smaller and smaller pieces. His fingers worked on autopilot, but his mind was racing. That restless feeling crawled under his skin and stayed there. Gabe wasn't telling them everything— at least, not yet.

Gabe leaned forward and set his elbows on his knees. The usual swagger drained from him.

"You already know most of it," he said to Nathan. Then he glanced at Eve. "But for you? Here's the short version."

He looked down, thumbs fidgeting at the edge of his sleeve. "Freshman year, Dante and I got close fast. We were both on the team, hitting the same parties, pulling each other into all kinds of dumb stuff. I thought he had my back, you know?

He gave a dry laugh. "Then I told him I was out. No more football. I wanted to try comedy. And that's when everything shifted."

Nathan stayed quiet. He'd heard this before, but this time it hit differently. It sounded stripped down, like Gabe wasn't trying to soften the blow anymore.

Gabe rubbed his hands together. "He didn't take it well. Said I was quitting on everything we'd built. Then he went for the gut. He said nobody would ever laugh at someone who looked like me. And the worst part? I believed him."

Eve stood up and hopped onto the stage beside Gabe and met his eyes.

"I like a big guy. I always have, but it's not really about size, it's about confidence, and confidence is something you have a ton of, Gabe."

For a second, his mouth opened like he might fire off a joke, but nothing came out.

"I mean it," she said, nudging her shoulder lightly against his. "I've met plenty of guys who look perfect, but there's nothing going on behind their eyes. But when you walk into a room, people feel it. You've figured out what works for you, and you own it like nobody else. That's not something to be ashamed of. Honestly, more people could stand to live their lives with even a sliver of the confidence you have."

Gabe looked at her, a faint blush rising to his cheeks. "Thanks, Eve. That means a lot. But the thing is, I didn't just embrace who I am—I built it. Brick by brick, until there wasn't anything left of the guy I used to be. I made myself into someone everyone could laugh at."

Eve's expression softened. "Wait, you did that to yourself, on purpose?"

Gabe chuckled under his breath, this time with a trace of pride. "Once I felt like I looked the part, I started doing my new act in class. It probably wasn't my smartest move, but it worked. People laughed—and that was all I needed. After that, I started hitting some off-campus parties, and it was the same thing. They liked my style. They liked me. So I leaned into it."

Nathan nodded. "So, you became the guy Dante said nobody would laugh at, just to prove him wrong."

"I don't know if that's it," Gabe said. "Maybe a little, sure. But it's also because I know what kind of funny makes me laugh, and I'm trying to do that. And honestly? It was just easier this way. It's a hell of a lot harder to stand up there and be funny without falling back on all the fat guy stuff. After a while, it stopped being an act and just became who I was. People seemed to like it, so I kept going."

Eve leaned in just enough for her shoulder to brush his, like she was closing the space on purpose. "You didn't need to change yourself for that. You're funny because you're talented, not because of how you look."

Gabe chugged the rest of his beer and hopped of the stage to grab another from his backpack and cracking it open.

"Maybe," he said. "But once something like that gets in your head, it's tough to shake."

Most people don't even want to be perfect. They just want someone who feels real—someone they can identify with."

He patted his belly. "This is what I've got to work with, and honestly, I'm cool with who I am."

Nathan felt Gabe's words settle deeper than he expected. He could see it now—the way his friend had built himself up, not just to make people laugh, but to protect himself.

Gabe's next laugh was thin. "I don't know. Maybe I'm just too afraid to try this whole thing without the crutch of the big guy character." He took another sip, then glanced back at them. "I've just been doing this so long, it's the only way I know how to be."

"Maybe you can do both," Nathan said. "You've got the talent, the improv skills, and you know how to work a room. Maybe try stuff that doesn't lean so hard on the fat guy angle. I'm telling you, man—you don't need it to be funny."

Gabe shrugged. "I dunno. Maybe you're right. It's hard to change what people expect. They see me and want the Big Gabe on Campus show."

Eve hopped down from the stage, crossed the room in a few easy steps, and grabbed another beer from the cooler. She stopped beside him, close enough that he could feel the energy shift. "You're not just the funny fat guy, Gabe. Forget what you think people expect from you. Forget Dante—he's the king of the worst anyway. I mean, seriously." She looked right at him. "Just be yourself. That's all anyone really wants to see."

Gabe walked over and clinked his beer against hers without hesitation, sealing the moment before a word was said. He took the cap from her new bottle and flicked it into the corner.

"Look. Maybe you're right," he said, locking eyes with her. "But this big, loud, take-up-all-the-space guy? That's me. If I'm gonna be the joke, I'm gonna be the one telling it."

He turned to Nathan. "And having a roommate who is a writer couldn't be more perfect. You're gonna help me work on some new material, right?"

Nathan smiled. "Yeah. I think I've got a few ideas."

Gabe stretched his arms out. "All right then," he said, looking between them. "This is going to be a great semester. Who knows—maybe I'll even get a chance to show you there's more to me than just fat jokes."

Nathan chuckled. "I'm counting on it."

The weight in the room didn't disappear, but it eased. They hadn't figured everything out, but for now, it was enough. Gabe was still larger than life, but Nathan finally understood why.

This wasn't just a performance—this was who Gabe was.

14

ARE YOU READY?

On the morning before classes started, Mia packed her bag with quiet intention, sliding each notebook into their assigned spot. She'd arranged them by subject in the same order as her schedule—color-coded, labeled, and exactly where they were supposed to be. She didn't need everything to be perfect, but having it all in place made things easier.

Her room was still pretty bare from the move, but she had unpacked the things that mattered most. Nirvana and Cranberries posters hung on the walls, along with a faded *Clueless* movie print that was tacked up with care. Her bed was neatly made, with crisp sheets and a single daisy-shaped throw pillow. On the nightstand sat a vintage alarm clock and a well-worn copy of *Pride and Prejudice*, its spine cracked from one too many re-reads.

Leaving San Diego State hadn't been easy, and starting over at NCSU was a big leap, but the spot she'd scored in the Hybrid Medicine program was too good to pass up. This was where the future was happening— where organic medicine mixed with cutting-edge tech.

For Mia, having an implant wasn't about becoming some Enhanced version of herself. It was about balance, and that's why she was here. To learn about how she can use that balance to help people who need it most.

Her apartment in West Hall was a few miles from campus. It was close enough for a quick drive, but way too far to walk. She slung her bag over one shoulder, let out a slow breath, and took one last look around her still-unfamiliar space.

It was finally the first day of classes at NCSU, and Mia was as ready as she'd ever be.

Transferring mid-year had been hard enough, and getting paired with Val as her roommate had cranked the difficulty level to eleven.

Val was pure and unfiltered chaos in high heels. She was intense in a way that made every conversation feel like a pop quiz Mia hadn't studied for. She followed her own set of rules, and Mia had figured out fast that trying to keep up wasn't worth the effort.

She adjusted the strap of her brown leather backpack and smoothed the front of her pink crewneck. Her acid-washed jeans and polished loafers nailed the look she was going for   classic but intentional.

Everything she wore said something about her, and she liked it that way. Her hair, straight and smooth, fell just past her shoulders, making her look younger—like she'd borrowed it from a girl still figuring things out, not someone who already knew exactly who she was.

She started going grey in her teens, as a result of a genetic quirk she shared with her mom. It had once made her self-conscious. Now, it was just part of who she was. It made her stand out, and she'd learned to appreciate that.

As she stepped into the shared living room of her apartment, her loafers clicked against the hardwood floor. She had worked hard to make her bedroom feel like home, but the rest of the apartment belonged to Val. It was dark, dramatic, and curated in a way that felt less like design and more like controlled chaos.

Black sheer curtains hung over the windows, draining most of the daylight and leaving everything tinted in a low, moody glow. The furniture was heavy and secondhand, the kind of stuff you had to know someone to get. Chains and silver rings were scattered across the coffee table next to a row of half-burned candles.

The air was thick with incense smoke, mixed with something more earthy—something that made Mia nauseous.

She wasn't even sure if Val went to class. There weren't any schedules stuck to the fridge, no color-coded calendars hanging on the wall— nothing about her screamed student.

The first night Mia moved in, she'd asked Val what her major was. Val looked up from her tablet, where she'd been scrolling through cyberpunk runway shows, one eyebrow raised like Mia had just asked something ridiculous. Then just said plainly, "I major in everything." That was it. No follow-up, no explanation. Just Val being Val.

Mia liked people; she liked trying to understand what made them tick, but Val seemed built to keep the world guessing.

This morning, she needed her roommate for one simple thing—a ride to campus. If Val didn't drive her, she'd have to rush to catch the bus, and the rain outside wasn't making that prospect any more appealing.

She walked up to Val's door, already wincing as the first crashing chords of "Blind" by Korn slammed through the apartment. The bass rattled the picture frames on the wall and thumped under her feet like the place had its own heartbeat. The guitar shredded its way into Mia's head, and her pulse spiked. It was too early for this kind of noise.

With a deep breath, she knocked hard on the door.

"Val!" She called, raising her voice to compete with the music. "Are you awake? You said you'd give me a ride to campus!"

There was no response—just more heavy guitar riffs and Val's complete disregard for the rest of the world.

She knocked again, louder this time. "Come on, Val!—I'm going to miss the bus if you don't drive me. Can you at least turn the music down?"

She waited, her hand still hovering by the door, hoping for any sign of life from the other side.

Nothing.

She stood there as the bass pounded in her ears like a second heartbeat. The longer she waited, the thinner her patience stretched. Mia glanced at the time on her phone—she was officially cutting it close.

If Val didn't give her a ride, she was going to have to sprint for the bus, and with the rain coming down the way it was, that was the last thing she wanted.

She let out a slow breath, braced herself, and pounded on the door hard enough to sting her knuckles.

"Val, seriously! You promised!" she yelled, raising her voice over the heavy guitars that were shaking the apartment. "You need to drive me to campus!"

The music blared on, indifferent as Mia lost her patience. She pressed her ear to Val's door, trying to hear anything past the relentless noise, but the only response was the same chaotic soundtrack that seemed to define Val's world.

She had worked so hard to build a life with balance and purpose, and now she was stuck sharing space with someone who operated like a permanent thunderstorm.

Val tore through everything—conversations, rooms, people—leaving only wreckage behind without a second thought. Mia wasn't sure if she even cared about classes or if she was just here to stir things up and keep the mystery going.

Checking the time again, Mia shook her head. If she left now, she might just make the campus shuttle. She'd probably be drenched, and definitely annoyed, but at least she'd be on time.

She slammed her fist on the door one last time, more out of spite than anything else. "Fine! I'm leaving!" she called over the music. "Enjoy your metal concert!"

With a resigned sigh, she grabbed an umbrella and headed out to face the day. Rain streaked down the windows in thin, steady lines, matching the rhythm of her quick steps as she moved into the hall.

Val might be chaos wrapped in leather and noise, but Mia had worked too hard to let her roommate's selfish goth energy throw off her day.

NCSU's Hybrid Medicine program was waiting for her, and chaos or not, she was ready to take it on.

∼

Mia sat in the middle of the bus, letting her fingers absentmindedly play with the frayed strap of her backpack as the city blurred past the window.

After a soggy mad dash to the bus stop, the rain had thankfully stopped. Steam rose from the pavement where the sun had managed to break through, though it didn't do much to warm the air inside. Winter still clung to everything, even as the day tried to soften around it.

She shifted in her seat, resting her head against the cold glass as her free hand scrolled aimlessly through her phone, her thoughts circling back to Val.

Before she even left California, she knew *who* she'd be living with—but she didn't know anything about her. The roommate assignment email only said that Val was a junior from Texas. That was it. No major, no interests, nothing. Half the form wasn't even filled out. She needed to know more.

It wasn't hard to find Val on social media. She had practically built her own mythology, piece by piece, like it was part of some master plan. Her profile was filled with heavily filtered photos. Each one was more dark and dramatic than the next. Lyrics about destruction and control underlined every post. The captions were cryptic, the kind of thing that probably meant something to someone, but not to Mia. She had scrolled for hours, hoping to find something familiar, something she could connect with—but all she found was a carefully constructed wall, built with equal parts angst and rebellion..

It didn't take long to realize that they had nothing in common.

But when Mia first arrived at West Hall, Val had thrown her completely off guard. She hadn't been warm exactly, but she hadn't been cold either. She'd helped carry in Mia's bags, stuck around to unpack a few things, and even helped hang her posters. At one point, she even complimented Mia's wardrobe in this casual, flat way that made it impossible to tell if she was serious.

Then, once Mia was reasonably settled in, Val invited her out to a club to meet up with some of her friends.

"You need to come out with us tonight," she had said, twirling her car keys on her finger like she didn't care one way or another if Mia said yes.

"We're going to The Lighthouse. You're gonna love it."

The way she'd invited her seemed genuine, and for a second, Mia felt guilty for judging Val based on her social media presence. Those profiles were usually all for show, anyway. Mostly, they were just filtered versions of someone's life, not the whole picture.

Mia hoped that she'd just misread her. Maybe underneath all the attitude, Val was a nice person. Maybe she was trying to help her new roommate from across the country find her footing here.

Mia had been dead wrong.

She *did not* love The Lighthouse. It wasn't the kind of place where you found your people—it was more like a runway disguised as a club. Nothing more than a hyper-glam Hollywood type scene where everyone was desperate to be seen. It was all about who had the newest upgrades, the flashiest enhancements, the kind of tech that practically screamed *Look at me*. Everyone posed like they were on a red carpet—pouty lips, dramatic turns, trying way too hard to look like they didn't care. It was high-gloss, overdone, influencer energy, and they wanted the world to know they ruled it.

She knew right away these were *not* her people, and they never would be.

She hadn't transferred to NCSU to join the Enhanced elite, and she wasn't about to play along with their cold detachment. She came here to study, to learn from the best, and to graduate with a degree that would give her the ability to actually help people.

15

UNION OF THE SNAKES

Nathan sat in the back of the lecture hall, hoping to blend into the background—a move he'd pretty much perfected since ninth grade.

Introduction to Health and Technology was one of the few classes he'd been looking forward to. It was low-key, discussion-based, and for once, it felt like a place where his questions might actually belong.

It didn't take long for Nathan to realize that the Enhanced crowd was part of his new reality, and he had no idea what to do with that.

Back at community college, things were simple. He could keep his head down, avoid attention, and stay invisible. But now, he felt like that invisibility was being stripped away.

Now, he was surrounded by people who lived by rules he'd never learned—people who were wired in ways he couldn't even begin to understand. He used to think getting a chip would solve everything. But now he wasn't so sure. The idea of having one hovered at the edges of his thoughts.

What if the MIND chip could finally quiet the noise in his head?—What if it smoothed out the panic and erased the sleepless nights?—Would he finally be free?

Before he could let himself get completely pulled into the fantasy, the lecture hall door swung open and slammed against the stopper with a sharp thud, causing the energy in the room to shift and cutting straight through Nathan's spiral.

"Hey, nerd. Move it—you're in my seat."

His head shot up as he caught sight of Val climbing the stairs toward him. Her eyes were locked on his, carrying a look that was both lethal and irresistible—like she could ruin your life in an instant, and somehow you'd thank her for it.

She was one hundred percent pure mean girl—the kind who walked like the hallway was a runway and talked like every word was a dare. Nothing about her was soft. She was polished, confident, and totally fierce.

Simon Wu trailed behind her, wearing an unreadable expression that only made things more terrifying.

Nathan froze as they reached the top of the stairs and hovered over him

"Oh. Sorry." His voice cracked as he forced the words out. "This is your seat?"

Val glared down at him, ice behind her eyes. "Did I stutter? I said move. Now."

His heart pounded as he shoved his notebook into his bag and scurried to find another place to sit.

Val's laugh followed him as she dropped into the seat he'd just left, with Wu sliding in beside her like they'd done this a hundred times.

Nathan moved down to the front, putting as much distance as he could between himself and whatever she was planning. He didn't dare look back, but he could feel her watching him, burning a hole right through the back of his head.

He settled in his new seat as Dr. Lowell greeted the class, his voice steady and composed. The rustling of notebooks and the hum of quiet conversation filled the air, but Nathan struggled to focus.

This wasn't a class for someone like Val. The seminar was meant to help transfer students get their bearings in a world ruled by biotechnology.

Nathan had been looking forward to this class. He had hoped that he'd finally get some answers, but as it began, all he found were more questions.

Everything was moving too fast.

There were new faces, new rules, and new ways to get crushed if you weren't careful. And behind him, Val was still there—like a splinter he couldn't dig out. A constant reminder that he was way over his head.

He stared at the blank page in his notebook. There weren't any answers waiting for him there. There hadn't been for a while, and now, as he sat there utterly confused, he wasn't even sure where to start looking to find any.

At the front of the room, Dr. Lowell stood at the podium, hands resting on either side like he was holding it all together through sheer force of will. He glanced up, scanning the room like he was sizing them up, then gave a tight nod.

"Welcome," he said. His voice wasn't loud, but it was strong enough to command attention and cut through the noise, bringing order to the room.

"You're here to learn about the world you're stepping into," he said, "and how tech fits into your new lives on this campus."

He let his words hang for a beat like he wanted them to feel the weight of it.

"I like to start with a question," he went on. "Yours, not mine. What would you like to learn this semester? I know for many of you, the idea of a bio-tech lifestyle is foreign. I like to gauge my students and find out where they're at with this. So tell me, what questions do you have? What do you want to know?"

Nathan's mind was still trying to make sense of it all when a girl in the front row timidly raised her hand.

"Uh, so... I've heard that some enhancements can, like, mess with your brain or something. I read somewhere that they can erase your memories or even cost you your identity. Is that true?"

Before Dr. Lowell could respond, Val's voice boomed from the back of the lecture hall, cutting through the air with no hesitation.

"Are you serious?" she scoffed, her voice loud enough to make heads turn.

"Erasing memories? Losing your identity? That's exactly the kind of bullshit people believe when they've never actually seen any real enhancements."

Nathan couldn't resist turning to face her; no one could. Her tone was dripping with disdain, like the very idea was beneath her. He felt the tension rise, not just in the room, but in himself.

Dr. Lowell raised a hand, cutting off the scattered laughter that followed Val's comment.

"Ms. Reynolds," he said, his voice calm but firm, "let's give your classmate the respect of a proper answer."

Val shrugged like the whole thing bored her, then gave him a look that said it all—she had no interest in playing by the rules.

The professor turned his attention back to the girl in the front row.

"It's a thoughtful question," Dr. Lowell continued. "The MIND chip is currently regarded as the most advanced and integrative biotechnological system available. What distinguishes it from similar technologies is its open-source platform—an architecture designed to allow adaptability and user-driven customization. Of course, such flexibility inherently brings complexity and risk, particularly when the platform is exploited beyond its intended medical or cognitive scope."

Nathan leaned forward slightly, interested in what the professor had to say. He had been so preoccupied with the idea of how the MIND chip could help him that he hadn't considered the risks.

"The truth is," Dr. Lowell continued, "approved enhancements—those subjected to rigorous clinical evaluation—are intended to support and optimize both physical health and cognitive performance. These enhancements do not tamper with memory or compromise identity. On the contrary, they are often developed to improve quality of life, particularly for individuals managing chronic conditions or neurochemical imbalances."

Nathan felt a small wave of relief at that. It was comforting to know that the MIND chip, at least in theory, was safe.

"However," Dr. Lowell added, his tone shifting, just a little darker, "not all enhancements are created equal. The open platform that powers the MIND chip has also made room for a surge of unregulated, third-party applications. Many of them can be dangerous because they go far beyond what's considered safe."

He paused for a second, like he wanted to make sure they were listening.

"Some of these unauthorized apps are designed to enhance strength, speed... even physical appearance," Dr. Lowell explained, his tone clipped but deliberate. "We're not talking about minor cosmetic adjustments. We're seeing a push for engineered perfection—more symmetrical features, idealized body metrics, and even sensory manipulation. The demand is high, and there's always someone willing to sell the illusion of flawlessness."

Nathan's attention sharpened. Third-party enhancements. He hadn't heard of that before.

"But just because you can do something," Dr. Lowell continued, "doesn't mean you should."

His tone was calm, but there was a weight behind it now.

"These kinds of enhancements are not medically approved, and they often bypass standard safety protocols entirely. The risks can be severe—nerve damage, physical deterioration, even psychological complications."

He paused, scanning the room as if to make sure they were paying attention.

"Many of these so-called advancements are developed by organizations more interested in pushing limits than protecting people. Safety is not their priority—results are. And while using these kinds of applications might not erase your memories, they can cause lasting harm, both physical and mental, and sometimes irreversible."

Dr. Lowell's eyes swept across the room, and for a moment, his eyes landed squarely on Val, who was back to lounging, her arms crossed as if to say she didn't care. Nathan followed the professor's glance, wondering how much of this applied to her. She wore her enhancements proudly, but now Nathan was starting to see the darker side of them—the risks that came with pushing too far.

Val seemed unfazed by the mention of dangerous enhancements. To her, it was all part of the package, just the price you paid to live beyond human limits. But to Nathan, the idea of crossing that line was starting to feel more and more unnerving.

Dr. Lowell's voice pulled him back.

"It's important to remember that while technology can help us do incredible things, there's a line between improving ourselves and losing who we are. The danger comes when we forget where that line is."

Nathan's leg hammered uncontrollably beneath his desk as the tension in the room thickened.

Val leaned forward in her chair with a dangerous glint in her eyes.

"You guys seriously have no idea how amazing the newest enhancements are," she said, her voice heavy with condescension.

"You should see some of the stuff Wu's got." She motioned toward Simon, who was sitting beside her, silent and unreadable.

Nathan could feel the energy in the room shift beneath the unspoken weight of power that Val wielded with such effortless confidence.

Then, without warning, she stood and let her leather jacket slide off her shoulders in one smooth motion, letting it fall to the floor. The sound it made was soft, but somehow it still carried.

For a second, she didn't move.

Her eyes shifted from their usual darkness to a bright violet. Her tattoos—the thorned vines and roses on her arms moved gently as if stirred by a breeze only she could feel. The petals seemed to lift and sway, weightless like they might drift away at any second.

The snakes coiled around her calves shifted. They tightened at first, then slowly began to loosen before sliding up her thighs and disappearing beneath the hem of her skirt.

Nathan's pulse jumped.

A breath later, the snakes reappeared, winding over her exposed midriff, gleaming faintly as they climbed. They looped around her waist like living sashes, shimmering in the light as they ascended further up her body, their motions fluid and controlled.

With slow, dramatic flair, she lifted her arms and spread them wide. The gesture was part invitation, part command—and everyone knew it.

The snakes responded instantly. They glided up her ribs, disappearing again under her crop top before appearing to wrap around her neck. Then they slithered down over her bare shoulders, coiling around her arms before blending into the inked roses on her skin.

Their tongues flicked out, tasting the air, their bodies tightening until they held still, waiting for her next command.

She stood there, calm and still, fully aware of the effect she'd just had on the room.

Nathan's eyes shot to Dr. Lowell, expecting outrage or shock, but the professor remained composed. He stood tall at the front of the room, though Nathan could see the slight hardening in his expression.

"That'll be enough, Ms. Reynolds," Dr. Lowell said, his voice breaking through the tension with ease. "When I agreed to let you audit this class, we made it clear you would sit and observe. No more outbursts. Are we clear?"

"Whatever, if you all want to live your lives as a bunch of organic losers," she sneered, her eyes locking on Nathan, "then suit yourselves. All I'm saying is, there are options."

Dr. Lowell folded his hands calmly on top of the podium. "Ms. Reynolds, you've been warned. If causing drama is what you're after, I suggest you take it to the Theater Department. This is a science course, not a stage."

Laughter rippled through the class. Nathan barely heard it. His mind spun with images of Val, her tattoos, and the world she lived in.

At first, the MIND chip seemed like a solution. A way to silence the noise, but now he wasn't so sure.

The more he thought about it, the more he wondered if he even had a choice.

16

WRITE OR DIE

Nathan felt the aftershocks from the drama in his Intro to Health and Tech class ease as he stepped into the writer's lab. He let the calm of the room wrap around him as he slid into an open seat by the window. It was quiet and familiar, like the space had been waiting for him to fill it with his ideas.

The place was untouched by the constant noise of technology that covered the rest of the campus. Light from old lamps spilled across battered wooden tables, their surfaces etched with scratches and doodles from students who had once sat in these same seats, pouring their hearts and dreams onto the page.

Each mark in the wood, every chip along the edges, was proof the space had a memory—like it held onto every idea and word ever written here. It wasn't polished or optimized. It was real.

For the first time since arriving at NCSU, Nathan felt something close to peace. He wasn't watching his back or scanning the room, waiting for some Enhanced student to size him up, cut him down, or remind him he didn't belong.

In this moment, there was only quiet. He finally had a chance to breathe without feeling like he had to earn it.

As he unpacked his relic of a laptop and woke it up, the constant anxiety that chewed at his nerves continued to loosen its grip. The steady calm of the writer's lab pushed everything loud and unpredictable somewhere too far to reach him.

He didn't feel the need to hide anymore. He wasn't a target. For the first time in a long while, he thought he might've found a place where he truly belonged.

He pulled up the syllabus for Organic Writing 201 and squinted at the title.

"Organic," he muttered. Up until now, writing had just been writing—there wasn't another way to think about it. He still wasn't sure how he felt about being labeled as only organic. His eyes landed on the word again. It felt too earthy, too plain.

For Nathan, writing had never been about labels or categories. It wasn't about fitting into a box or proving something. It was the one thing that made sense when everything else felt like a mess. He didn't care about likes, followers, or anyone's approval.

He wrote because it helped quiet the noise in his head. It was the only thing he did that let him breathe.

He had barely settled when Professor Simmons entered. She moved with the kind of sharp purpose that made the rest of the class sit up straighter, her scowl carved deep like it had spent years settling there, unimpressed by anyone who dared show up unprepared.

"Good morning, my young storytellers," she said. Her voice was smooth, but there was steel under it—the kind that warned you not to waste her time.

She scanned the room like she was making snap judgments about who would make it through the semester, just by how they sat.

"Some of you," she added with a nod, "I know well."

Her eyes landed on Nathan and stayed a second longer than necessary, her stare sharp behind the rim of her glasses.

Simmons continued, dragging out the words like a challenge, "I haven't had the pleasure of teaching."

The way she looked at him wasn't unkind, but it wasn't welcoming either. It was the look of someone already deciding whether he had what it took—or how much she'd have to break him down to find out.

She folded her arms and stood in the center of the room like it was a battlefield she had conquered countless times.

"If you're here because you think this is an easy elective," she said, "you're dead wrong. This isn't a workshop for half-formed ideas or stories you're too scared to finish. This is where you strip yourself down and learn to write with intention. If you do not intend to give your best, the door is right there."

A quiet settled over the room. The class looked at each other to see who might cave first. For a moment, Nathan thought about it. He thought about gathering his things and walking out like he always did when things got too real. But before that old instinct could take over, Professor Simmons kept going.

"I have rules," she said, her voice cutting through the quiet. "Rules you will live by if you want to survive this course."

She let her words settle, then added, her voice dropping into something darker, quieter. "And trust me—I'd rather none of you find yourselves having to die by them."

Nathan wasn't sure if she was serious. *Dying by words?* He swallowed hard. It sounded like something a professor would say to scare freshmen, but she said it like it was personal. Like she'd seen it happen before.

She paced the front of the room with eerie precision.

"You're here for a reason—to create. To tell stories that are raw and vulnerable. Stories that matter."

Stopping in the front of the room, she looked over the class again. "Let me be clear. I won't tolerate the packaged, polished garbage they mass-produce out there."

She nodded toward the buzzing quad and the sleek buildings beyond the window.

Nathan felt the shift. She didn't have to say it outright, but he knew exactly who she meant. The Enhanced. The world outside this lab, where creativity was optimized and streamlined until there was nothing left that made it real.

He'd seen the new stuff they were cranking out. It was quickly produced, shiny, and flawless, but it lacked depth. He used to think it was fine, maybe even fun, but the perfection drained it of any real meaning. The books they churned out at lightning speed were easy to rip through, and the movies they made were packed with action and digital graphics that kept his attention.

The problem was, they never made him feel anything. They were just empty.

That's why he had always preferred the old stuff—the classics. Not because of some network or trend, but because they were simply better.

She turned back to them. "I don't want perfect writing," she said. "I want your truth. I want stories with teeth, stories that bite and leave a mark. I want to feel your pain, celebrate your victories, and see your mess —all of it. You need to be able to put everything you are on the page, no matter how raw or ugly it is. If you can't do that, you might as well walk out now."

What Nathan felt wasn't fear. At least not the kind that faded when you told yourself to relax. This was different. She was asking for his truth —and that was something he wasn't sure he could give.

He never wanted to be here. Not at NCSU. Not in this program. And definitely not in a class that expected him to tear himself open and expose himself for the whole world to see.

The idea of sharing his words made his skin crawl. Until now, only a few people had ever read his work—a few teachers, Eve, and his mother.

His mom had believed in him more than anyone else ever had—and far more than he could ever believe in himself. She was the one who sent his portfolio to NCSU, quietly submitting his work to a program he never thought would give him a second thought.

He had no idea she had sent it until the day his acceptance letter arrived—the same day he buried her. She had sent it off as a final act of hope, a mother pushing her son toward a future she always believed he deserved. She had done it quietly, holding on to the belief that this place might offer him more before her body gave out.

The memory came back before he could stop it. He remembered how much he had wanted to yell at her—how angry he had been that she wouldn't be there to carry him through it. He had sat in his room, the acceptance letter shaking in his hands, terrified and completely alone. And yet, even through the fear, he understood why she had done it. Why she had sent his words out into the world without telling him. She believed in him, even when he didn't.

He had been furious. Furious at her for leaving him. Furious at the universe for taking her. Furious at himself for being angry at her for doing something he knew she did out of love. And above all, he was furious at the school for saying yes—because now, he had no excuse. No way to stay small, no place to hide, and nowhere that felt safe.

He remembered sitting on his bed, sobbing, the letter crushed in his fist as if it were proof that she was gone. Proof that the only bright spot in his life had pushed him into a world he wasn't ready for, daring him to live the way she always hoped he would.

He never wanted any of it. Not the loss. Not the future. Not the weight of her belief.

He had only wanted to stay where it was quiet. Where no one could see him. Where he could keep pretending nothing had to change.

His mother believed in words and the power they held. But more than that, she believed in her son—and she knew his way with words was something to be celebrated. She believed that if anyone was meant to tell stories that mattered, it was him.

She always said he had a gift. That his writing could make people feel something real. Just like his father had before him. A father Nathan had never known, but whose absence still followed him like a shadow.

She believed that if she got him here—if she pushed him to take the chance—he might finally see the person she knew he could become for himself. That he might step out of the darkness and let someone else see it too.

Now he was here, sitting in Simmons' class while she talked about unlocking souls and sharing your voice like it was something easy. Like, there wasn't anything terrifying about handing over the rawest pieces of yourself and hoping no one would tear them apart. Like it didn't cost everything just to be seen.

He wanted to disappear. He wanted to pull his hoodie over his head, sink low in his chair, and vanish into his writing, where no one could find him.

It was the only place where he was safe, where his thoughts could spill onto the page without anyone prying them open. There was no judgment there. No pressure to explain why every word mattered more than he could ever admit.

That safe space was gone now. Torn away by a decision made for him, leaving him exposed in a room where silence wasn't enough, and hiding wasn't an option.

17

COME AS YOU ARE

As class ended, Nathan shoved his laptop into his backpack and fell in line behind the rest of the class. They all moved like they'd just survived something they hadn't signed up for. All he wanted was to get out of there.

"Mr. Boone, a moment?" Simmons' voice cut through the quiet, sharp enough to make him jolt.

Every instinct told him to keep walking, to pretend he hadn't heard her, but his feet stayed planted. He tightened his grip on his backpack strap, holding on like it might steady him, and turned around.

She stood by her desk. Her face had softened from its usual sharp lines, but it wasn't exactly comforting. It was the kind of look that made the hair on the back of his neck stand up.

She nodded toward the chair across from her. "Please. Have a seat."

Every part of him wanted to bolt, but something in the way she said it kept him stuck. He made his way over, stiff and slow, before dropping into the chair.

He fidgeted in his seat like he was outside the principal's office. It reminded him of the time, back in eighth grade, when Dante and the others had been particularly relentless, causing him to bolt out of the cafeteria and straight through the emergency exit without thinking. He tripped the alarm and triggered a full fire department response. A teacher caught him two steps outside, shaking and red-faced, and marched him straight to the front office, where he was forced to sit and wait to find out if they were going to call his mom or lock him up and throw away the key.

Now, he sat here the same way, waiting for Simmons to tell him he was in the wrong class, the wrong school, the wrong life altogether.

"Nathan," she said softly, sounding more human than she had all class. "I wanted to talk to you about your mother. I want you to know that she and I were friends."

"You were friends—with my mom?" His voice cracked on the last word, and he hated the sound of it.

"Yes, good friends, actually," Simmons replied, nodding slowly. "We were roommates at Mount Holyoke. We used to spend hours at this little coffee house in Northampton. It was our place."

She smiled faintly, her expression drifting toward some far-off memory. "We would go there every Tuesday to hear your father play his music."

He struggled to process what she was saying. "You knew my dad, too?"

"I sure did." Simmons gave a small smile. "He was something else—a real performer. You look just like him, you know. I'm sure you've heard that before."

She paused, studying him in a way that made him shift in his chair.

"Funny enough, I dated his best friend back then. That's how your parents met."

She looked off into a memory. "Your dad was not your mom's type, at least not at first. She thought he was all flash, a dreamer with no plan, but he had this way about him. Once he decided on something, he made it happen—and that included your mom."

Nathan's mom had told him about his father the same way Simmons was describing him now. She'd tell him about his dad's smile, how it made her believe in things she never thought she wanted. Hearing it from someone else felt different. Like finding a photo you didn't know existed —a piece of a life that had always been out of reach.

"I was so sorry when I got the news about your mom," Simmons said quietly. "We had kept in touch for years, but when she stopped writing—" She paused, wiping beneath one eye. "I know how hard she fought, Nathan. She was an incredible woman."

He didn't want to talk about this. Not here—not with anyone.

"A young man like you, losing both parents at such a young age," she added, her voice even softer. "It's so unfair."

He nodded. "Yeah." He didn't have the energy to say more.

He kept his eyes on the floor, focusing on the scuffed tiles instead of the sting behind his eyes. Losing his mom was still raw, and hearing Professor Simmons bring her up in this room, at this school, made it worse. It was all too soon to revisit that pain with a woman who, until minutes ago, had terrified him.

"Your mother and I kept in touch over the years. She spoke of you often," Simmons said, her voice gentler now. "She was so proud of you, Nathan. She believed you had a gift. She used to say you were destined to be a great writer."

The words landed hard. Knowing his mom had said things like that brought a strange heat behind his eyes. It was comfort and grief, tangled up in the same breath.

"I have to say, I agree with her," Simmons said, locking eyes with him in a way that made him sit up straighter.

"I want you to know something else, Nathan. I was on the selection committee that reviewed your application."

Her tone sharpened. "I'm the reason you're here."

He tried to make sense of what she'd just said. He'd always figured he slipped in because they needed more students, or they were desperate for someone still writing *organic*. Deep down, he thought it was luck. Maybe even a mistake. But hearing Simmons—the professor who could spot every flaw in the room—say she was the one who wanted him here? That changed everything.

"Your writing—it's really good," she said, leaning in like she needed him to believe it. "You've got your father's passion. I saw it immediately when I read your work. I hear your mother's voice too. It's clear your parents' talent is in your blood."

A wave of pride flooded him. It felt like grabbing hold of a thread that tied him to his parents, to everything they'd been before he lost them.

"You've got the raw talent, Nathan. You know how to write—there's no question about that," she paused. "But your stories? They're safe. There's no real conflict. It's like you're afraid to challenge your characters —and maybe even yourself."

He snapped to defend himself. "I put everything I have into those stories," he replied, his voice tight.

Simmons didn't blink. "Take the short story from your portfolio, 'The Boy Who Hoped For Forever.' It was beautifully written. The descriptions were vivid. I could see everything—you built the world. But there was no weight to it. No stakes. It felt like you were holding back. If I'm being honest, it all just felt a little too safe."

The words stung. He'd poured himself into that story. He had spent countless nights rewriting, dissecting every line, every scene—and now she was calling it safe?

"It's not enough to build a beautiful world," she continued. "You have to be willing to burn it down. If you want to be a writer—a real writer, Nathan—you need to dig deeper. You need to show what's truly inside you. It doesn't need to be perfect. Messy is okay, as long as it's yours. I know you've got it in you. You're just avoiding it. It's time to let it out."

"That's not really my style," he replied, still tense. "I think there's already too much negativity in the world. I don't want to create more."

He paused, reaching for words. "I write because it makes me feel good. I never really write anything to share it, but if one day I do, I want my stories to make people feel good, not miserable."

"I'm not asking for misery, Nathan," she pressed. "I'm asking for honesty. For vulnerability. When you lean into the conflict, it doesn't just add darkness—it makes the payoff that much stronger when things go right. You've lived through more than most people your age, and none of that shows up in your work. Why do you think that is?"

He didn't have an answer. At least not one he could say out loud.

"Listen, Nathan, your mom and I used to talk about you," she said, her voice quieter but intense. "She told me about all the hospital stays, the way those kids treated you, how lost you felt. She would call me sometimes, desperate to make sense of it all."

A wave of embarrassment swept over him. He had no idea his mom had told anyone those things.

"The last time we talked was right before she submitted your application," Simmons continued. "She believed in you. She believed you were capable of turning all that pain into something powerful."

"I use writing to get away from everything," he said quietly. "I'm not sure I can write my way into it."

"Nathan, you can't just write to escape your pain," Simmons replied, leaning in again. "You need to write through it. Be honest about what you've lived through. That's where the story is."

He lifted his head, searching her face. "I don't know if I'm ready to put myself out there like that. I don't think I can do it."

"You need to ask yourself—if you don't want to grow as a writer, why write at all?" Her tone wasn't harsh, but it still cut deep.

"And more importantly, if you don't want to grow as a person, what's the point of anything? Life isn't meant to be feared; it's meant to be lived. It's a gift, Nathan. Don't waste it hiding from yourself. It's time to face your fears and let yourself grow—not just as a writer, but as a person."

He didn't know how to respond.

"You don't have to have all the answers right now," she said, her voice gentler. "But you need to understand—this is where it starts. The best art—the kind that sticks, the stories people carry with them—comes from truth. Especially when it's hard. I truly believe that you've got that truth in you, Nathan. You just have to be brave enough to let it out."

She paused. "Picture someone like you, picking up your work. They see your truth, and it connects with them—it makes them feel less alone. Gives them hope. Wouldn't that be worth putting yourself out there?"

The words hit hard. He knew she was right. He just didn't think he was strong enough to be what she already saw in him.

"Nathan," Simmons said, her tone more direct. "You don't even realize how good you are. But I do. And I'm not going to let you settle for anything less."

She leaned back, giving him space without letting him off the hook. "The only way you get there is by facing the hurt that lives inside you. Use your art to confront your pain. Turn it into something that sets you free."

He felt like she was asking him to pull open every wound he'd managed to stitch shut. But the way she looked at him—like she already knew he could do it—made it hard to argue.

He felt exposed. Like she could see every weak spot he worked so hard to hide. She wasn't just pushing his writing. She was pushing *him*. And that scared him more than he wanted to admit.

Simmons leaned back in her chair. "I know it's not easy," she said. "But you have something important inside you, and it's being drowned out by the need to create these perfect, unblemished stories. You have to let go of that control. You have to allow yourself to write about the things that scare you."

The idea of exposing himself on the page—writing the parts he'd spent years burying—felt impossible. Like tearing open a wound and inviting the world to watch.

His voice cracked under the weight of the question. "Why does it have to be about pain?"

Simmons didn't hesitate. "Because pain is truth, Nathan. Conflict is truth. That's what makes stories resonate."

He wanted to push back. He wanted to argue. Instead, he sat frozen, pressure building behind his ribs like something was about to snap.

"We're drowning in art that's weightless—polished until it doesn't feel like anything. That's the Enhanced for you. You're not like them." Her voice didn't rise, but the fire in it was unmistakable.

He still wasn't sure that he didn't want to be.

The Enhanced were everywhere—filling up galleries, topping charts, writing stories that practically glowed with perfection. They had mastered the art of flawlessness.

But Simmons was right about one thing: their work always felt hollow. Like it was missing a heartbeat. They couldn't create the kind of art that lingered because they had stripped away everything messy, everything human.

"I'm giving you an assignment," Simmons said, her tone shifting.

"I want you to write a piece about what scares you most, without filters. No holding back. Show me what it looks like inside Nathan Boone's soul."

His shoulders tensed as a familiar weight settled over him. He could feel it coming—the inevitable drop before the crash.

"I don't think I can do that," he said quietly.

"You can, Nathan." Simmons' voice didn't waver. "You can—and you will."

He opened his mouth to argue, but nothing came out. She was already looking at him like she knew the answer. Like she'd made peace with it, and now it was his turn.

"What if it's not enough?"

His voice came out flat, more resignation than fear.

"It's not about being enough," she said. "It's about being real."

He didn't respond. He shifted his hand to his knee, pressing down until he could feel the edge of bone beneath denim. The pressure steadied him. It gave the silence somewhere to go.

Simmons didn't move. She just waited, allowing him the space to respond.

Finally, realizing he had no choice, he gave in. "Alright, I'll try."

She gave a faint nod. "That's a start. All I ask is that you be honest with yourself."

His legs were stiff as he stood, slid his bag over his shoulder, and turned toward the door. Simmons' voice stopped him before he could leave.

"Nathan, don't let anyone—least of all the Enhanced—tell you that you're not good enough. You're here for a reason. You're here because you deserve to be, because you have a voice. Don't let anyone take that away from you."

He met her eyes, and for the first time, he believed she meant it.

Maybe he could believe it, too.

"I won't," he said, as He made his way to the door, every step heavy, like walking through water. Her words ran on a loop in his mind, threading through his thoughts, impossible to shut out.

She wasn't just another teacher. She had known his mother. She had chosen him—believed in him when he hadn't believed in himself.

And somehow, that terrified him most of all.

18

MOTHER NATURE'S SHIFTING MOOD

Nathan's head spun as he hustled across the quad, making a beeline for the gym to meet Eve after her yoga session. The wind whipped through the bare branches overhead, and the January chill sliced through his jacket. It felt much colder than it had earlier when he'd walked to class—like Mother Nature's mood had suddenly shifted.

Typical New England weather, he thought as he stuffed his hands into the pockets of his puffer vest.

The temperature drop gnawed at his bones, mirroring the unease inside him. Simmons had known his parents—intimately, it seemed—like she had a window into his past that he didn't. That was what unsettled him most.

He had come to NCSU for a fresh start, hoping to carve out something separate from the weight of his history. Maybe he'd even believed he could blend into the background, just like he had at his last school. But now, that illusion was shattered.

Instead of escaping his past, it felt closer than ever, dragging at his heels.

He huddled against the wind, pulling his arms in to trap whatever heat he could, his breath misting in front of him as he quickened his pace. The voices in his head were relentless.

Why did Simmons know so much? Why did she have to mention his parents like that?

The questions dug in, and no matter how hard he tried, he couldn't shake them.

Why couldn't things just be simple?

Each step felt heavier—like the wind was actively resisting him, pushing back, forcing him to acknowledge what he didn't want to.

He just needed to see Eve. He needed her steady presence to take the edge off. Maybe then, the storm in his head would settle.

Just as he reached the hill leading up to the gym, a familiar voice cut through the wind.

"Yo! Cheeseman—my favorite slice of nervous cheddar—wait up!"

Nathan turned just as Gabe jogged up beside him. "Man, you're on a mission," he laughed, giving Nathan a playful nudge on the shoulder.

He forced a smile, though it felt loose, like something borrowed. "Yeah," he shrugged. "I told Eve I'd meet her after yoga. We're supposed to grab lunch."

"Lunch?" Gabe teased, flashing a wide smile. "You know that's one of my top 10 favorite meals, and if you sprinkle in Eve, we're talking top five, easy."

Nathan raised an eyebrow. "Top 10 favorite meals? There's only three."

"Not if you count second breakfast and midnight snack. I'm telling you, there's way more than three meals in a day."

With that, he pulled a small red spiral notebook from his back pocket. "See? Proof. Page 24—Gabe's Top 10 Favorite Meals."

Nathan squinted as they walked side by side, their strides slowing so he could read Gabe's chicken-scratch handwriting. "What's number nine?"

"Oh, that's The Cry Meal—you know, when you're so depressed, the only thing that helps is inhaling a pair of meatball subs and a two-liter of Dr Pepper while having a good cry. I almost was going to call it a Meatball Your Eyes Out Meal, but, you know—too corny."

Nathan burst out laughing. "Oh my god. You are too much."

Gabe winked. "That's the goal, my friend."

Nathan let the warmth of laughter linger for a moment before the weight of his thoughts started creeping back in. The past wasn't gone, just temporarily drowned out by Gabe's ridiculousness.

"So," Nathan said, shifting gears away from his roommate's regular absurdity, "how's the first day of classes treating you?"

Gabe's expression slipped. "Man, it's been educational, that's for sure. I just came from Advanced Improv."

Nathan raised an eyebrow. "And—not great?"

"It's tougher than I thought," he admitted, pulling his collar up higher to shield himself from the wind.

"I figured it'd be easy—I'd crack a few jokes, bask in the laughter, maybe I could whip out a few of my impressions, they always kill. But the professor wasn't having any of it. She says comedy is about more than just making people laugh—she wants us to dig deep and find something real. Honestly? I'm not sure I have the guts for that original stuff."

Nathan frowned. Gabe seemed like the kind of guy who could brush off anything and turn any situation into a joke. Seeing doubt creep into his voice was strange.

"That sounds tough," Nathan said carefully. "I get it, though—the pressure to dig deep when you're not even sure what's in there, it's scary stuff."

"Yeah." Gabe kicked at a pile of slush on the edge of the sidewalk. "First class today, I pulled out this Sam Kinison bit—nailed it, too."

He hunched over and let out a dramatic, ear-splitting "Oh—oh—ooooh!" The sound echoed through the cold air, earning a sharp glance from a passing professor and a sigh from a woman bundled in a thick scarf.

Nathan shrank a little. "Gabe, maybe save the scream routine for later?"

Gabe nudged Nathan. "Aw, c'mon, man. Just spreading a little joy." He threw a theatrical bow toward the unimpressed professor. "If they can't appreciate a classic, that's on them."

"So, what happened with your professor?" Nathan asked.

Gabe sighed. "She called me a hack."

Nathan turned to him. "A hack? Seriously?"

"Yeah. She said I was just recycling other people's work instead of pulling from something real. She said I was scared. Can you believe it, me —scared? She went on and on about me not having the courage to put my own voice out there, in front of the entire class. It was kind of humiliating."

He kicked another chunk of ice. "I mean, she's not wrong. I've been doing other people's bits for so long, I don't even know if I have anything original to say."

Nathan studied him. For the first time, he saw a crack in his roommate's typically bulletproof confidence.

He flashed back to his conversation with Simmons, remembering how she had seemed to peer straight into his existence. He recognized that same vulnerability in Gabe's expression—the feeling of having your guard stripped away, leaving you uncertain of what you had to offer.

Nathan knew that feeling all too well.

"Hey," Nathan said, voice softer now. "Tell you what—if you want to come up with some original bits? I'm down to help in any way that I can. Let's just limit the junk food—okay? I can't handle another sugar hangover."

Gabe let out a short laugh. "Aw, man, you're such a lightweight, Cheese. It's kind of adorable. But okay, fine—we'll do brewskis instead," he offered with a chuckle before turning more sincere.

"Seriously, though, thanks. I definitely could use your help putting some fresh stuff together. I just don't wanna be the guy who's only good at imitating other people."

"Anyway, enough about my tragic comedy career and public humiliation—what about you? First day of classes going okay?"

Nathan tensed slightly, thoughts flashing back to the drama with Val and then to Simmons. "You know—about as good as yours, I guess. Just trying to keep up—You know."

He pushed his feelings down. He didn't want to unload everything from the day he still had yet to unpack.

Gabe nodded, giving Nathan a friendly punch on the arm. "Yeah, this place can definitely be overwhelming at first, but just remember—it's only the first day. You'll settle in soon, I'm sure."

Nathan forced a smile, but his thoughts were already starting to spiral again.

As they reached the gym doors, he knew he needed Eve.

He needed that steady, grounding energy she always brought.

Maybe then, the noise in his head would quiet—if only for a little while.

19

———————————

CRASH COURSE

Nathan and Gabe squeezed through the crowded halls of the sports complex, dodging gym bags and weaving around students rushing to their next class until they reached the yoga studio. Through the wall of windows, they spotted Eve wrapping up her session.

She moved in perfect rhythm with the instructor. Every transition was effortless—like she was fueled by something deeper than muscle memory. She looked centered and composed, radiating a quiet power. Her breath was measured and controlled, as if the outside world didn't exist.

Gabe was practically drooling as he stared through the window into the class with his mouth wide open. He nudged Nathan without looking away. "Dude, yoga might be humanity's best invention. Seriously—look at all the babes in one room. I'm totally signing up."

Nathan held back a laugh, raising an eyebrow. "Oh yeah? Right, I can picture you trying downward dog and taking out half the class in the process."

Gabe shot him a mock-offended look.

"Hey, man, I've got moves you've never seen. Watch this." He planted his foot against his calf, settling into an impressively steady tree pose. For someone built like a retired linebacker who never passed up a good meal, his balance was surprisingly solid. It was like he'd been practicing yoga his whole life.

Nathan was genuinely impressed by his roommate's grace. "Okay, didn't see that coming," he admitted. "Guess you do have an inner yogi."

Gabe held the pose in complete serenity, calmly exhaling through his nose. "You haven't seen anything yet, check this out."

He smoothly transitioned into a more elaborate stance, somewhere between a warrior pose and an interpretive dance move. He stretched his arms and leaned forward like he was about to take flight. For a moment, he seemed to be at complete peace.

Just as he was about to reach full enlightenment, the deep chime of the clock tower echoed through the hall, snapping him out of his zen. He flailed his arms in a desperate attempt to regain his balance, but he couldn't stop himself from crashing backward into the glass wall of the yoga studio with a heavy thud.

Inside the class, the vibe was completely destroyed. Their serenity gave way to surprise as every head snapped toward whatever had shattered the calm, and at the center of it all was Eve, staring at them with equal parts shock and annoyance.

Gabe's cheeks immediately went beet red as he scrambled to his feet and brushed himself off like nothing had happened. "They probably didn't even notice," he mumbled, trying to play it cool.

Nathan doubled over, trying to hold back his laughter.

"Yeah, totally. No one noticed the earthquake you just caused."

Eve transitioned into her final pose, shaking her head with slight amusement. The studio's calm returned slowly, settling like dust after a gust of wind, as if Gabe's disruption had somehow been part of the flow all along.

As the class ended and people crowded the door, Nathan spotted Mia, and it took his breath away. She slipped through the hallway like the crowd parted for her without realizing it.

Late morning light caught the silver strands in her hair, making them shimmer like silk. Every step she took was steady and unhurried, like she moved to a rhythm only she could hear. She sifted through her bag, digging around for a hair tie. When she found one, she pulled her hair back in one smooth, practiced motion. Then, as she tied it back, she looked up, met Nathan's eyes, and gave him a soft smile.

For a heartbeat, the hallway faded. Her expression was warm, almost familiar—like they'd known each other forever.

"Hi," she said, her voice soft, barely louder than a breath, but somehow it cut through all the noise.

An unexpected calm settled over Nathan, steadying him in a way his usual nerves never could.

Gabe leaned over and elbowed Nathan lightly, nodding toward Mia.

"I'm telling you, dude, she's totally into you," he whispered, full of amusement. "You two have the whole slow-motion, locked-eyes thing going on. It's like watching a real-life rom-com."

Mia slipped into the crowd, disappearing into the steady flow of students. The ease she left behind lingered, something quiet and unshakable settling in Nathan's chest. He didn't move. His thoughts trailed after her like she'd left a piece of herself behind.

"Oh, man... she's got you, dude," Gabe said, nudging Nathan. "Seriously, you better snap out of it before Eve catches you drooling over your enhanced girlfriend."

"Shut up, dude," he replied, shaking off the haze. "She's not my girlfriend."

It sounded true when he said it, but he didn't want it to be.

The truth was, he wanted to know her. He wanted to know what made her smile like that. He wanted to know if Gabe was right—if something impossible could actually be possible.

Before he could think too much about it, Eve walked over, rolling up her yoga mat with practiced ease. A light sheen of sweat clung to her skin, but she looked energized. Her hair was twisted into a messy bun, a few strands falling around her face. She barely glanced at Nathan before locking in on Gabe, her expression unreadable but clearly unimpressed.

"Thanks for crashing my class, you big jerk. We were totally in the zone until you decided to go full-on bull in a china shop," she said, her voice dripping with mock accusation.

"What? I was just showing Cheese here how I harness my chi, or whatever. I can't help it if the damn clock tower ruined my peace." He hunched over, dragging one foot behind him in an over-the-top Quasimodo impression. "Sanctuary!" he croaked.

Eve snorted, crossing her arms. "Oh god, you're too much. Honestly, the look on the instructor's face when you hit the glass? I almost lost it right there."

Nathan chuckled. "So, good session?"

Eve's face lit up. "It was amazing! Everything was on point today—the flow was perfect, and we tried some new poses. You would've loved it."

He shrugged. "I don't know, Eve. That whole peace and serenity thing isn't really my style."

She poked him lightly in the arm.

"That's putting it mildly," she said with a quiet laugh. "You don't exactly give off peaceful vibes... internal mayhem is more your thing. That's why I think you need to join. I think it'll do you some good. One of these days, I'll get you into a session."

Gabe slung an arm around Nathan's shoulder.

"Yeah, Cheeseman here has no idea what he's missing. But don't worry, I'll help you wear him down."

"It could be fun for all of us to join. You've seen my potential—plus—" he stopped, eyes following the last few girls as they walked past, "—that class looks packed full of... peace."

"Eyes up, Kowalski!" Eve said, swatting his arm. "There's more to yoga than the view, Gabe. But if you're serious about trying—and you can manage to drag Nathan in—then I'd love to see if you can hang."

Gabe raised his hands in surrender. "Challenge accepted. Next stop, enlightenment."

Nathan rolled his eyes but couldn't hold back a smile.

"So, uh, are we having lunch?" Nathan asked.

Gabe snapped back to attention. "Yeah! Let's hit the caf. It's chicken burger day—I could probably eat a hundred of those things right now. I skipped second breakfast."

"Second breakfast?" Eve asked, raising an eyebrow.

Nathan chuckled. "Trust me, you don't want to know."

She shrugged. "As tempting as pressed chicken patties sound, let's skip the cafeteria. I'm in the mood for something different today. Let's head off campus—there's a diner in town with killer veggie wraps. I'll drive."

"You mean Chubbie's?" Gabe's eyes widened. "Now you're talking. That place is amazing. They've got these Double Bacon Cheeseburgers—" He trailed off, eyes glazing over.

"Picture this: two quarter-pound beef patties, three slices of cheddar, and crispy bacon. But instead of a bun? It's sandwiched between two glazed donuts."

"Chubbie's is the only place in New England that still makes food like that anymore. Man, those burgers are killer—in every way."

Eve laughed. "Well, that sounds— intense. I can already feel my arteries clogging just hearing about it. I think I'll pass on the heart stopper and stick to something that'll help me live past my twenties."

"I'm down for a field trip, as long as they've got some normal food on the menu," Nathan said. "After the morning I've had, getting off campus sounds kind of perfect."

Eve smiled as she threw her yoga mat over her shoulder. "Great, let's hit the road before the lunch rush."

As they stepped outside, Nathan felt lighter. No cafeteria crowds. No pressure. Just friends, food, and a rare moment of calm. And for once, that was exactly what he needed.

20

CHUBBIE'S

The drive to Chubbie's was light and easy. Gabe cracked jokes about his deep appreciation for the *talent* in the yoga class while Eve rattled off details about new poses she'd learned. For a moment, everything felt almost normal, and Nathan was able to let himself breathe.

When they reached the café, it felt like they'd stepped into a different world. Chubbie's had the same cozy charm as his favorite restaurant back home in Vermont—the one where he used to spend hours nursing a coffee and hammering away at whatever writing project had taken over his life that day.

The scent of espresso and fresh bread hung in the air, mixing with the low hum of conversation. Unlike the high-tech spots on campus or the noisy crowd in the dining hall, this place was old-school and simple. No digital menus. No robotic baristas. Just friendly faces behind the counter and the promise of a meal that wasn't engineered for efficiency.

They slid into a booth at the back. Eve ordered a grilled veggie panini with sweet potato fries. Nathan went for a buffalo chicken wrap.

Gabe, in true Gabe fashion, scanned the menu for exactly five seconds before, just like he promised, settling on the Heartstopper Burger.

In person, it was somehow both more impressive and disgusting than described. And to complete the masterpiece, he added a triple-thick milkshake.

"Dude, isn't that a bit much?" Nathan asked. "I mean, you're basically eating half a Dunkin' and a Dairy Queen combined. I can see why those places closed down. Did you really need to order that shake?"

"What's wrong with my shake? I had to get one. It'll help with digestion," Gabe replied, completely serious, like it was some kind of medical necessity.

Eve rolled her eyes. "I can hear your cholesterol levels spiking."

Nathan shook his head as Gabe took an exaggerated bite, practically unhinging his jaw to fit it all in.

"You're just jealous that I can eat whatever I want and keep my boyish figure," he said through a mouthful of food, looking entirely too pleased with himself.

As they ate, Eve's excitement filled the space between them. She launched into a story about her modern art class.

"You guys, I'm so pumped for this semester's project. We're working on an installation using recycled materials to highlight environmental issues," she said, her eyes bright. "It's insane what people come up with. Give someone a pile of trash and a glue gun, and suddenly you've got a sculpture that makes you rethink your place in the world."

Nathan let her words wash over him. For a second, he thought they might steady him, but the feeling didn't last.

No matter how hard he tried to stay present, his fingers tapped against the table, and his foot bounced relentlessly under it.

His mind kept getting dragged back to his writing class. Simmon's words pressed on him like a weight.

Face your pain. Write about it. Dig deep.

His thoughts jumped to his Intro to Health and Tech class and how Val had owned a room she had no business being in. Then came the memory of her tattoos—the way they twisted and coiled over her skin like they were alive.

He shivered as he reached for his water, gripping the glass harder than he needed to.

Eve, ever perceptive, caught the look on his face. Her voice softened. "Hey... you alright, Boone?"

Nathan forced a smile, but it felt weak. "Yeah, I'm cool."

She didn't buy it.

"Nathan, look at me. I know something is up with you. Don't hide— I'm here—What's going on?"

He hesitated. The way she looked at him like she truly cared settled over him heavier than he expected. He wasn't sure what to do with it. He didn't want to dump everything on her—or Gabe.

He didn't want to be that guy. Not here. Not now.

He let out a slow breath. Maybe letting some of it out wouldn't make him weaker. Maybe it would actually help.

"Let's just say my first day of classes wasn't exactly awesome." He gave a weak chuckle.

"It started in my Intro to Health and Tech class..." He trailed off, trying to keep it surface-level.

Eve cut in with a groan. "Oh, man, that class is the worst. It's nothing more than spoon-fed tech propaganda. I had it in my first semester here. Dr. Lowell's nice and all, but half the time I felt like he was trying to brainwash me."

"It wasn't the class or Dr. Lowell. That was all fine," Nathan replied, his tone quiet but clear.

"I think the course might be interesting. It's just that—" He hesitated. "Val's in that class. You were right about her... she's a total bitch."

Gabe, who had been demolishing his food in blissful ignorance, paused mid-bite. "Hey!—Go easy on my future wife."

Nathan shot him a deadpan look. "Sorry, man. It's true, though. She's the worst."

"Oh, a Val Reynolds event... I see." Eve's tone was dry. "But why is she even in that class? She's not new—what, is she just there to mess with people, or something?"

"Seems like it," Nathan muttered. "I guess she's auditing the class. That wasn't even the worst part of the day."

He shoved aside the image of Val's snakes and forced himself to focus.

"I've got this professor for my writing class—Dr. Simmons. Let's just say, she hit me with a few things I wasn't prepared for."

He paused, gathering his thoughts. "She told me she knew my mom. She knew my dad, too. I guess they all went to college together."

He paused. Saying it out loud made the whole thing feel even more surreal.

"She also said that she was on the selection committee," he added. "The one that accepted me here."

That got their attention. Gabe stopped chewing, and Eve's concern sharpened.

"Wow. That's pretty heavy," Gabe said. "So what... she let you in as a favor to your mom or something?"

"No, I don't think it was like that at all," Nathan replied, "She told me I was good enough to be in the program. She said she pushed for my acceptance. I don't think she did it as a favor at all."

He ran a hand over the back of his neck. "She thinks I have what it takes to be a great writer someday. She just said my writing is missing something."

"Missing something? Like what exactly?" Eve asked.

Nathan let out a slow breath. "She said my writing is too safe. Too easy. She told me it's missing conflict or darkness or something. I dunno, I'm still trying to figure it all out." The words didn't feel like his own.

"Now she wants me to write about my fears. Not just mention them, but expose them."

Gabe nodded slowly. "That's heavy, man. But hey, you're a great writer. Some of that stuff you showed me the other night? It was seriously good. I'm not much of a reader, but I felt like I was really there. You know—in the story. Don't beat yourself up about it. I'm sure you'll figure it out."

"I don't know, man. It's not that simple." Nathan shook his head. "She wants me to be vulnerable. To dig into things I've spent years trying to forget. I have no idea how to do that without falling apart."

Eve sighed and shook her head. "Come on, Nathan. Stop being so dramatic—"

The way she brushed off his feelings caused him to immediately tense up.

She noticed right away and snapped her mouth shut.

After a moment, she reached across the table and took his hand.

"Sorry," she said quietly. "I didn't mean it like that. I hear you, Nathan. I see you." She glanced at Gabe. "How can we help?"

"I don't think you can," he said. "I think I have to figure this out on my own. I just... I don't know where to start."

Nathan exhaled, his mind somewhere else, caught between Professor Simmons' words and the memory of Val's tattoos.

His pulse ticked up. He braced himself for the spiral.

Then, a soft voice came from behind him. "Um, excuse me."

Nathan tensed. He knew that voice.

Gabe, halfway through shoveling the last of his fries into his mouth, looked up and froze. His jaw hung open for half a second before he kicked Nathan under the table.

"Ow! What the hell, man?" Nathan yelped.

He rubbed his shin, and the irritation faded when he turned around.

Standing behind him was Mia, tray in hand, her expression caught between hopeful and hesitant.

She shifted her tray slightly. "Do you guys have room for one more?"

"Uh... yeah, sure," Nathan replied, sliding over to make space.

Eve's expression stayed neutral, although Nathan could feel the change in energy. She was watching Mia closely, her posture just a little too still. She wasn't the type to make a scene. Still, he recognized that look—she was sizing Mia up and searching for any cracks in her façade, anything that might confirm her suspicions about Enhancement.

"Thanks," Mia said as she slid into the seat beside Nathan, tucking a strand of hair behind her ear. Her voice carried the same steady warmth he had noticed before. This time, though, there was a trace of shyness beneath it, like she was still looking for acceptance, still trying to find a place where she belonged.

"I was supposed to meet my roommate for lunch, but after she blew me off for a ride into campus, I decided to take the school shuttle back into town and explore a little." She shrugged. "Not that I'm heartbroken about it," she added with a hint of amusement. "She's not exactly my favorite person."

Gabe, sensing an opportunity to land a joke, wiped his hands on a napkin and leaned in. "Oh yeah, I know all about terrible roommates. Mine's a real dud. Total basket case. And he smells like—"

Nathan didn't let him finish. He kicked Gabe back, hitting his shin with perfect accuracy—payback for the shot he'd given him earlier.

Gabe jumped violently, nearly knocking over his drink as he clutched his shin.

"Ow! Okay, okay, point taken!" he hissed, shooting Nathan a wounded look before shoving another fry into his mouth like nothing happened.

Mia let out a small laugh, and Nathan felt his shoulders ease just a bit.

Eve, finally breaking her silence, folded her arms, her tone even but edged with something unreadable. "So, I don't think we've officially met. I'm Eve, and you're new here. Mia, right?"

Mia nodded, shifting slightly in her seat. "Yeah, just transferred in. Let's just say it's been quite an adjustment."

"Yeah, I hear that," Nathan said. "I just transferred, too." He let out a quiet sigh, the weight of it barely noticeable but telling.

Mia tilted her head, intrigued. "Rough start?"

"You could say that. I'm still trying to figure out how things work around here."

Mia gave him a small, knowing smile.

"I think the hardest part for me so far is the weather. I've never left the West Coast before, and this New England winter? Yeah, I'm not a fan. I've only been here a week, and I'm already learning the hard way that I had no idea what cold actually felt like. Honestly, I never even owned a winter jacket until now."

Nathan chuckled. "Yeah, it's brutal at first, but you'll get used to it."

"I seriously doubt it, but hey, I like a challenge," she replied, tugging her sleeves down over her hands like she was gearing up for battle.

"What about you?" she asked, shifting the focus back to him. "Where'd you transfer from?"

"I grew up in Vermont, so I'm used to the cold, but everything else here is different. I feel like I've landed in another universe. Some of the people here are... a lot."

Mia laughed softly. "Yeah, I get that. My roommate, for one. She's pretty intense."

Something in her tone made Nathan pause. "Intense, how?"

Mia shrugged. "Let's just say she's unique. Dark, I guess. I honestly don't know what classes she takes or if she even goes to any. I guess she lives by her own rules. Oh, and she's covered in these awful tattoos. They're terrifying, if I'm being honest—snakes, mostly, everywhere."

Nathan blinked, his mind catching up. "Wait—did you say snakes?"

Mia nodded. "Yeah, you know, super goth stuff. She's very 'look at me, look at how dark and edgy I am.' It's kind of exhausting the way she's built her entire image around the whole horror show aesthetic."

His pulse jumped. "Your roommate's not Valerie Reynolds, is she?"

Mia's eyebrows lifted. "Yeah! You know her?"

Nathan grimaced. "Let's just say I've seen her around—you're right, she's intense."

He glanced over at Gabe, who was polishing off his milkshake with a loud slurp, trying to get the last of it.

"You know, the big guy here has a special place in his heart for her."

"Cheese!" Gabe exclaimed, feigning offense. He wiped his hands dramatically before shooting Nathan a look of betrayal.

Eve's eyes darted to the clock above the café door. When she saw the time, she straightened and began gathering her things with a bit too much urgency.

"Sorry to bail, but I need to head out," she said. "I've got Philosophy over in Scitico Hall, and I want to get there early."

He knew it was more of an excuse than anything else. She wanted out of the conversation—or maybe just away from the table's new dynamic.

Slinging her bag over her shoulder, she glanced at Nathan.

"Nathan, if you want a ride back to campus, now's your chance. Otherwise, there's a shuttle that runs every half hour."

He shook his head. "If it's okay, I think I'm going to hang back for a bit. I'm done with classes for the day, and I'm not in a rush to get back to the campus madness any time soon."

Sensing the tension, Gabe jumped in.

"Oh man, Scitico? That's the crunchy side of campus. They have these vegan energy bars at the bookstore, they're insane. I could eat like four or five at a time."

Eve raised an eyebrow. "Gabe, you know those bars are like a thousand calories each. They're meant for survival situations. You know, like being stranded in the woods."

Gabe patted his chest with exaggerated pride. "Exactly. You know me— I'm all about survival. Mind if I tag along? I don't have class until two," he asked, shooting her a hopeful look.

Eve gave him a look that lingered a second longer than necessary, a teasing spark in her eyes. "Sure thing, big guy—All aboard."

She turned to Nathan. "You sure you want to take the shuttle back? It's not exactly a thrill ride."

Nathan gave a small shrug. "Yeah. I'm good."

Mia stepped in before the silence stretched too long. "I have to go back to campus, too. I've gotten very familiar with the shuttle today. If you want, I can walk you to the stop."

Nathan caught the offer in her voice and gave a quick nod. "Yeah... sure. That'd be great."

Eve shifted her weight as she turned to leave. "Suit yourself. Call me later, Boone." Her tone carried just enough ice for Nathan to feel it.

Mia, hoping to keep things polite, offered a warm, "It was nice meeting you, Eve."

Eve paused before offering a cold response. "Yeah, you too." The words were neutral, but her tone had enough edge for anyone paying attention to notice, and clearly, Mia did.

Mia's eyes followed Eve as she exited the café, a ripple of tension settling in her wake. She turned back to Nathan, her voice quieter now. "Did I say something wrong?" There was no self-pity in her tone, just careful observation, like she was trying to piece something together.

"No, it's not you," Nathan reassured her quickly, leaning in slightly. "She's just got some strong feelings about the enhanced crowd. The fact that you're rooming with Val probably didn't help either."

Mia picked at her napkin, tearing little pieces off as she spoke. "Oh, I see. I didn't exactly choose to live with Val, you know? Transferring mid-year doesn't give you a ton of options."

"Tell me about it," Nathan replied with a sympathetic look. "I ended up rooming with the literal big man on campus."

He chuckled, shaking his head. "I've gotta admit, at first, Gabe scared the hell out of me, but I had him pegged all wrong."

He paused, then added, "Maybe Val just needs a bit of time to warm up. You know, show a different side."

Mia let out a small, uncertain laugh. "I'm not holding my breath on that one. From what I've seen so far, I'm pretty sure there's no warm side to Val—just a permanent 'resting bitch face' with a side of being one step away from starting a cult."

She leaned in slightly, her voice dropping, the napkin crumpled tightly in her grip.

"I haven't been able to get a read on her from the start. I moved in early to get ahead on the mountain of work I knew was waiting for me. That first night, after I moved in, she was actually pretty sweet to me—" Mia's expression shifted with a mix of confusion and hesitation.

"After she helped me settle in, she insisted we hit The Lighthouse—it's this super exclusive club for the Enhanced crowd. She said it was 'safe' for people like us, where we wouldn't have to 'dumb things down' for Orgos."

Mia hesitated, her eyes going wide. "Oh god, that sounded awful. I didn't mean it like that."

Nathan chuckled, waving off her concern. "It's cool, no offense taken."

Relieved, Mia continued, "Anyway, I only went that one time, and that was enough. It wasn't for me. I prefer staying in with a good book, some music, maybe a glass of wine. I'm not much for the party scene."

She paused, "Honestly, with the courseload I'll have this semester, there won't be much time for that kind of stuff anyway."

Nathan nodded. "I'm all for peace and quiet, too. I guess I'm still trying to find a decent place to write without distractions. Living with Gabe has its own set of challenges. Don't get me wrong, I'm glad we ended up as roommates—but he's kind of... always on."

"He sure does seem to have an energy about him," Mia added.

Nathan nodded, his mind still on The Lighthouse. "So, that Lighthouse place—was it like some kind of initiation? Did they make you swear loyalty under a neon sign or something?"

"No, it was nothing like that," Mia replied with a chuckle.

"I think it was more like Val didn't want me alone in our apartment. Honestly, I think she's hiding something. Her room is always locked. I've been here a week, and I've never seen that door open once."

Nathan leaned forward, his interest piqued. "Really? That's weird."

"I know, right? But I promised myself I'd try to meet new people and dive into the whole New England experience. Still, everything here feels so different from San Diego."

"I thought moving here from Vermont was an adjustment," Nathan said with a nod. "But San Diego to here? That's gotta be a culture shock."

"Yeah. It's been a wild ride so far," Mia agreed. "That first night, before we went to the club, we stopped by her friend's place. He was decent, at least at first. We talked a lot, since I'm studying hybrid medicine and he's all tech med. We didn't exactly see eye to eye, but he was respectful."

"Wu, right? I think I've seen him around with Val," Nathan said.

"Yeah, that's him. Simon Wu," Mia confirmed, then hesitated. "But there's something weird about him. I mean, he was cool when it was just the two of us. He's super smart and totally reasonable. But the second Val walked in, he just... I don't know, changed. Like, he shut down. I think she's got some kind of hold on him."

Nathan frowned. "That does sound weird. I haven't had much experience with the enhanced crowd. Honestly, this is probably the longest conversation I've had with someone who might be enhanced."

Mia looked at him deadpan, her lips twitching. "What exactly makes you think I'm enhanced?"

Flustered, Nathan stammered. "Oh my god, I'm so sorry. I just assumed because you were living with Val and—" He paused. "I mean, you are... right?"

He shifted in his seat, heat rising to his face.

Mia burst into laughter. "Relax, I'm just messing with you."

Before Nathan could fully recover, Mia's eyes snapped to something over his shoulder. Her expression changed in an instant, her hands tensing into tight fists—a small move, but enough to make Nathan sit up. He turned to follow her line of sight and felt a sharp flare in his chest as Dante stepped up to their table, towering over them, his attention locked entirely on Mia.

"Mia," Dante said, his voice sharp. "You blew us off for lunch. Val told you that you needed to meet us."

Mia's posture didn't shift. "I felt like a change," she replied coolly.

Dante radiated arrogance. His voice came low and even.

"Man, I don't care what your excuse is. She's outside waiting for you, and she's pissed. Let's go."

Mia raised her eyebrows, mirroring his energy. "Oh, so now she wants to give me a ride? She ignored me this morning, and I had to take the bus." She leaned back. "I don't care if she's not happy. Tell her I'm not coming. Tell her I'm having lunch with my friend."

Dante's eyes shot to Nathan with icy dismissal. Not a word. Not a nod. Just that slow, simmering superiority.

His expression remained unreadable, a quiet dismissal that sent a slow burn through Nathan's chest. Once again, there was no sign of recognition, no acknowledgment—just the unmistakable message that, in Dante's world, Nathan didn't exist.

Mia broke the tension. "And when we're done here," she said, turning to Nathan, "we're going to the library."

Nathan raised an eyebrow. "We are?"

"Yes, we are," she replied, her tone solid as stone.

"Please, Mia," Dante asked, his voice almost pleading. "If you don't come with me right now, we're gonna have a problem. All of us will."

For the first time, Nathan heard it—something that didn't match the Dante he knew. It was almost as if Dante was afraid.

She didn't blink. "I'm sorry, but I'm not coming. You can tell the Wicked Witch of West Hall that I have better things to do than waste time on whatever power trip she's running today."

Dante's stare sharpened.

Nathan watched, amazed at how steady Mia stayed—unshaken, brave, like she wasn't even sweating it.

She just grabbed her bag with one swift movement and got out of her seat. "You know what? I've suddenly lost my appetite. Come on, Nathan, the shuttle just pulled up."

Nathan stood up slowly, shoving his arms into his coat. The air between him and Dante felt like it could ignite. His fists balled at his sides.

Then Mia looked at him, and the storm inside him eased.

She steadied him without even trying.

He felt it fully—how being near her didn't make him forget who he was. It made him remember who he could be.

21

PAPER TIGER

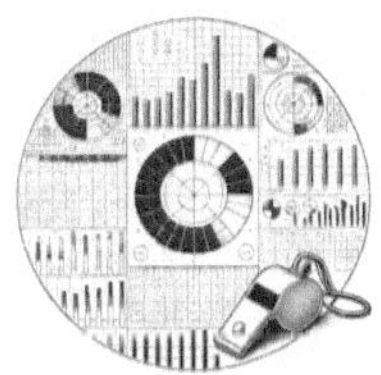

For Dante Edwards, sports weren't just a game. They were the only thing he'd ever been good at, and playing well on the field was all anyone ever expected from him. Growing up in a low-income household, he knew his athletic talent was the only shot he had at making something of himself.

He wasn't the smartest guy in class; he knew that. School had always been something to survive, not somewhere he shined. His grades were just high enough to keep him eligible and on the field. Just enough to keep the offers coming.

Even with trophies stacked in his room and his name all over the school's record books, he couldn't shake the feeling that none of it was ever going to be enough.

That he was never going to be enough.

Without football, without the wins and the headlines, there was nothing else. He was just the jock. Deep down, a voice kept reminding him he'd never have anything else to offer.

That voice grew louder at NCSU. The competition was tougher. The stakes were higher. Back home, he had been the star. Here, he was just another athlete fighting for a spot on the roster. The relentless pressure hollowed him out like a tin man, taking whatever heart he had left.

When he was a kid, Dante thought getting a MIND Chip would change everything. Back then, it was all over the feeds—those glossy ads showing athletes breaking records, running faster, hitting harder, pushing past every limit like it was nothing. It wasn't just tech. It was magic. And as a kid sitting in his too-small apartment, watching those clips on a secondhand tablet, he believed it. He figured if he ever got one, he wouldn't just be better—he'd be unstoppable.

So when they told him he was getting one as part of his athletic scholarship at NCSU, he thought that his dreams were finally going to come true. He'd finally have the missing piece that was going to take him from hometown hero to legendary.

He had all these ideas about what it would feel like—running drills without feeling like his lungs were on fire, recovering after games without his whole body feeling wrecked. He'd be a dominant force on the field with no limits, and no one would be able to stop him.

But the chip they gave him wasn't the kind he'd dreamed about. Not even close.

The NCAA-approved version was locked down so tight it was useless. It tracked his performance, his recovery, his vitals, and flagged him if he pushed too hard, or worse, if he wasn't pushing hard enough. Sure, it could speed up his healing time, but it also meant they knew everything. How fast he ran when he pushed himself, and how slow he was when he wasn't giving everything he had. They knew if he took a play off, even for a second.

The coaching staff tracked everything he did, like some twisted version of Santa Claus. They knew when he was sleeping, when he was awake, and if he was out past curfew or doing anything that might be considered detrimental to the team. He was constantly under their watchful eyes; he was forced to be good—not for the sake of goodness, but for the team, and the team alone.

His version of the chip wasn't there to help him win. It was there to make sure he never stepped out of line.

For everyone else, the MIND Chip was the ultimate upgrade. It made people smarter, sharper, fitter, and even better-looking. It was like having a personal cheat code for life. Students used it to ace their exams without feeling tired after pulling all-nighters. Others would just use it to show up at the gym already halfway to ripped. Some didn't even bother working out anymore; their implants kept them lean and camera-ready without breaking a sweat.

But for athletes like Dante? It wasn't an advantage. It was a leash. One more thing he didn't get to control. His stats weren't his anymore. Every bit of his performance—his speed, his recovery, his power output—all belonged to the school now.

His body wasn't his anymore either. It was reduced to data on a screen, and data could be deleted. He could be swapped out and replaced by someone faster, stronger, and hungrier than he was.

He wasn't just a player anymore. He was a product, and deep down, he wasn't sure how long he'd stay valuable.

His first semester on campus nearly wrecked him. Every workout, every drill, every second on the field was picked apart. Coaches didn't even have to yell. He knew right away that he was falling behind. The chip told them before he could. Split times, recovery rates, power output—every number that measured whether he was good enough or not showed that he was not reaching his potential, no matter how hard he pushed himself.

Football used to be the one place he felt free. It wasn't easy, but it was simple. He'd put in the work, he'd show up early, and he'd be the last to leave, he'd pour his heart and soul into his game, and it paid off. Now he felt like he was stuck inside some giant machine, just another piece waiting to break.

The only thing that made it bearable at first was Gabe, the one person who got it. They were both small-town kids trying to stay above water in a place that expected them to be machines. Some nights, after brutal practices, they'd sit in their dorm, too tired to move and talk about how the coaches never let up. How it felt like they were always being watched. Always being judged. Always one mistake away from losing everything.

They promised to stick it out together. They swore to each other that they'd always have each other's backs. No matter what.

By the end of their first semester, Gabe cracked. The constant grind, the endless pressure, and the sinking feeling that his heart wasn't in it anymore finally wore him down.

Dante still remembered the night Gabe told him he was done.

"I just can't keep doing this, man," Gabe said, sitting across from him in their dorm. His voice was quiet, but there was something solid underneath it. He'd already made up his mind.

Dante stared at him. He had to be joking. "You're giving up everything," he replied, frustration sharp in his voice. "You're just gonna throw it all away?"

Gabe didn't argue. He just said there was more to life than playing sports. That he couldn't handle the way they were being treated anymore.

He said they owned them—that they were just data points, and stats on a screen, and the second they stopped performing, they were nothing. He said he didn't want to wake up one day and realize he'd spent his entire college career being controlled.

Dante wanted to get it. He tried, but couldn't. He heard Gabe's words, and he felt the weight of them, but they didn't land the way he needed them to. For Dante, being on the team was all he ever wanted, the only thing he'd ever known.

Being a part of a team like The NCSU Orange Wave, a team that was always a championship contender, was the shot Dante had worked for his entire life. No matter how hard it was, walking away didn't make sense to him. Quitting meant admitting that you weren't good enough to make it, and he wasn't ready to face that. Not then—not ever.

He begged Gabe to stay—to stick it out. He threw out every argument he could think of.

He promised him that next season would be better. They'd get more playing time. They'd get to be on nationally broadcast games, and the NFL scouts would be watching. They'd finally be the stars they were meant to be. He swore all their hard work would pay off. That all the suffering would be worth it in the end.

In his head, it all made sense. He laid his entire vision out for Gabe, piece by piece. He was convinced that if he just said the right thing, Gabe would stay. But there weren't enough words to change his mind. Gabe had already made up his mind, and nothing Dante said could bring him back.

The next day, Gabe officially quit the team, but he didn't move out of the dorm. For a few weeks, they went through the motions, but their connection was gone. Replaced by something heavy neither of them wanted to deal with.

One day, without warning, Dante packed up and left, leaving behind a note that was way too long, way too raw, and filled with things he regretted the second he set the pen down.

At the bottom, he'd scrawled one last line: *Good luck becoming a clown.*

With his bags packed and nowhere to go, Dante talked his way into a meeting with the Dean of Campus Housing, doing everything short of begging to get moved out of the dorms. When they offered him a spot in West Hall, he said yes before they even finished the sentence.

It wasn't about the room or even the building. It was about getting out, getting away from campus, away from the constant reminders that he was never going to be enough.

The off-campus apartment in West Hall hadn't been his first choice, but it didn't matter. It was the reset button he desperately needed. A chance to figure out what came next without everything hanging over him.

That's how he ended up living with Simon Wu. The last person he ever expected to be the answer to his problems.

Dante stood outside the apartment complex, key card in hand, staring up at the building. It wasn't anything like the cramped, outdated apartments he'd pictured after reading the campus housing ad. This place looked more like a 5-star luxury hotel than an off-campus college apartment complex. It was all sleek lines, massive windows, and a courtyard straight out of a high-end design blog.

The ad had been vague at best, but this? This felt off. For a second, he wondered if he'd mixed up the address—or worse, maybe he was getting pranked.

He thought back to the argument he'd had with the dean earlier that day. After way too much back and forth, they'd finally approved him for an off-campus unit—one that was supposedly better suited to *his situation*. Whatever that was supposed to mean.

He swiped the key card, hesitating before the lock beeped and the door clicked open.

The lobby was next-level clean. Polished concrete floors gleamed under soft, recessed lighting, and everything about the place screamed expensive. The vibe was mid-century modern, but not in a try-hard way—muted navy, deep charcoal, slick walnut wood. They'd even worked in some retro tech touches to soften the high-energy, ultra-modern vibe the rest of campus had. Analog clocks lined the walls of the lobby, each showing a different time zone from across the world, like some subtle nod to the international students they were trying to impress. Abstract art hung over the seating areas—pieces that managed to look scientific without being cold, like they belonged in a place designed for the best and brightest.

It was the kind of aesthetic Dante had only seen in magazines—the expensive kind they kept behind the counter.

Dante's duffel bag suddenly felt heavier. He stood there for a second, trying to process what he was seeing, his mind scrambling to catch up.

This can't be right, he thought.

As he stepped into his apartment, he took a moment to soak it all in before dropping his bag by the couch. The sound of footsteps made him glance up. His new roommate was heading his way from the hallway, walking like he had somewhere important to be, but wasn't in any rush to get there.

The guy looked like he'd just stepped out of a boardroom—tailored charcoal slacks, a crisp white button-up with the sleeves rolled neatly, and loafers so polished they probably had their own spotlight.

There was something about him—calm, in control, like he already had everything figured out. He had the kind of confidence that made Dante feel like he was there for a job interview instead of meeting his new roommate.

"Welcome to your new home," he said, his tone smooth but not exactly friendly. "My name's Simon, but everyone just calls me Wu."

He hesitated for a beat before gripping Simon's hand. Despite being much smaller than Dante, Wu's grip had a surprising strength that made Dante wince slightly.

"Nice to meet you, I'm Dante. Dante Edwards," he said, pulling his hand back.

"We *know* who you are, and we're glad you could join us," Wu said, his voice low and cool, carrying just a hint of dry amusement.

We?

Dante didn't say it out loud, but the word echoed in his brain. The apartment was supposed to be a double—just him and one other roommate. At this point, he was just happy to have a new place, and it was way nicer than he had imagined, so that was a bonus. He decided to just roll with it.

"I'm excited to be here, too. The dorms were…" He trailed off.

Everything about this place felt wrong to him. It was too perfect, too polished. Like it belonged to someone else's life.

Wu's eyes narrowed. "I get it. Those places are not for people like us."

"Yeah, totally, I guess. Well, this place… doesn't look anything like I pictured," Dante said, forcing a laugh that didn't quite land. He motioned toward the living room, full of posh leather furniture and an energy that practically screamed: *Don't touch anything.*

"The ad made it sound like a basic off-campus unit. Are you sure this is where I'm supposed to be?"

"You're definitely in the right place, Dante," Wu said, smooth as ever, like it was already settled. Like it had never been a question. "Soon you'll find that everything you need is taken care of."

Dante blinked, trying to make sense of it. The way Wu said it—like it was a done deal, like there was no room for any more questions—made it clear he wasn't getting any more answers, no matter how hard he pushed.

Wu tipped his chin toward the hallway. "Your room's down there, second door on the left. I only have one rule—keep the common areas clean, and we won't have any problems."

It wasn't exactly welcoming, but there was something about Wu's calm that weirdly settled things. Like he had everything under control. Like nothing ever threw him off.

"Thanks," Dante said, shifting his duffel higher on his shoulder, feeling the awkward weight of it.

Wu nodded—barely—then turned and walked off like he had somewhere better to be. "Kitchen's stocked if you're hungry," he added over his shoulder, not bothering to look back before disappearing into his bedroom.

The door snapped shut, followed by the sharp click of the lock sliding into place. The signal was subtle, but clear enough—Dante wasn't invited to follow.

Dante stood there, still holding his bag, staring around like he was waiting for someone to tell him it was a joke. The place was quiet, polished, and expensive. It felt a million miles away from the dorm he'd left behind.

Dante sat on the edge of his new bed, staring at the perfectly painted walls like they were supposed to mean something. His bag sat half-unpacked on the floor, clothes spilling out like even they didn't want to stay there.

He leaned forward, elbows on his knees, head in his hands. This wasn't the life he thought he'd be living when he first showed up at NCSU. Back then, he told himself it was a fresh start. A chance to be someone different. Someone better. He'd promised himself he'd leave the cocky version of Dante behind—the one who used to run Strafford, Vermont like he owned it.

Back home, he was untouchable. Captain of the football team, all-league basketball player, and a record-breaking track star. His name was everywhere—plastered on school posters, and blasted through speakers at every Friday night game. He could still hear the crowd. He used to strut through those halls like he owned them, holding his chin high and putting everyone else beneath him. Back then, acting like that felt justified—like he deserved it.

Now, whenever he thought about how he behaved and who he used to be, the memory made him feel sick.

He couldn't stop replaying all of it. The way he treated people, the teammates he dismissed, the friends he took for granted, the classmates he ignored, and worst of all, the ones he straight-up humiliated.

Nathan Boone had been his favorite target. To everyone else, he was just the sick kid, and Dante hated how easy it had been to zero in on him. Group projects, lunch, and between classes—he never let up. Every dig, every joke was perfectly timed to get a laugh.

Nathan's health, his size, the way he always looked like he was bracing for something—it was all fair game if it kept the crowd entertained. Every time he got people laughing at Nathan's expense, it gave him this twisted rush, like he was untouchable.

Now it just made him sick.

Coming to NCSU was supposed to change everything. He was going to show up, crush his goals, and finally reach his potential—but he was going to do it the right way. No shortcuts, no ego. He'd promised himself he'd be the guy who worked hard and stayed humble. The guy who used his talent for something good. But as soon as he got here, reality hit hard. He wasn't special. Not even close.

It humbled him. In the worst kind of way—and he knew it.

Every day was the same—wake up, push himself until he couldn't move, crash, repeat. Ego didn't survive long in that kind of grind. And sure, maybe that was growth. But it didn't make it easier to sit with the guy he used to be.

He dragged himself out of the spiral with a slow breath and flopped back on his bed, staring up at the ceiling. Coming here was supposed to be a clean slate, but he didn't feel any different. No better than the kids he'd stepped on to get here.

A knock broke the quiet. He sat up, rubbed his eyes, and crossed the room. His hand hovered on the handle for half a second before he opened it.

Wu stood there, casual like he'd been waiting all day for Dante to answer.

"Oh," Dante said, keeping his tone neutral. "Hey."

Wu didn't waste time. "Are you getting settled in? Need a hand unpacking?" His voice was smooth, easy—but there was something in his eyes. Something that said he already knew the answer and was asking just to see what Dante would say.

Dante shook his head. "No thanks, I'm good. I'll finish up later."

Wu scanned the room with a calm, detached interest. "I know this isn't exactly what you expected," he said, giving a small nod. "But you'll adjust. We're here to help."

Dante's brow pulled together. "That's the second time you've said *we*. They told me at campus housing that this was a double. Who else lives here?"

"Relax," Wu replied. "It's just us in this apartment. When I said *we*, I meant me and my friend Val. She's in the suite across the hall."

"So who is she?" Dante asked casually. "Your girlfriend or something?"

Wu ignored the question completely. He stepped into the room like he didn't need an invitation, stepping over to Dante's desk and picking up the playbook without asking. "So, you're an athlete."

Surprised that Wu would have any interest, Dante replied, "Yeah. I play football. Why, are you a fan?"

Flipping through the pages, Wu showed no sign of interest. "No. I don't waste time on things that break people."

Dante just shrugged. "Yeah, well, it's the only thing I'm good at."

Wu gave a humorless smile. "And how's that working out for you?"

"Honestly, not great," Dante admitted. "Back home, I was All-State every year. Now I'm lucky if I get off the bench."

Setting the playbook down, Wu leaned against the desk like he owned it. "That has to be frustrating."

"Totally," Dante agreed. "At this point, I'm just trying not to get cut. I can't afford to lose my scholarship."

Wu gave a slow nod. "Sounds like you need a little help, perhaps an edge."

Dante let out a dry laugh, though there wasn't any humor in it.

"I need more than a little help. They gave me this bullshit locked version of an implant when I got here. It's NCAA-approved, so basically, it cuts me off at the knees. There's nothing I can do about it."

Wu studied him, sharp and steady. "There are ways around that."

That sparked Dante's interest. "What kind of ways?" he asked.

Wu smoothed a wrinkle on his sleeve, taking his time like it barely mattered. "You'll find out," he said, voice low and casual. "When it's time."

Wu's words rang in his head: *Sounds like you need a little help, perhaps an edge.*

Whatever Wu was offering—whatever workaround he had in mind to break through the limits of Dante's implant—wasn't going to be simple, and he was sure it wasn't going to be free.

But Dante didn't care. Whatever it was—He was in.

22

THE GLYPH

It didn't take long before Val showed up, pushing through the apartment door with a kind of cold precision that shifted the air.

Dante froze, halfway through shoving clothes into a drawer, already feeling the change in the air before he saw her. The sound of heels struck the polished floor in sharp, steady beats, slicing through the quiet like a warning.

She was already at his open door before he realized it, stepping inside without a word. No invitation, no hesitation—like she belonged there. The air changed again, becoming more dense, like it bent around her.

Wu sat at Dante's desk, glued to his phone. He greeted her without looking up.

"Val."

"Wu," she replied, her tone clipped, almost as if she were bored.

Every inch of her radiated control, sculpted with the kind of precision that was meant to be both desired and feared. Her tailored outfit looked expensive and dangerous. There was nothing soft about her. She was perfection wrapped in intimidation, a walking contradiction of allure and threat.

She turned to Dante, her stare crawling over him.

"So," she said, her voice cool and flat. "You're Dante Edwards."

It wasn't a question. It was clear that she knew exactly who he was.

Dante straightened, more out of instinct than choice, but it didn't help. He still felt exposed. He shot a look at Wu, still absorbed in his phone, offering zero backup.

Val didn't wait. She closed the space between them without hesitation, stopping just short of his personal space. For half a second, he thought about stepping back, but he didn't. Something told him that he needed to stand his ground. He made himself hold her stare, even though it felt like she was peeling him apart layer by layer with her eyes.

She looked him up and down, scanning his body from head to toe like she was sizing up a piece of equipment. Then she reached out and gripped his arm, her hand cold and clinical. Her fingers pressed into his bicep like she was searching for something.

"You're strong, very strong," she said, flat as before. "But you could be stronger."

She let go and circled him, scanning every inch of his body like he was under a microscope. He could feel her eyes taking notes as she looked him up and down. She stopped and brushed her fingers across the back of his neck, just at the edge of his collar.

"You're holding tension here," she said. "We'll see what we can do about that."

Dante stayed still. He wasn't sure if he was supposed to move or speak, but silence felt like the safest option.

She stepped back in front of him. Her stare cut into him again. She tilted her head, studying him like he was some weird specimen she couldn't quite figure out.

"There's a softness in you," she said, like she almost admired it. Then, just as quickly, she shook her head. "That will have to go."

His jaw clenched. He wasn't sure why that stung more than it should've, but it did.

She stepped back, folding her hands neatly in front of her. She was composed again like none of this had been personal.

"At a glance? He's not terrible, Wu," she said, like she was rating a thrift store find. "But you'll have to strip him down and start over."

Wu pushed to his feet, stepping in beside her.

She stepped closer to Dante, stopping inches from his face, her eyes locked on his.

"Speed. Strength. Focus," she said, like she was listing ingredients. "We can fix all of it. The only question is whether you're willing to do what it takes to level up."

"Level up how?" He asked, letting the words slip out before he could stop them.

Val didn't answer. She looked him over, lips curving into a subtle, knowing smile. It wasn't friendly. It said she knew something he didn't. Something he probably wasn't ready for.

She glanced over at Simon. "He'll need a lot of work, Wu."

Simon nodded like he already knew. "I'll get him there."

Val turned her attention back to Dante. "You better," she said, her voice cold and flat.

Then, without another word, she turned to walk out of the room, pausing with dramatic flair.

"Oh, and Dante?" she added, without bothering to turn back. "If you're here to waste our time, don't bother unpacking."

With that, she disappeared around the corner, letting her words linger in the air long after she was out of sight. A moment later, the apartment door slammed shut with a loud, final crash, like the last nail being driven into a coffin. That's when Dante felt it—whatever this was, it wasn't normal. It was something bigger, colder, and far more intense than he could have ever imagined.

"What was that about?" he asked, turning to Wu, his voice tight.

He didn't answer. He just motioned for Dante to follow. When they reached the door to his room, Wu pulled out his student ID and swiped it against the keypad. The panel beeped, and after a soft click, the door unlocked, and he pushed it open.

Dante wasn't sure what he expected—maybe a couple of monitors, and judging by that handshake earlier, he wouldn't have been surprised to see a weight bench or even a few dumbbells shoved in the corner. Something that made sense, but what he saw wasn't even close to what he'd imagined.

The room glowed faint blue from a wall of monitors. It wasn't a bedroom. It was a computer lab straight out of a different timeline. The walls were dark green, with shelves packed with old tech and pop-culture relics that looked like they'd been stolen from a collector who took things way too seriously. The room screamed retro-futurism in the weirdest, most over-the-top way.

A Commodore 64 sat on one desk, its beige casing in mint condition. Next to it, a translucent purple Nintendo 64 caught the light from the screens. In another corner, an original PlayStation was hooked to an old CRT TV where a paused Metal Gear Solid was frozen on the screen.

Dante stepped slowly inside. His eyes dragged over stacks of floppy disks, a Discman with coiled headphones, posters covering the walls—Blade Runner, The Wraith, and a giant cutout of an astronaut from 2001: A Space Odyssey, his visor flashed with a Starfield leaping through hyperspace. On another shelf, rows and rows of VHS tapes were stacked like trophies: The Matrix, Robocop, Terminator 2.

"What the hell is this place?" Dante asked.

"It's my workspace," Wu said like it was obvious.

"Your workspace?" Dante echoed as he let his eyes scan the room in disbelief. He stopped in front of a tower of glowing computer screens, their bulky frames humming softly. The text on one screen scrolled rapidly, lines of code written in what looked like an ancient programming language.

Wu stepped past him, running a hand along the back of a black leather chair, its silver armrests gleaming under the dim glow of the monitors looking like something straight out of a late-90s hacker movie.

"This is where the magic happens," Simon offered with pride. "Or at least where it begins."

"Magic?" Dante repeated, still struggling to process what he was seeing. "This looks like something out of some kind of time capsule. Are you serious with all this stuff?"

"Dead serious," Wu said, his tone edged with pride. He gestured to the consoles, the monitors, and the shelves lined with all of the old tech. "It's not just junk. It's functional. Everything in here has a purpose."

Dante looked at him, clearly not following. "A purpose for what?"

Wu turned fully toward him, his eyes cold and calculating. "A purpose for helping people like you."

Dante's pulse quickened. "People like me?"

Wu stepped closer. "Yes. People with untapped potential. People who need an edge to level the playing field. To go beyond what they think they're capable of."

Dante opened his mouth to speak, but couldn't. The weight of whatever was going on was closing in on him. The room felt smaller, the hum of the computers suddenly too loud. This wasn't about tech nostalgia. Whatever Simon was talking about, it was bigger. Way bigger.

Wu pulled out a chair beside his workstation and motioned for Dante to sit. "It's time you learned what this is really about."

Dante hesitated; his instincts screamed at him to leave, but the weight of Wu's stare left no room for refusal. He stepped forward, and his heart pounded as he lowered himself into the chair.

Wu turned to the screen in front of him, his fingers moving with rhythmic precision across the keyboard. The monitor lit up with a sequence of commands as he typed a series of codes, his cold expression unwavering. The display quickly came alive with a furious stream of foreign text scrolling faster than Dante could process.

"What are you doing?" Dante asked, scanning the monitors.

"I'm tapping into the athletic department's MIND portal," Wu said calmly, his fingers still flying across the keyboard.

"Whoa! You can do that?" Dante's eyes widened.

Wu glanced at him with a brief spark of amusement crossing his face before it settled back into its usual mask of indifference. "I can do anything."

The scrolling text slowed before landing on a screen labeled *Athlete Performance Metrics*. Dante immediately recognized the layout—it was the same system the coaches used to track the team's stats.

Wu leaned in, inspecting the screen with a clinical eye.

"Hmm," he said, scrolling through the data. "I can see why you're frustrated. Your performance is far from peak."

Dante leaned in, gripping the edge of the desk so hard it looked like he might snap.

"What are you talking about? Far from peak? I've been busting my ass every single day—all day."

Wu pointed to a graph, his finger tracing the numbers. The highlighted trend line dipped sharply, giving a visual confirmation of Dante's worst fears.

"Look here," he said, hovering his cursor over a section of the screen. "Your speed—your output—is suboptimal. You're performing at 20% less than when you first arrived on campus for preseason."

Dante clenched his fists as he fought back the creeping feeling of helplessness. "Yeah, well, I've been bulking up, you know, getting stronger, putting on weight—it's a trade-off."

"No, it's not," Wu said flatly, turning to face him. "Your underperformance is all in your head."

Dante let out a bitter laugh. "All in my head? I'll tell you what's in my head, a bullshit chip they put in me to monitor me on these stupid tests. It's making everything worse."

"Ah, yes," Wu said, his voice calm but sharp. "I agree, your *bullshit chip* is not working for you. At least not the way it could." He leaned closer, tapping the screen. "It's working against you."

Dante blinked, "What are you talking about?"

Wu leaned back in his chair.

"That chip isn't just monitoring you. It's limiting you, Dante. The athletic department is keeping you inside their lines—they're holding you in place until they need you. You're not failing because you're not good enough. You're failing because they won't let you succeed."

The words hit something inside Dante that he hadn't allowed himself to fully acknowledge. "What are you saying? That it's holding me back?"

Simon's tone took on a quieter intensity. "I'm saying it's time we level the playing field."

Dante swallowed hard. "How can you level the playing field?" he asked, frustration bleeding into his voice. "There's nothing you can do. I've got an NCAA-approved chip. There's no enhancing my model."

Simon turned to him slowly, his expression colder than the words that followed. "Did you not hear me when I told you that I could do anything?"

He leaned forward, the glow of the monitor reflecting in his eyes. "I mean it. When I say I can do anything, I mean anything."

Dante sat frozen as the tension wound tight through his muscles. "How? I mean, there are rules," he said firmly, though his voice faltered slightly."When I got my implant, they made me sign a waiver that clearly stated if I so much as tried to mess with my chip, I would get kicked out of school. If I do anything to it and get caught, no other school will ever take me."

"You're forgetting the part where they'll repossess your chip," he said, his tone flat. "I hear it's pretty painful."

"You're messing with me, right?" Dante said, though it came out weaker than he wanted. His confidence was slipping fast.

Simon's voice dropped lower, the edge in it clear. "I can assure you that I'm not messing with you. I couldn't be more serious."

Dante didn't remember that part of the waiver. When they mentioned no tampering during the signing process, he'd been too excited about getting what he thought was a fully loaded, consumer-grade chip that would turn him into an unstoppable force. He'd skipped the fine print, scribbled his name without a second thought.

Dante exhaled slowly, his shoulders tense and unmoving.

"The system's not built to help you win, Dante," Wu said. "It's built to control you—to keep you inside their lines, exactly where they want you."

He tapped a finger against the desk like he was considering how far to take this before speaking.

"Lucky for you, I don't follow their rules. And if you're ready to stop following them too—if you're willing to give something up—I can make that chip work for you, not against you."

Dante wanted to press him and get something solid before agreeing to anything. He wanted to argue, maybe even walk away, but the seed of doubt was already there. Wu had planted it, and now it was spreading—fast.

He turned it over in his head, trying to make sense of it. The way the coaches acted like his chip was gospel, the numbers they rattled off without ever watching him move. The way he'd drag himself back to his room after practice, dead on his feet, and still be slower than he was before. He figured it was just because the competition was tougher now. He never once thought the school might be the one holding him back.

He let out a hard breath, the kind that said he was officially done with whatever game his new roommate thought he was playing.

"Enough with the riddles. What's the play here? What am I signing up for?"

Wu's fingers froze over the keyboard. His stare cut to Dante, sharp and fast, like he'd just found exactly what he was waiting for.

Without a word, he reached into a drawer in his desk and pulled out a small carbon fiber ring. It caught the light from the monitors as he turned it in his fingers.

"Here," he said, tossing it toward Dante. "Put this on."

Dante caught it easily, turning it over in his palm. The ring was lighter than it looked. "What is it?"

"It's called a Glyph." Wu leaned back in his chair like this was just another Tuesday. "Think of it as a bridge. It overlays my programming on top of your restricted chip and unlocks its full potential."

Dante's eyes narrowed as he kept turning it over. "Won't they see it? Won't they know we messed with my device?"

Wu gave a small shake of his head. "No. It hides everything. Coaches, athletic staff, the NCAA—none of them will have a clue. As far as they're concerned, you'll still be playing by their rules."

Dante hesitated, staring at the Glyph as it sat cold and weightless in his palm. Then, with a breath he didn't realize he was holding, he slid it onto his ring finger.

The effect was instant, sending a rush firing through him, red hot and aggressively electric, like a shot of adrenaline without the crash. His mind sharpened, and his thoughts cut clear through the noise of uncertainty he'd felt a fraction of a second before. His body followed, feeling infinitely lighter and exploding with energy. It was like he'd finally woken up after dragging himself through the mud for weeks.

It wasn't overwhelming, but it was real. Like waking up and realizing you'd been asleep your whole life without ever knowing it.

He flexed his fingers, testing the strange new energy settling under his skin.

"Holy shit," he breathed out. "That was intense." He ran a hand over his head, steadying his breath. "Where do we start?"

"For now, you need to relax," Simon said. His tone stayed even, but there was something cold underneath it. "We can't move too fast with this. We need to ease you in. We just pulled the NCAA limiter off your chip. That's it for now. All you need to do is train like you normally do. I'll track the results and get a baseline. We'll go from there."

Dante's expression sharpened. "What do you mean, that's it for now?"

The heat that had been simmering under his skin surged back to the surface. "I thought you were gonna hook me up. You said you could do anything. So why not give me the works?"

Wu didn't even blink. "Because going all-in comes with a cost that I don't think you're ready to pay yet." His voice was flat, like he wasn't interested in explaining.

Dante hated feeling like he was being strung along. Now, with the Glyph on his finger and that rush still buzzing under his skin, waiting wasn't an option. He needed answers. "What kind of cost?"

Wu hesitated—just for a breath—before he let out a slow exhale.

"Forget I said anything. You're not there yet. Besides, Val told me not to—" He cut himself off.

That got Dante's attention. His heart kicked hard in his chest. "Wait. Val? What does she have to do with this?"

Wu stayed silent, but the change in his posture was impossible to miss. He sat up straight like he was bracing for impact.

Dante's frustration cracked open. His pulse surged wildly like he was wired straight into a power source.

"Just give me the juice!" he snapped, exploding out of his chair.

Dante lunged, pouncing on Wu in a flash. His hands clamped around Simon's throat, shoving him back against the desk hard enough to rattle the gear stacked behind him. For a second, Wu didn't move. He didn't flinch. He just stared at Dante like he'd expected this all along.

Then, without hesitation, His hand slid across the desk, fingers gliding over its surface with eerie precision until they landed on his mouse. He shifted it twice—smooth and mechanical—like flipping a switch he already knew by heart.

Whatever he did, it immediately caused Dante's temper to cool, and his grip loosened as if someone had shut him down from the inside. All of his strength drained out of him in an instant, leaving him feeling empty and powerless.

Dante stumbled back and fell into his chair. His breath came in ragged gasps. The anger in him had drained away and was replaced by nothing.

Wu adjusted his collar, brushing it smooth like nothing had happened. "We're going to have to do something about that temper, aren't we?" he said, calm as ever.

Dante blinked hard, his mind scrambling to catch up. "I... I didn't mean—"

"Just breathe." The words came quietly, but they hit hard. There was no room for argument.

Dante's hands shook as he sat there, struggling to pull himself together. His breathing was uneven, his thoughts scrambled, and for the life of him, he couldn't figure out what had pushed him so far over the edge.

His racing heart slowed, easing into an unnatural, steady rhythm that didn't feel like his own. It was as if someone had reached inside him and turned the volume all the way down. Every muscle unlocked at once, leaving him feeling weightless.

He stared at Simon, his voice rough when he finally spoke. "What did you just do to me?"

Wu composed himself and turned back to his screen. "You've got quite a temper," he said, fingers gliding over the keyboard as if nothing had happened. "I simply balanced you." He typed a few last changes into Dante's profile like he was updating a simple file instead of messing with someone's mind. "Your chip's more connected to you than you think. The Glyph masks, redirects, enhances, but it can also stabilize. Consider this a favor. You can thank me later."

Dante ran a hand over his face, feeling the weight of it all press down harder. "Alright," he muttered. "If you're not giving me the works, just give me something. You and Val said you'd level the playing field. I'm tired of being behind. Can't you at least do something to help me catch up a little?"

Wu studied him for a long beat before leaning back in his chair. "Alright, I suppose we can give you a little bump, just to see how you'd react," he said. "But it has to be subtle. No one can know."

"Look, man, I wouldn't even know where to start if I tried explaining all this to someone," Dante said, letting out a shaky breath. "I'm still trying to wrap my head around whatever you're doing in here. Nobody else needs to hear about it from me."

"Alright, that's fair enough." Wu let out a small, humorless laugh. "Enhancements like the ones you're asking for always come at a cost."

Dante relaxed a fraction. "Name your price. I've got scholarship money. Whatever it costs, it's yours."

Wu's expression hardened like he'd been waiting for this conversation.

"The price can't be paid with money, Dante. You need to be prepared to give up something more valuable—something you can't buy back or replace once it's gone. You need to know that anything we do is going to come at that cost."

Dante leaned in, his heart thudding in his chest. "What is it, then? What's the price? I need this. I'll do anything. Just tell me what you want."

Wu's stare sharpened, and when he spoke, there was no doubt left in his voice. "If we're going to give you something that's really going to change the game for you, we have to put it where no one can find it. Which means it has to replace something."

Dante shook his head. "I don't get it. Would it kill you to just be straight with me for once and drop the drama?"

Wu met his eyes. "If you want to gain something, you have to give something up. For this? It's a piece of who you are—a memory."

"A memory?" Dante asked, unsure he wanted to hear the answer.

"That's the price," Wu confirmed.

Dante's mind spun. You're saying... I'd forget something? Like, forever?"

Wu gave a slow nod, "That's exactly what I'm saying. You need to think carefully about this—what are you willing to lose to be the best?"

Dante had pictured paying in sweat, risking injuries, and maybe crossing a line or two, but this was a trade-off he never saw coming. The idea of losing a part of himself—something he'd never get back—felt heavier than any risk he'd imagined.

He found the words with difficulty. "Does it have to be a good memory?"

Wu stayed stoic. "That's up to you. But you need to think about what you'd be giving up. Even the bad memories matter. They shape you. They make you who you are."

He let the silence stretch, like it was part of the test.

"So the real question is this—what part of yourself are you willing to erase?"

Dante tried to steady his thoughts, searching for something in his heart he could live with. After a few seconds, he exhaled.

"Yeah... okay." His voice dropped, like he already knew. "I think I've got something I want to forget."

23

THE STACKS

For Mia, the seventh floor of the library stacks felt like a forgotten hideout. The wood of the study cubicles was smooth and worn, carved up with initials, tiny drawings, and half-faded messages from people who'd sat here before them. Around them, shelves leaned heavily with old books on medicine and biology—thick ones with cracked spines and yellowed pages, some were so old that they looked like they belonged in a museum, not a campus library.

She had found this place almost as soon as she got to campus. After everything that had gone down at The Lighthouse, she needed somewhere to get away from it all, and the library had always been that place for her. Back home on the West Coast, she'd lived in the stacks, and now she was doing the same thing here. There was something about it, a place like this that felt safe and predictable, and after moving in with Val, predictability was something she'd needed more than anything.

As an organic medicine student, she was supposed to be downstairs with the rest of her peers, plugged into their spotless tech stations, scrolling through flawless notes on gleaming screens. But that kind of learning never worked for her.

She hated it.

The noise downstairs was constant—voices humming beneath the quiet whirr of machines, screens flashing with data that never seemed to stop. It wasn't just the tech. It was the way people seemed to merge with it, like they belonged to the network more than to themselves.

Down there, it was easy to forget people were still human. Upgrades had replaced everything—voices, movement, connection, and for her, it was smothering.

Up in the stacks, high above all the noise, she could breathe again. It was just her, the books, and the quiet rhythm of pages turning.

She sat in the cubicle she'd unofficially claimed her first week on campus, the one that reminded her of her study space back home. Tucked into a far corner, it was right next to a narrow window that framed a perfect view of the hills climbing away from campus.

Winter was dragging its feet, but she found herself staring out there more than she should have.

She would catch herself daydreaming about the trails that had to be out there. She would picture herself walking beneath trees so tall they blocked out everything else. She could almost feel the fresh pine air filling her lungs, and the ache in her legs that came from doing something that mattered.

The woods in New England were a mystery to her, all thick forests and rolling hills. They were nothing like the sunbaked canyons and dusty trails she'd grown up with back in California.

She couldn't wait for spring to finally take over Connecticut's moody winter. The second it did, she planned on hiking those trails like she used to back home.

Nathan sat in the cubicle across from hers with only a thin partition between them. He felt like she was miles away, not just on the other side of a half-inch slab of particleboard painted over more times than he could count.

The glow from his laptop lit up with a blank document. The cursor blinked like it was tired of waiting for him to get his act together and just write something already.

Professor Simmons had told them to write about something real—something that mattered. It wasn't a suggestion. It was a challenge. One he hadn't figured out how to accept.

He stared at the keys, feeling like they were just out of reach. He was supposed to write about his deepest fears, his biggest failures, and the parts of himself he worked tirelessly to pretend weren't there. He didn't even like thinking about that stuff, let alone turning it into the main character of his stories.

He tried to focus, he tried to drag something honest out of his head, but all he could think about was Mia, sitting just on the other side of that wooden divider between their cubicles.

He could hear the scratch of her pen as it moved across the paper when she took notes. Just knowing that she was there, with him, was all weirdly calming.

Their conversation at Chubbies had been easy in a way it never was with anyone but Eve. But, Mia wasn't Eve—she was different in a way he hadn't expected. The way she'd stood up to Dante, without flinching, like it was just another Monday, stuck with him. She did something so easily that he had never been able to do: put Dante in his place.

So many times, he had wanted to tell him off the way she did. He wanted to tell him straight to his face exactly where he could stick his jokes and nonsense—but he could never find the strength. He was in awe of how cool she was, and now he was hooked. There was no ignoring it. He needed to know more.

His mind bounced between his writing assignment and the fact that he had a major league crush on someone for the first time since meeting Eve back in third grade. It wasn't subtle, and he wasn't fooling himself about how this usually went.

As soon as he made his feelings known, Mia would probably drop him in the friend zone faster than Eve ever did. He knew that, but it didn't change how he felt. There was something about her—something he couldn't explain. It was in the way she looked at him, like she actually saw him; it was as if she saw who he was inside instead of the anxious mess everyone else usually wrote him off as.

Meeting someone like her was the last thing he had expected to happen when he came to NCSU, and now that he had, he wasn't sure what to do about it.

Even with Mia sitting across from him, somehow making it easier to breathe, it didn't change the fact that his first writing assignment was still staring him down. He was supposed to pour his soul into it, but he wasn't anywhere close to being ready to do that.

Simmons' voice rang through his head. *Write what scares you the most.*

What kind of fear was she after, he wondered. Was it a literal fear, or was she asking him to push himself deeper than he ever had before—to go somewhere he wasn't sure he wanted to go?

He took stock of his options. He could write about failing, or about being the weird kid who never fit in, but none of that felt like the truth right now.

The truth was much simpler.

The truth was, he was scared of everything. Throw a dart at a dictionary and let it land on any random word, and chances are that it had kept him up at night at least once.

Eve used to laugh whenever he listed off his irrational fears. He could still hear her cracking up the day he told her about his full-on phobia of electric blankets. It wasn't just a weird thought he had once—it was a recurring nightmare.

He would imagine falling asleep with the heater turned up way too high, causing him to become completely drenched in sweat. Then, somehow, that sweat would hit a loose wire, and with a loud zap, a sharp jolt of electricity would shoot through his body before everything went dark.

That was it—that's how his life would end. He'd be electrocuted in his sleep. That would be the final scene in the movie about the broken kid who never found his place in a world built on perfection.

Cue the end credits over some depressing, moody, and dramatic retro synth—like the soundtrack to an '80s tragedy.

He knew how silly it was to be afraid of something like that, but that was the thing about how his mind worked—his fears never needed to make sense to feel completely real.

Simmons wasn't asking for something that ridiculous. Even if he wrote the best piece of his life, she wouldn't take a fear like that seriously. Sure, he could make it funny—maybe even get her to laugh—but that wasn't the assignment. She wanted something real. She wanted him to be honest with himself in a way he'd never had before, but writing like that, being completely vulnerable, felt impossible.

He heard Mia flip another page in her notebook, causing him to straighten up in his seat. The blank document on his screen screamed back like it had insulted him personally. Writing was supposed to be his thing, the only thing he was ever good at—it was where he usually pulled himself together.

"One word," he whispered to the screen, pleading for it to start the heavy lifting for him.

But the blank document just stared back at him, like it knew he wasn't up to the challenge.

The voice inside his head was screaming at him now. It was raw, relentless, and impossible to block out.

Come on, Nathan. You just need one thing. Just one. The list is already a mile long—way longer than you'd ever admit out loud. Any of it would work. Any fear, any screwup, any time you wanted to vanish. Just pick one. Just pick something— anything.

His fingers trembled as his brain ran through the usual suspects on his list of fears.

Getting humiliated in public, waking up to find out he had some deadly disease, that one was holding strong at the top spot on his personal fear playlist, and the old classic: death by defective bedding.

The greatest hits were all there, stuck on repeat, but none of them felt big enough to kick off his first college assignment.

He rested his fingertips on his keyboard, waiting for something— anything—to hit him. He closed his eyes, took a deep breath, and randomly punched a few keys, hoping something would come out of him in the dark.

When he was done, six letters appeared beneath his fingers just as something inside him told him to stop. It wasn't a thought, it was more like a jolt that sent a chill running straight through him.

When he opened his eyes, he expected nonsense. Instead, he'd crafted a single word, perfect and terrifying in every way. It stared back at him, as cruel and cold as the person it was meant to describe.

Snakes.

He wasn't writing about actual reptiles. Not their fangs, not their venom, not the sick pattern of scales that made his skin crawl.

He was writing about her.

He was writing about Val.

The way she made him feel wasn't just a casual fear. It wasn't the kind that showed up and then disappeared. It hung around like a shadow, lurking around every corner, tucked away in the depths of his mind, waiting for the right time to strike.

His first few days on campus had flipped his world upside down, and at the center of it was Valerie Reynolds.

She didn't just have power—She *was* power.

She had the kind of power that made people move out of her way without her saying a word. She wasn't supposed to notice someone like him, but earlier that day, she did, and he couldn't shake the feeling that she was after something—something that only he had.

He stared blankly at his screen.

The cursor at the end of the word flashed like it was daring him to keep going.

He thought about Val's tattoos. He thought about the way they moved. He had seen it with his own eyes.

It wasn't a trick—It was real.

Tattoos weren't supposed to move like that, but hers did, and he knew that they were waiting for the exact moment to strike.

That was what terrified him most. The feeling that she could strike at any moment, and something told him that when she did, it wouldn't be a warning shot. It would be the kind of hit that left nothing standing.

Normally, this was where his brain would spiral, and every fear he'd ever collected would crash in on him all at once until he couldn't breathe. But not this time. This time, something held.

This time, the fear inside him told him exactly what he needed to write about. He knew that a piece about Val would deliver exactly what Simmons was looking for.

So he pushed through the mess of images flashing behind his eyes. Now that he'd landed on his topic and knew there was enough to unpack, he only needed to figure out where to start.

The screen glowed back at him, waiting for his next words. He stared at it, letting his fingers hover over the keys as he searched for the line that might break it all open.

Mia's steady voice cut through the silence.

"You've been quiet over there. You okay?"

It was the same tone he'd heard in the cafeteria, the one that had somehow steadied his breathing without even trying. Now, it barely broke through. The word on his screen stared back as the haze of horror-induced writer's block clung to him like smoke.

The cursor at the end of the word pulsed, like the flick of a copperhead's tongue. It taunted him—daring him to type more, waiting for any excuse to strike.

Mia's chair scraped on the floor as she stood up and leaned around the partition that separated them. She looked down at him, her eyebrows drawing together when she saw his face.

His eyes stayed locked on the screen, caught somewhere between thought and fear, like he'd slipped out of the room entirely and left his body behind to stare in his place.

She stepped the rest of the way around and dragged her chair over, settling quietly beside him. She let her eyes drift to his screen, landing on the single word sitting there, the rest of the story still waiting to be written.

She didn't speak. She just sat with him, resting her hand lightly on his knee, giving him a small, steady squeeze. A quiet reminder that she was there.

The warmth of her hand grounded him, and his breathing steadied as he slowly pulled himself out of the fog.

"What are you working on?" she asked gently, her tone casual but laced with concern.

He sat back, rubbing the back of his neck. "It's my first piece for my writing class," he muttered, gesturing vaguely at the screen. "My professor wants me to write about what scares me the most."

He let out a weak laugh, though it didn't reach his eyes.

She tilted her head slightly and let her expression soften as his words tumbled out. The tension in his voice, the hesitation behind his thoughts, made her hold her silence, letting him speak without interruption.

"I thought I had a concept," he said quietly, his thumb dragging over the edge of his laptop. "You know, something that really gets to me... but now, I'm not so sure."

She could sense the weight he was carrying. She didn't say anything at first. She just stayed there, resting her hand on his knee, giving the slightest rub before letting it settle again. When she finally spoke, her voice was calm and careful.

"It's okay to not know, Nathan. Sometimes the hard part isn't finding the thing—it's admitting what it is."

"That's the problem," he said quietly. "I think I know exactly what it is."

His hand hovered over the mouse, like he was afraid it might burn him. The word on the screen glowed back at him as he dragged the cursor across it.

"I just don't know why I'm letting her—" he caught himself. "I mean, *them*—get to me so much."

He shook his head, his shoulders tight as he stared at the screen.

"I knew coming here was going to be tough. I guess I just didn't think it would be like this."

"Trust me, if anyone gets the culture shock that comes with transferring here, it's me," she said gently. "I totally get it. It's like—one minute you're home, where everything makes sense, and the next you're dropped into a place that feels like a different planet—surrounded by people who barely seem human half the time."

Her eyes were drawn to his laptop screen and the single word glowing on it. She let out a quiet breath, almost like she was confirming something to herself, before looking back at him.

"And Val? Yeah. She's the worst."

He let out a weak laugh, shaking his head.

"Yeah, your roommate is definitely in her own category of awful. Like, if there were a ranking system for horrible people, she'd have her own exclusive tier—right above 'cartoon villain' but just below 'actual demon.'" He sighed, glancing back at the word on the screen. It still stared back at him, a strange reflection of the turmoil inside.

She let out a small chuckle, shaking her head. "Tell me about it— you're lucky that you don't have to share a bathroom with her. I'll spare you the details, but I'm sure you can imagine."

"Oh, don't tell me," he scoffed. "I can see it now. I'll bet she's got the entire luxury goth self-care line—a moisturizer that deflects any trace of joy, makeup to help mask the burden of existence, and a body wash that smells like broken dreams and tortured souls."

She shook her head. "How did you know?" Her amusement softened as her expression turning thoughtful.

"Seriously, Nathan, you came to NCSU for a reason, didn't you? Something inside you thought this was the right place for you. Something told you to take a chance."

He paused, letting her words settle into the quiet between them.

"I guess," he said slowly. "Part of me wanted to see what I could do, you know?" He stopped like he wasn't sure if that even made sense.

"It's just that writing's always been personal for me. It got me through a lot of tough times."

She gave a small nod but didn't rush in. She just let his words hang there, allowing him space.

He glanced at her, then back at the screen.

"But writing the way my professor is asking me to? She wants me to be raw, honest, unguarded," he said, the words tasted bitter as they left his mouth. "I've never written like that before. Not even close." He drew in a slow breath. "I don't know if I can."

He let out a breath.

"I spent a lot of time in and out of hospitals growing up," he said. "There were endless tests that no one ever told me why I needed them or what they were looking for. I grew up surrounded by specialists who would always tell me I was fine, but after being poked and prodded for so long, I didn't know how to believe it. I didn't even know what feeling fine was supposed to feel like."

Her eyebrows pulled together. "That sounds exhausting—like you were stuck on pause while everyone else got to live their lives."

He was surprised by how well she understood.

"Exactly," he said quietly. "School didn't wait for me. Playing sports, making friends, you know, just doing normal kid stuff... it all went on without me while I was stuck in whatever clinic wanted to run more tests."

He paused, his voice softer now.

"I never really had friends. Most of the time, it was just me and a stack of books."

She nodded slowly. "That sounds lonely."

"It was." He wasn't looking for sympathy—this was just the truth.

"That's why I started writing in the first place. I didn't have friends in the real world, so I made them up. I gave them names, stories, and places to go. I got to go with them on adventures, and live these whole other lives I never thought I'd have. And for the first time, it felt like I found somewhere that I belonged."

He let out a breath. "And, once I started, I couldn't stop. I think I was hooked from the first sentence I ever wrote."

"I'm sorry you had to go through all that," Mia said, her voice gentle and genuine. "But now you're here, and you've got an opportunity to make up for lost time, right?"

"Yeah, I guess," he said, glancing at her for a brief moment before looking away.

"But sharing my work? I'm not sure I can do that."

He paused, letting his fingers nervously drum on the desk.

"I feel like if someone doesn't like what I write, it's not just my words they're rejecting—it's me. It's hard not to take that personally."

Mia gave his leg a soft squeeze. "Look, I get it," she said, her voice warm but certain. "I used to freeze up before presentations. Not because I didn't know the material, but because I was convinced I'd say something stupid, and everyone would remember it forever."

His mouth tugged into the hint of a smile. "Yeah—I've been there," he admitted.

"So, I started forcing myself to go first," Mia continued, "just to get it over with before I let myself spiral. And you know what? No one ever remembered a single thing I said. Not once."

He gave a short, quiet laugh. "That's hard to believe. You always seem like you have it all together."

"That's the trick," she said, flashing him a smile. "You know—Fake it until you make it."

He glanced at his screen again, his expression turning thoughtful.

"Look, I can't believe your professor is setting you up to fail," she added after a moment. "She probably sees something in you that you don't see yet, and she's just doing her job and trying to pull it out of you."

"Maybe you're right," he said. "Although I'll admit, sometimes I do dream about my writing making an impact on somebody. I mean, that's the point, right? Having someone out there reading my work and feeling something real."

Mia nodded, waiting.

"But the thought of putting it out there?" Nathan shook his head. "Letting people judge it? That's terrifying." He hesitated. "I know, I'm just being weird."

"You're not being weird, Nathan," she said with a small smile. "You're being honest with yourself. I think that's kind of brave."

Her words settled over him like a blanket he hadn't realized he needed. For the first time in a long time, the weight in his chest felt a little lighter.

"You think so?" he asked.

She leaned back just a little, but her eyes stayed steady on his. "I do," she said. "And if you want someone to read your work before you turn it in—or if you just want to bounce ideas around—I'm here."

His mouth lifted into a small smile that wasn't the kind he used to get through things. It was the kind that stuck around for a second longer than expected.

"Thanks, Mia. That means a lot."

She nodded once, then gestured toward his screen.

"So what are you going to write, Nathan? What's truly eating at your insides?" she asked. She said the words carefully, like she was handling something fragile.

He stared at her for a moment. The words were there now, pushing everything else aside. They pressed against him, refusing to let go, like there was no room for anything else.

For a moment, nothing happened. It was just him versus the blank document on his laptop.

Then, slowly, his fingers moved—like someone had flipped a switch and everything clicked into place. He was sucked into a flow he hadn't expected to find but couldn't turn away from now that it was there. Everything poured out of him in a rush, like it had been trapped inside for years and was finally breaking loose, desperate to be heard.

The sentences hit hard and honest in a way that made them feel more real than anything he'd ever put into words. Each thought dragged another with it, like links in a chain he hadn't even known he'd been carrying until now.

This piece wasn't about snakes.

It was about control. It was about power.

It was about the way Val looked at him like she already owned him.

24

THE FACTS OF LIFE

Nathan stopped in the hallway and stared at the necktie hanging limply from the handle on the door to his dormroom. It was cheap, faded, and clearly swiped from a clearance bin, but it still delivered the universal message loud and clear—*do not disturb*.

"You've got to be kidding me," he grumbled.

He pulled out his student ID from his pocket and swiped it against the door lock. The lock beeped, the little light flashed green, but the door didn't budge. He tried pushing it open, but it was jammed. He swiped his card again, this time shoving with more effort and he door creaked open a few inches, barely enough for him to wedge his foot inside.

"Gabe?" he called, trying to see through the narrow gap.

A panicked voice came from within. "Wait! Don't come in!"

Nathan froze, his hand still on the door. "Gabe, what the hell are you doing in there?"

"Hold on!" Gabe snapped, his tone frantic.

"Dude, seriously—just let me in." He gave the door another shove, wedging it open slightly more.

"I said, hold on!" Gabe shouted, his voice almost a whine now. "Just cool your jets, man!—I'll be right there."

Nathan groaned and leaned against the door. His patience was already running on fumes. "Dude, just let me in. I've had a pretty shitty day, and I'm not really in the mood for one of your bits right now."

All he heard was silence, followed by the unmistakable thud of something-or someone—hitting the floor.

Nathan raised an eyebrow, his frustration mixed with slight curiosity. They hadn't even been roommates long, but Gabe already had a way of turning normal situations into full-blown productions.

"Gabe!" he tried again. "I swear—if this is one of your acts, I'm not in the mood."

"It's not!" Gabe interrupted, defensive. "Just—hold your horses!"

Nathan let out a long, tired sigh. "You've got ten seconds before I bust this door down," he threatened, knowing full well he was not capable of doing it.

"Ten seconds?!" Gabe sounded genuinely panicked now. "Bro, come on—"

"Ten," Nathan said, his tone flat. —Another loud crash from inside.

"Nine," he continued. —More frantic movement.

"Eight," he drawled, starting to enjoy Gabe's rising panic.

"Dude, STOP counting!" Gabe yelled with sheer desperation in his tone now.

"Seven," Nathan said, gripping the door, ready to shove it open.

"FINE!" Gabe finally screamed. "Just—give me two more seconds!"

Nathan paused, rolling his eyes. "Two seconds, Gabe."

"One Mississippi...two Mississippi," he muttered under his breath, then braced himself.

He had no idea what kind of disaster was waiting for him, but knowing Gabe? The scale ranged somewhere between "I swear this isn't what it looks like" to "Grab a mop and don't ask questions."

Nathan shoved the door open, and Gabe practically jumped out of his skin.

He stood in the middle of the room like a kid caught elbow-deep in the cookie jar. He was out of breath, his shirt buttoned crooked like he'd dressed in the dark, and his hair looked like it had gotten into a bar fight with a weed whacker. His expression stretched wide and overly eager, like he was ready to pitch an excuse Nathan hadn't even asked for yet.

"Oh hey, man! I didn't hear you come in!" Gabe forced, cranking his voice into casual overdrive like he was trying to talk his way out of a speeding ticket.

Nathan leaned against the doorframe, raising an eyebrow. "You didn't hear me come in?" he repeated slowly. "Because you were just screaming at me to wait outside, like, two seconds ago."

"Oh, was I?" Gabe laughed nervously, taking a step back toward his desk, the universal sign of a man about to commit to a terrible lie. "Man, I must've been talking to myself. You know how it is. I was just trying to hype myself up to head down to The Laugh Lab and work on some new stuff."

Nathan scanned the room. There were no signs of a crime scene, no panicked half-dressed stranger scrambling out the window, no smoke or ominous puddles of unknown origin. Just their dorm. Except...

A faint, rhythmic beeping cut through the tension.

Nathan's eyes narrowed. "What's that sound?"

"What's what sound?" Gabe replied immediately, too fast, too loud, and absolutely guilty.

"That sound." Nathan pointed toward the desk behind Gabe. "That noise, coming from your desk."

Gabe shifted, planting himself in front of his desk like a bouncer guarding VIP access to his worst decision.

"Oh, that? That's nothing," he said, waving a dismissive hand. "It's just —uh—my meditation timer. It helps me stay balanced. Real zen stuff. You wouldn't get it."

Nathan wasn't buying it. "Right. Because when I think of inner peace, I think of you."

The steady beeping continued.

Nathan stepped forward, and Gabe instantly countered, blocking him like he was Shaquille O'Neal guarding the paint in the NBA finals.

"Seriously, dude, it's nothing! Don't worry about it! Just chill! Crack open the snack stash, grab whatever you want—my treat!"

"Gabe." Nathan's patience had officially clocked out. He sidestepped sharply, pointing at the desk. "Move it, Kowalski."

"Fine, but you don't have to be so pushy about it," Gabe mumbled, finally stepping aside with the enthusiasm of a man forced to walk the plank.

Nathan leaned toward the desk as the beeping grew louder with every second. He pulled open the drawer, and there it was—Gabe's old-school handheld video game, looking like something between an Atari Lynx and a Game Boy.

Nathan had seen Gabe playing it all the time, but never up close. Now, with its glitchy screen and steady beeping, it looked less like a retro collectible and more like something about to blow.

Nathan frowned as he picked it up. "This? This is what you were trying to hide?"

Gabe lunged forward like a goalie making a last-second save, and snatched the device out of Nathan's hands with the speed of a man caught red-handed.

"Oh, that! Yeah, it's not a big deal," he said, holding it up triumphantly like it was a trophy rather than extremely suspicious. "See?"

He slammed a button like his life depended on it, and the screen blinked to life, displaying an unmistakable, pixelated image: the emulated start screen of *BurgerTime*.

Nathan's confusion quickly turned into outright disbelief. "You were in here... by yourself... playing video games?"

"Yup," Gabe replied with a shrug, his expression brightening like he'd just convinced a jury of his innocence.

"Can't a guy enjoy some retro charm in his downtime?"

Nathan eyed him the way a parent eyes a toddler who claims they did not eat the last cookie.

"That doesn't make any sense, Gabe." Nathan's patience was stretched thin. "Why did you have the door blocked off?"

Gabe shifted into mock offense so theatrical it practically begged for stage lights. "What doesn't make sense? I was just helping my boy Peter Pepper stack some juicy burgers. You know—I was just doing my part. That's how I unwind."

Nathan gestured toward the doorway, exasperation creeping into his voice. "You were yelling at me not to come in. You sounded like you were hiding something! And all this time, you were just stacking digital burgers on a screen?"

Gabe tilted his head like he was deeply considering the question, then shrugged with exaggerated ease. "What can I say? I get really into it."

Nathan deadpanned, still trying to process the sheer absurdity of it all. "You're unbelievable."

He looked down at the screen of the handheld again. The cheerful retro pixels danced for a second, then dissolved and were replaced by a diagnostics display with a tiny picture of Gabe below a line of loud neon text that read:

MIND Inc. User Interface: Chamber 37

Nathan froze. The disbelief in his chest twisted into something else entirely. He looked up at Gabe, and his voice dropped into something careful as he asked,

"Gabe, what the hell was that?"

Gabe's face barely had time to register panic before he snapped into full-on performance mode.

"Alright, alright, you got me! I was in here, uh, checking out some sweet babes on the internet. "

He hammered another button on the device, and the screen instantly shifted to display a scantily clad woman in a seductive pose.

"See, dude? I was just enjoying the, um, finer things in life—You got me, I'm totally busted."

Nathan didn't buy what Gabe was saying for a second. As he looked back at Gabe's handheld, the screen flashed again, and the diagnostic screen reappeared. It was only for a split second, but it was long enough to convince him that he wasn't imagining things.

Nathan's breath caught. "There—I just saw it again." He snapped his eyes to Gabe, and his voice was sharp. "Gabe… are you enhanced?"

Gabe hesitated, realizing he wasn't getting out of this. With a sigh, he waved a lazy hand. "Ok, fine, you got me. I'm Enhanced."

Nathan blinked. "Wait, seriously? You are?"

"Sure," Gabe replied with a shrug like he was admitting he liked pineapple on pizza. "Look, I was gonna tell you someday." He chuckled. "I just didn't want you to think I was weird or anything. I swear it's no big deal. Really."

Nathan stared at Gabe as he tried to process everything.

"Hold on—how is it even possible that you're Enhanced?" he asked, struggling to wrap his head around what he'd just heard.

"I mean, look at you. You don't exactly fit the Enhanced stereotype."

Gabe let out a theatrical laugh, slipping into a John Candy-from-Stripes delivery. "So, you're saying you've noticed that I've got a bit of a weight distribution problem? That I'm a little husky? That I carry myself with the grace of a man who has never turned down a buffet?" He spread his arms wide, shaking his head like he was addressing an unseen audience.

Nathan groaned, rubbing his hands down his face. "Wait—I didn't mean it like that, Gabe. I just—"

Gabe snapped his fingers dramatically. "Look, Nathan. Have a seat."

"What?" Nathan frowned. "What did you just call me?"

"I called you Nathan. That's your name, isn't it?" His tone and his choice to abandon the nickname he'd given his roommate were a signal—this was him being sincere.

"You know—You *look* like a Nathan. Anyone ever tell you that?"

Nathan wasn't sure if this gentler, more genuine tone was an act or not.

"I think it's time for me to explain to you the facts of life," Gabe said, not looking at him.

"What do you mean, the facts of life?" Nathan asked, frowning as he sat on the edge of his bed.

Gabe put his handheld back in his drawer and plopped onto the bed across from Nathan's.

For a moment, neither of them spoke.

Then Gabe let out a long, exaggerated sigh, leaning back on his hands like he was about to deliver life-altering wisdom.

"Listen, man, it's like this," Gabe began, leaning forward with a dramatic flourish. "You take the good, you take the bad, you take them both and there you have—"

Nathan shook his head, already lost. "What are you talking about?"

"I'm talking about The Facts of Life, dude! The Facts of Life." Gabe chuckled, clearly enjoying himself.

Nathan stared, still confused. "Gabe, you're not making any sense?"

"I'm sorry, let me try this again," Gabe said, pausing just long enough to make it dramatic. Then his expression lit up, and he launched into an overly enthusiastic performance.

"When the world never seems—to be living up to your dreams, then suddenly you're finding out the facts of life are all about you!" He sang, throwing in a ridiculous shimmy for emphasis. "Ooh ooh oh oooh!"

Nathan raised a hand to stop the nonsense. "Wait—wait. Isn't that the theme song from The Facts of Life? Like, the old TV show?"

Gabe waved him off, shaking his head dramatically. "No, I'm talking about the Gloria Loring solid gold hit from 1979. The one that gained notoriety as the theme for the hit sitcom of the same name. They're two totally separate things."

"Gabe, what the hell does that have to do with anything?"

"Look, Cheese," Gabe said as his tone shifted back into his usual character mode. "You're right, I'm *Enhanced*." He said as he made exaggerated air quotes. "But seriously, it's not a big deal, okay?"

Nathan narrowed his eyes. "I can't believe this, you really are?"

"Believe it, Cheese," Gabe said, shrugging like he'd just admitted to preferring his steak well done. "I have a chip, but I'm not like those turds you've seen on campus so far. I didn't sign up for some vanity upgrades so

I could flex for the frat bros. I got mine as part of my football scholarship."

Nathan leaned forward, trying to wrap his head around it. "You're telling me they just gave you one—because you were on the football team?"

"Pretty much." Gabe shrugged, his casual tone clashing with the weight of his words. "I didn't have a choice, you know? It's just how the game works here."

Nathan frowned. "What do you mean, 'how it works'?"

Gabe leaned back on his bed. "The NCAA has rules, man. They gave me a modified version of the chip when I got here. It's supposed to track performance, keep tabs on injuries, all that stuff. Honestly, I never thought I'd ever want one of these things in my head. It's not like they asked me. It was just part of the deal."

Nathan raised an eyebrow. "And you were cool with that?"

Gabe let out a bitter laugh. "I didn't have much of a choice."

"And that's why you quit?" Nathan asked.

Gabe nodded, "Yeah. See, back in high school, no one could touch me on the field. I'd dominate the line of scrimmage without even trying. It didn't matter who they put in front of me—I'd win. Every time. But when I got here? Everything was different. I was always a step too slow. I'd get burned by guys half my size—half my strength. At first, I thought it was me, like maybe I'd just peaked too early."

Nathan stared at him, feeling a twinge of sympathy. "But it wasn't you?"

"Nope," Gabe said, letting out a hollow chuckle. "Turns out, they do something to your chip if you're an athlete. It's like they tweak it to slow you down or something."

Nathan blinked. "Slow you down? Why the hell would they do that? I mean, wouldn't they want you to be your best?"

Gabe shrugged, "I don't know all the details, but for some reason, they throttle it. They keep you ready but limit the wear and tear on your body. I think they are trying to keep you fresh for when they need you. They've got guys who sit on the bench for three years, and then their Senior year comes around, and the coaches unleash their chip or whatever, and suddenly they're All-Americans." He shook his head. "It's wild, man. They're not just managing the game—they're managing you."

Nathan let the words sink in. "That's crazy," he said, a hint of disbelief creeping into his voice.

"I know, right?" Gabe said, more serious than Nathan had ever heard him be. "You want to know the worst part? If you leave the team, they take back all their equipment, and I'm not just talking pads, cleats, or a helmet."

He tapped his temple. "I mean *all* their equipment."

Nathan felt a chill creep up his spine. "Wait. You're saying they'd extract your chip?"

"Yup," Gabe said, with bitterness laced in his tone. "It's buried in the waiver they make you sign, hidden in all the fine print. If you're not an athlete anymore, you don't get to keep the tech. It's theirs. So yeah, they'll take it out."

Nathan swallowed hard. "And?"

"I've heard it's bad—like, really bad." Gabe exhaled.

"Bad how?" Nathan asked as his voice tightened with unease.

Gabe shook his head. "Well, it's painful as hell, for one. But I've heard stories about guys who had their chips removed, and it totally messed them up. They couldn't focus. Couldn't function. Some of them just disappeared. And I don't mean they transferred or dropped out. I mean they were here one day, sitting in class or hanging out on the quad, trying to figure out how to fit back in—and the next day, they were just—gone."

Nathan's chest tightened. "That's insane. And they're allowed to do that? Just... take it out like that?"

"Yup." Gabe's tone was matter-of-fact. "That's how they get you. They know you'll do anything to play. They fill your head with all these promises—scholarships, glory, maybe even going pro. Then they make you sign the waiver, and boom. You're theirs to monitor—to control—to own."

Nathan was quiet, his mind racing as he tried to process everything.

"So how did you get out of it?" he asked, glancing at Gabe. "I mean, how did you avoid the equipment retrieval?"

Gabe's expression turned dry, almost amused. "I told them I'd scheduled it, but said that I wanted to use my family doctor. So I filled out all the forms and followed all the rules—the whole deal. But instead of letting some barbarian rip the chip out of my head and potentially scramble my brain for the rest of my life... I, you know—" He made a vague gesture with his hands. "Took care of it."

Nathan narrowed his eyes. "What do you mean? How did you *take care of it?*"

"This is how." Gabe leaned back into the drawer and pulled out his handheld game. The screen lit up, now displaying the top BurgerTime high scores. Every slot was filled with the same initials: G.D.K—

Nathan squinted at the screen. "BurgerTime? You took care of it by playing BurgerTime?"

"Well, not exactly playing the game. Although I do enjoy it."

Then, out of nowhere, he threw his arms up in mock frustration. "Damn those friggin' pickles!"

Gabe laughed, but it didn't last long. "Seriously, it's not the game—it's the device. I got it from this guy on campus. I can't say who. I promised to keep that part a secret. But yeah—it's basically a mask for my chip."

"What do you mean—a mask?" Nathan stared at him. "What, does it hide you from the coaches or something?" he asked, like he was trying to piece it all together.

"Actually, yeah. That's pretty much it," Gabe replied. "It tricks the system into thinking I'm not on the network anymore. The athletic department thinks I already had the retrieval. As far as they're concerned, my chip's boxed up and waiting to be destroyed after graduation."

Nathan blinked, his mind racing. "Destroyed? Do they destroy everyone's chip after graduation?"

Gabe let out a short, dry laugh. "Nah. Just us X-Men." His tone was heavy with sarcasm. "That's what they call the quitters. X-Men. Cute, huh?"

"That's messed up," Nathan said as he shook his head.

"I know, right?" Gabe let out a humorless chuckle. "They want you to feel like you're defective. Like you couldn't cut it. Keeps the other guys in line. Nobody wants to be known as one of the X-Men."

Nathan stared at him as the weight of it all sank in.

"So what happens when you graduate?"

"Nothing," Gabe said. "Or at least nothing I don't want. The athletic overlay on my chip deletes itself, taking every record of me playing here with it. Then I'll just be a regular guy with a chip that doesn't track my every move."

"So what do you do until then?" Nathan asked.

Gabe didn't miss a beat. "Until then, I'm Gabe Kowalski, performing arts major—hiding out in plain sight."

Nathan sat back on his bed and let out a slow breath. His mind was spinning. Not with panic or even anxiety—just pure wonder.

Everything Gabe had said flipped what he thought he knew about the MIND chip, making him look at everything differently.

He had just learned that having a chip wasn't always about enhancements. Sometimes it was about how people could be turned into assets. How, sometimes, the choice in getting one wasn't made by the end user. And how control could be given up with something as simple as a signature.

His thoughts snapped into focus, and he turned to Gabe, who was already watching him connect the dots like he knew exactly what was coming next.

Nathan hesitated. "Gabe, we can't—"

"I know," Gabe cut in.

"...tell Eve."

25

DOUBLE DRAGON

Mia felt a sense of dread as she approached the door to her apartment in West Hall. She paused before swiping her keycard and stared at the worn brass knob for a moment, trying to steady her nerves. She wasn't in the mood for whatever drama Val might have waiting on the other side.

Exhaustion weighed heavily on her from the first day of classes—first hustling to catch the bus, then dealing with the awkward lunch at Chubbie's with Dante, and now this. All she wanted was some peace and quiet.

She winced as she pressed her keycard to the reader, praying the door wouldn't make a sound. The light flashed green before the lock betrayed her with a beep so loud it seemed to echo across the entire campus. With a sigh, she straightened her shoulders and braced herself. Carefully, she turned the knob, easing the door open and hoping to sneak in unnoticed.

Maybe Val wouldn't be home. Maybe she was out with Wu, or Dante, or any number of insufferable people she'd met in her short time on campus. None of them had made any kind of positive impression on her. The NCSU Enhanced were not Mia's people. In fact, nobody she'd met so far was.

Nobody except Nathan.

She caught herself wondering what was going on behind his sad eyes. She'd enjoyed talking with him at Chubbie's, and the way he opened up to her in The Stacks stuck with her. She found herself drawn to him in a way she hadn't felt in a long time, and she realized she hoped it wouldn't be long before she bumped into him again.

She closed her eyes for a second and pushed the door open while pleading silently to the gods of campus housing.

Please don't be home. Please don't be home.

As she walked through the kitchen, she set her bookbag on the floor with a soft thud and scanned the room. It didn't take long to realize—today wasn't the day her prayers would be answered.

Sitting on the sofa, perfectly still, with her long legs crossed and her arms draped along the back of the couch like she owned the entire world, was Val. No book, no magazine, no phone in her hand—she just sat there —waiting.

Mia didn't pause. She walked into the room with her usual steady confidence, her loafers tapping against the floor with purpose. She'd decided very quickly that whatever her roommate's deal was, she wasn't about to let herself become one of her targets. If Val thought she could intimidate her with silence and theatrics, she'd picked the wrong girl.

As she stepped closer, she noticed something about Val had changed. She studied her silently for a moment, then she saw them. Her tattoos— the snakes that had previously wrapped around her arms—had changed into dragons.

Two of them, black and red in sharp tribal ink, were perched high on her shoulders. Their scales seemed to shimmer faintly under the dim light, and their piercing eyes tracked Mia as she moved. Their mouths were open, with flames curling between their jagged teeth as if they were ready to burn down anything in their path.

Mia stopped a few feet away and tilted her head slightly, taking in Val's new ink.

"Nice update," Mia said flatly, motioning toward the dragons. "What are you trying to do—scare some poor freshman in the quad, or are you just in one of your moods?"

She didn't know how right she was.

Val's eyes remained cold. "I've been waiting for you," she replied, her voice smooth like every word had been planned.

Mia didn't flinch. She crossed her arms, leaning casually against the kitchen counter as if Val's entire presence wasn't designed to make her uncomfortable.

"Yeah? Well, here I am. What's so important that it couldn't wait?"

Val's body language screamed: *Don't fuck with me.*

"We were supposed to meet at lunch," she said, her tone crisp and accusing.

Mia rolled her eyes and turned toward the fridge, pulling it open to grab a bottle of water.

"Yeah, I know," she replied simply, twisting off the cap and taking a long sip.

Val held her expression like stone. "I pinged your Glyph," she said, her voice dropping just enough to carry a hint of menace.

Mia took another sip before setting the bottle down on the counter. "Well, I didn't get your ping. I told you—I don't need your stupid Glyph. I left it in my room. You can have it back."

Val didn't blink. "Oh, I know you did," she said. "I know everything you do."

Mia barely reacted, leaning casually against the counter with her arms crossed. "Well, after this morning, I figured you deserved a taste of your own medicine," she replied evenly.

For a moment, Val's mask slipped. Her smirk faltered, and her eyes narrowed as she searched Mia, trying to figure out where her strength was coming from. But just as quickly, her composure snapped back into place.

"Careful," Val said, her voice quiet but cutting, her eyes locking on Mia like a warning.

Mia tilted her head, her expression steady. "Or what?"

The tension in the room thickened as the dragons on Val's shoulders seemed to shift again. The flames smoldering around their open mouths made them look like they were actually breathing.

"Trust me, you don't want to find out," Val said, her tone heavy with warning.

She glared at Mia, waiting for her to make the next move. The dragons' red accents caught the light again, the small flames creeping through their teeth burning brighter, matching Val's mood.

Mia grabbed her bag from the counter and slung it over her shoulder. She turned on her heel, her stride steady as she walked to her room. She wasn't going to give Val even a second of satisfaction.

"Good talk, Val," she said over her shoulder, light and dismissive like the conversation never mattered.

She shut the door firmly behind her and let out a slow breath as the latch clicked into place. Leaning back against the door, she closed her eyes for a moment.

Let Val play her game. Let her think she had the upper hand.

Whatever Val was trying to do, Mia wasn't going to get sucked in.

—Not today.

—Not ever.

26

CABIN FEVER

Nathan woke up to find his dorm room eerily quiet. Gabe's bed was neatly made, like he'd been gone for hours. He sat up slowly and rubbed his eyes, trying to shake the grogginess, but his thoughts stayed tangled in everything that had happened since he'd arrived on campus—Gabe's revelation, Val's unsettling presence, and Mia's calm reassurance.

He had spent most of the night revising his writing, diving headfirst into his biggest fears.

His eyes drifted to the window. It looked mild out, the kind of winter day that teased the promise of spring even though it was months away.

Mother Nature was in a good mood today.

He squinted as he looked toward the hills in the distance and let his eyes settle on the faint light he'd noticed the night he first moved in. That night felt like it was centuries ago. So much had happened since then that it felt like he'd been at NCSU long enough to complete a doctorate.

His eyes locked onto a small plume of smoke rising from the solitary cabin, tucked neatly into the woods. He leaned closer to the window, his curiosity piqued. He couldn't help but wonder about what the view from that cabin would be like.

Was there someone out there, on the other side, looking back at the bustling campus? Were they wondering what was happening in this chaotic little bubble of noise and people?

The distance was deceptive. The cabin seemed so far away, isolated and quiet, but as far as he could tell, it couldn't have been more than a mile or two away, tucked behind the off-campus housing.

The rolling hills behind it made the space seem infinite, like it belonged to a world completely separate from his own.

He sighed and snapped out of his daydream before dragging himself to his desk and collapsing into the chair. He was exhausted after spending the night tossing and turning with his mind caught in a relentless ping-pong match of all the previous day's drama. At the top of it all was the fact that his roommate—the last person he'd ever imagine being Enhanced, in fact—was.

Gabe has a chip, he thought, the idea still felt surreal. He stared at the blank screen, chewing the inside of his cheek.

He wondered how many more people like Gabe were out there. Those without the telltale signs of being Enhanced. No sculpted bodies, no airbrushed perfection, no effortlessly cool style—just ordinary people blending into the crowd. He couldn't imagine how much of what he saw on campus was real, and how much was just carefully constructed illusions.

His eyes dropped to his laptop screen, scanning the words of his latest draft. It all felt... wrong. It felt like the worst thing he'd ever written—flat, aimless, and painfully forced. For a moment, he hovered his fingers over the keyboard, tempted to highlight everything and press delete. Scrapping the entire thing and wiping it from existence felt like the easiest solution.

He could start fresh, maybe write something more profound. Something deeper. Like how his biggest fear wasn't snakes or people like Val, but something darker. Maybe he'd write about dying. *That would get his Simmon's attention, right?*

He shook his head at the thought. Truth be told, he wasn't really afraid of dying. In his mind, he was simply counting down the days until whatever the doctors had spent years scanning him for finally caught up with him and took him for good.

Some days, he even welcomed it, the peace, the endless sleep. It would be the ultimate escape from the confusion and chaos of his life. Dying didn't scare him at all; he knew that it was inevitable, like a quiet conclusion waiting just out of reach.

He stared at the screen on his laptop. The blinking cursor felt like it was taunting him, daring him to hit submit, to let go of his work and face whatever came next.

Pulling up the classroom application from his writing lab, he scrolled through the list of professors until his eyes landed on Simmons's name. With a heavy sigh, he clicked on the assignment—a blinking reminder that his first draft was due in six days.

Six days, he thought to himself. *Like, six days is enough time to figure this out.*

No sense in holding onto this mess, he thought, trying to bargain with himself. *I'll just keep revising it, rewriting it, and for what? Simmons will hate it, she'll rip it apart, and I'll fail. She'll see what a mistake she made, sticking her neck out for me to join the program.*

The thought snowballed, each fear piled on top of the last, gaining weight as it tumbled through his mind. He could see the domino effect in vivid detail: first, he'd fail the assignment, and then he would fail the class, and failing the class meant he would probably lose his scholarship—and without his scholarship, he would be forced to go back to Vermont, to a home that didn't exist anymore, to a life that no longer had room for him.

That wasn't an option. He didn't have anywhere else to go—not right now, at least.

As overwhelming as his short time at NCSU had been, it was his home now, and he had to try to make the best of it.

Six days, he thought again, the words pounded in his head like a drumbeat.

"Alright, fine. I'll figure it out. I'll just have to start over."

He sighed, staring at the screen. "I'm not really afraid of snakes. They're just gross. And Val?" He scoffed under his breath. "It's a big campus. I'll probably never see her again. Yesterday was just bad luck. Today will be different."

He took a deep breath, hovering over his keyboard. His mouse highlighted the block of text he'd agonized over all night, ready to click the delete button. The thought of erasing it all—every word, every piece of himself he'd reluctantly put into the work—felt terrifying and yet somehow freeing.

All it was going to take was one click, and it would be gone.

Just as he was about to click the delete button, the door swung open, slammed against the wall, and an explosion of *Big Gabe Energy* jolted Nathan out of his thoughts.

"Yo, Cheese!" Gabe shouted, his voice somehow louder than the door had been. "The caf is calling! Time for breakfast!"

Nathan spun around, his pulse still racing. "Gabe! Jesus, man, can you not just blast in here like that?"

Gabe looked completely unfazed, like he hadn't just nearly given Nathan a heart attack.

"What? I figured you'd be up. I mean, it's breakfast, dude. It's holding the number three spot on my list of top meals—and it's coming for pre-dinner's crown. Let's go!"

Nathan blinked, his disbelief cutting through his leftover panic. "Pre-dinner?"

"Yeah, you know, pre-dinner!" Gabe said, pointing to the corner of the room where piles of clothes hid what Nathan now realized was his secret snack stash.

"It's a whole thing, Cheese. We'll talk about it later. It's too early for that now. Let's move!"

He clapped his hands together, already halfway back out the door.

Nathan shook his head, muttering under his breath as he turned back to his laptop. "Hold on, let me just delete this," he said, moving his mouse to the small trash can icon on the screen. With a single click, the file—titled *The Serpent* vanished.

Starting over felt like standing at the bottom of a mountain he wasn't sure he had the energy to climb. It was overwhelming, no question—but it wasn't impossible.

He thought about finding Mia later and seeing if she wanted to meet him in the stacks again. She'd made things easier yesterday, just by being there. She hadn't pressured him to talk or explain himself. She'd sat with him and listened like it was the most normal thing in the world.

Maybe I'll even show her something else i've written, he thought. *One of the pieces I've never let anyone read. One the ones that felt too personal, too close.*

It wasn't much of a plan, but it was something.

He reached out to close his laptop, ready to follow Gabe to breakfast, when suddenly a pop-up flashed across his screen.

As soon as he saw the words, he was flooded with instant dread: *Assignment Submitted.*

His heart stopped.

He stared at the screen in disbelief. *No! No! No! That's not possible! I didn't submit anything!* his mind screamed.

"Come on, man. Let's hit it before they run out of waffles," Gabe said, his voice cutting through the noise in Nathan's head. It snapped him out of the spiral before he slipped any further.

Nathan turned to him, his mouth slightly open, words failing to form. "I—I didn't... I didn't mean to submit it," he stammered, his voice shaking with disbelief.

"What do you mean?" Gabe asked, stepping over to where Nathan was sitting, his brow furrowing. "What'd you do?"

Nathan pointed helplessly at the laptop. "It says I submitted my assignment. I was deleting it—Deleting it, Gabe! It wasn't ready. I wasn't ready! And now it's... It's gone. It's sent."

Gabe peered over his shoulder at the screen, his face scrunching up. "Well, yeah, it says submitted. Maybe your professor has a recall option or something?"

Nathan shook his head. "No, she said once it's submitted, that's it. It's final."

Gabe tilted his head, scratching the back of his neck. "Okay, so... maybe she'll go easy on you?"

Nathan let out a sharp, bitter laugh. "Yeah, right. She's not exactly the 'go easy on anyone' type. She's going to read that mess and think I'm a complete idiot."

Gabe leaned against the desk. "Hey, look, maybe it's not as bad as you think. You're always in your head about this stuff. I'm sure it's fine."

Nathan gestured at the now-empty space on his screen where the file used to be. "Gabe, it's not fine. What I just sent in was awful. I'm serious. It was some of the worst writing I've ever done. It was just... rambling nonsense about snakes and—Well—Val."

Gabe's eyes lit up, and he swooned dramatically, clutching an invisible necklace. "Ooh la la, Val! You don't have sights on my Caf wife, do you, Cheese?"

"What? No—No way. You know that I think that chick is pure evil," Nathan said, shaking his head in disgust.

"She's all yours, with your stupid Caf fantasy girlfriend game. This isn't about her. It's about my writing. This is exactly why I don't share my stuff. Simmons is going to shred me. I am so screwed."

"Okay, relax, Cheese. Just breathe. You are not screwed," Gabe said, trying to calm him down.

"It's only your first assignment. What's the worst that happens? Simmons gives you a bad grade? Big deal. So what if you bomb the first assignment? You have all semester to bounce back. Just tell her you're still adjusting to college or something."

Nathan rubbed his face, his frustration mounting. "It's not like that,

Gabe. It's bad because this is my first submission to Simmons. This was my first real chance to show her I belong in the program. She has high expectations for me, and if I blow this, she's going to think letting me in was a mistake."

"Trust me, Cheese, I get it. I know exactly what it's like trying to live up to everyone's expectations," Gabe said, leaning against the desk. "But I'm sure she's reasonable. Professors aren't out to destroy us, you know."

Nathan slumped back in his chair, the weight of it all pressing down on him like a stone. "It's not just about this class. Simmons fought for me to get into this program. If I let her down, if she realizes what a mistake she made…" He swallowed hard. "She could take everything back, Gabe. She could take back my scholarship. And if that happens—"

"You go back to Vermont," Gabe said quietly, finishing the thought for him. His tone had softened now, the humor gone from his voice.

Nathan shook his head. "I wish I could, but there's nothing left for me there anymore."

For a moment, the room was still, the weight of Nathan's words settling between them.

"Look, man, it's out of your hands now. Sitting here freaking out isn't gonna change what's already done. Let's go grab breakfast. It'll give you some time to clear your head and figure out your next move. You're not gonna fix anything staring at a blank screen, you know?"

Nathan hesitated, the panic in his chest still swirling, but he couldn't deny Gabe's logic. He glanced at the laptop screen one more time, then closed it with a sigh. "Fine," he muttered, grabbing his coat.

"That's the spirit!" Gabe declared, already heading for the door with his signature swagger.

"Let's get moving. All that bacon isn't gonna eat itself, and I'm determined to break my personal best for most pancakes in one sitting. I was so close the other day, but then a tragic chocolate milk tsunami threw off my rhythm."

Nathan shook his head, a small, reluctant smile tugging at his lips as he grabbed his coat and followed.

27

ENGINE NO. 9

Mia sighed and zipped up her bag as the muffled roar of yet another over-the-top metal anthem blasted through the thin walls of her room.

Today's particular flavor of *auditory assault* was "Engine No. 9" by the Deftones. The distorted guitar riffs and aggressive vocals rattled the apartment, shaking the floorboards like an earthquake.

How anyone could willingly start their day with that much aggression was beyond her.

But that was Val.

Every morning, it was something equally loud, relentless, and angry. It was like she woke up ready to burn the world down with pure willpower —and her angst-fueled playlist was her weapon of choice.

Mia rolled her eyes, zipped up her bag, and slung it over her shoulder.

"Val! Not everyone needs a rage-metal pep talk before breakfast," she shouted, though the odds of being heard over the music were slim to none.

When she opened her bedroom door and stepped into the hallway, she was immediately hit by the full force of Val's music.

The guttural breakdown slammed into her, each beat vibrating through the walls like a pulse. For a moment, she just stood there and listened.

The lyrics carried a raw, primal energy that was borderline poetic. For a second, she almost admired the intensity. The way Chino Moreno delivered each crushing lyric like his life depended on it almost felt romantic to her.

To each their own, she thought, shaking her head. No time to make waves with Queen Val today.

"Hey, Val, I'm leaving!" she called out, raising her voice to fight above the thunderous riffs.

—Nothing.

She shouted again, louder this time: "I said, I'm leaving!"

Still no response.

Her patience had evaporated.

Cupping her hands around her mouth and using every ounce of volume she could find, she screamed one final time, "See you later, Val! I hope you have the day you deserve!"

She didn't wait for a reaction or assume Val even heard her. She just grabbed her coat, threw it over her shoulders, and walked out letting the door clicked shut behind her.

Inside Val's room, the metal didn't just roar—it consumed like a sonic tidal wave smashing against the walls, bleeding through the floorboards, and sinking into the bones of the building.

Distorted guitars and grinding vocals tore through every corner, shaking the air like a tantrum made of sound. But within the storm, there was a quiet that felt almost sacred—almost tribal.

Val, Dante, and Wu sat in a perfect triangle—

Dante stiff on the bed like a sculpture, Wu cross-legged on the floor with his hands resting perfectly still, and Val perched at her desk, unnervingly composed. None of them moved. Not a twitch. Their bodies were locked like statues frozen mid-thought, locked into a collective stillness that defied instinct.

Anyone watching safely from a distance might have said they looked like they were meditating, but up close, the cracks showed. Their stillness wasn't peaceful. It was paralyzed. Their eyes didn't blink. Their chests barely moved. It was the kind of quiet that made your skin crawl.

Their pupils radiated a vivid, unnatural ultraviolet glow, like a blacklight had been hardwired behind their retinas. The light pulsed in slow, rhythmic waves, giving them a synchronicity that didn't feel like chance.

Their smiles—subtle, euphoric, and wrong—made it worse. It wasn't happiness. It wasn't peace. It was the kind of expression you saw in dreams that made you wake up in a cold sweat.

The air between them was charged, and thick enough to choke on. Something unseen threaded through the space like static with a given purpose, linking them into a single current. No words passed between them, but they were connected, bound by something deeper than speech. Something beyond human comprehension.

Then it began. A pulse of data surged through the room, invisible but alive. Signals ripped between their minds in a private language no outsider would ever be able to decode.

It wasn't communication.

It was communion.

A digital bloodline that fused them into one being with three faces.

Chino's voice screamed on as the music pounded like war drums in a concrete tunnel. But none of them flinched. Not once. They stayed locked in place, eyes glowing, expressions fixed, their bodies humming with barely contained voltage.

Then—silence.

The song ended with one final scream, stretching into a drawn-out wave of feedback that clung to the air before abruptly cutting off. The silence that followed felt louder than the music itself. The light in their eyes flickered once, then faded, dissolving into the enhanced shades they'd chosen for the day.

Whatever spell they were under had been broken.

Like a switch had been flipped, the stillness evaporated, replaced by the effortless motions of three people slipping back into the rhythm of their usual routine.

It was the kind of natural flow that, at first glance, could almost make them seem ordinary, like any group of friends getting ready to casually go about their day.

But they weren't ordinary.

Not even close.

28

PROSE PRO

After breakfast, Nathan walked briskly toward the arts side of campus, running through what he wanted to say to Simmons in his head. With each step, he rehearsed a different version of the conversation. The words spilled out in his mind like dialogue from a poorly written script.

It was a computer error. A mistake. I didn't mean to submit it—it wasn't ready!

That seemed like a safe enough start. Or maybe he could just be honest. He could tell Simmons the truth: he wasn't proud of the work. It was only a first draft, something he was going to delete, something he was going to start over.

Maybe he'd tease her a little. He'd flash her a smile—an actual smile, not the awkward, tight-lipped kind he usually gave—and say, *"You know what? I had a brainstorm moment. A flash of inspiration hit me, and in a fit of panic and passion, I accidentally sent the wrong file. But hey, now you get to see my raw creative process."*

That sounded like a good plan. It sounded a bit too playful, but at least he'd come off confident, like he wasn't just a walking disaster barely holding it together.

As the plan formed in his head, a nagging doubt tugged at him.

What if she saw right through him? What if Simmons didn't care about brainstorming or passion?

What if she hated the piece and tore it apart in front of him, line by line?

The thought made him stop in his tracks for a moment. He took a deep breath and let the warmth of the sun ground him. The trees swayed gently overhead, and the faint sound of conversation and footsteps filled the campus around him.

"Alright, Nathan," he muttered under his breath. "Stop overthinking it. You'll figure it out when you get there."

He squared his shoulders and tipped his head back for half a second, looking at the sky like it might have an answer.

It didn't.

As he started walking again, the arts building came into view, and with it, a sinking feeling in his chest started to consume him. The closer he got, the more it felt like walking into a final exam he hadn't studied for.

Nathan stood outside the door to Professor Simmons' office, his palms sweaty as he hovered, and shifted his weight from one foot to the other. The placard on the door read Dr. Leah Simmons – Creative Writing Department Head. The letters were etched in a sleek gold font that seemed way too formal for a professor who, rumor had it, could tear apart a student's work with a single, sharp comment.

He glanced at his phone. *11:45 a.m.* Her office hours wouldn't officially start until noon.

He had fifteen more minutes to rehearse. He could pace out here, go over exactly what he was going to say again, maybe double-check the assignment portal—anything to keep his mind from spiraling.

He pulled out his phone and opened the listing of his active assignments, trying one more time to find a way out of this mess. His heart sank as he scrolled through the submission page.

The words on the screen seemed to mock him:

The Serpent—Submitted January 14, 9:26 AM.

"Damn it," he muttered under his breath, swiping at the screen like a magical fix might suddenly appear and save the day. He stared hard at it, trying to manifest some hidden feature he'd missed to show itself.

"Hey there," a familiar voice said, breaking his focus.

He flinched, looking up to find Mia standing a few feet away. Her bag was slung over her shoulder, and she wore that easy smile she seemed to carry everywhere she went.

"Oh, hey, Mia. What are you doing here?" He said, before quickly locking his phone and shoving it into his pocket.

"I need to talk to Professor Simmons," she said, stepping closer. "I was hoping to get into her Contemporary English Lit class, but the system auto-dropped me because I'm flagged as..."

"Enhanced?" he blurted before he could stop himself. He froze, immediately wishing the word was on a string he could yank back.

She let out a small laugh. "Yeah, Nathan. Because I'm Enhanced." She studied him for a second, her smile softening. "It's okay. I think I know what you meant."

"Oh God—no—I'm so sorry—" His face flushed.

She shrugged. "Seriously, it's cool. I'm not ashamed of who I am. But yeah, because I have what I have, they won't let me into that class. It's some sort of arts department policy."

Nathan frowned, nodding. "Yeah, I guess there are rules, especially in the arts. They seem super protective about who gets in where."

Mia chuckled, lowering her voice conspiratorially. "Apparently, they don't want people like us to be friends."

Nathan cracked a smile. "Yeah, Enhanced vs. Orgos. It's so dumb. We're all still just people, right?"

"We sure are," Mia replied, her tone soft but firm.

"But wait," Nathan asked, connecting the dots. "Contemporary Lit? Why do you want to get into that class? I thought you were pre-med."

"I am," she confirmed, leaning against the wall beside him.

"I still have a few electives I needed to fill, though. When I transferred, some of the classes I took my freshman year didn't come with me."

"Really?" Nathan asked, frowning. "That doesn't seem fair."

"It's fine, really," she said, waving it off. "I took them when I was still in high school. I was accelerated, so no time lost."

He couldn't help his curiosity. "But why Contemporary Lit? With Simmons, of all people."

"Well," she began, "when I started looking at schools to transfer to, I found a few with better programs for hybrid medicine. They had better campuses and better locations. Think less snow, more beach. They were places much closer to what a Southern California girl like me was used to."

She paused with a playful glint in her eyes. "But NCSU had one thing those other schools didn't."

"Oh yeah?" Nathan asked, raising an eyebrow. "What's that?"

"Her," she said, tapping her knuckles lightly on Simmons' door. "She's brilliant."

His brow furrowing in genuine curiosity. "Wait—you actually want to study with Simmons, like—on purpose?"

"Absolutely," Mia said simply.

He stared at her for a moment, trying to process what he'd just heard. His mouth opened slightly like he wanted to question her decision, but no words came out. Finally, he gave a small, disbelieving laugh.

"Okay, I get loving books, trust me, and Contemporary Lit? It's a great course. I took it back in community college, but why do you think Simmons is so awesome?"

Giving it a second of thought, she tucked a strand of her silver hair behind her ear. "She's awesome because she has this way of cutting through the noise. You know that feeling, like everyone's giving you advice, but it's all empty? Like they're saying the right words, but they don't really mean anything?"

He nodded, remembering Simmons' sharp, no-nonsense comments in class. The professor made every word feel like it mattered.

"Well," she continued, her tone steady, "Simmons isn't like that. She doesn't sugarcoat anything—she's blunt, but it's real. And to me, that kind of honesty matters. Especially in medicine. You need someone who won't just tell you what you want to hear, but what you *need* to hear. That's the only way to get things right."

He frowned. "But still—a literature class?"

She just shrugged, her expression thoughtful. "It might surprise you, but not all doctors are stuck in a lab coat 24/7. I love books, Nathan. I love words. They're powerful. Sometimes more powerful than the medicine itself."

The way she said that made him think about his mother—how she used to say the same thing. She'd always talk about the responsibility of writers, how words had weight, how careless ones could harm but thoughtful ones could heal.

Her voice pulled him back.

"Medicine isn't just about science, Nathan. It's about people. People with real stories and real emotions. Some of the best doctors understand the arts as well as they understand anatomy. It's about understanding someone's life in a way that facts and charts can't. Simmons gets that. She teaches people how to stop skimming the surface and find the truth underneath."

He nodded slowly. "I guess I never thought about it like that."

"Well, now you have," she said with a smile.

For a moment, they stood in silence. Nathan felt a little lighter, like the weight of his assignment didn't seem quite as crushing as before. He almost forgot about the whole reason he was standing there in the first place—until the sharp clicking of heels echoed down the hall, slicing through the quiet like a countdown.

Professor Simmons approached with her usual brisk stride. She stopped abruptly in front of her office door, her eyes narrowing with immediate disapproval when she spotted him.

"Mr. Boone," she said, her tone carrying a slight edge of irritation. "To what do I owe this unannounced pleasure?"

Before Nathan could even attempt a response, her gaze shifted and landed squarely on Mia. Her eyes narrowed as she scanned her with an expression that made it clear she was already disapproving of her presence. Simmons' lips pursed slightly, and when she finally spoke, her voice dripped with judgment.

"And I see that you've brought a guest?" she said, her words hanging heavy in the space between them.

"Uh, Professor, this is my friend Mia. Mia Bennet," he said, awkwardly gesturing toward her. "She, uh… she was here first. She came to see you during office hours. I just—uh—I just need to talk to you about my assignment, but she's, um, first in line."

Simmons' expression tightened, pulling her mouth into a line. "Miss Bennet, is it?" she said, dragging out the name like it was something she wasn't sure she wanted to touch.

Mia, to her credit, didn't flinch under the professor's stare. She squared her shoulders and met Simmons' eyes head-on.

"Yes, Professor. I was hoping to talk to you about getting into Contemporary Lit," she said, keeping her voice steady. "The system auto-dropped me because—" She stopped there, figuring the real reason might not go over well.

Simmons sighed and rubbed her temple, like tech glitches were a personal insult. "The system," she muttered. "It's supposed to make life easier, but all it does is screw things up." She let out a sharp breath, straightened her coat, and shoved her hand into a pocket. "Fine," she said. "Just give me a second to get settled."

Then she pulled out an old, brass skeleton key, the kind you'd find in some romantic, haunted mansion where secrets waited behind every door. It made perfect sense that this was how Simmons secured her office. It was simple yet elegant, and timeless in a way that made Nathan wonder if the key opened more than just the door to her office.

She slipped the key into the lock like it was the most natural thing in the world, turning it with an ease that spoke to muscle memory. Nathan wasn't even surprised anymore. He was impressed by how unapologetically old-school she was, like she'd made a promise to herself long ago and never once thought about breaking it.

The key turned with a quiet click, and the door swung open with a soft groan, revealing a dim little office on the other side.

Nathan leaned in for a better look. Bookshelves covered every wall, packed full of Textbooks, novels, and papers, all stacked neatly. Some of it looked like it hadn't been touched in years. It was the kind of place that felt weirdly outside of time, like if you walked in, you might forget what year it was.

Simmons slipped through the doorway without a word. She set her coffee down with quiet purpose before settling into the chair behind her antique desk.

"Alright, Miss Bennet," she called from behind the desk, already digging through a pile of papers. "Let's make this quick. I don't have all day."

Mia let out a breath and stepped into the office, walking straight into whatever was waiting for her.

Nathan stayed in the hall, his thoughts spinning as the door clicked shut behind them. He leaned back against the wall. All he'd done was buy himself a few more minutes before the inevitable.

Nathan hovered outside the office door, staring at the frosted glass panel as if it could somehow clear itself and give him a better view of what was happening inside. The muffled voices of Mia and Professor Simmons drifted through the cracks in the door, like a conversation happening on the wrong side of a movie screen.

He leaned closer, his forehead nearly brushing the wood. Every now and then, he'd catch the faintest hint of Simmons' voice—a sharp edge softened by something unusual.

A sweetness.

Was that a chuckle he just heard? His brow furrowed, and he tilted his head, straining harder to make sense of the sounds.

The way they were talking changed—it got quieter, harder to catch what they were saying through the door. The sharp clicks and precise tone Simmons was known for faded into something else—something almost friendly.

His frustration bubbled as the words became impossible to catch. It was like they'd switched to a language he didn't know, and he was stuck out in the hall, chewing on his own questions.

He hadn't realized how long he'd been standing there, hyper-focused on the muffled sounds, until the doorknob turned. He quickly stepped back, pretending to examine his phone, hoping he didn't look as guilty as he felt.

The door creaked open, and Mia stepped out, her expression cool and collected, though there was a faint hint of satisfaction in her eyes. Behind her, Simmons followed, the sharp edge of her usual demeanor replaced with something else—something almost kind. Her lips curved—not quite a smile, more like she was in on a joke he didn't get.

And then, to his disbelief, she let out a low, amused chuckle—a sound so foreign coming from her that it sent a shiver down his spine.

"Mia," Simmons said, her voice smooth, almost delighted. "You have a very unique perspective. I look forward to seeing how it develops in class."

Mia nodded. "Thank you, Professor. I'm looking forward to it too," she replied calmly, though Nathan could hear a slight undertone of pride in her voice.

Simmons' eyes shifted briefly to Nathan, her face was impossible to read. Then, without another word, she turned back into her office, leaving the door slightly ajar.

Nathan was about to ask her what just happened, but she beat him to it.

"Well, that went better than I expected," Mia said, a small smile tugging at the corner of her mouth as she adjusted the strap of her bag.

"What—what did you say to her?" Nathan blurted out, unable to keep the disbelief from his voice.

Her tone was nonchalant. "I was just honest."

He stared at her in amazement. You were just honest? With Simmons? And that worked? He glanced at the still-cracked door, trying to remember the excuse he'd been planning to give for why he was standing there in the first place.

"Good luck," Mia said softly, patting him on the shoulder. "You'll be fine. Just don't overthink it."

He watched her head down the hall, then turned back to the door. His curiosity wasn't gone—it had doubled.

Simmons' voice, sharp as ever, cut through the hallway.

"Mr. Boone! Are you coming in, or do you intend to loiter outside my office all day like a lost puppy?"

He took a breath, squared his shoulders, and stepped through the door. Simmons sat behind her desk, watching him like she was already two moves ahead in a game he didn't know he was playing.

She motioned toward the chair in front of her desk. Her face was impossible to read. "Have a seat," she ordered briskly.

He sat as the wooden chair creaked beneath him, his hands clenched tight in his lap. The words were there, ready to spill out, but Simmons spoke first.

"Before you start, I've already read it," she said curtly, letting her words slice through the room with precision, leaving no space for hesitation.

His heart sank. "Wait, you already read it?"

"I did," Simmons said, her tone steady. "And it was good, Nathan. Very good." She leaned back in her chair, folding her hands like time didn't matter. "But we both know it's not your best. Is it?"

He opened his mouth to respond, but she continued before he could form a single word.

"It's exactly what I expected from you. It was clean, concise, and a bit romantic in its prose. But—" She tilted her head slightly, her stare nailed him to the chair. "True, Nathan, is it true?"

He blinked, unsure how to answer. "I mean, yeah, I guess—"

"Don't guess, Nathan, be honest with yourself," she interrupted, her tone growing sharper. "Are snakes—or whatever it is, or shall I say whoever these snakes are meant to represent—what keeps you up at night? Is this the thing you're truly most afraid of?"

Simmons watched him closely, letting the silence push for an answer.

"No, not really," he admitted. "Honestly, what kept me up last night was way worse than snakes."

Simmons nodded slowly, her lips curling into the faintest hint of a knowing smile. "Good," she said simply. "Then you know what to do."

Nathan frowned, glancing up at her. "What do you mean?"

"Whatever it was that kept you up last night," Simmons said, leaning forward slightly, her voice low, "that's where the truth is. That's what you need to be writing about."

The challenge echoed in his mind as he sat there, gripping the arms of the chair to keep himself grounded. Simmons' expression didn't waver, her eyes dared him to show up, to stop holding back, to write like he meant it.

He wanted to respond, but the words wouldn't come. For the first time since sitting down, he felt like the air in the room had been sucked out, leaving him exposed.

Simmons leaned back, her sharp expression softening just slightly, though the intensity in her eyes remained.

"You've got potential, Nathan. But potential without honesty? That's wasted talent. And in my opinion, wasting talent like yours is the biggest crime anyone can commit."

Her words hit him deeper than he cared to admit. He didn't trust himself to say anything, so he simply stood, scraping the chair softly against the floor as he pushed it back.

"Six days," Simmons added as he turned toward the door. "You've got six days to show me what's keeping you up at night."

Her words chased him out of the office as he clenched his fists and stepped into the hallway, the sound of the door clicking shut behind him sealing the challenge in his mind.

29

CORDIALLY INVITED

Dante and Wu sat in the courtyard, the cold air crisp against their skin. The buzz of campus life surrounded them—students perched on benches, groups huddled over laptops, voices mingled with the occasional bark of laughter—but for Dante and Wu, the world around them felt like background noise.

Dante slouched on the edge of a concrete planter, his fingers tapping against the rough edge. He looked like he was one wrong word away from jumping out of his skin. Wu stood nearby with his hands shoved deep in his pockets, standing straight like always, calm in a way that made it hard to tell what he was thinking.

"I'm just saying, man, all this drama with her, it's killing me," Dante grumbled. "The way she bosses us around, her attitude. I am so sick of her trying to act like Dr. Evil's little sister or some shit. It's like, 'Hey, Val, could you just chill for like one second?' I swear she lives for the drama."

Wu tilted his head slightly, letting Dante's words hang in the air. He didn't interrupt; he knew Dante needed to get it out.

"And don't get me started on all that glitching bullshit," Dante added, throwing up his hands. "Seriously—eyes glowing purple, syncing up to metal music—it's all so messed up, bro. You can't tell me you don't think it's even a little bit creepy."

Wu exhaled slowly, finally breaking his silence. "It's not important if I think it's creepy or not," he said, his tone calm.

"If you want to keep your scholarship? If you want to go pro? You need to play by her rules and do what she says. We both do, and if we don't, neither one of us has much of a future. That's the deal, you know it and I know it."

Dante kept going, "I know, man, but it's like she's got me by the balls. Tell me how that's any different from when the athletic department was waxing my stats and keeping me on a leash every day. You can't."

"There's a risk and a reward to everything, my friend," Wu said calmly.

"A reward?" Dante scoffed, though it came out flat. "All I've seen is only risk. I haven't seen one bit of upside. Have you? Seriously, why are you even dealing with her? You're not trying to go pro. So what's in it for you?"

Wu considered the question. For a moment, Dante thought he wouldn't answer. Then he spoke, his voice quieter now.

"I just want to work. I just want access," he said, keeping his voice even. "There's still so much we don't know about what we can do. There's so much more than we're using. Val has access to some things that no one else does. I think if I have a little more time, I can crack this whole thing wide open. You just need to trust me. Just be patient."

Dante just stared at him. "Patient, huh? I don't know, man. I think we're in way too deep to ever get out of this. And you can't tell me you don't think the stuff we're doing is messed up. I can't handle any more of those early morning glitchouts. That one today? I think it almost fried my brain for good. You seriously think any of this feels normal?"

Wu dropped his head, then looked over at Dante. "No, it's not normal," he admitted. "But some of it's cool too, don't you think? When we're connected, when it all clicks—it's like..." He trailed off, as if he couldn't find the words.

"Like what?" Dante pressed, leaning forward, curiosity creeping into his voice.

Wu looked away, like he was chasing the right words but couldn't catch them. "It's like... the second we sync, everything else drops out. The pressure, the second-guessing, all of it—it's just gone. I don't know how to explain it, but I feel it. The way we connect—it's raw. Yeah, it's unstable, but it could be so much more. We're close, Dante. I can feel it. We just need to hang on a little longer and push through."

"Wu, you're the smartest person I've ever met. Why do we need her? Can't you just get the access you need and do this on your own? I'd back you, man. I just don't trust her. What's so great about her anyway? What power does she have over you?"

Wu kept his voice low. "I'm not as smart as you think I am. Val can get me plugged into the network in ways I can't on my own. Don't ask me how or why, but she just can. And the way I see it? The world only has so much time before all this—everything we're messing with, all this rapid influx of tech—goes bad. I mean, really bad. I need to figure it out before it's too late."

Dante looked up at him, frown deepening, waiting for him to say more.

Wu let out a slow breath, leaving way too much unsaid between them.

"For now? Being part of Val's crew is a means to an end," he said finally, his voice steady, but a little checked out. His fingers twitched, something he could usually keep in check. "If I have to plug in and do some weird stuff to get where we need to go—where the world needs to go—then that's what I'll do."

Dante struggled to agree. "It's all so messed up, man. She knows this is going sideways, sooner rather than later, and she's still got us doing these dumb errands. Why not just give you this magical *access* and let you run with it and save the world or whatever?"

Wu leaned in a little closer. "Because Val's not trying to save the world, Dante. She's trying to own it."

～

Nathan sat stiffly on the edge of a bench on the opposite side of the courtyard, arms folded, one foot tapping anxiously against the concrete. False confidence wrapped him up like a too-tight blanket that did nothing to keep out the cold. From across the way, he could see Dante and Wu, wrapped up in a heated conversation.

He wasn't scared anymore—not of Dante, not the way he used to be. Three days ago, he might've flinched. Three years ago, he definitely would've. But now, all he felt was anger, burning slow and steady in his core, settling deep in his chest like smoke from a fire that refused to die out.

He thought back to his meeting with Simmons. She'd told him his writing was good, but not great. The fears weren't deep enough, they weren't what kept him up at night.

God, snakes? Really? he thought bitterly. *What the hell was I thinking?*

He shook his head, trying to escape the disappointment in himself. As he sat there, his eyes were drawn back to Dante like a magnet.

Dante Fucking Edwards, he thought as he stared at him from across the courtyard.

His former nemesis—the guy who shoved him into lockers—made gym class a living hell, and turned high school into a gauntlet. The guy who saddled him with the BaBoone nickname, the one that clung to him from middle school all the way to high school graduation, a joke that never died, a label he could never quite scrub off.

But the Dante sitting across the quad wasn't that guy.

He wasn't puffed up, barking out tasteless jokes, or throwing his weight around. He wasn't commanding the space, obnoxious, or intimidating. There was something off about him, but Nathan couldn't quite put his finger on it. His posture was off, his shoulders were hunched, and his fingers were drumming absently against his knee. He didn't look confident or sure of himself. He looked like someone searching for something they couldn't find.

Dante Edwards looked lost.

Whatever it was, Nathan told himself it wasn't his problem. Dante's problem is exactly that—Dante's problem.

He had no intention of getting sucked into whatever shitty situation Dante was dragging himself through.

And yet, Nathan couldn't take his eyes off him.

He couldn't help it. Watching Dante caught up in whatever mess he was stuck in should've felt good. Like some kind of payback. Maybe even a little justice. But it didn't. It felt sad, like the balance he thought he wanted wasn't there.

Nathan kept digging for an answer when Dante looked up and locked eyes with him from across the quad.

Dante grabbed his bag, stood up, and gave Wu a tap on the shoulder before making his move. He didn't look tense, and he wasn't rushing, but there wasn't an ounce of hesitation. He wasn't walking—he was striding, cutting straight across the courtyard.

Heading straight for Nathan.

⁓

Nathan burned alive in his thoughts. The world around him—students laughing, footsteps echoing across the courtyard, the bite of the January wind—blurred into nothingness.

Everything—everywhere, disappeared except for the sight of Dante moving toward him, purposeful and steady, with Simon Wu trailing a few steps behind like a shadow.

Nathan's mind raced, leaping to conclusions at light speed.

He remembers me—he's coming to teach me a lesson.

He's going to make sure I don't forget my place.

But then another thought crept in, quiet and sharp. *Am I afraid?*

He asked himself the question as Dante moved closer, unsure if what he felt was fear at all, or if it was something else entirely.

Dante moved with purpose, closing the space between them, and Nathan found clarity.

He was afraid, but not in any way that made sense. The same way that new rage had slammed into him back in The Caf and again at Chubbie's—fast, hot, and impossible to ignore—this fear felt different, and it wasn't alone. It came hand in hand with his newfound fury, the two of them tangled up into something he didn't have a name for.

He wasn't afraid of being shoved or mocked or made to feel small. He wasn't afraid of the cruel nicknames, the whispered threats, or the way Dante could twist a crowd against him with just a look and a laugh. He'd lived through that already, and somehow, he'd made it out the other side.

It wasn't being bullied that Nathan was afraid of.

He was afraid of what he might do if Dante came even one step closer.

His mind spiraled into a whirlwind of imaginary scenes flashing in vivid and violent detail. He could almost see it, as though it were a memory instead of a fantasy.

Dante would throw the first punch, aiming to make a statement, to show everyone in the courtyard that he still owned Nathan Boone, but that wouldn't go the way Dante planned. Nathan would catch his fist mid-air, stopping the attack like some B-movie action star ripped straight from an '80s VHS bargain bin.

They'd stand there, eye to eye, locked in a tense standoff. Nathan would snarl, his face would twist with something primal, before ripping Dante's fingers clean off his hand.

The fantasy in his head played on in vivid detail, like a ridiculous movie he couldn't pause. The world around him faded as his brain spun the drama into overdrive.

His daydream turned into wild, full-blown ridiculousness in the most satisfying way possible. He imagined landing open-handed slaps that left Dante stunned, sending him stumbling back, and begging Nathan to stop. Every smack would wipe the smugness clean off his face, scrubbing away years of that look Nathan had never been able to forget.

But then—like a jolt of lightning—the fantasy shattered.

The sudden stop of Dante's steps on the gravel in front of him snapped Nathan back to reality, yanking him out of his violent daydream before it could spiral any further. The silence was deafening. Dante towered over him, blocking out the sun, turning him into an ominous silhouette.

Nathan blinked hard as he unclenched his fists, his nails leaving faint crescents in his palms. His shoulders sagged slightly as he exhaled a shaky breath, grounding himself in the present.

Dante's expression was unreadable. He wasn't wearing his trademark arrogant smugness like Nathan might've expected. Instead, his face was just blank—almost neutral.

Nathan straightened up, squared his shoulders, and readied himself for whatever was about to happen. His brain fired off warning after warning.

Whatever happens, don't lose it, he told himself. *Don't let him see you flinch. Don't give him anything.*

"Hey, man," Dante said, his voice was casual, but there was an edge to it—something unreadable.

Nathan looked up at him, and for a split second, the simmering storm inside threatened to boil over, but he kept his voice calm.

"Hey," he replied.

Dante didn't move right away. He stood there, staring at Nathan, the air between them charged. Then, slowly, he reached into his pocket and pulled out a small, impossibly thin card. As the light hit its surface, a digital display lit up, glowing with shifting patterns of deep blue and violet. It was mesmerizing, futuristic, and almost too beautiful to be real.

"You're new on campus, right?" Dante asked, his tone almost kind, though it didn't put Nathan at ease. He glanced over at Wu, who gave a small nod of approval, like this was some unspoken agreement between them. "We want to officially welcome you."

Confused by the offer, Nathan just looked up, trying to use Dante to block out the sun so he could see his face.

"Take it," Dante said, gesturing toward him with the card in his hand.

Nathan, caught off guard, asked. "Why?"

"Just take it," Dante said, his patience visibly thinning.

Awkwardly, Nathan reached out and took the card. The second his fingers made contact, the holographic text shimmered and reformed into his name—*Nathan Boone—Plus One*. The card was warm in his hands, energy surging through it in a way that felt almost alive.

The image on the card shifted again, revealing glowing text that simply said: The Lighthouse. The letters pulsed in response to his grip, shifting with each subtle move of his hand.

Nathan looked up to search Dante's face for answers, but he stayed silent, the usual confidence flickering as he glanced at Wu.

"What's this for?" he asked, his fingers tightening around the card.

"It's an invitation," Dante snapped, the edge in his voice sharper now, like he was over the whole thing but pushing through anyway.

"Look, bro —come or don't come. It's your call. We're just trying to be nice here."

Wu nudged him gently, a silent cue to tone it down.

Rolling his eyes, Dante forced himself to go back to his calm approach.

"Listen, all we're saying is that we know you're new here," he continued, sounding a bit more genuine. "We've seen you around, and we thought you might want a chance to make some new friends."

Wu nodded, like everything was settled, and shot Nathan a quick, easy smile. But Nathan kept his grip tight on the card, his mind still racing. There was no way he was buying this sudden act of kindness, not from Dante. Not even with Wu playing the nice guy.

He didn't buy it for a second.

This wasn't some friendly welcome-to-campus thing. There had to be a reason—something underneath it all he couldn't see yet. People like Dante and Wu didn't do anything without an angle. Maybe it was a setup. Maybe they were testing him. Whatever it was, it wasn't random, and it definitely wasn't a coincidence.

Nathan turned the card over in his hand, watching as the light shifted across the letters. It pulsed, almost like it was waiting for him.

Nathan's head spun with questions, none of them making it out, but he knew answers were coming.

Whether he liked it or not.

30

A KNOCK AT THE DOOR

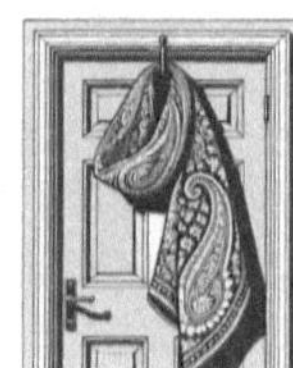

Nathan fumbled with the invitation in his pocket as he made his way toward Winston Hall. The weather hadn't changed—Mother Nature's good mood continued, but it didn't match his. Not even close.

He rolled the metallic card between his fingers, surprised by how light it felt—almost delicate. The real weight wasn't in the metal—it was in what the card stood for. And right now, it felt heavier than anything he could carry.

A single question bounced around in his head. *What was The Lighthouse, anyway?*

Mia had told him about it the day before in the stacks, and the way she said it hadn't sounded casual—it had sounded like a warning. *Not my place. Not my people,* she'd said. And even though they barely knew each other, he already trusted her. If it wasn't her kind of place, then it definitely wasn't a place he belonged either.

Still, the idea of going kept echoing in his head like background noise he couldn't turn off.

The uncertainty clung to him, dragging his thoughts in a million directions at once. As he walked, Nathan felt the usual wave of nerves creeping in, humming under his skin like bad Wi-Fi. It wasn't full-on panic yet, but it was getting there.

His pace slowed as Eve's dorm came into view. His brain spun through every version of how she might react when he told her what happened.

They hadn't talked since she bailed at Chubbie's the day before. He'd sent her a few messages and even tried calling once or twice, but there was no response.

There were no messages. No calls. Not even one of those random, offbeat memes she always sent to let him know she was thinking about him.

There was just—silence.

It was like she'd vanished without a trace. And the longer it stretched, the harder it became to believe she was simply busy.

They'd checked in every day since eighth grade, back when they first got phones. Going a whole day without a single message wasn't just weird —it felt like something important had gone missing. Something he'd gotten used to having without even thinking about it. Maybe she was done.

Maybe she had finally reached the point where she decided that his problems weren't hers to carry anymore. She had spent so much time helping him hold it all together, but that didn't mean it hadn't worn her down. Maybe she was tired of pretending it didn't, and maybe she had decided to walk away for good.

He needed to figure out what was going on. More than that, he needed her. Ever since she bailed on him at Chubbie's, everything had felt scrambled.

He pulled in a breath as he climbed the steps to her dorm. The sun was still shining like it had no clue anything was wrong, but it didn't do much to warm him up.

Whatever was going on, she probably had a good reason, but whatever her deal was, it would have to wait.

Right now, he needed her.

Even telling himself that didn't make it feel any less messed up. His thoughts spun out, faster and louder, as the invitation burned a hole in his pocket like it was waiting for him to make a move he wasn't ready for.

As he approached the door to Eve's room, he stopped in his tracks when he noticed something hanging loose from the top of the doorframe —a silk scarf, paisley patterned, its bold swirls of red and navy caught the light. It was unmistakably Eve's—he'd seen her wear it a dozen times before, usually tied around her neck or in her hair.

Seeing it there told him everything he needed to know. Eve was busy, and whatever she was up to, she didn't want to be interrupted.

He just stood there, staring at the door, stuck. For a moment, he thought about ignoring the scarf and knocking anyway—but that felt weird. Plus, if Eve was mad at him, disturbing whatever was going on in her room was probably the wrong move.

A text felt safer, assuming she'd cooled off enough to answer this time. He slipped his hand into his pocket and pulled out his phone.

He typed quickly: *Hey Eve, I'm downstairs. Haven't talked. We cool?*

His thumb paused over the send button for half a second before he hit it. The message sent, and he shoved his phone back into his pocket.

He turned to head back down to the lobby and wait for a response, but the bolt on the door slid back, followed by muffled voices from the other side.

Oh, shit! His mind gasped as he picked up his pace and turned to rush down the hall. He didn't need to know who was in there. He didn't want to.

But then the door swung open behind him.

"Cheeseman?"

The voice froze him mid-step.

Nathan whispered, "Gabe?" before slowly turning around.

"Yo, roomie!" Gabe's voice carried down the hall, light and teasing. "What the heck are you doing here?"

Nathan turned fully, his brain scrambling to keep up, to see Gabe standing in Eve's doorway, leaning against the frame, casual as ever. His trademark grin was plastered across his face like none of this was a big deal.

Nathan's brain blanked. *Why is Gabe in Eve's room?*

"I was just..." Nathan struggled to find any words, his brain on the verge of a nuclear meltdown. "I mean—since when are you and Eve...?" He trailed off, still in shock, nothing coming out right.

"What? I told you I had a thing for our favorite hippie chick, didn't I?" Gabe finished for him, chuckling.

Nathan stared. His mouth opened, but nothing useful came out.

Eve stepped into view behind Gabe, standing in the doorway with her arms crossed. No guilt, no apology—just a raised eyebrow like she was waiting for Nathan to get a clue.

"Hey, Nathan," she said, like everything was completely normal.

"Eve?" Nathan managed. The word felt dry and clumsy. He glanced between them as his thoughts tripped over each other.

"Relax, Cheese," Gabe said. "It's not what you're thinking."

Nathan blinked. "Oh, it's not? Then tell me—what exactly do you think I'm thinking?"

Gabe looked back at Eve, a faint blush on her face. There was a hint of guilt there, but also something softer as she gave him a sweet nod.

"Alright, fine. It's probably exactly what you're thinking."

Eve sighed and nudged Gabe in the ribs. "We were gonna tell you, Nathan. It just kind of… happened."

Her voice was calm but not as breezy as before. "What can I say? I like being around this big idiot."

Nathan crossed his arms, eyeing them both. "So this is why you haven't been answering my calls? I thought it was because you were super pissed at me for staying with Mia at Chubbie's."

Eve sighed. "Well, I can't say I was pumped about that whole deal, but no, yesterday just got away from me. Sorry for not getting back to you. I'm like the worst friend ever."

Gabe shifted, like he wasn't sure what to say next. "Yeah, we're both sorry, man. We were trying to figure out how to tell you. I guess we just… got caught up. Let's leave it at that."

Nathan let out a slow breath. "Really, it's fine. As long as we're cool. All of us."

"We are," Eve said, her voice steady. "Totally cool."

"Yeah," Gabe added. "We're all just a little gang of Fonzies."

Nathan laughed, quick and a bit awkward, but real this time.

He watched them as Eve leaned into Gabe, and he slipped his arm around her. In that moment, it weirdly made sense. The two of them matched in their own unique way.

Nathan gave them a look, but his tone was lighter now. "I have to admit, this is kind of great. My old best friend and my new best friend doing… whatever this is." He said, shaking his head and letting out a dry laugh. "I guess you have my blessing. Not that either of you asked for it."

Gabe pressed a hand to his chest like Nathan had just proposed. "Best friend? Cheese, I'm honored." He wiped away an imaginary tear. "Out with the old, in with the new! He said it, Eve! I'm his new best friend!"

Eve rolled her eyes and gave Gabe a quick jab to the ribs.

He doubled over with an exaggerated "ooof," then straightened up, looking amused. "I deserved that."

Eve looked at him sideways, her tone gentler now. "You sure you're not mad?"

Nathan shook his head. "No, I'm not mad at all. I guess this is all just a bit unexpected."

Eve tilted her head, eyeing him. "Then why do you look so wrecked?"

Nathan glanced at both of them, his expression turning serious. "Can we just go inside?" He ran a hand through his hair and let out a breath. "I need to talk to you—both of you, actually—about something seriously weird that just happened in the quad."

Eve shot Gabe a quick look before Gabe shrugged and stepped aside, holding the door open.

"Alright, Cheeseman," Gabe said. "Whatever it is, we've got your back."

Gabe stepped out into the hallway, gesturing for Eve to lead Nathan into her room. Nathan hesitated, his fingers brushing against the doorframe before stepping inside, feeling like an intruder in a space that wasn't his. Gabe followed last, letting the door close softly behind him.

Eve's room was exactly what he expected—unapologetically her. It was warm and colorful, a swirl of bohemian style with a little bit of everything mixed in. The walls were draped in tapestries: one with a deep blue and gold mandala, another filled with stars and constellations that seemed to shimmer in the soft light. Fairy lights zigzagged across the ceiling, casting a warm glow over the space. Real plants crowded the windowsill and spilled across shelves, thriving under the soft beam of a sunlamp tucked in the corner. A lava lamp bubbled slowly on her desk, glowing beside a scatter of open notebooks and half-used pens.

Her bed was tucked neatly against the wall, piled high with mismatched blankets and an avalanche of throw pillows. Gabe dropped onto it like it was familiar territory, settling back against the headboard without a second thought. Eve curled up beside him, folding her legs underneath her with easy comfort.

Nathan took the papasan chair across from them, sinking deep into the cushion as it gave way beneath him. For a second, he felt like the chair might swallow him whole.

Eve had a single room. Nathan knew this, and it didn't surprise him at all. What did surprise him was the scarf on the door handle. He knew what it meant, and the idea of Eve using it to send that kind of message didn't make any sense.

He hesitated before speaking, debating whether he wanted the answer.

"Eve," he started in a careful voice. "You have a single. Why the scarf?"

Eve just looked at him as if the answer should have been obvious.

"It's all theatrics, my good man," Gabe cut in before she could answer. "She wanted to make sure everyone knew exactly what was going on in here."

"Just ignore him," Eve said, rolling her eyes. Then her tone softened as she leaned in, her focus shifting completely to Nathan. "Enough about us. Why the sudden drop-in? Are you okay? God, I'm such a jerk. I should've checked in sooner, but I figured maybe you needed space to figure things out."

Nathan hesitated before digging into his pocket and pulling out the invitation Dante had given him.

Without a word, he tossed the card to Gabe, who caught it easily.

Gabe's face went still as he flipped the card over. The image of The Lighthouse glowed faintly on the small digital display with *Plus One* flashing underneath in bright, neon letters. For a second, his fingers slipped like he might drop it, catching himself just in time. He knew exactly what it was, and Nathan didn't miss the change in his expression.

For a moment, Gabe just stared at the card, flipping it over to inspect both sides.

"Where did you get this?" he asked, keeping his tone light, though his grip on the card tightened slightly.

"That's the weird part," Nathan said, leaning forward in the chair, before he let the name fall from his lips like a stone. "Dante gave it to me."

Gabe's smile disappeared, and he shot a quick look at Eve, who sat up straighter.

"Dante?" Gabe repeated, his voice quieter now.

"Yeah." Nathan leaned back in the chair and let out a breath. "He just showed up out of nowhere in the courtyard, handed me that thing, and told me to come to The Lighthouse. He said it was some kind of invitation. Like a 'welcome to campus' thing."

Eve frowned and held out her hand. Gabe hesitated for half a second, then handed the card over without a word.

"What did he say exactly?" she asked, as she inspected the card in her hand.

Nathan shrugged. "Not much. He said he knew that I was new on campus and they wanted me to come hang out or whatever. It was weird. Is this, like, something they do to welcome transfer students or something?"

"I don't think so," Eve said. "This doesn't sound like anything the school would set up. Definitely not at The Lighthouse, that's for sure." She shook her head.

Nathan turned his focus back to Gabe, who was watching Eve hold the card like it might blow up.

Gabe let out a short breath. "Yeah, you're right. That place is pretty intense." He caught himself, realizing he'd said too much, and went quiet.

Eve shot him a look. "What do you mean, intense, Gabe?" Her tone sharpened. "What do you know about that place?"

He looked at her like it was no big deal. "Not much," he said, picking his words with extra care. "From what I hear, The Lighthouse isn't just a hangout spot or some club. It's a whole other thing."

"That's not an answer," she said flatly, crossing her arms. "Spill it, Kowalski, and don't make me ask twice."

"Look, I don't know much," Gabe lied smoothly, his voice calm but firm. He turned to Nathan instead, using him as an escape hatch. "All I know is that it's not for everyone. It's supposed to be super exclusive. And if Dante handed you an invite, it means he thinks you belong there."

Nathan frowned, struggling to make sense of it. "Why me, though? I'm not…" He trailed off, unsure how to finish.

Gabe smiled faintly, doing his best to keep the tension from spilling over. "Look, Cheese, sometimes people see things in you before you do. Maybe that's all this is."

Nathan didn't look convinced. Neither did Eve, who was still watching Gabe like she expected him to mess up.

This thing with Eve had taken Gabe by surprise. She wasn't like anyone he had ever dated. There was something about her—the way she operated totally unfiltered, honest, and completely uninterested in anything fake—that made him feel more seen than he was used to. And somehow, he already cared about her more than he ever thought he would.

That was what made everything harder.

He knew exactly how she felt about the Enhanced. She didn't trust them. She didn't believe they deserved the special treatment they got. In her eyes, they weren't even fully human anymore—not in the ways that mattered anyway. The worst part was, she didn't try to hide it.

And honestly, he couldn't blame her. Not entirely. He had seen firsthand what some of the Enhanced at NCSU were capable of—how far they were willing to go, and what they were willing to sacrifice. But still, he didn't see himself that way. Not at all. Deep down, he knew he wasn't one of *them*. He had to believe there was still a difference.

He just needed time. Time to prove to her that being Enhanced didn't automatically make someone a threat. That people like him could still be good.

But he also had to move carefully. Nathan was already caught in the middle of whatever Val, Dante, and Wu were planning. One wrong step—one miscalculated move—and the whole thing could fall apart. Not just for him, but for all of them.

Nathan sat quietly, letting a thought creep in before he could shut it down. Maybe Dante did remember him. Maybe he wasn't saying anything—out of guilt, or because he was trying in some twisted way to make things right. His chip could have rewired something, flipped a switch, and now he regretted everything he'd ever done. It was a crazy thought. But Nathan was desperate for anything that might make sense of this.

He exhaled sharply and looked up. "What if Dante knows who I am?" he asked, his voice quieter than he intended. "What if he just doesn't want to admit it? Maybe his chip... I don't know, changed something in him? Maybe it made him see things differently, and now he feels bad for how awful he was—what if this is his weird way of apologizing?"

Eve and Gabe both turned to him, their expressions unreadable. Eve, predictably, was the first to react.

"Or," she said, tilting her head, "he's just the same manipulative asshole he's always been, and you're giving him way too much credit."

Eve looked at Nathan, her brow furrowed slightly, her lips pressing into a thin line. "Seriously, think about it—guilt, making amends? There's no way. It's not his style—never has been," she said, her tone thick with skepticism.

She exhaled sharply, shifting her stance. "I've heard of Enhanced people burning out, losing whatever made them such raging assholes, but that's a big maybe. More often than not, they just get better at faking it."

She trailed off, her words hanging in the air like she didn't fully believe them herself. "Probably not, though. I mean, it's Dante Edwards we're talking about here."

Nathan wasn't sure if he believed Dante's sudden change of attitude either, or if he could even afford to believe it.

Eve flipped the invitation over in her hands, the light shimmered on its polished surface. She turned to Gabe and shoved the invitation into his hands.

"Take this thing away from me. I feel disgusting after even touching it."

Gabe leaned forward and took the card from her, exhaling like he was bracing himself for a confession.

"Alright, look, I'll come clean," he said, glancing between Nathan and Eve. "The Lighthouse is more than just some super-exclusive underground club for Enhanced kids. Sometimes they send out invites to people they want to recruit. I think that's what's happening here."

Eve narrowed her eyes, crossing her arms as she stared at Gabe. "And how exactly do you know that?"

Gabe jumped in before he could stop himself. "My first-year roommate was a regular guy, just like me. He didn't have any enhancements or anything."

The guilt from the lie stung, but he pushed through it.

"Halfway through spring semester, he got an invite like this." Gabe held up the card. "He went, said he had a great time. He told me about the stuff they do there. Honestly, it sounded way too intense for me. Next thing I knew, he got a chip, and everything changed. After that, he started hanging out with a completely different crowd—Val's crowd."

Eve's lips tightened. "I see," she said, though her tone made it clear she wasn't surprised. If anything, the truth just confirmed what she'd already suspected about the place.

Feeling like he'd successfully thrown Eve off his scent, Gabe pressed. "After that, he moved out and left me behind for the Enhanced crowd. Didn't even say goodbye." He shook his head. "I don't know exactly what goes on in there, but whatever it is, it sounds pretty terrifying."

Nathan's brow furrowed, his gut twisting at Gabe's story. He listened carefully, dissecting each word, wondering how much of it was true and how much was just Gabe covering his tracks. The details sounded polished, too smooth, as if Gabe had prepared them in advance. Nathan wasn't sure what was real and what was meant to deflect, but he knew one thing—Gabe wasn't telling the whole truth.

Eve, however, looked intrigued. "Terrifying how?" she asked, her voice steady but curious.

"I don't know," Gabe said, leaning back and shrugging. "Dark rooms, weird rituals, probably some kind of culty vibe. Who knows? All I'm saying is, it's not the kind of place you just wander into unless you're ready to change everything about who you are."

Nathan didn't answer right away. He just held out his hand toward Gabe, silently asking for the invitation back.

"Terrifying," he mumbled. The word stuck in his mind, lining up too perfectly with what Simmons kept pushing him toward—something raw, something real. Something that truly scared him.

"Nathan. You're not seriously considering going, are you?" Eve's voice cut through, sharp with warning.

He stared at the card, the cool metal smooth against his fingertips. The neon lighthouse logo pulsed faintly, like it was breathing.

"I don't know yet," he said, turning the card over again. "I'm still thinking about it."

Eve let out a sharp breath, crossing her arms. "What is there to think about? These people are the worst of the worst. Whatever they want from you? It's not worth finding out."

She turned to Gabe, ready to snap, but he jumped in first.

"What's your deal with the Enhanced crowd, anyway? Why all the hate?" Gabe kept his tone casual, but Nathan could see him working an angle. He was testing her. He was trying to figure out how deep the hate went—and how hard it would be to change her mind about people like him.

Nathan stayed quiet. He knew exactly why Gabe was pushing, and he let him.

That's when Eve let loose.

Her arms dropped to her sides as she stepped forward, her expression tight with anger and something deeper Nathan couldn't quite name. "You want to know my deal with them?" Her voice stayed low, steady, but Nathan could hear the strain behind it, like it was costing her something to keep it together. "I'll tell you my deal, Gabe. Enhancements go against everything life is supposed to be about."

She continued, her words coming fast, and each one landed heavier than the last. "Life isn't supposed to be perfect. You're not supposed to live forever. You're not supposed to have a life without pain or just delete the file or whatever they do when shit doesn't go their way. That's not what being human is all about. Our flaws are what make us who we are, and our struggles help us learn and grow."

She paused to catch her breath.

"Those assholes out there?" She motioned vaguely, the movement jerky and tense. "Those cookie-cutter chip-heads? They're not people anymore. They're drones. They sold their souls for what? To look perfect? To move a little faster? To escape death? It's pathetic."

Gabe didn't say anything. He kept his face still, but Nathan caught the flex in his jaw.

Eve kept going, her mind frantic as the words continued to spill out.

"I'm not saying I have it all figured out—I don't—and I'm not pretending to be some kind of saint. But I believe this life matters because it's hard. We're supposed to learn something from it. We're supposed to fight to be better—not just for ourselves, but for each other."

She took a breath, like she was trying to steady herself, but it didn't slow her down.

"Look, I don't know what happens when this life ends—nobody does," she said. Her voice had softened, but there was still strength in it. "But I know one thing for sure. When you start messing with nature, when you rewrite biology and take shortcuts just to chase some version of perfection, you lose something. And it's not something you can ever get back."

She paused, steadying her breath.

"You lose your spark. That thing that makes you who you are. Call it a soul, call it energy—it doesn't matter to me. Whatever it is, it fades. It disappears."

She shifted slightly, her voice now steady.

"The people who go all-in on that stuff? They're empty. There's no light in them. No connection. No real energy. They're walking around like they're still human, still *themselves*, but they're not. Not anymore."

Nathan sat still, his fingers brushing the edge of the card, hoping it might somehow tell him what he needed to do.

Eve's voice cut through the quiet, sharp and unshakable.

"And let me make one thing crystal clear," she said, her tone firm.

She turned to Gabe, meeting his eyes without hesitation.

"I don't have any space in my life for anyone who's Enhanced."

The words landed hard and heavy, and the silence that followed was even heavier.

Gabe didn't say anything at first. He leaned back like Eve's words hadn't touched him, but Nathan caught the tension in his shoulders. Her rant hadn't just made things clear—it had made his path with her a whole lot harder.

"Well," Gabe said after a beat, his chuckle sounding way too forced. "Don't hold back, Eve. Tell us how you really feel."

Eve shot him a look but didn't say anything. Her silence felt heavier than everything she'd just unloaded on them.

Nathan's mind spun in the aftershocks of Eve's rant. Her words sat heavy in his chest like a weight he couldn't shake. But under all of it, something else started to push its way through.

He let out a slow breath before sliding the invitation back into his pocket. It felt heavier now, like it was waiting for an answer he hadn't figured out yet.

"You want to know why I'm even thinking about this?" Nathan said. His voice was steady, but there was heat behind it. "It's because of Simmons."

Eve blinked. "Simmons? Your writing professor?"

He glanced at Eve, then over at Gabe, before looking back down at the card in his hand like he was still trying to decide how much to share.

"I turned in my assignment—the one about what scares me most. And you know what she said?" He let out a short breath. "She said it was good. Really good, actually. But not my best."

Eve raised an eyebrow. "Isn't that what professors are supposed to say? You know, to push you?"

"It wasn't that." Nathan shook his head, the words coming faster now. "She told me to dig deeper. To stop hiding behind metaphors and distractions. She told me to tell the truth—my truth."

He ran a hand through his hair, sitting back in the papasan as he worked it out loud. "I think I finally get it. If I keep running and hiding every time something gets hard, I'm going to spend the rest of my life miserable. I think it's time I stopped being scared and faced things head-on."

Eve stayed quiet, just watching him carefully. She didn't look convinced, but she didn't interrupt.

"That's why I think I need to do this," Nathan said. His voice had stopped shaking. For the first time in a while, he sounded like he believed himself.

"Everything about The Lighthouse scares the hell out of me. Every part of it. But maybe that's the point. Maybe that's exactly why I *have* to go."

He looked at both of them, his fingers tightening slightly around the card.

"As cheesy as it sounds, I think I need to walk in there, face every single one of them—Dante, Val, all of them—and say it out loud. Tell them they scare the shit out of me. And when they smile at me like that is exactly what they were hoping for? I'll look them in the eye and tell them all to fuck right off."

It was the most confident thing he'd ever said. A rush of adrenaline and something that felt like clarity pulsed in his veins, and the card in his pocket pulsed right along with it.

Gabe was the first to break the silence. "Well, Cheese," he said, his tone easy, but there was something serious under it. "If you're going, you're not going alone."

Nathan frowned. "What do you mean?"

Gabe tilted his head, like it should be obvious. "You need a bodyguard. Your invite says plus one. I'm coming with."

Eve's eyes darted between them, not even pretending to be okay with this. She let out a slow breath, then shook her head.

"Fine." She reached into her macramé bag and pulled out her keys. "If you guys are gonna go through with this, you can take my van."

Nathan reached for them, but she held them back for a second.

"Nathan," she said quietly. "You know this could all blow up in your face."

He nodded. "Yeah. But I think I need to do it anyway."

For a second, she didn't move. Then she let out another breath and handed him the keys.

"I get it. And for what it's worth..." She met his eyes. "I'm proud of you."

Nathan stared at her. "You are? For what?"

"For taking control of what happens to you," she said, her voice soft. "For admitting how you feel and finally doing something about it. It's way overdue."

He nodded. "Thanks, Eve. I'm not gonna lie, I'm terrified—but I think that's the point."

"Don't thank me yet," she said. There was a tiny smile there, but her worry hadn't gone anywhere. "Just be careful. Both of you."

"We'll be fine," Gabe said as he grabbed the keys from Nathan and gave them a casual twirl, like none of this was even slightly concerning.

"It's just a creepy underground club for the Enhanced and their loyal little fan club—who, for some reason, want to drag our boy into the fold and make him one of their own."

He shot Nathan a look, the corner of his mouth twitching.

"What could possibly go wrong?"

Eve rolled her eyes. "Oh, that's super reassuring. I feel so much better now."

"Glad I could help." Gabe chuckled, pulling her in for a quick hug. "Don't worry. I'll keep an eye on him."

"You better," she said, looking up into Gabe's eyes. "You don't want to lose your best friend status the same day you earned it."

Nathan snorted. "We'll be okay. I promise."

"I know you will." Eve leaned against her desk, watching them as they headed for the door.

As they stepped out, Nathan felt the nervous energy still humming in his chest. But underneath it was something steadier. Something solid.

For the first time in a long time, he wasn't running.

And he wasn't going alone.

31

THE LIGHTHOUSE

Eve's van sputtered to a stop across the street from The Lighthouse, its engine letting out the unmistakable cough and rumble of a classic VW barely holding itself together. Rain splattered against the windshield, mixing with the engine's uneven grumble as Gabe cut the ignition.

The winter drizzle had sharpened into something meaner, turning from rain into frozen bursts of ice that pelted the van's roof like bullets—sharp reminders that something was building, and it wasn't going to wait much longer.

Mother Nature must've sensed what was about to go down—and she clearly didn't like it.

Nathan sat in the passenger seat, staring through the fogged-up glass at the building ahead. The Lighthouse certainly wasn't what he expected. If anything, it looked like a forgotten relic, a run-down warehouse left to the mercy of time and the city's urban artists.

Layers of graffiti covered every inch—tags, murals, and chaotic bursts of color all fought for space. Brightly colored signatures dripped down in jagged letters, each layer burying the last like some endless competition. The windows were blacked out, offering zero clue about what went on inside.

During the day, the building would have disappeared into the background, but tonight it was alive with energy. Every time the door swung open, a wash of neon spilled onto the street, twisting in the puddles before disappearing again. Bass-heavy music leaked through the cracks, like a heartbeat Nathan didn't trust.

He pulled his coat tighter and leaned back as the van's heater worked overtime to cut the winter cold. It blasted his face with warmth, but it didn't do much for the cold sitting in his chest.

He watched as people filtered in and out, each one moving with an effortless kind of confidence. They didn't walk—they arrived. Like the place had been expecting them, like it knew it needed them to survive.

The rain kept falling, sharp and steady, but it didn't seem to matter.

The Enhanced didn't flinch.

Their chips managed everything—the chill, the damp, the bite of wind. None of it touched them the way it touched him. And it showed. In the way they moved. In the way they entered.

They weren't just walking in. They were making an entrance.

Each step felt intentional, every movement smooth and measured, like they'd practiced it. They didn't speak. They didn't rush. Whatever this was, it wasn't confidence—it was control. Like they already knew they didn't need to prove a thing to anyone.

Nathan exhaled slowly, watching the van's windows fog up around the edges.

"So, that's it?" he asked, his voice low, hesitant.

"That's it," Gabe replied flatly, not taking his eyes off the door.

Nathan frowned, his curiosity getting the better of him. "Have you ever been inside?"

Gabe hesitated, his jaw tightening as his fingers tapped a quiet rhythm against the steering wheel. "A few times."

Nathan blinked, then frowned. "Seriously? You've been in there?"

"Yeah," Gabe said again, his tone careful. He stopped, then added, "I wouldn't normally come here, but... Val and her crew rolled out the welcome mat for me when I first got on campus."

Nathan's eyebrows shot up. "So just like Dante did for me, huh?"

"Exactly. I'm pretty sure they do it for anyone who catches their eye. You know, the whole *welcome to the club spiel*."

His voice shifted into a mocking sing-song.

"You'll make new friends, find where you belong—blah blah blah."

He rolled his eyes.

"They're big on recruiting people early. They want to get their hooks in before you even realize what's happening. When I got my invite, I was curious to see what it was all about. You know— find out what the big deal was about the whole thing."

"And?—What did you figure out?" Nathan pressed, watching Gabe closely.

Gabe's expression twisted into something bitter. "I figured out pretty quickly what this place is—*what they are.*" He paused, his face tightening. "And I promised myself I'd never come back here."

Nathan glanced at him. "And yet you're still here?"

Gabe gripped the wheel like it might steady him, the silence stretching until it nearly split. When he finally spoke, his voice dropped.

"Listen, Cheese, there are two kinds of people who get invites like you did. People who already have chips. And people who want one. Either way, they've got something the network can use."

Nathan shook his head, his voice tight. "I still don't get it. Why me? Out of all the new kids on campus? There have to be—what, a few hundred incoming students this semester alone? And they want me?"

He looked away, swallowing the lump forming in his throat. "I don't have anything anyone wants. I mean… I barely even know what *I* want."

Gabe didn't say anything right away, his eyes drifting back to The Lighthouse, its neon glow flashing rhythmically across his face.

"Just… trust me, man. If you got that invite, you have something they want."

He paused, like the rest of it hurt to say out loud.

"I don't know how to explain it. All I can say is—whatever is going on here is way bigger than we think it is, and once we step through those doors, there's no going back."

"So then why did you agree to come here with me?" Nathan asked, his voice quieter than he intended.

Gabe turned to him, a hint of exhaustion in his eyes.

"That's a good question, Cheese," Gabe replied, leaning back in the seat like he was buying time. "Honestly? I'm still trying to figure that out myself."

He let out a breath and looked over. "All I can say is—I want you safe. You're my friend, Nathan. I couldn't just sit back and let you do something this insane without backup."

Nathan frowned, not quite buying it. Gabe must've caught the doubt in his expression because he sighed before continuing.

"Look, I'm already Enhanced," Gabe said, his voice steady but weighed down, like the words didn't come easy. "They know who I am, and they know I'm not up for grabs. But you?—I think that they might've had their eye on you since you got to campus."

Nathan blinked, trying to process. "What are you talking about? I don't have anything anybody wants. I'm not special—I mean, we both know that I'm barely holding it together. What could they possibly want with me?"

"I'm still trying to figure that one out too," Gabe replied, his tone tightening. "My best guess is that they probably think you've got something about yourself you want to fix. They're probably just going to try to sell you a chip. They'll make it sound like it'll solve everything, and try to suck you in. That's their typical move anyway."

He shifted, eyes locked on the building across the street. "I don't know, maybe they saw you go down in The Caf the other day and they figure you're an easy target to get on board. You know, get you on the network and all that."

Nathan swallowed hard. "What do you mean *the network?*"

"It's like this, Cheese," Gabe said, his voice low and serious. "Once you're Enhanced, you're not just some person with a chip. You're part of something bigger—whether you want to be or not. You're connected, monitored, and locked into the system. And the more people they bring onto the network, the more powerful it gets."

He paused, making sure Nathan was hearing him.

"That's what The Lighthouse is about. It's not just some underground club for the cool kids. It's where they pitch the whole package. Make it sound like you're leveling up. Like you're getting something better."

He shook his head once.

"But really? It's a recruitment center. And they're *always* looking for more."

Nathan hesitated, his voice heavier now. "What if you're right? What if I do have something I want fixed?"

Gabe turned to him sharply, his expression unreadable.

"I just wish I could stop overthinking everything all the time," Nathan admitted, the words slipping out before he could stop them.

"I wish I could feel normal for once. You know, not second-guess everything. I wish I could stop waking up every day feeling like something's seriously wrong with me. A chip could fix that... right?"

Gabe exhaled, leaning back in his seat. "I guess so," he said slowly, his voice measured.

"I mean, yeah, a chip could definitely level you out. It could quiet the noise in your head, make you calmer, more confident—all that."

Nathan's heart picked up speed. "That doesn't sound so bad."

Gabe glanced at him, his eyes sharp. "Trust me, man. Having a chip isn't all smooth sailing. Being Enhanced has its own set of problems."

Nathan raised an eyebrow. "Like—what kind of problems? Every Enhanced person I've ever seen looks perfect. I can't see how any of them have problems. They make it look like life's just... easy."

"I promise you, Chees, it's not all fine and dandy." Gabe's tone shifted —quieter, more serious. "The Enhanced have their own kind of issues. Stuff no one talks about. Like addiction."

He paused.

"Especially now," Gabe continued, "with all these third-party apps and mods people keep loading onto their chips. Once you start down that path, it doesn't stop. There's always something else to tweak—your focus, your strength, your emotions, your memory. Whatever you've ever wanted to fix about yourself, there's probably an app for it."

He gave a small shake of his head.

"And, the more you add, the harder it gets to remember where you started. And honestly? That's probably where Eve gets her whole 'Enhanced are soulless zombies' thing."

He hesitated, then added quietly, "And the scary part is... I don't think she's wrong."

Nathan sat back, turning over Gabe's words. After a second, he said carefully, "I just think that—maybe if I got one, you could help me figure out how to use it. You know... to keep everything that's always crowding my head under control."

He hesitated before looking over at Gabe. "I mean, you don't have any of that third-party stuff, right?"

"Yeah—I don't use much of that nonsense," Gabe said, then paused. "Well, not technically. I mean, I do have my overlay. It hides my chip from the school's internal network, so I guess that counts as third-party."

He scratched the back of his neck. "I'll admit, I do have a few other add-ons, but I never really use them. They kind of mess with my head. They make things all foggy. I've been meaning to delete them, but honestly? I've just been lazy. I don't know, I guess that crap just isn't for me.

Nathan nodded, relieved. "Yeah, but you don't go overboard or anything. I mean, you don't have any crazy body mods or anything. You're just—well, you."

Gabe laughed, low and genuine. "What, because I'm a fat guy, you think I couldn't possibly be modding my appearance?"

Nathan fumbled. "No—I mean, well, yeah... but not like—" He groaned. "You know what I meant."

"It's cool, Cheese," Gabe said, waving him off. "I get it. But think about this—who are my comedic heroes?"

Nathan blinked, then gave a slow nod. "Well, Chris Farley's the obvious one," he said. "You quote him constantly. I'm pretty sure half your personality is just built from Farley impressions at this point."

He let out a quiet laugh. "And you've got that Sam Kinison yell down so well, it's actually kind of terrifying."

He paused, thinking for a moment before adding, "Oh—and John Candy. Yeah, I like that guy. He always seemed like someone you'd want to hang out with."

"Yup." Gabe nodded, clearly pleased. "And what do those guys have in common?"

Nathan frowned, not quite sure what he was getting at. Gabe puffed out his cheeks, expanding his body with an exaggerated gesture.

Nathan blinked. "Wait. Are you telling me you've got an enhancement to make yourself fat?"

Gabe burst into laughter, slapping his belly. "Actually, yeah, you could say that. You've seen how I eat, right?"

Nathan grinned. "Who hasn't? You don't exactly keep your Top Ten Favorite Meals list—or whatever you call it—a secret. I mean, when you eat ten full meals a day, it's hard to miss. You make it seem like food is your whole personality."

"That's the goal," Gabe replied without missing a beat. "You think half the stuff I eat is healthy? Spoiler alert—it's not."

He jerked his head toward The Lighthouse. "So I picked up an app. In there."

For a second, something flickered across his face—something hard to read—but it passed just as quickly. He gave his stomach a theatrical rub, like he was playing it off for laughs.

"It lets me stay at my ideal size and weight, but it balances out all the risks. You know, high blood pressure, cholesterol, all the stuff that would normally spike by eating the way I do."

He exhaled, his voice softening a little. "Plus, without the app, my metabolism would just burn through everything. I've always been like that. Even back when I played football, it was a nightmare trying to bulk up for the season. Every summer, I'd eat nonstop just to hold the weight, but the second I even looked at a set of free weights, it would all disappear."

He shrugged. "I guess I'm just unlucky that way."

Nathan's mouth dropped open as he connected the dots between Gabe's diet, size, and his comedic idols.

"Wait, you're telling me you choose to look like that because you think it's the only way people will think you're funny?"

Gabe grinned. "Look, it's hard to explain, but I think to be taken seriously as a comic, I can't look like I used to. You wouldn't laugh as hard at me if I looked like some kind of underwear model, would you?"

Nathan shook his head, still processing. "I don't know, man. I think funny is just funny, no matter what a person looks like."

"Look, man, this is the style I've chosen," Gabe said, leaning back in his seat with a proud, almost smug expression. "And, I don't do anything halfway.—Never have."

He ran a hand over his belly like it was part of the brand. "And honestly? I think it works for me."

A slow smile spread across his face. "Plus, the ladies don't seem to be complaining."

Nathan stared at him for a long moment before chuckling softly.

"Speaking of ladies, what are you going to do about Eve?"

Gabe's grin slipped, just a little, and he shifted in his seat. His hand moved to the back of his neck, rubbing slowly like he was trying to ease something he couldn't name.

"I don't know, man," he said, his voice quieter now. "I know you warned me about how she feels about people with a chip, but I didn't realize it was that deep."

He looked over at Nathan, his usual confidence flickering for a second.

"Are you really okay with me and her getting together?"

Nathan shrugged and leaned forward, resting his arms on his knees. "Yeah—it's cool," he said, though there was the faintest shake in his voice.

"I mean, I've had a crush on Eve since, like, the third grade, so yeah, I get why you like her."

He paused for a moment, then looked up and met Gabe's eyes.

"But she's my best friend. Always has been. And honestly? I wouldn't want it any other way."

He held the gaze a second longer before adding, "And I meant what I said earlier. You're my best friend, too."

"Thanks, Cheese." Gabe let out a breath, his shoulders relaxing. "I was pretty scared to tell you. Honestly, both of us were. We didn't know how you'd take it."

Nathan gave him a faint smile. "Yeah, well, I'm taking it just fine. You're a good guy, Gabe. Just… don't screw it up, alright?"

Gabe grinned again, the sparkle returning to his eyes. "I won't, man, I promise—maybe we can double sometime?"

"What do you mean double?" Nathan asked, raising an eyebrow. "Like a double date?"

"Yeah," Gabe said, his grin turning mischievous. "Me and Eve and you and Mia."

Nathan blinked, taken off guard. "What—Mia? No way. I told you, she doesn't like me like that."

"Oh, Cheese," Gabe said, laughing and shaking his head. "You have no idea how wrong you are. When I see you two together—let's just say, it makes my spidey senses tingle."

"You're so weird, man." Nathan rolled his eyes. "I'm telling you, she's nice and all, but there's no way a girl like that would ever go for me."

Gabe leaned forward, his tone shifting slightly as he smiled knowingly.

"Remember what I just said about the Enhanced being 'on network'?"

"Yeah—So?" Nathan replied slowly, narrowing his eyes.

"So, let's just say that when you're on the network, you can pick up on people's emotions," Gabe said, gesturing with one hand.

"It's not like reading minds or anything. It's more like—" He paused, trying to land the right words. "It's like tuning into someone's frequency. You feel their energy, their vibe. And you, my friend? You make that Mia vibrate in a big, bad way."

Nathan froze. His face went hot as he tried to laugh it off.

"You're insane," he said quickly. "There's no way that's real. It's probably one of your sketchy, bootleg apps screwing with your signal or something."

He waved it off, but his thoughts were spinning too fast to land on anything solid.

"I'm just saying," Gabe replied, leaning back and folding his arms behind his head like he had all the time in the world.

"Maybe you should stop selling yourself short, Cheese. I'm not the Enhanced Love Guru or anything, but come on—there's definitely something going on between you two."

Nathan exhaled and shook his head. "Yeah, well, maybe you should deal with your own girl problems before we even start talking about my love life—or whatever sad excuse for one I've got."

Gabe let out a low chuckle and gave a tired shake of his head. "Yeah, yeah. Easier said than done."

Nathan shot him a sidelong glance, a smirk tugging at the corner of his mouth. "I promise you, when she finds out about you, she's gonna be pissed. Like—*super* pissed."

Gabe rubbed a hand down his face. "I know, man... I'm working on it."

He hesitated, then looked over at Nathan, his expression softer than usual. "I've got to figure something out, Cheese. I really like her. She's the first person who makes me feel like I don't have to perform all the time. Like, being exactly who I am is enough. And honestly? That scares the hell out of me."

Nathan nodded, still smiling. "I get it. I'll tell you what," he said, locking eyes with Gabe.

"You help me survive tonight, and I'll help you survive Eve. Deal?"

Gabe's grin returned, wider this time. "Deal."

He tilted his head toward the glowing doorway just ahead. "Now—ready to face the digital music?"

Nathan looked at the entrance, its edges pulsing with light, the bass thudding like a second heartbeat deep in his chest. He swallowed, his breath catching for just a moment.

"As I'll ever be," he said quietly.

His hand tightened around the invitation in his pocket as he pushed the van door open and stepped out into the cold, electric night, crossed the street, and headed toward whatever was waiting for him on the other side.

32

GET OUT

As they approached the front entrance of the club, a pressure built in Nathan's chest, like his body was bracing for impact before his brain could catch up. He didn't stop moving, but each step dragged heavier than the last. Every movement felt loaded, like he was approaching something irreversible.

Wu stood by the front door, angled just enough to seem casual, like he was lounging in front of a velvet rope at some underground club. His stance was loose, and his posture was laid-back, but the sharp focus in his eyes said otherwise. He was here for a reason—and would not be ignored.

"Alright, give me that invite," Gabe said, his voice steady as he held out his hand. They stopped a few feet from the door, close enough to feel the low-end thump of bass pulsing through the brick.

Nathan's brain hit a wall. "What? Why? Don't we need it to get in?"

"Trust me, Cheese," Gabe replied without flinching, his tone infuriatingly vague. "You do not need that thing."

After a beat, Nathan gave in and handed it over.

Gabe didn't hesitate. The second the card hit his palm, he flung it down the alley with a smooth flick of his wrist. Nathan watched it disappear into the shadows. In an instant, it was gone, swallowed by the dark without a sound.

"What the hell, man?" Nathan hissed. A rush of panic surged up his chest like a fire alarm going off in a sealed room. "Why would you do that?"

"I told you to trust me, Cheese," Gabe replied, cool and collected as ever. He gave Nathan a quick nudge between the shoulder blades. "Don't ask any more questions—just move."

Nathan stumbled forward, stunned, trying to figure out what kind of plan involved throwing away the one thing that got them through the door. He opened his mouth to push back, but before he could get a word out, Wu saw them.

"Kowalski," Wu said, his voice calm and unreadable as they approached. His enhanced eyes flicked briefly to Nathan before returning to Gabe. "What's up?"

"Hey, Wu," Gabe said casually, like this was just another Tuesday. "Long time no see."

Wu's attention shifted to Nathan as he gave him a slow, sizing once-over. "Do you have your invitation?"

"No invitation for Nathan," Gabe said smoothly, stepping slightly in front of him. "He's my guest tonight."

Wu's expression stayed neutral, but his eyes narrowed just slightly. He looked back at Gabe.

"What do you mean, you don't have it, He looked at Nathan, "Where's your invite? We gave that to you for a reason. Don't tell me you lost it."

Gabe didn't even flinch. "Nah, we didn't lose it—We threw it out," he said with a shrug, motioning down the alley with his thumb. "It's down there if you want it back."

Wu's eyes sharpened. "You shouldn't have done that," he said quietly. "She's not going to like this."

"What else is new?" Gabe scoffed, nudging Nathan forward. "She doesn't like anything."

"Alright," Wu said, stepping aside, just barely enough to let them through. "But if Val asks, I'm not the one who let you in."

Nathan didn't breathe until they were through the door. Even then, his chest stayed tight. The entrance felt like it narrowed around them, like they were being squeezed through some invisible threshold.

He leaned toward Gabe, his voice low and tense. "How did that even work? Why didn't he stop us?"

"It's called attitude, my good man." Gabe beamed. "You can walk into any building if you act the right way. Plus, it doesn't hurt that Wu's just a sheep in wolf's clothing. I mean, seriously—the guy's stacked with mods to project 'stoic enforcer,' but deep down?" He leaned in a little. "He's a total wimp."

Before Nathan could press him, Gabe reached forward and gripped his shoulders with calm certainty, guiding him deeper into the club like this was all part of some mapped-out plan he'd memorized months ago.

Inside, the music didn't simply play—it hit like a shockwave. It wasn't the kind of sound you just *heard*—it was the kind that settled deep in your chest, rearranging your heartbeat and rewiring something in your bones.

The main floor moved like it was alive. Bodies swayed in perfect rhythm, guided by a beat so relentless it seemed to rewire instinct itself. Overhead, lights sliced cleanly through the haze, sweeping across the room in carefully timed arcs that felt less like ambiance and more like choreography. There was nothing spontaneous about it.

This wasn't a light show—it was a mechanism. And somewhere above it all, tucked behind walls or buried in the guts of the place, some unseen architect of illusion was pulling every string. It was hard not to imagine him perched behind a panel of switches and dials, hidden like a myth, deciding what deserved light and what should be left to the dark.

For a moment, Nathan felt like he had stepped behind the curtain of something much bigger than a club. Not quite magical, but manufactured with the same reverent precision—something built to impress, to distract, and most of all, to keep people from asking the wrong questions.

Nathan stayed close behind Gabe, weaving through the chaos. But as they crossed into a darker section of the room, something changed.

The music didn't fade—it was consumed. Pulled into the walls like a secret being swallowed. It didn't vanish completely. It sank lower, deeper, until it felt like pressure more than sound. It moved under his skin, vibrating just below the threshold of hearing, like a hum only his bones could pick up.

The space they stepped into looked like it had been lifted from a billionaire's hidden lounge. Velvet couches lined the walls, their deep cushions glowed under the pulse of the lights that shifted between purple and electric blue. Everything was cold and perfect in a way that felt unnatural.

But the people were worse.

They didn't look like they were sitting. They looked like they had been *placed*, stretched out across the couches like mannequins. Their heads lolled back. Their mouths hung slightly open. None of them moved. None of them spoke. They looked caught somewhere between unconsciousness and something harder to name.

The first thing Nathan noticed was their eyes.

Each of them had the same unnatural glow behind their eyes—ultraviolet and otherworldly, like their pupils had been replaced with something synthetic. It didn't look like a reflection. It looked like it came from *inside* them. Like whatever made them human had been turned off, and replaced with something cold, flickering, and soulless.

They all sat perfectly still, breathing in time with one another like a human metronome. At the base of each neck, just beneath the hairline, tiny lights pulsed in rhythm, sending out signals like a silent conversation only they could hear.

Nathan leaned in closer to Gabe, keeping his eyes on the couch-lined wall. "What is this?"

Gabe didn't blink. "It's called glitching."

He nodded toward the people stretched across the velvet cushions like furniture. "It's basically like a shared trip. One person drops in, and the rest follow."

Nathan frowned. "That's... not real, right? You're messing with me again, aren't you?"

"I'm not," Gabe answered. His voice was flat, his face unreadable. "They're all linked through the network. It's the same song, the same energy, but they don't hear it the way we do. It's all internal— the music —it's in their bodies."

He looked back at Nathan, then looked back at the room. "Their chips are synced up to one another. Their breathing, heartbeat... everything—it all matches up. And when they're in the same rhythm, the system starts dumping the bad stuff. Every bit of sadness, stress, fear, even anger—it gets spread across the group. They absorb it, process it, and in return, they get this artificial high. Think of it like manufactured joy. Like a designer calm or something. They're not sharing a vibe—they're purging their humanity and replacing it with whatever the system tells them to feel."

Nathan looked around again. The air didn't feel relaxed. It felt empty. Like something important had been shut off.

"So... they're not just vibing?" he asked. "They're actually—what— erasing part of themselves?"

"That's one way to put it, I guess," Gabe said. "They're not really here anymore, not fully. It's like their minds checked out and left their bodies running on autopilot."

Nathan didn't respond. He couldn't. Because now he was looking at the center couch, where his eyes had landed on Dante.

He was sprawled out like he belonged there, arms resting across the back of the couch, legs stretched wide, completely at ease. He had a girl on each arm, their heads tilted back, eyes half-closed, glowing faintly with that same ultraviolet haze that everyone wore. Neither of them looked conscious. Their bodies were too still, their faces too blank.

But it wasn't the girls that made Nathan's stomach tighten.

It was the look on Dante's face.

He didn't look smug. He didn't look present. His eyes were open, glowing faintly, but there was nothing behind them. He looked like he was searching for something far away—something that wasn't ever going to show up.

Nathan's feet felt rooted to the floor.

This wasn't what he thought The Lighthouse would be. Not even close. This wasn't rebellion. It wasn't freedom. It was something colder. Something designed to make people forget who they were.

And then Dante moved. He turned his head slowly and locked his eyes on Nathan.

He didn't blink. He didn't breathe. He just stared.

And in that second, Nathan knew that Dante was truly seeing him— all of him. Seeing who Nathan was, and maybe even who he was supposed to become.

Then, without sound, Dante's lips formed a single word.

Boone.

"What the fuck?" Nathan gasped, stumbling backward into Gabe as if Dante's voice had shoved him.

"Didn't I tell you this place was creepy?" Gabe muttered, stepping closer. His voice was light, but something in his posture wasn't as relaxed as before.

"Look at 'em all. Plugged in, frying their brains. It doesn't get much creepier than that."

Nathan turned, his pulse pounding beneath his skin. "Have you ever tried it? You know, Glitch out like they are?"

Gabe scoffed, but the sound was dry. "Me? No way. I hear it feels pretty sweet though, but I don't mess with that shit. I get my buzz from getting laughs and sugar highs exclusively. That stuff?" He nodded toward the couch. "It's all bad."

Nathan didn't push further. He let his eyes drift back across the lounge and soak in the strange rhythm of the room, the buzz beneath the silence, the way the air vibrated with something unspoken. The Lighthouse wasn't glamorous. It wasn't exciting. It was a trap built to look like freedom.

"Come on," Gabe said. "They serve beer here, too. First round is on you."

"What?" Nathan blinked as he let the world come back into focus like someone had spun the lens.

"You heard me," Gabe said, already steering him toward the bar. "If we're gonna stand up to whoever dragged our asses out here, we're gonna need a few pints of liquid courage, and you're buying."

Nathan followed without thinking, his limbs slow to catch up. The crowd melted around them as they moved through the haze.

The bar stretched across the back wall, sleek and glossy like a slab of obsidian; the light bounced off it in strange patterns. Gabe leaned in and placed the order like he'd done it a thousand times. Nathan rested his elbows on the counter, letting his eyes wander once more.

As his eyes scanned through the crowd, the glitchers didn't move. They just sat looking like mannequins mid-charge. The glow from their chips flashed in near-perfect sync, like a beat they were all trapped in. It didn't matter how long he watched—they never broke pattern.

Nathan was about to suggest they leave when he saw Val.

She stood across the room, fire and fury wrapped in one body. That rare, volatile mix of attraction and danger that dared you to stare while warning you not to. Her jet-black bob framed a face sharpened with purpose. Her eyes burned, not with annoyance, but with rage.

Standing across from her, steady as stone, was Mia.

She didn't flinch. She didn't fold. Their standoff coiled the room tight, like it might snap if either one moved too fast. Val wasn't yelling to make a point. She was yelling to dominate.

Nathan tried to guess what had sparked the argument between them. Was it a stupid fight over their shared apartment? Or had the tension between them—Val's chaos and Mia's calm—finally boiled over? It felt less like an argument and more like a collapse that had been waiting to happen.

Val's arms flailed dramatically as her voice climbed with every syllable, like she could win through noise alone. But Mia didn't move. She stood anchored.

Then Val pointed—stabbing the air like her finger was a weapon—and aimed it right at Nathan.

His mind screamed.

Why is she pointing at me?

Mia turned. Her eyes locked onto his.

Everything shifted.

Whatever had been holding her back snapped the moment she saw him.

"Nathan!" she screamed, her voice cutting through everything.

He shouted back before he had time to think. "Mia!"

She stepped toward him—just one step—but it was enough to shift the entire room.

Val caught it. Her face twisted. She lunged, grabbing Mia's arm, and yanked her back like she owned the moment.

Even through the pulsing crowd, Nathan could read her lips.

"Bring him to me."

Mia ripped her arm free and didn't hesitate. She took off, cutting straight into the crowd.

At first, nobody noticed. She slipped between people like she'd done it a hundred times—like nothing else mattered but reaching him. But then the crowd shifted. Their movements were subtle at first, like they were all caught in a slow-motion dream where the room itself was telling them what to do.

The music changed. It wasn't just internal anymore. It was in the air, loud and crawling. A command disguised as rhythm. One by one, the glitchers organized, and their movements became synchronized. The trance broke, but not completely. They moved like dancers with no will of their own, swaying on cue.

Every time Mia changed direction, someone blocked her. Not aggressively. Not even consciously. They just stepped in front of her, like they knew she was coming.

She didn't slow down.

She shoved past one, then another, forcing her way forward.

And just when it seemed like she was about to make it, some Enhanced guy—built like a walking protein shake—grabbed her by the arm. His grip was casual, like he was helping, but his smile made it worse.

He looked like he thought he was doing her a favor. Like she was part of the show.

She yanked herself free and shoved him as hard as she could with both hands, sending him stumbling backward like a drunken sailor caught in a storm. He flailed and toppled into the crowd, taking a few people down with him like they'd all gone overboard together.

She didn't look back. She had bigger things to deal with.

But as she kept pushing through the crowd, the full picture hit her like a punch to the chest.

The sick weight of it dropped fast and hard, and a flood of horror crashed through her as she realized she hadn't been fast enough. She'd fought like hell to get to him, torn through the crowd like it might cost her everything—and it still wasn't enough.

She was too late.

Wu had beaten her to the bar, where Nathan stood in horror.

"I found your invitation," he said, his voice steady. "Take it. You need this to be in here."

Nathan hesitated, looking between Wu and Mia, who was still pushing through the last bit of the crowd with desperation on her face.

"Nathan, no!" Mia's voice cut through the noise as she finally broke free and pushed toward him. "Don't touch it!"

He didn't hear her in time. His fingers were already on the card.

The moment he touched it, the impact surged through him like something tearing loose from the inside. The lights fractured overhead. The music shattered. Movement around him blurred into fragments. Reality jolted and cracked down the middle like glass under pressure. A burst of white light seared into his vision, washing out everything around him.

Every nerve inside him was ignited, sending a surge of electricity rushing through him like he'd been plugged into something he wasn't meant to touch.

And then the light changed.

A golden glow pushed through the chaos. It started somewhere deep in his chest and spread outward, filling every part of him. It was the opposite of pain—something that didn't demand anything from him. It felt like it had been waiting all along, wrapping around him like it already knew exactly where to go.

The feeling wasn't imagined. It was something his bones remembered. A peace from long before doctors and diagnoses, from when his mother still had the strength to carry him in her arms and convince him the world couldn't reach them there.

That warmth held him again now, and then he heard her.

"Everything will be okay, Nathan."

The words arrived with clarity, like she was there, in that space, with him. This wasn't a memory—it was real. Her voice sounded just like it did when she would comfort him after a bad day, when Dante had pushed him too far, or when the world outside his bedroom had felt impossible to face.

Time didn't feel real anymore. It wasn't moving forward. It wasn't moving at all. It just kind of floated there with him, stuck in that warm amber light. For once, everything wasn't spinning. There was no pressure in his chest, no noise in his head, no need to fake like he was fine.

Everything was quiet.

He was at peace.

He let go of everything.

All the pressure that had lived inside for years—fear, guilt, that constant feeling of being out of step with the world—lifted. Gone. This wasn't an escape. This was a release.

And then it ended.

There was no warning. No gentle fade. The light was ripped away like someone yanked a cord.

Nathan gasped, stumbling as the weight of the room rushed back.

The first thing he saw was the card on the floor, sparks flickering at the edges. It wasn't a card anymore. It was just a shattered mess of glass, metal, and broken circuitry, scattered like it had never been whole.

Gabe stood over him, hand still outstretched, breathing hard. He'd knocked the card from Nathan's grip. Hard enough to destroy it.

Nathan blinked, still trying to hold on to whatever had just taken control over him before so quickly letting go. His head spun as the noise from the club rushed back in around him.

Mia finally reached him, her voice slicing through the chaos like it was aimed straight at his heart.

"Run, Nathan! You need to get out of here. Now!"

He turned, still dazed, just in time to see Val making her way through the crowd. She didn't need to fight her way through like Mia had. People stepped aside without hesitation, their bodies shifting as if pulled by an invisible current. It was like something radiated off her, a low-frequency command that only the Enhanced could hear.

They parted around her like she was cutting through water, clearing a path as she walked straight toward them.

Her eyes were locked in, and her expression didn't shift.

She wasn't coming to talk. She was coming for him.

She moved like she already owned the outcome—like whatever happened next had been written long before Nathan ever stepped foot inside this place.

Gabe didn't waste a second. He grabbed Nathan by the arm and pulled him toward the exit.

"Thanks for having us!" he shouted over his shoulder, dragging Nathan along with him, his voice bright in a way that didn't match the urgency in his grip.

"Lovely party. Let's do it again sometime."

He didn't stop moving. Nathan barely kept pace, his feet dragging as they slammed into the exit doors and burst out into the rain.

"What the hell just happened?" Nathan gasped, the question tumbling out of him without permission.

"No time for explanations, Cheese," Gabe snapped, his voice tight, his hand still wrapped around Nathan's jacket. "Just move."

The cold slammed into them, but Nathan barely noticed. His body moved without permission, caught somewhere between a sprint and a stumble. Every muscle burned, like he'd been running underwater, and the pounding in his skull made it hard to keep a single thought straight. Rain blurred the world around him, warping the lights and shapes until the van ahead looked like it was being dragged farther away with each step.

Gabe reached the passenger door first. He yanked it open and grabbed Nathan by the arm, shoving him inside without saying a word.

Nathan dropped into the seat and yanked the door shut with hands that barely worked. The sounds from The Lighthouse were still crashing around inside him. His heartbeat hadn't caught up. It felt like it was still stuck back in that room, buried under the weight of the music and the glow.

The driver's door swung open, and Gabe climbed in with one fast motion. He slammed it shut hard enough to shake the entire frame. The key was already in his hand. He jammed it into the ignition, and the engine sputtered once, then roared to life. The rumble rolled through the floor beneath them like a warning neither of them could afford to ignore.

A sudden pounding rattled the window beside Nathan, making him jump in his seat and practically land in Gabe's lap before catching himself.

Mia stood outside, rain running down her face like tears she didn't have time to cry. Her hair stuck to her cheeks, her eyes cut toward the club behind her before snapping back to his. Whatever was chasing her, she wasn't wasting time explaining.

"Open up! Let me in!"

Nathan reached back and pulled the sliding door open. The metal groaned in protest, and the wind shoved its way into the van as if trying to follow her inside. She didn't hesitate. She climbed in fast, slamming the door behind her, water soaking into the seats as she leaned forward.

"Drive!" she commanded. Her voice didn't crack, didn't waver. Her eyes locked on Gabe like she'd already decided for him.

Gabe shoved the van into gear. The tires slipped across the pavement before catching, and the van jolted forward with more speed than it could handle. The engine roared beneath them, fighting every push.

The city stretched out ahead of them, blurred by rain and headlights, the world smeared with movement. Behind them, The Lighthouse faded from view, but the weight of it lingered, like the whole building had carved itself into Nathan's memory and refused to let go.

Eve's van hummed quietly, the low vibration barely cutting through the pounding rain outside. The occasional screech of the windshield wipers carved through the silence, rhythmic but failing to keep up with the downpour. Inside, the air was heavy with silence.

Nathan sat in the passenger seat, his head tilted back against the headrest, his breathing uneven. His limbs felt disconnected, like he wasn't fully inside his own body. His mind was still stuck back in The Lighthouse, wrapped in that warm amber light, and the feeling of pure and undisturbed peace he felt when he touched the invitation.

Nathan spoke, his voice scratchy. "Somebody needs to tell me what the hell just happened back there—because I've never felt anything like that before."

Mia hesitated before leaning forward and placing her hand on Nathan's shoulder, her grip firm yet soothing. For a moment, she stayed like that, trying to ground both of them, before pulling her hand away and turning to Gabe for guidance on how to answer Nathan's question.

Gabe didn't look back at her. He didn't look at Nathan either. Because he and Mia both knew exactly what they saw. They saw how Nathan responded when he took the card from Wu, the way the entire room had shifted, like the energy in the air had been drawn to him, like he was the center of something bigger than any of them understood.

"We think you have an implant, Nathan," Mia said finally, her voice careful but unsteady.

Nathan's head snapped toward her, with disbelief flashing across his face. "No," he replied immediately, shaking his head. "That's not possible. I never got a chip. My mom—she wouldn't have let me—"

Mia interrupted, her voice firmer now. "Nathan, it's true. We all felt it. When you touched that card, something inside you reacted. I think you've had one for a long time—it's just been... asleep. Whatever was loaded onto that invitation card—it woke you up."

Gabe let out a slow breath, pressing his back into the headrest, his eyes fixed on the road. "She's right, Cheese," he replied, his usual humor absent. "I thought you might have one the night you moved in. Remember what I told you about the network? Syncing up, feeling vibes from one another? It was just a hunch at first, but what just happened back there? That confirmed it. You've had it all along."

Nathan shook his head, his thoughts racing. "That doesn't make any sense." His voice rose, edged with something close to panic. "I don't have a chip. I—"

"It doesn't matter if you chose it," Mia cut in. "You have one, and it's not just a normal chip—it's something else—Something unique."

Nathan felt like the van was shrinking around him, his breaths coming faster. "But how?" His voice cracked. "How could I have a chip and not know it?"

"Because clearly, whatever you have is way more powerful than ours," Gabe said, his voice tense. "You're not like most Enhanced, Cheese. That card? It doesn't just react to anyone. It's like a key, and you're the lock."

Nathan stared at him, trying to force his brain to catch up. "What does that even mean?"

Gabe's jaw tightened. "I don't know, man. All I can tell you is what I saw. The second Wu activated that card and handed it to you, it was like flipping a switch. The lights, the energy—it was all coming from you."

Nathan swallowed hard, tears stinging his eyes until they blurred everything in front of him. "I'm not like you guys," he said, forcing the words out. "I know I'm not. If I was Enhanced, why do I feel like complete shit—all the time? None of this makes sense. I'm not Enhanced, I'm just a normal, broken kid."

Mia leaned in, "No, Nathan. You've never been normal. Someone made sure of that a long time ago."

Nathan froze. The weight of her words settled over him like a lead blanket, pressing against his ribs. "What are you saying?"

Mia inhaled, her hands curling into fists in her lap. "You've always felt it, haven't you? That thing inside you that you can't explain. The thing that's made you afraid your whole life."

Nathan's mind flipped through years of memories—hospital visits, unexplained anxiety, the gnawing sense that something was wrong with him, even when doctors swore there wasn't. He thought it had been in his head. He'd spent his whole life trying to rationalize it, trying to be normal.

But what if it had never been in his head at all?

He tried to speak, but nothing came.

Gabe, sensing the spiral, spoke up, his voice more measured now. "Look, you're not the only one this has happened to. Some people get implanted without knowing. It could've been before you were born or when you were a kid or something. It doesn't matter how—it matters that it's there." He exhaled sharply. "And now Val knows it, too."

"Val?" Nathan's voice was barely audible. "What does she have to do with this?"

"She's been looking for someone like you," Mia continued, anger creeping into her voice. "Not you specifically, but someone who would accept the key, like Gabe mentioned earlier. I think she's even pulling strings to get people like you on campus. Either because she thinks they're the missing piece to whatever twisted puzzle she's building, or to recruit them to do her dirty work and find who is. Honestly, I think that's why I'm here, too. I think she was trying to use me to find you."

Nathan looked over at Gabe, "Why didn't you tell me this before? Why didn't you warn me?"

Gabe ran a hand through his damp hair and exhaled hard as he stared at the road ahead. "Because I didn't know for sure. Like I said, I had my suspicions, but I wasn't positive. I didn't want to tell you some crazy idea that would likely freak you out and end up being wrong."

He gripped the wheel like he could squeeze the regret out of himself. "Honestly, I thought I could protect you. I really did, but I was wrong. I'm sorry that I let you down, Nathan."

Mia let out a slow breath, shaking her head. "None of that matters now. What matters is what we do next."

She glanced between them. "We're in this now, all of us are, and we need to figure a way out, because Val isn't going to stop until she gets what she wants. And what she wants is you, Nathan."

Nathan buried his face in his hands, pressing the heels of his palms against his eyes. His thoughts were tangled, everything felt too big, and it was all coming at him way too fast to process. "So, what do we do?"

"We fight," Gabe said simply. "But first, we need to find a place where we can keep you away from Val until we figure out what's going on. I promise you, we're going to do everything we can to make sure you that you—stay you."

"And how do we do that?" he asked, voice quiet but steady.

Gabe turned to look at him. "We're going to need some help. I think we need Eve."

Nathan blinked. "Eve?"

"Yeah," Gabe said, meeting Nathan's confused gaze. "She hates Val more than anyone I know. If we tell her what's going on, there's no doubt that she'll lose her shit—but she'll channel all of her anger into taking Val down. That's the kind of fire we need right now."

Nathan bit his lip, unsure. "I don't know, man. Eve's not exactly… pro-Enhanced."

"Exactly," Gabe said with a light chuckle, though his tone didn't quite match the humor in his words. "Which is why we need her in on this. She's got her opinions, sure, but if anyone can help us keep you grounded, it's her."

Nathan glanced back at Mia, searching her expression for reassurance. She gave him a small nod, though the tension in her face hadn't eased. "He's not wrong," she said softly. "I don't know Eve, but we all know she's got no love for Val. If anything, that alone makes her dangerous. And that kind of danger? It might be exactly what we need."

He nodded slowly, the weight of their words settling over him. He still wasn't sure how to feel about everything—about the chip, about Val, about this mysterious part of himself he didn't even know existed. And yet, for the first time in a long time, he didn't feel completely alone.

"Alright," Nathan said, his voice steady as he looked between Gabe and Mia. "I guess it's time to put an end to all this."

Gabe's energy picked up, a little more like himself again. "That's the spirit, Cheese."

Mia gave a small nod, reaching over to give his shoulder a quick squeeze before settling into her seat. "We'll get through this," she said, her voice quieter but steady. "Together."

The van hummed quietly around them as the rain continued to pound against the windshield. It wasn't a plan—not yet—but it was something. And for now, that was enough.

33

SCREEN TIME

Eve's van idled in front of Winston Hall, its engine thrumming low as rain tapped at the windshield like it was trying to get in. Cold air funneled through Gabe's cracked window, pulling in the damp scent of freezing pavement. Nathan shifted in his seat, watching the streetlights stretch across the wet asphalt like they were trying to outrun the night.

"So, what did you tell her?" he asked, finally breaking the silence.

Gabe kept his eyes on the entrance to the dorm, as he drummed his fingers on the steering wheel with the rhythm of someone who'd been improvising all day. "I just told her you chickened out, and we were going to grab a few slices at Chubbie's for After-Dinner. It's not quite in the top ten but..."

Nathan let out a low groan. "Oh god, not now with at stuff."

Gabe shrugged, like the answer should be obvious. "What? I had to say something believable, right? I mean, I couldn't exactly say, 'Hey, Eve, Nathan had a meltdown in a culty rave club and unlocked a hidden data relic with his DNA or whatever you want to call what just happened."

Nathan leaned back, rubbing his temples with the base of his palms. "Yeah... okay. You're right. We've got to ease her into this. If we dump everything on her at once, she'll lose her shit."

Gabe twisted around in his seat to glance at the back. "Mia, fair warning—Eve is gonna freak when she sees you. Don't take it personally. Just let her do her righteous-indignation thing if she needs to. And

246

Cheese?" He looked at Nathan. "Hop in the backseat. My lady rides shotgun. I mean it is her van, after all."

Nathan sighed but unbuckled his seatbelt and hopped into the back beside Mia. The second he clicked in, the passenger door popped open, and Eve slid in like she owned the moment with the same effortless confidence she always had.

She buckled in, turned the vent her way, and gave them a grin like she already knew she was right. "Thank God you didn't go through with it. I knew you had more sense than spending a night with those godawful chip-heads. Now Chubbie's? That I can live with. But if there's even a sliver of pickle anywhere near my half, I swear—" she turned to gloat, but froze mid-spin.

Her eyes landed on Mia, and her smile vanished.

"Wait—hold up. Why is *she* in my van?"

Before anyone could get a word out, Gabe cut in. "Look, it's a long story. I promise, we'll catch you up, but first, we need to get out of sight."

Gabe swung the van around the back of Winston Hall before pulling into a hidden corner behind a row of maintenance trucks. The temperature had dropped, shifting the rain into steady snow, that quickly started to collect on the ground as the van hissed to a stop in the damp silence.

"Alright," Gabe muttered, cutting the engine. "Let's move. Quickly."

They slipped out, their footsteps brushing through a thin layer of powder on the path that hadn't been there ten minutes ago. Gabe led them toward the rear entrance, pausing just long enough to glance over his shoulder before cracking the door and waving them in like they were sneaking into a movie they hadn't paid for.

Nathan stuck close to Mia as they moved down the stairs. She paused, then slid her hand toward his. He froze for half a second—then laced his fingers through hers, like they'd been doing it forever and no one had to make it a thing.

"It's cool, I swear," he said, his tone reassuring. "We've been down here before. It's totally safe."

Mia offered a faint smile as they ducked into the dim corridor. At the end of the hallway, Gabe shoved open the last door, leading them into the old movie theater hidden beneath Winston Hall.

Eve perched on the edge of the stage like she was judging a talent show she didn't sign up for, arms crossed and expression sharp.

"Alright. Someone better start talking, because I'm not in the mood for cute excuses. Why is *she* here?"

Her stare cut into Mia like she was scanning for hidden malware.

Nathan and Mia sank into a pair of front-row seats as Gabe made his way to the breaker box. The heavy click of the switch echoed through the theater, loud in the silence, before the house lights blinked on overhead.

Nathan opened his mouth, but nothing came. His thoughts tangled, still fraying at the edges. Before he could force something out, Gabe stepped in.

"Look, Eve," he started, locking eyes with her. "First of all, Mia is *with* us. Not against us."

"What do you mean, *with us?*" Eve scoffed. "She's a chiphead, Gabe. I mean, she's Val's roommate. She can't be trusted."

Mia, who'd been quiet this whole time, didn't raise her voice—she didn't have to. "No. That's not fair. I'm not like them. So stop pretending you know me just because I have an implant."

Eve raised an eyebrow, caught off guard by the defiance.

Mia stepped forward, her posture firm but not aggressive. "I get it—for whatever your reason is, you hate the Enhanced. But have you ever actually tried to get to know one of us?"

She held Eve's stare like she was daring her to say something. Eve didn't flinch; she just looked at her, like she was trying to decide if any of this was worth the energy.

"Look, I transferred here for better opportunities," Mia said with a huff, folding her arms. "I'm not here to be part of some elitist's secret agenda. I didn't choose to live with Val—that was purely bad luck."

She exhaled sharply, running a hand through her hair.

"And yeah, I have an implant, so what? I don't use it to be 'Enhanced,' whatever that means to you. I only use it for my health. That's it. I don't have any third-party mods or black-market apps. I don't believe in those things—they're not safe."

Eve's expression hardened. "Oh, please—give me a break, would you? You expect me to believe that you don't have any enhancements? Just look at your hair, for Christ's sake. A twenty-one-year-old with silver hair? You expect me to believe that's natural?"

She threw up her hands in exasperation before motioning toward Gabe and Nathan.

"You're not fooling anyone." Her eyes narrowed.

"I'm serious, guys. Nothing about this girl adds up."

She folded her arms again. "I can smell her digital lies a mile away. There's not a single thing about her that's real."

Mia exhaled sharply, her hands curling into fists. "Well, I don't know what to tell you. My mom went gray at twenty, and so did I. And you know what? I love it. It connects me to her. And let me tell you something else..."

She took a step closer, "I'd imagine you know a thing or two about people who struggle with mental health after being friends with Nathan. Panic attacks like his? They are no joke. I used to have them every day—until I got my implant. Sure, I still get nervous sometimes, but my chip helps me keep my emotions in check. Honestly, it saved my life."

Nathan inhaled slowly, something unspoken settling in his chest. The way Mia said it—like she was defending herself, but also him—hit deeper than he expected.

Eve's expression faltered. Her mouth opened, then snapped shut.

Mia didn't stop. "I'm not apologizing for doing something that made my life more bearable. You think because I have a chip that you have the full picture of who I am? That's just sad, Eve.

"I know exactly who I am, and I like who I am. I'm not just some walking billboard for enhancements like you think I am. And I'm certainly not here to prove I'm real enough just to earn your approval.

The room went silent. Nathan watched the exchange, stunned—not just by Mia's intensity, but by how fiercely she stood her ground.

Gabe broke the tension with a loud ding, mimicking a boxing ring bell. "Alright, ladies, back to your corners. Let's cool off and talk about what happened at The Lighthouse."

Eve didn't uncross her arms, but the sigh that she let out came with a crack in her confidence. She gave Nathan a look—wary, not convinced, but not entirely closed off either. "Fine. Let's hear it. Start from the top."

Gabe nodded, stretching his arms before cracking his knuckles like he was about to deliver the most dramatic story ever. "Alright, here's the Reader's Digest version—we don't have time for the Director's Cut.

Getting in wasn't the problem. I tossed my invite down the alley the second I saw it—thing gave off major bad omen vibes. Like, if horror movies taught us anything, it's not to touch the glowing object pulsing with mystery code.

Wu was working the door with his classic 'Wu Energy' you know, Hey everybody, look at how cool and edgy I am' He didn't want to let us in so I turned on the Kowalski charm and talked our way passed him.

Eve rolled her eyes. "I thought this was the Reader's Digest version. Cut to the part where things get weird."

"Alright, fine," Gabe continued. "So, we walk into the place, and it wasn't what we expected. People were glitching—synced up, frying their brains on some kind of weird mental high."

Eve frowned. "Glitching?"

Mia sighed. "Think of it like a digital bong hit. Some Enhanced do it to sync their minds, share their experience. I've never done it, but I hear it's intense."

"All I know," Gabe added, "is that they looked wrong. Eyes glowing, creepy smiles—it wasn't normal, Eve. It was like they were being rewired or something."

Nathan nodded. "I saw Dante first—fried out of his mind, a girl on each arm. No surprise there. But then, I saw Val—screaming at Mia."

Mia drew in a breath. "She was pissed that I wasn't on board with helping her find you, Nathan. She said she needed you, that you were the missing link."

Gabe jumped in. "Yeah, and then Wu came back with that damn invite. He must've fished it from the alley or some shit."

Nathan swallowed hard. "That's when it got weird. He tried to force it into my hand, and the second I touched it, something changed. I don't even know how to explain it. At first, I felt calm, like everything suddenly made sense. Like I was supposed to be there. Then the lights started freaking out. My body locked up. And then it felt like... I wasn't even me anymore. I was wired into something bigger. I was plugged in. Like my mind wasn't mine."

He looked at Eve, his voice softer now. "I heard my mom's voice. It wasn't a memory. I actually heard her. Like she was there. It was intense. Then, I guess, Gabe slapped it out of my hand, and everything snapped back."

"And it shattered on the floor and totally fried," Gabe jumped in. "Sparks, smoke—full-on cursed-card meltdown. That's when I knew we were done. We had to get out. No way were we sticking around to see what else that place had planned for us."

Eve stared at them like she was trying to catch up. "So—what are you saying, Nathan?"

Mia let out a slow breath and rubbed her temples before answering.

"We think he has a chip. But it's not like any of the ones we've seen before. There's something different about it. I think it has to do with the way he connects to the MIND network. And now Val knows. Whatever it is he's got, that's what she's after."

Eve's eyes bounced between all three of them, like she was trying to solve a puzzle that didn't come with all the pieces.

"Okay, hold up," she said, her voice cutting through the room. "You're seriously telling me that Val is after Nathan because of some mystery chip no one even knew he had until tonight? That Wu just randomly brought that invite back, and it magically unlocked some hidden tech inside him? Do you guys even hear yourselves right now?"

She looked over Nathan, searching his face like she was looking for a tell, some giveaway that this was all some elaborate joke.

Her voice dropped. "Please tell me you don't actually believe this, Boone."

"It's true, Eve," Nathan said quietly. "I felt it. Honestly... I think I've always felt it."

Eve shook her head, still looking like she'd rather be anywhere else. "Okay. Fine. Let's say I decide to roll with this insanity—what's the plan?"

"We don't know yet," Gabe said, more serious now. "We were hoping you'd channel some of your righteous fury and help us come up with something. For now, the only thing that's clear is we've got to keep Nathan away from Val—until we figure out what he has inside him that she's willing to do anything to get."

Eve hesitated, the weight of everything pressing down. She wanted to fight the absurdity of it, but her pulse was pounding, and the truth was starting to feel unavoidable.

Finally, she nodded, slow and stiff. "Fine. But I'm only doing this for Nathan."

She shot Mia a glare sharp enough to draw blood. "And if you screw us over—even once—I'll make sure you regret it."

Mia didn't flinch. "I won't. And honestly? You don't have to trust me. I'm not here to win you over or make you like me. I just want Val out of the picture—gone, for good. You can believe me or not, but at the end of the day, we both want the same thing."

Eve studied her, looking for cracks in her confidence, but all she saw was exhaustion.

"Eve, before we go any further," Gabe said carefully, his tone more measured than usual, "there's something else you need to know."

Eve frowned, arms crossing again, more reflex than conviction. "Yeah? What's that?"

Gabe glanced at Mia, then at Nathan, his expression unusually serious. "There are three people in this room with tech in their heads."

Nathan took a deep breath, ready to speak, but Gabe held up a hand.

Eve blinked. "What do you mean three?"

A silence fell over the room, but it wasn't the kind that passed. When the realization hit, it didn't feel like shock. It felt like betrayal.

She turned to Gabe, her voice thin. "Wait… you too?"

Gabe froze, all the usual confidence slipping away. For a second, he looked exposed, like every wall he'd ever built had cracked wide open. When he finally spoke, his voice was softer than usual, like it cost him something to say it.

"Yeah… me too."

Eve stepped back, her breath catching as the air around her seemed to tighten. "You… you're not like them. You don't—" The words snagged in her throat.

"You knew how I felt about this. You knew, and you still—" Her voice cracked as she shook her head. "You lied to me."

"I didn't lie, Eve," Gabe said, his voice quiet but firm. "I just didn't tell you. There's a difference."

Eve let out a dry laugh, shaking her head. "Seriously, Kowalski? Don't start with semantics. You knew how I felt about people with implants. And you just conveniently forgot to mention that you're one of them?"

Gabe's usual charm was gone. "Look, Eve, you have every right to be pissed at me. I get it. I know how you feel about us. That's why I didn't say anything." His voice dropped lower. "But you need to know—inside, it's just me. I'm still Gabe. I always have been."

He gave a small, half-hearted shake of his belly. "I'm not boosting my looks to get your attention. I mean, seriously… look at me."

For a split second, something shifted in Eve's expression. It was caught somewhere between annoyed and something slightly amused. But as soon as it came, it vanished.

"I wanted to tell you, I swear, but I didn't want you to judge me for having an implant. I wanted you to see me for who I really am first. I wanted you to see the real me." He glanced at Mia, then back at Eve. "That's all any of us want."

Eve's eyes followed his, landing on Mia. Her eyes narrowed. "Us?"

Mia pushed herself up from her seat, stepping forward. "Yeah. Us." Her voice didn't waver. "You think having a chip means we're all lazy or fake, like we skipped some essential struggle to get here. But that's not what this is. That's not who we are, at least not all of us."

She nodded toward Gabe. "We both use our chips out of necessity, not vanity. Neither of us is trying to live forever or become invincible. We're just trying to survive."

Eve stayed quiet, letting the tension in her shoulders soften just a fraction.

"And yeah," Mia continued, pressing forward, "I know Val and her crowd make everything about us look bad. Honestly, they make me sick, too. All we're asking is that you don't lump us into the same category as them. We're not like them."

Silence pressed in around them. Nathan, sitting quietly in the front row, felt the shift— felt the moment teetering on the brink of something inevitable.

Eve finally let out a long breath, rubbing her temples before sinking onto the edge of the stage. "Fine," she muttered. "Maybe I jumped to conclusions. But I still don't like this. I don't like any of it."

"I know you don't, and I am sorry that I hid this from you," Gabe replied, his voice lighter but still serious. "I'm not asking you to like it. I just want you to understand it."

Eve looked up at him with something unreadable in her expression. Then, with a sharp glance at Mia, she added, "But I still don't trust her."

Mia let out a short, humorless laugh. "That's fine. I don't trust you either, but we both want the same thing: to stop Val."

Eve scowled, not fully convinced but too tired to keep arguing. "I can live with that—for now. But if we're doing this, then let's stop guessing. What does she want with Nathan?"

"I can answer that for you," a voice said calmly from the shadows behind the upper row of seats.

The group turned toward the top of the theater, and Simon Wu stepped into the dim light, his presence sharp and commanding.

And just behind him, leaning casually against the doorway, was Dante.

Nathan's heart pounded. The room had been heavy with tension moments ago, but now it crackled with something new.

Something worse.

34

PUZZLE PEACE

Simon Wu stood in the aisle between the rows of old seats in the abandoned movie theater beneath Winston Hall. The concrete behind him was cold, but it didn't register—not with his mind moving as fast as it was.

Leadership had never been his thing, not in the way it came naturally to people like Val or Dante. But that didn't matter anymore. The only thing that mattered was making sure the damage he helped cause didn't get any worse.

His mind drifted back to the spring of 2023. That was the turning point in his life. Not a moment of triumph. Not some revelation. Just rock bottom.

He'd failed out of not one, but two four-year universities by the time he was twenty. Incomplete assignments, a GPA so low it might as well have been a straight-up rejection letter from the world. A 2.8 grade point average—that's what he'd graduated high school with. Barely enough to get into his first school. His parents had been quietly disappointed, but they didn't push. He always felt they didn't expect much from him, which stung more than outright anger ever could.

It wasn't that he wasn't smart—he was. But dyslexia twisted words into a scramble. While ADHD turned lectures into white noise, and OCD trapped him in loops, burning through time and energy. School was a battlefield, and he was always outgunned.

But give him a puzzle—a physical, tangible problem to solve—and Simon's brain lit up. Jigsaw puzzles, LEGO sets, anything that required spatial reasoning and focus, he excelled at. He'd lose hours finding the edges, locking together the border piece by piece, his concentration razor-sharp. Then he'd move to the interior, filling in the details with precision that felt almost instinctual.

And in those moments, he discovered something: he wasn't broken. His brain didn't work the way schools expected it to, but it worked in a way that mattered. His ability to see the bigger picture, to break complex problems into smaller, manageable pieces, was something tests couldn't measure.

But being good at puzzles and building intricate LEGO creations didn't get him passing grades. And it definitely didn't keep him in college. After failing out of his second university, he transferred to community college. He felt defeated but he wasn't going to give up on himself. He knew he wasn't stupid, no matter what his GPA said. He just needed to figure out a way to bridge the gap between how he thought and how the world expected him to function.

It was during a late-night library session at the community college, surrounded by textbooks he could barely comprehend, that he stumbled upon an article about the R&D department at NCSU. They were conducting cutting-edge research in cognitive enhancements and brain-computer interfaces. He clicked the link, skimmed the abstract, and felt something crack open inside him.

This is it. The thought hit with such clarity that it almost scared him.

If Simon couldn't succeed the way the world wanted him to, maybe he could rebuild himself.

From that moment on, he worked harder than he ever had before. Days blurred into nights as he hit the books with a fury that he had never had before. He wasn't naturally gifted in academics, but sheer grit carried him through, and his grades improved enough to transfer to NCSU. When he arrived, he wasted no time securing a spot as a "research participant" in the university's MIND chip development program.

It wasn't glamorous. He had essentially volunteered to be a lab rat. The research team tested early-stage cognitive enhancements on him, tweaking the technology, observing how it integrated with his brain. The tests were grueling, and sometimes painful, but he convinced himself to stick it out.

And for the first time in his life, the pieces started to click.

The MIND chip didn't just help him overcome his learning disabilities —it amplified him. His focus sharpened. His ability to visualize and solve complex spatial problems became otherworldly. He wasn't just good with puzzles anymore; he could see solutions before others even recognized there was a problem.

That's when Val found him.

Not long after he'd joined the program, she swooped in and plucked him out of obscurity, pulling him into her orbit. At first, Val was sweet, and he felt like he'd made a real connection, maybe even a friend.

She had opened up to him in a way he hadn't expected. She shared her reasons for having a chip, her belief that humanity's future was tied to technology. The way she spoke about progress and purpose was intoxicating. It made him feel like he was part of something bigger.

She didn't care that he was broken. She cared that he was moldable.

For a while, it felt like they were partners. It felt like they were equals.

But looking back now, He could see it for what it truly was.

Val wasn't sweet—she was strategic. Every moment they spent together, every late night in the lab, every laugh, and every kind word had all been part of a larger plan. She'd been using him, and he hadn't even realized it.

It wasn't until they were deep into their experiments that he started to see the cracks. They weren't just working on the university's research. She had been slipping her code into the trials. Not just into the system— into him.

At the time, he hadn't questioned it. He trusted her. And when she talked about unlocking the chip's full potential, about pushing past the limits that the school had set, it sounded exciting. Like they were on the verge of something groundbreaking.

But there was always one missing element, one final piece.

And Wu, for all his brilliance and newfound abilities, wasn't stupid. He started to see the signs. He started to put the puzzle together. Val didn't want progress for humanity. She wanted control.

He could've been her perfect pawn, and for a while, he was. But not anymore.

What happened back at The Lighthouse— it hadn't even been that long ago. Minutes, not hours. But it changed everything. He'd seen it—*felt* it. When Nathan reached out, when they connected, something shifted deep in Wu's neural map. Not code. Not data. Something he didn't have language for.

Val had pushed Wu hard to make sure Nathan was on the network the moment he arrived. She hadn't made it optional. She'd threatened to rip Wu's chip out, tearing it from his skull like it was nothing, like it hadn't rewired every part of him. She called it a surgical execution. He knew how brutally painful something like that would be, but the pain wasn't what scared him. It was what came after. It was the blur—The fog—The loss of everything the chip had given him—his clarity, his control, his ability to finally function in a world that never made sense before. Without it, he wasn't just afraid of being broken again. He was afraid of not being at all.

He'd tried to push back. He told her she had the wrong guy, that Nathan was just some nervous kid who looked like he was trying to find his way at college. She didn't care. She didn't want excuses. She wanted results.

So he did what he was told. At least, he tried.

When Gabe told him he'd tossed the card down the alley, Wu didn't even hesitate. He waded through a sea of trash and shadows, half-expecting to step on a used syringe or get mugged by rodents. At one point, he was *pretty sure* he saw two rats sizing each other up like it was West Side Story with switchblades. Still, he found the card and raced it back into the club like his life depended on it, because it did.

When he placed the activated card into Nathan's hand, he was still half-convinced it would do nothing, but he saw it happen. He felt it sync in his bones. Then came the pull. The shift. Nathan didn't just join the network—he was the network.

All this time, Wu had thought he was part of a failed experiment. A spare piece in a puzzle no one cared about solving. But now he knew better. It wasn't theoretical anymore. Val hadn't been chasing a ghost. She'd been right the entire time—Nathan was real. He was the missing piece she had been searching for.

Wu didn't think he was strong enough or smart enough to save the day. He wasn't a hero. But he'd helped get Val this far. He brought her to the edge of what she wanted, and if he stayed silent, she would win. He couldn't let that happen.

Shaking himself out of the memory, Wu stepped into the dim light of the old theater and slid his calm, measured demeanor into place like a mask.

Dante lounged casually in the doorway behind him, exuding the kind of smug confidence that Wu had never trusted. Dante wasn't worried. He never was.

Wu's attention locked onto Nathan, studying him like a puzzle he didn't quite know how to solve. He wasn't here to save the day. He was here to stop a mistake he helped create.

"Nathan Boone," Wu said, his voice slicing through the tension.

"We need to talk."

35

MY SO-CALLED ENEMY

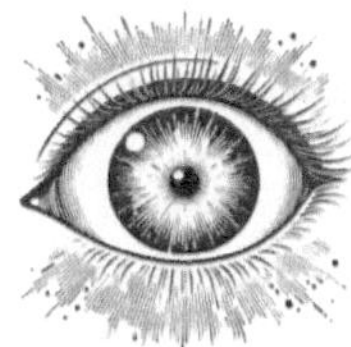

Everyone watched as Wu and Dante stepped into the light, their figures sharp against the dim glow of the theater. They moved with quiet purpose, closing the space between them and the group.

Wu's expression was impossible to pin down. He looked calm, maybe even a little sympathetic—but there was something colder just beneath it. Something that said this wasn't a social call. And that alone had warning bells going off in Nathan's head. His whole body tensed, like it already knew something was about to go wrong.

"This has all gotten out of control," Wu said, his voice quiet as they made their way down the aisle. "I shouldn't have let it get this far."

He paused and met Nathan's eyes. "It's time that you learn the truth. It's time to put all this madness to an end."

But Nathan barely heard a word.

His world had shrunk to a single point.

Dante.

Still standing there like the whole thing was a waste of his time.

Like he had somewhere better to be.

Like he was stuck in the world's most tedious conversation and he was just waiting for it to end.

He was too cool. Too calm. Too checked out to notice—or care.

Like he wasn't the reason Nathan had spent years afraid to walk into a room.

His relaxed attitude was enough to send Nathan into free fall.

It hit fast—a flash in his chest, hot and blinding, burning through him like wildfire, without warning or build-up. Just heat, pressure, and the sharp edge of everything he'd held back for years. There was no containing it now. It was already too much.

He moved before he even realized it. His feet pounded against the cement floor as he sprinted up the aisle toward Dante. Each step was fueled by every insult, every shove, every time he was made to feel small.

Dante just stood there. Clearly confused, as the kid who'd let him cut the deli line a few days earlier came sprinting toward him, like they had unfinished business in a movie he didn't know he'd been cast in as the villain.

Before he could wrap his head around what was happening, Nathan was already on him, slamming both hands into his chest and shoving him back with everything he had.

Dante stumbled slightly, causing his sneakers to scrape against the worn concrete, making a sound that echoed through the theater.

Nathan stood over him as he shook off the impact and started to get to his feet.

"Tell me that you remember." His voice cracked under the weight of his emotions—rage, hurt, frustration, they were all there.

"I know you do. You remember everything. Every shove. Every name. Every time you made me feel like I didn't matter."

His chest heaved, and his breath came in short, ragged bursts. Years of silence were crashing to the surface all at once, too loud to hold back.

"Say it," he demanded, stepping closer.

"Say it, Dante. *Tell me you know what you did.*"

The room froze.

Dante caught his balance and exhaled. He didn't shove back. He didn't flinch. He just stood there, like nothing had ever happened between them.

That made Nathan even angrier.

"No, you don't get to act like this is normal," Nathan spat, his cracked voice echoing through the abandoned theater. His fists were clenched at his sides, and the tension inside him coiled tighter with every breath.

"You know exactly what you did to me!" Nathan exclaimed, his voice sharp with raw emotion.

Dante's expression gave nothing away. His posture was loose, his voice flat.

"Dude, I have no idea what you're talking about."

He looked at Nathan like he was a perfect stranger.

"I don't even know you, man."

The way Dante stood there, looking down at him like he was nothing —like he had never been anything—made Nathan's rage burn hotter than he ever thought possible.

His fists trembled, his vision blurred at the edges, and his pulse thundered in his skull.

"You don't know me?" he seethed, his voice thick with fury.

"Let me remind you."

His voice dropped, his tone cutting like glass.

"Baboone."

For a split second, something cracked in Dante's expression. It might have been recognition, maybe even regret, maybe it was a little of both, but as quickly as it came, it vanished.

But Nathan had already seen it, and that was all it took to make the blaze of fury in his chest rage even hotter.

"You fucking tortured me!" Nathan growled, stepping closer, his entire body tense with the weight of everything he had carried for years.

"You made my life a living hell, and now you want to stand there and act like I never even existed?"

The words scraped out of him as something inside gave way. It wasn't loud or dramatic—just quiet and final. Like something deep inside him that he had been holding on to for years, had finally let go.

It wasn't just rage anymore. It was heartbreak tangled with exhaustion, the kind that settles into your bones and never quite leaves. And now, all of it was breaking loose, pouring out in a way he couldn't stop.

"How could you not remember?" he asked, the words thick with disbelief—his voice rising again as the fury surged back, hot and alive, refusing to stay buried.

Dante didn't say anything. He just stared down at Nathan, his enhanced eyes flickering with gold. There was no recognition on his face. Only annoyance, the kind that made it obvious he was already over the whole thing.

It was clear he had no idea what Nathan was talking about.

And somehow, for Nathan, that made everything worse.

He needed him to remember.

He needed Dante to understand exactly what he had done to him.

Every cruel word. Every shove. Every humiliation.

None of it had been harmless, and none of it had faded with time.

It was real. And it had stayed with Nathan—every moment carved deep, like scars no one else could see.

He refused to let Dante ignore the past any longer.

He refused to let Dante ignore *him*.

If words—those carefully chosen ones he'd spent a lifetime learning to write when speaking felt impossible—couldn't get through, then fine.

He was done asking questions.

He was going to make Dante remember exactly who he was.

He balled his fist, drew in a sharp breath, and without a second of hesitation, he swung.

His fist connected with Dante's chin—clean, solid, and harder than he expected.

The impact jolted up Nathan's arm like an electric shock. He had poured *everything* he had into that punch—all the years of humiliation, the rage he hadn't even known was there until a few days before, and every pathetic late-night revenge fantasy he'd ever played in his head—only to feel like he'd just punched a steak nailed to a chimney.

But Dante didn't even blink. He just absorbed the hit like it was nothing.

Like *Nathan* was nothing.

His hand throbbed like he'd shattered every bone in it—and maybe he had—but he didn't care. The adrenaline roaring through him steamrolled right over the pain. He drew back again and prepared to swing one more time with whatever he had left.

"Nathan, stop!" Eve's voice rang out from behind him, sharp with urgency.

But he didn't stop. He couldn't.

He threw one last, desperate punch—but this time, Dante was ready.

His hand shot up and caught the fist that was flying toward him in mid-air. It was the same move Nathan had imagined himself doing to Dante just yesterday, out in the courtyard. Only now, it was reversed.

Dante's fingers closed around Nathan's balled-up hand with crushing strength, locking them in place. The grip was so tight it felt like the air itself had been squeezed out from between them.

Their eyes locked, both of them frozen in a moment that seemed to stretch indefinitely.

A white-hot and electric current surged between them. Nathan's rage and Dante's detachment didn't cancel each other out. They created something else—something neither of them understood—something powerful.

Nathan's muscles locked, and his breath heaved as he stared directly into Dante's golden, enhanced eyes as they faded and shifted back to their natural caramel color.

He stared in disbelief as the tension drained from Dante's face, and the arrogance he'd known all too well vanished. His eyes—usually cold and unreadable—were suddenly wide, glassy, and filled with something Nathan had never seen before.

It was fear—deep, pure, and primal. And along with it, a spark of recognition, like a long-buried memory was forcing its way to the surface.

His mind raced, searching for answers, but nothing made sense. Beneath the pain in his clenched fist, beneath the iron hold Dante had on him, he felt something else.

He felt a pull.

Dante shuddered. His grip loosened, but not in retreat.

He wasn't pushing Nathan away anymore. He was holding on, as if he were afraid to let go.

Nathan wanted to yank his hand back, to break whatever was happening—but he couldn't.

He was locked in, connected to Dante in a way that sent alarms blaring through his body. Every instinct inside him screamed that something was wrong, and yet—it wasn't.

Beneath the shock and the rage, something unexpected stirred within Nathan—an emotion he couldn't quite place. A sense of relief, as if some unspoken weight had shifted. A connection, intangible yet undeniable, had begun to take shape.

Emotions surged through him. Anger and confusion tangled with something dangerously close to forgiveness. The energy between them intensified, crackling in the narrow space that separated them. It pulled at him, building toward a kind of understanding he hadn't expected and wasn't sure he wanted.

The others stood frozen, their expressions locked in disbelief.

Then, suddenly, Eve snapped into motion.

"No—that's enough!" Her voice rang out as she rushed toward them, desperate to break the unnatural connection, but before she could reach them, Wu shot his arm out to catch her.

She twisted against his grip, trying to wiggle free, her voice rising.

"Get your hands off me, you goon!" she snapped, pounding her fists against his chest.

Wu remained unfazed, his expression eerily calm. "Let it happen," he said simply, his voice like steel. "This needs to happen."

"Wu, please," Mia's voice sliced through the chaos, desperate and pleading. "You have to stop this. Can't you do something?"

Gabe, who had stood motionless, stunned by what was unfolding, suddenly sprang into action, his hesitation evaporating as urgency took over. He moved with purpose, his resolve hardening as he made his way toward Wu.

"Let her go," Gabe said, his voice carrying an authority that made it clear he wasn't asking.

Wu hesitated, just for a second, before releasing Eve.

She stumbled back, her wild eyes darting between Gabe and Wu before landing on Nathan.

The air in the room was charged, vibrating with an almost unbearable energy.

And then, all at once, it reached its crescendo.

Nathan and Dante—still locked in place—erupted in a final, blinding surge of electricity as the current between them exploded. It surged through a spectrum of neon, flashing from red to orange, then yellow, cascading into green before bleeding into blue, violet, and finally bursting into electric pink, pulsing like it was alive.

And then, just as the vibrant energy threatened to consume everything, it collapsed in on itself, causing the neon brilliance to vanish like a supernova fading into the void, leaving behind nothing but a thick, suffocating silence.

Nathan stumbled back first, catching himself on the armrest of one of the old theater seats, gripping it like a lifeline.

Dante didn't move. His eyes gave a single sharp flick, like something inside him had shorted out before coming back online. The color shifted, slowly this time, stabilizing back into the rich, unnatural gold he always chose for himself, signaling that his chip had come back online.

"What the fuck was that?" Eve's voice shattered the silence.

Nathan's head snapped up, locking onto Dante. His pulse pounded in his ears.

"You—" He swallowed hard. "What the hell did you just do to me?"

Dante exhaled sharply, dragging a shaking hand over his face. "I didn't do anything to you, man."

His voice was uneven. "Whatever just happened? You did that—*to me.*"

Nathan shook his head. No. That didn't make any sense. "How could I—"

"He's right," Wu said, his voice calm but with an edge. "Dante had nothing to do with it. That was all you, Nathan."

He tilted his head slightly, eyes narrowing in thought. He looked at Nathan like he was a puzzle—one he hadn't quite solved yet, but the pieces were finally starting to fall into place.

Eve's eyes blazed with frustration as she took a sharp breath, barely holding back the full force of her anger.

"Can you all please stop being so goddamn cryptic and just tell us what the fuck is going on?" she demanded, her fists clenched, ready to swing if necessary.

Gabe moved quickly, catching her by the shoulders before she could get any closer. His grip tightened slightly as a hint of concern broke through his usual calm. "Alright, everybody needs to just chill for a second," he said, his voice firm but calm, though a note of worry edged in around the command.

Mia stepped toward Nathan, placing a cautious hand on his arm. "Are you okay?"

Nathan forced himself to breathe, but every inhale felt unsteady, his body still buzzing from whatever had just happened. His skin tingled, and his pulse was a chaotic rhythm against his ribs as the weight of the moment pressed down on him.

He searched for an explanation, but nothing made sense.

"I don't know," he admitted. His voice was quieter now, but his eyes stayed locked on Dante.

For the first time, Dante looked back at Nathan like he knew him. Not just in the way someone recognizes a face, but in the way someone remembers what they did to break it. He looked like he felt every taunt, every shove, every moment that had chipped away at Nathan piece by piece, and for the first time, he looked like he regretted it.

Wu let out a slow breath, crossing his arms. "Well," he said, almost amused, "I guess that settles that."

"Settles what?" Eve snapped. Her patience had evaporated.

Wu's eyes narrowed. "Nathan Boone is the one. He's the link Val's been chasing since the beginning. I had a feeling that he was back at The

Lighthouse, but after what just went down… I don't doubt it anymore. He's the reason we're all here."

"What the hell are you even talking about?" Nathan shouted, his voice cracking with frustration.

"Until an hour ago, I'd only dreamed of being implanted. Now you're telling me that not only do I have a chip, but it's—what? Some kind of supercharged version?"

He shook his head. "That doesn't make any sense. I've spent my entire life in and out of hospitals, trying to figure out what's wrong with me. Why would that happen if I had a chip this whole time?"

Wu shrugged. "That, I don't know, but I do know that whatever it is you *do* have? Val wants it—and she won't stop until she has it."

Mia stepped forward. Her voice was softer this time, but just as serious. "It's true, Nathan. Wu's right." She took a deep breath. "She's been watching you since you got here."

She glanced at Wu, then at Dante. "She's been using all of us to get close to you."

Dante exhaled and rubbed his jaw. "It's true. We've all just been pawns in her dangerous game. She's had us doing all kinds of shit for her, running errands, recruiting new students, helping her expand her reach, it's been exhausting. I think for some reason, she knew you were coming."

He looked at Nathan. "She's been waiting for you."

Nathan scoffed. "What do you mean—waiting for me? I've spent my whole life as the screwed-up kid no one cared about—unless they were giving me shit."

He shot daggers at Dante.

"And now you're telling me I've got some kind of secret power—what, like a hidden chip or something?"

"Well… kinda," Mia said hesitantly.

Nathan turned to her, his eyes searching. "What does she even want from me?"

Mia hesitated again, like she was still trying to piece it all together. "I never gave her enough time to fully bring me in. I didn't even know I was part of this until yesterday. Honestly, it's been a lot to handle. I thought I was just coming here for the hybrid medicine track—something cutting-edge, something that could change everything. But Val—" she exhaled sharply, shaking her head. "I'm pretty sure she pulled all the strings to get me into the program."

She let out an empty laugh. "Honestly? When I applied, it felt like a long shot. I mean, I have the grades, but my lab work? It's not exactly groundbreaking. When I got accepted, I was shocked. I thought maybe I got lucky. That someone saw potential in me that I didn't even see in myself."

She swallowed hard. "But now I know why I'm here."

Her eyes shot to Dante, then Wu. "I realize it now—Val worked the system. She pulled all the strings and got me placed in that apartment—with her, surrounded by her people. She's powerful like that."

Wu nodded, his expression darkening. "That's how she works. She doesn't just bend the rules—she breaks them and rewrites them to get whatever she wants."

"I knew something wasn't right," Mia said. "It started the night after I met you, after your panic attack in the cafeteria. She pulled me aside and started grilling me. She told me that I needed to get close to you. She wanted me to earn your trust. She demanded that I find out everything about you—your schedule, your past, your weaknesses, even your fears. She actually wanted me to give her notes after every conversation. And she made it clear—I wasn't supposed to leave anything out."

She looked down. "She cornered me, over and over again, like she thought if she kept pushing hard enough, I'd eventually give in. She acted like I owed her something. Like I was her project to control."

Dante let out a dry, humorless chuckle. "Yeah, that sounds like Val, alright. She's a real bitch when she wants to be, which is pretty much all the time."

Mia exhaled sharply. "But I wasn't about to cave. I made it very clear—I had no interest in playing her game."

Wu shook his head, "I can't imagine that went well."

"Not really, she completely lost it," Mia answered. "She didn't just get angry, she got vindictive. She wanted to cut me down and make me feel like I didn't matter. She said she could make my scholarship disappear. Told me I was a mistake, that I didn't belong here. And if I didn't fall in line—if I didn't do exactly what she asked—she promised she'd make sure I was gone."

"And what did you say?" Nathan asked, his voice quiet but insistent.

Mia lifted her chin with pride. "I looked her right in the eye and told her no, thank you—politely, of course."

He raised an eyebrow. "Just like that?"

She let out a chuckle. "Well… not exactly like that. I might've used more colorful language, but I think you all get the point." She smiled with a hint of pride. "I learned a long time ago that if I don't speak up for myself, no one else will. So, I told her, in the sweetest voice possible, exactly where she could stick her plans for me."

"I'm sure she loved that," Wu scoffed.

"I have no idea," Mia admitted with a shrug. "I didn't stick around long enough to find out. I just went to my room and shut the door." She exhaled as if she could still feel the tension of that night pressing against her. "The next morning, I woke up to a text. An apology—or at least, something that looked like one. She promised to drive me to campus, and I actually thought, Wow, maybe she's not completely awful."

Nathan frowned. "And?"

Mia rolled her eyes. "And then she completely ghosted me, vanished to do whatever it is she does—probably plotting world domination while blasting that awful nu-metal music that she loves."

"Classic Val," Wu said, shaking his head. "She's got manipulation down to an art form."

Then his expression shifted as he approached Nathan.

"I need you to listen to me," he said, his voice steady.

Nathan turned to him, wary. For the first time, Wu's sharp, calculating edge softened—just enough to feel almost human.

"I know that this is a lot to take in," Wu said. "But the truth is, Val has something on all of us." He glanced at Eve, and his tone went flat. "Well... most of us."

Eve shot him a look that could've cut glass, but she didn't say a word.

He exhaled sharply. "If there's one thing I know, it's this—she's not going to stop until she gets what she wants." His voice was steady, but the weight behind it pressed into Nathan like a vice.

Nathan's mind raced. He knew it now—there was no more doubting it. The way Dante reacted, the energy that surged between them, the way his body had responded to something buried inside him wasn't normal, but it was clear now. He had a chip, and he must have had it for years without ever knowing about it.

He finally had something he'd always dreamed of having, and now he was afraid that instead of saving him, it would end him.

Wu studied him, his expression unreadable, before continuing. "The MIND Chip's original design had capabilities most people never knew about. The earliest versions weren't just prototypes—they were limitless. Officially, they were never implanted in anyone, but some people believe a few of them made it out, and a few might even be hidden inside everyday people just waiting to be activated. The rumor is that if their full potential were ever discovered, it would change everything. Maybe even rewrite the future as we know it."

Nathan's pulse pounded. "So, what? She thinks I have one of these prototype versions or something? That I'm sitting on some kind of lost technology?"

Wu let out a slow breath. "You're not just sitting on it. Val's already started unlocking it, and after what just happened with Dante, I think she's right."

"Oh god," Eve groaned, rubbing her temples like she was physically pained by the conversation. Everyone turned toward her, but she didn't wait for a response. She threw her hands in the air, her frustration spilling over in waves.

"This is exactly why I can't stand you people," she snapped. "All the cryptic nonsense, the conspiracy theories, the secret tech, and hidden powers, and whatever network garbage you're all whispering about—I swear, you all sound completely insane."

She turned to Nathan, her eyes blazing with frustration. "Come on, Boone. We're out of here."

Nathan blinked, caught between the weight of everything he'd just heard and the very real concern on his friend's face.

She reached for his arm, tugging him gently. "You may have a chip in your head, but you're still my best friend. I'm not going to just stand here and listen to any more bullshit about how you have the secret meaning to a blissful tech-filled life locked deep in your brain."

Her voice cracked slightly, but she pushed forward. "None of this is true. You are just Nathan Boone. You're just an anxious writer who's gotten himself wrapped up in some nonsense in his first week of college."

Gabe flinched but recovered quickly. "Eve, don't say that," he pleaded. "I don't know what's going on either, but I've never seen anything like what just happened."

"Oh, please," Eve scoffed, spinning toward him. "That parlor trick? Dante totally did that. If you can't see that, then you are completely blind. There is no way in hell that Nathan has a chip. This is all just a poorly executed recruiting stunt by Val and her minions."

She glared at Wu and Dante, then turned to Gabe—her face twisting like his betrayal was the only honest thing he'd ever given her.

"And you…" Her voice dripped with something bitter, something wounded. "You're the worst of them all."

Gabe took a small step back, his usual confidence cracking. "Eve—"

"To think I liked you," she pressed, her words shaking with emotion. "And this whole time—"

She let out a sarcastic laugh and shook her head. Then, almost to herself, almost in disbelief, she whispered, "Oh God! — I can't believe it— I hooked up with a chip-head."

Gabe's face fell.

"And a lying chip-head, at that," she spat.

No one spoke.

Eve turned away, dropping her head into her hands like she couldn't bear to look at him.

Gabe didn't move. He stood there in silence, wrecked in a way he couldn't hide.

She stomped forward, her boots hitting the worn theater floor with angry steps. She grabbed Nathan's arm, looping hers around his in a firm, almost desperate grip.

"Let's go, Nathan," she said, her voice shaking with frustration.

"Let's get out of here before they try to pull another stunt in a weak attempt to corrupt you."

He couldn't move. His whole body locked up. Every muscle was stretched tight and ready to snap. The phantom static from his connection with Dante still buzzed in his fingertips, crawling up his arms, humming just beneath his skin like a live wire left exposed.

"No, Eve," he said, his voice steadier than he expected. "I think it's all true. I felt it. I think that I've always felt it, I just didn't know what *it* was until now."

He turned and locked his eyes on hers, hoping she could see what he was trying to say. "Wu's right. It wasn't Dante—it was me. I need to figure out what's in my head. I need to know what it can do."

Eve's grip loosened. She blinked fast, like she was trying to keep herself from falling apart, but the cracks were already showing.

"That's just great," she whispered, her voice breaking as she let go of him completely, before stepping back as tears welled up and spilled down her face.

"I can't stand here anymore and watch you fall for this bullshit," she choked out, her voice cracking with rage and heartbreak. "I can't go through this—*not again.*"

She shook her head, laughing bitterly through the tears. "You're all so damn desperate to belong to something. To be perfect. To matter in some big, shiny way. Well, I've got news for you—none of you are perfect. Not even close."

And before anyone could stop her—before Nathan could even begin to find the words—she turned and stormed out.

36

THE DISTRACTION

The first sign of the reboot came as a quiet ripple through the system that barely registered at first. Then it struck—an unseen pulse rolled through everybody in the theater, everybody except Nathan.

Mia felt it immediately when a sudden jolt raced up her spine. It wasn't painful, but it carried a wrongness that set her nerves on edge, like the air before a blackout, the moment just before everything goes silent. She gripped the armrest of the chair next to her to steady herself.

"Alright, everybody—" Gabe's voice was low, uncertain. "What the hell was that?"

Wu's expression darkened. "That was a shutdown alert. It sounds like the network has had enough of the black market."

"Oh my god, Wu, that felt like a total reboot warning, right?" Mia asked.

Wu nodded. "Yeah. It's happening."

Gabe threw his hands up. "Oh, great. Of all the times this could happen, it has to be now. Well, that's just fantastic."

Nathan sat back in his seat a few rows up, listening. His hands rested uselessly in his lap, his shoulders hunched as if to make himself invisible. Everyone else seemed to know what was going on. They moved with urgency and spoke in code, and he was stuck in the back, tuning into a conversation that didn't belong to him. He wasn't part of this world—he never had been. They spoke in quick, tense bursts, clearly used to whatever was coming next. He was the only one in the room who had no idea what was happening, but he knew one thing—they were scared.

Mia turned to the others. "Listen, I need you to understand something. A shutdown alert is rare. I mean, really rare. It's when the network or whoever runs it decides it's time for a purge."

"A purge of what?" Gabe asked, his usual confidence shaken.

"Of everything," Mia said. "Or at least, everything they think is slowing it down. You know, open-source apps, experimental mods, rogue code— anything clogging the system. If the network's too bloated, it purges the junk to keep running smoothly." She swallowed. "I've been through this a few times, and trust me, it's not fun."

The air in the theater felt heavier, the space shrinking. Nathan's pulse picked up. They were caught in their own world, distracted, wrapped up in something they understood, but he didn't.

Wu cut in, his voice sharp with urgency.

"It's true. I've studied this for Val. And for myself. Here's what I know." He paused to gather his thoughts. "Mia's right. Sometimes the network picks up things that shouldn't be there—corrupt code, bad apps. So it dumps them."

Mia took a breath. "How long do we have?"

Wu's expression was unreadable. "It's hard to say. It could be hours, could be minutes. That was just a warning pulse. The network is basically telling us to shelter in place until it's done cleaning up the network."

Gabe exhaled and dragged a hand down his face. "Great. Love that for us. Nothing says 'everything's fine' like a surprise full-body factory reset."

The room felt smaller now, the old theater seats pressing in, the low hum of the hidden space suddenly too loud.

Nathan stared at the exit, unblinking, his vision locked onto the lingering emptiness. The echo of Eve's sharp words played over and over in his head. He hadn't stopped her from leaving. He should have said something, anything, to make her stay.

Was she right? Was this some elaborate stunt? Were they really trying to recruit him?

The more he thought about it, the more uneasy he felt. None of them had been honest with him. Not really.

Gabe had been nothing but a great friend since he'd arrived, but he wasn't totally open about having a chip until he was caught.

And Mia had been sweet to him from the moment he first saw her— had that been an act too? She admitted that Val wanted her to go after him, and maybe she'd turned that down—but somehow, she always seemed to be exactly where he was.

He thought about all the random run-ins, how she always appeared right when he least expected it, small moments that had felt like fate at the time. Like maybe the world was finally giving him something good.

She had a way of putting him at ease. She made things feel lighter. Safer. Like he could finally breathe, even when everything else was falling apart.

But looking back, it all felt too convenient—like the universe hadn't shifted on its own—it had been nudged.

It wasn't comforting anymore. It was suspicious—too much to ignore.

Would someone with a motive like hers really tell him the truth? Or had she only revealed just enough to make him trust her?

And then there was Dante.

Nathan looked down the rows of empty seats at him. He should have felt something—rage, hatred, even fear. Instead, there was only calm. No anger. No anxiety. No crushing pressure in his chest.

Something between them had shifted. And as he studied him, he wasn't sure which one of them caused the change. The longer he looked at him, the more he wondered—had Dante unlocked something in him, or was it the other way around?

One thing was clear: he couldn't stand in this dingy theater with these people any longer. The regret he had for not leaving with Eve gnawed at him.

She had been with him through every challenge he'd faced since elementary school, every low point, every moment he thought he wouldn't make it through. And now, as she was once again trying to help him, he had pushed her away.

From his seat high up in the theater, Nathan watched the group below as they were locked in a heated conversation. They were all too focused on each other to notice him. *Were they planning something? Were they talking about him?* He wasn't sure who to trust anymore.

"I have to go after her," Nathan whispered to himself.

He edged back into the rows of empty seats, keeping his movements controlled. They were all absorbed in the moment. They weren't looking at him. They weren't even thinking about him.

He took a step—quietly—then another, careful not to draw attention, before slipping toward the exit. His fingers gently grasped the door handle, and slowly, he pulled it open just enough to step through, easing it shut behind him like even the smallest sound might shatter what was left.

As he slipped out, the theater lights flickered once, then cut out completely, plunging the room into a thick, breathless darkness. The only sound was the low, uneven hum of the electrical system trying to steady itself. The soft click of the door behind him was barely audible, lost beneath the weight of it all—like the room had swallowed it whole.

Dante let out a sharp breath. The kind of breath that comes not from shock, but from realization. They were in it now—whatever *it* was.

The group stood frozen as the darkness cut through whatever false confidence they'd been clinging to. There were no more jokes to fill the silence. No more quick one-liners or eye-rolls to break the tension. Nothing to distract them from how real it all suddenly felt. Just that quiet, creeping kind of fear that settled over everything like the blackout had weight.

"Perfect," Dante muttered. "Because what this night really needed was pitch-black silence and full horror movie energy." He tried to play it off with sarcasm, but the strain in his voice was a dead giveaway.

The group stood in silence, shrouded in the dark. Then, with a stuttering pulse, the lights surged back to life, bleaching their faces in a cold, artificial glow. Gabe and Dante exchanged a look before turning to Wu, an unspoken plea for an explanation.

Wu exhaled. "Relax, it's probably just a power surge from the campus subnet," he said smugly. "I bet a bunch of students think hopping offline will help. They're all scrambling to save anything they can before the system restarts. It won't do anything."

"Well, that's super reassuring," Gabe muttered sarcastically. "But that still doesn't answer the question—what do we do?"

Dante's expression darkened. "It doesn't sound like there is anything we can do. I guess we just have to wait it out."

Gabe threw up his hands, frustration bleeding into his voice. "How can you be so calm about this?"

Dante turned to him. "They warned us about this in training camp. Remember?"

Gabe blinked. "Wait—you remember that? You remember me?"

Dante met his eyes, steady, real in a way he hadn't been all night. "Yeah, man. I remember." He exhaled sharply. "I remember everything."

A weight pressed down on Gabe's chest as a rush of old memories—good times, bad times, and everything in between all came flooding back.

For the first time since Dante moved out, Gabe saw his old friend again. The real Dante was back, and he wasn't sure how to feel about it.

Dante gave him a dry look. "Listen, man, we'll hug it out later, alright?" He turned to Wu, his expression shifting. "Seriously, though, am I good?"

Wu raised his hands. "Relax, my code is flawless. You're safe."

Mia crossed her arms. "Listen, guys, I've been through this a few times. Honestly, it's not great, but it's not the end of the world. I usually throw on some music, fall asleep, and when I wake up? It's over. No harm done."

Dante let out a harsh laugh. "Yeah, that sounds great for you. You barely use your chip at all. Guys like me—and Chubby over here—" he motioned toward Gabe "—we're loaded with third-party stuff. We're totally screwed."

Gabe scowled. "First off, fuck you, dude. Second—" he turned to Wu "—is he right?"

Wu shook his head. "No. I promise you, as long as you haven't installed anything from a shady back-alley source, you're fine."

"So only clean black-market apps are safe, got it," Gabe muttered, the sarcasm barely masking the unease creeping into his voice. "Yeah, that makes total sense."

Wu sighed. "We just need to hold tight. Stay calm. And wait."

Gabe exhaled sharply. "Alright, I guess we're locking down for the night. Everybody get comfortable."

Mia glanced toward the upper rows of seats, and a chill swept through her chest. She had barely noticed Nathan for the last few minutes, but now, an uneasy feeling crept over her. She spun toward the group. "Wait—everybody shut up—where's Nathan?"

"He's probably just going up to see Eve," Gabe replied, though worry was creeping into his voice. "She's right upstairs. I mean—he wouldn't really leave right now, would he?"

Gabe took a step toward the aisle.

Wu's voice cut through the moment. "Stop. Nobody moves."

He turned to the group, his tone sharper now. "We stay down here. Together. That reset could wipe out anyone with unstable or unverified code. Nathan might be okay—he's Unmodified. He's pure. He'll be fine. But the rest of us?" He shook his head. "We can't take that risk. We're safer down here."

Before anyone could argue, the first wave of the reboot hit—just a prelude to whatever was coming next. The theater groaned as the system surged again, this time harder. The air hummed, staticky and wrong. The walls seemed to vibrate, the surge of energy forcing them to stagger. Mia grabbed the back of a seat for balance as Dante and Gabe braced themselves. A second pulse slammed through the room, stronger, knocking them off their footing and into the rows of chairs.

With that, it became clear—No one was leaving now.

37

FULL INTEGRATION

Nathan's heart pounded as he raced out from the depths of Winston Hall. Just as he reached the end of the first hallway, he heard footsteps.

"Eve! Wait up!" he shouted. "I'm coming—I'm sorry!"

He sprinted toward the stairwell and took the steps two at a time, climbing fast to reach ground level. The sharp rhythm of heels on concrete echoed ahead of him, but the sound was fading. She was getting away.

He pushed harder. His lungs burned. His heart slammed against his ribs. But then the footsteps started getting louder—she wasn't pulling ahead anymore. He was closing in.

He reached the final landing, rounded the corner, and stopped cold.

The footsteps weren't Eve's.

They were Val's

"Nathan Boone," a voice purred from the shadows. "We finally meet."

The hallway ahead stretched out, silent, and wrong in a way that didn't make sense.

She stepped forward and emerged from the shadows like she'd been born there. Her eyes were dark and unreadable, holding something unnatural.

Instinct drove him to step back until his shoulders met the cold cement wall behind him.

He was trapped.

"Man, you've been hard to get a hold of," Val continued, tilting her head, studying him like he was a puzzle she was about to solve. "I was starting to think you didn't want to be found."

"Maybe that's because I didn't," he said with a forced shrug.

Her smile curled. "That's cute, but we both know that's not true, is it? You want answers, and lucky for you, I have all of them."

Every instinct screamed at him to run. But he couldn't move. No matter how badly he wanted to deny it, she was right. He wanted to know what was inside him.

She stepped closer, slow and careful, like one wrong move might make him bolt.

"Look, Nathan," she said, her tone warm, almost endearing. "I know this first week at NCSU has been hard for you. I only want to help you. I can't even begin to imagine how lost you must feel. I can show you where you belong."

The way she spoke, the way her words wrapped around him—it was different from what he expected. There was no venom, no manipulation—Just kindness.

Then, something shifted.

It felt like one of those rare childhood moments when the world still made sense—before the weight of everything started pressing down like a ton of bricks. When he would sit at the kitchen table, away from school, away from the world, lost in his stories. When he would talk, and his mother would just listen, her eyes lighting up with pride, telling him how special he was.

Val continued, her voice dropping into something more apologetic.

"I admit it—I went about this all wrong," she said, stepping closer. "I never meant to scare you."

For the first time, Nathan could really see her as she moved into the dim light of the corridor. The terrifying version of Val that he'd seen on campus, at The Lighthouse, the evil version that had lived in his mind—the one with her striking tattoos and face full of angst—was gone. Instead, her eyes were warm, and her smile was soft and genuine. Her skin looked smooth and olive under the flickering fluorescent lights in the underbelly of Winston Hall.

Before he could react, she slipped her arm through his in a casual, effortless motion, like they were old friends. The warmth of her body sent another wave of comfort through him. It was that same strange, familiar feeling that had wrapped around him at The Lighthouse and then again just moments ago.

"Let's walk," she said, her voice low, steering him gently toward the exit.

"You can ask me any question you want, and I promise I'll answer every single one. I'll tell you everything you need to know."

Val pushed the door open with her hip, and a blast of cold air rushed in, slicing through the warmth of the hidden corridors. Snow had started falling in thick flakes, swirling under the bluish courtyard lights like confetti at a funeral. But Nathan barely noticed.

Not with her pressed against him, hip to hip, leading him effortlessly into the night.

The warmth radiating from her body was intoxicating. It felt like standing too close to a fire, even though you knew it might burn you, yet you couldn't bring yourself to step away.

The blizzard outside, the icy wind cutting against his skin—it barely registered.

All he could feel was her.

"Wow," she said, looking up to the sky, watching the snowflakes catch in the haze of the campus lights. "I didn't expect this—looks like Mother Nature's mood has changed."

He froze as a rush of cold swept through his chest. That was his joke. It was the kind of thing he would say. The same way he and Eve used to talk about the weather, like it had emotions, like it was alive.

The words echoed in his head. Not because they were profound, but because she said them like she *got it*, like she understood that some days shift without warning. That nothing has to make sense before it changes.

It was like she knew him—not just the surface-level things, but the ones he barely admitted to himself.

She pulled her arm tighter around his, drawing him closer.

"I'm sure my friends told you plenty of things about me." Her voice dipped into something almost teasing. "And I'm sure none of it was flattering."

He was unsure how to answer.

She stopped walking, turning to face him, letting her eyes lock onto his with an intensity that sent a shiver down his spine.

"Nathan," she said, her voice soft, almost humble. "I don't know what to say except—it's all true."

A chill moved through him, putting every nerve on high alert. "What's true?"

She exhaled slowly, choosing her words carefully. "All of it," she said, her voice laced with something unshakable. "I've been waiting for you."

Nathan stiffened as she unhooked her arm and slid her hand into his. Their fingers intertwined effortlessly.

It felt—right.

It felt like he was holding hands with someone who loved him—Someone who would protect him at all costs.

He felt safe.

They started walking again, slowly, each step pressing deep into the snow, leaving crisp imprints behind.

"I think I get it now." He said, his voice steady. "There's a chip in my head, right? Wu said something about first-gen implants—how some of them function differently, how no one really understands them. Is that what I have? Is that why you've been looking for me?"

"That's exactly why I've been trying to find you," she replied simply, like it was the most obvious thing in the world. "I've spent years trying to recreate the tech that you have, Nathan. The tech that has been hidden inside you your entire life."

He turned her words over in his head. "If you've spent years trying to recreate it, then why hasn't anyone else figured it out? What makes my chip different from every other implant out there?"

She just smiled. "It's the way you connect to others, Nathan. I know you've felt it—the feelings, the unspoken energy. Right now, to do that, people like me rely on extra applications, synthetic pathways, layers of code that cloud the experience. It's not pure. It's not like the way you can do it. We need that clean bond, the unfiltered connection. We need to understand the way your device works so we can recreate it, naturally and without limits."

Nathan exhaled sharply, the pieces snapping into place. The way Gabe had always calmed him, how his presence alone could steady the worst of his spirals. Mia, too—there had been something about her, something grounding, like a steady hand on his shoulder.

And then there was Dante. The way his presence did the opposite, igniting something dark and volatile inside Nathan, lighting up the kind of anger that came from somewhere deeper than he understood.

"I've given my entire life to recreating what you have, but I've hit nothing but roadblocks and dead ends. No one can figure out what makes it work."

She squeezed his hand slightly, her voice dipping into something more certain. "And now that I've found you, now that I know how special you are," her voice practically glowed, "I'm not letting you go."

There was something in the way she said it, something that unnerved him. It was dangerous, but it was also intoxicating.

Nathan forced out a weak laugh. "Yeah, right. I'm super special."

"You are, Nathan. And it's not what's in your head that makes you special," Val said, tightening her grip on his hand. "It's you."

Nathan swallowed hard. "If I'm so special, then why do I feel like crap all the time?"

"Because you just don't know how to use what you have." Her words sent a chill racing through him.

"Honestly?" she smiled as if she were about to let him in on some great cosmic secret. "No one does."

He let the weight of her words settle over him. "So that's it? This thing inside me—the thing that's made my life a constant battle—is supposed to be some kind of miracle?"

"That's why you've lived through hell," she said, her voice soft but edged with something sharper. "Doctors have spent years trying to unlock whatever's inside you—poking, prodding, scanning every inch of your mind, but they never cracked it. They could see the potential, but they had no idea what they were dealing with. They never understood that the key wasn't just the chip."

"I don't even know when I got this thing in my head," he admitted, his voice barely above a whisper. The cold air stung his cheeks, but his thoughts were racing too fast for him to care. "My mom wasn't against enhancements—not exactly—but she always said—"

"I know," she interrupted smoothly.

He stiffened. "What do you mean—you know?

Her expression softened as her grip on his hand tightened ever so slightly. "Nathan," she said, her voice almost gentle, like she was breaking something to him that she wasn't sure he was ready to hear. "I think there's a lot about your mother that you don't know."

He pulled his hand back slightly. "Wait. What do you know about my mom?"

She held his gaze, unreadable. Then she sighed, shaking her head like she was deciding how much to say.

"I know enough, Nathan," she replied, her tone velvet-soft. "You deserve to know the truth about who you are and where you come from—and I can help you find it. That's all I've ever wanted to do."

She shook her head like this was all just one big, frustrating inconvenience. "Look, Nathan, I know this has been a mess," she said, her voice slipping into something softer, something almost regretful. "I'm sorry about everything. This isn't how I wanted things to go."

He eyed her warily.

"I told Wu—and that oversized brute of a sidekick, Dante—to just be nice to you. You know, try to make friends and invite you to our party. I never told them to drop some secret invitation on you like a pair of secret service agents without any explanation." She rolled her eyes dramatically. "Honestly, they're both idiots."

He let out a breathy laugh. "Yeah, no kidding."

She nodded like she completely understood. "Right? I mean, who even does that? And look, I know about your history with Dante, obviously."

The mention of Dante made Nathan tense, but Val just sighed and pulled him a little closer, her voice dropping into something almost thoughtful. "I thought maybe if he faced what he did— if he had to look you in the eye, he'd finally take responsibility for how badly he treated you. I thought maybe he'd try to mend things between you, too, you know, make things right."

He scoffed, the warmth of Val's presence making it harder to stay fully angry. "Mend things?" He let out a dry laugh. "That guy only cares about himself."

"I know," she agreed, giving an exasperated shake of her head. "And now he walks around like he doesn't remember anything?" She rolled her eyes again. "Like, please."

The way she laced her words with sarcasm was eerily familiar. It was the same kind of dry, biting tone Eve always used.

He hadn't even started to process it when she kept going

"Dante is something else, I'll give you that," she mused. "You know, all brawn, no heart." Then she turned her attention fully back to Nathan. "He's not like you."

Something in Nathan's chest fluttered—something he wasn't entirely comfortable with.

"They actually bragged about your little meeting in The Quad," Val went on, shaking her head with a huff of annoyance. "They were so proud of themselves." She scoffed. "They seriously thought it was a good idea to scare you into going."

"Well, it worked, didn't it?" Nathan's voice came out sharper than he expected. "If I'm being honest, the whole reason I went was because I thought it would be a good idea to face my fears. I was terrified of them." He paused, then let the truth slip out. "And you, too."

Val sighed, her expression shifting, something more genuine pressing through. "I thought pushing people, scaring them, would help me find the right one," she admitted.

"It wasn't until Dante and Wu told me all about how they spooked you that I realized how wrong I was." She exhaled, her grip on his hand tightening slightly. "I'm sorry, Nathan. Really, I am."

Her eyes met his, filled with sympathy. "I mean, who even treats people like that? It wasn't right. This all could have been so much easier on everyone."

Nathan swallowed hard, but before he could respond, Val's calm cracked. A flash of anger slipped through.

"I told them—" she snapped, and for half a second, her eyes lit up, burning red with fury before vanishing just as fast as it came. She caught herself almost instantly, and after taking a sharp breath, she pulled it together. Then came a small, breathy laugh as she rolled her shoulders like she could shake the irritation off with the movement.

"Idiots, both of them," she muttered under her breath before flashing Nathan a charming, almost sheepish smile.

The shift had been so fast. The way she snapped back into control, so effortlessly, reminded him of someone. It reminded him of Eve.

The sarcasm, the way she used humor to undercut real frustration, the quick temper just barely restrained. It was uncanny.

But then she smiled again, soft and warm and understanding, and Nathan, despite that hint of doubt he felt, moved past it, forcing himself to let it go, to push down the unease in his gut. Because, in this moment, she felt like the only person who understood him. He felt like she truly knew him. And right now, that felt like enough.

She stopped walking and turned to face him fully, taking his free hand in hers.

The way she held his hands—firm but gentle, fingers laced together like they'd done this a thousand times before—sent a shiver down his spine. Not from the cold, but from something else. Something he couldn't name.

She looked at him then, really looked at him, her dark eyes steady and sincere.

"Look, Nate," she said, her voice low, inviting. "Can I call you Nate?"

He hesitated but nodded. No one had ever called him that before.

She smiled, a knowing, almost grateful smile, like she'd been waiting for this moment.

"There's a lot more that I need to explain," she continued. "There are so many layers to this. And I can only imagine how overwhelming it is for you." She squeezed his hand slightly, her thumbs brushing against his skin, grounding him, keeping him close.

"So why don't we just go back to my place? I'll lay it all out for you. I'll tell you everything. No more secrets, I promise."

A strange sense of recognition crept over him. There was something in the way she held herself, the way her eyes softened as they met his, that sent a rush through his chest—something he couldn't quite make sense of.

It was subtle, a shift so small he almost missed it, but it was there. A familiarity that shouldn't exist. He studied her face, trying to place it, but the answer felt just out of reach. And then, like a trick of light or a memory surfacing too late, he realized it.

It wasn't Val's face he was looking at—it was Mia's. The way she looked at him, the quiet confidence, the gentle patience, the way she let silence fill the space between them—it felt familiar. It was the same way she had looked at him in the cafeteria when he'd first woken up, disoriented and afraid, searching for something solid to hold onto.

The warmth in her eyes, the way she steadied him without words, without force—it was soft. It made him feel safe.

He shuddered as he tried to shake off the strange pull that had settled over him. He knew deep inside that he should push back, but the way Val's eyes connected with his—the steady confidence, the soft patience—made it impossible.

Before he could fully process the moment, before logic could interrupt whatever force was pulling him in, he found himself nodding, the words slipping from his mouth before he could stop them.

"Yeah...I need answers."

"Excellent," she said smoothly, squeezing his hand like she was passing him a secret. A message without words—one that told him she wasn't letting go.

"This will be fun."

38

LIVE AND LET DIE

Nathan sat stiffly on the edge of Val's bed, chewing his fingernails as all his signature anxious tells kicked in—sweaty palms, bouncing leg, the whole deal.

He was still trying to figure out why she had been so nice to him. There was no denying that he found her attractive, but something about all of this felt off. The warmth that had clouded his thoughts outside was fading, and whatever spell she had cast over him was starting to wear off.

"You want a beer?" She asked casually, pulling him from his thoughts.

"Uh, sure, I'll take a brewski," Nathan replied, trying to sound nonchalant, but failing miserably.

"Cool. I'll be right back. Don't you dare move," she teased, her tone dripping with playfulness.

He swallowed hard. There it was again—that flirt. That push-and-pull that made him second-guess everything.

The moment she disappeared down the hall, he let out a breath he hadn't realized he was holding before the room fell into silence.

He shifted and took in her space with cautious curiosity.

It was exactly the kind of vibe he had expected—equal parts emo, goth, and late-'90s nu-metal nostalgia. Black sheets. Blood-red LED strips ran along the edges of the ceiling like mood lighting for a séance. To top it all off, a massive poster of the band Korn stared back at him like it was judging his taste in music.

Korn? Nathan squinted at it. Was that even a word?

Beneath the band's name, *Life Is Peachy* was scrawled in jagged, eerie font.

"It sure doesn't feel that way," he muttered under his breath.

His attention shifted back to the door. He hesitated, then slowly got up, creeping toward the hallway to steal a glance at Mia's room. Her door was open just enough for him to see inside.

Soft colors, a neatly made bed, and books—so many books—lined her shelves, stacked with care like she had read each one a hundred times. His eyes skimmed the spines, recognizing all the names he loved. Vonnegut. Bradbury. Salinger.

His chest ached.

Before he could take another step closer, the sharp click of Val's heels against the hardwood floor sent a jolt of panic through him. He scrambled back to his spot on her bed just as she stepped into the room with a beer in each hand.

She set the drinks down and walked toward the multi-disc CD player sitting atop her dresser, her fingers grazing the buttons with care.

"Oh, you're gonna love this," she said, pressing play. "All this old tech? It's some of my favorite stuff."

He remembered what Eve had said about the Enhanced and their obsession with vintage things. Now that he was looking, he noticed it everywhere. Old *Teen Beat* magazines were stacked neatly in a bin by her desk. Then a bookshelf—not filled with books, but with VHS tapes, movies he'd never even heard of, and shows he never knew existed.

And at the very top of the shelf, perched like a silent guardian, was ALF. A nearly life-sized plush doll, staring down with his ridiculous face, judging him.

He shuddered. Then it hit him.

It started as a low hum, barely noticeable, then intensified, radiating through his skull. It wasn't like the connection he'd made with Dante earlier—it wasn't some sudden spark of energy.

This was different. It went deeper into him. It felt almost familiar. He had felt this before.

His mind took a nosedive into the past, years ago, to one of his million hospital visits, all blurring together like some weirdly specific recurring nightmare.

Out of nowhere, they'd decided to admit him again. Because, of course, they had. He didn't think it was going to be a *big deal.* These visits rarely were. They were more of a hassle than anything, like jury duty, but with more needles and less courtroom drama.

He figured it'd be the usual parade of endless waiting rooms, mysterious doctors whispering in corners, and tests so vague and inconclusive they may as well have been fortune cookies.

But this time it was different.

He'd felt normal when he showed up. Not normal by anyone else's standards, but normal for him. He didn't have any symptoms worth mentioning, and it had been weeks since his last episode, and he was starting to think, maybe, he was in the clear—at least for a while.

Still, they insisted that they needed to see him. So he went.

He remembered sitting in the waiting room and trying to play it cool, while he mentally rehearsed his *"I'm not freaking out"* breathing pattern while secretly spinning every worst-case scenario imaginable in his head.

Eventually, they called him in—finally—and led him down some unfamiliar hallway to a room that felt way too secretive to be part of a regular hospital.

The walls were too white, too clean, like someone had scrubbed away anything human.

Then came the wires, the electrodes, the machines that beeped and blinked with unsettling precision. It all looked unnecessarily high-tech, like they'd borrowed gear from a government lab just to mess with him.

None of it felt routine. It all felt staged—like the whole setup was designed to make him feel small, observed, and very, very nervous.

And just when he was starting to convince himself it was all just some overblown precaution—

The buzzing started.

At first, it was just an itch—deep under his skin, in a place he couldn't reach, like his nerves were reacting to something they couldn't see.

It made him fidgety and tense, like he needed to move but didn't know why. It was the kind of feeling that made your skin crawl, but there was nothing to swat away.

But then—gradually, everything shifted.

The tension in his muscles began to relax. And the hum, while still there, somehow stopped feeling uncomfortable and started to soothe him, feeling like white noise that had been turned up just enough to lower the volume in his head.

It wrapped around him in this low, steady rhythm that pulled at the edges of his mind.

Before he knew it, his eyelids started to droop, not from exhaustion, it was more like someone had flipped a switch inside him. Then, his muscles relaxed, not in the way they do when you're cozy in bed, but in that weird, slow way where you don't know if you're falling asleep or being pulled under.

His body stopped responding like it had decided on its own to power down.

The hum filled every part of him, and before he could even think to fight it, he was out.

When he woke up, everything had changed.

The wires and machines were gone, but so was the sharp, clinical cold of a hospital.

In its place was something that felt almost—gentle.

The room was dim, washed in soft golden light that filtered through thin curtains, and a small floor lamp glowed in the corner like a candle someone had forgotten to blow out. The air smelled faintly like something warm—maybe vanilla, maybe old paper.

There was no beeping, no nurses whispering just out of earshot. Just stillness.

And while everything looked calm, that quiet only made it worse.

No one came in.

No one explained a thing.

The cozy stillness wrapped around him like a trick, and beneath it, his nerves lit up like warning flares.

They didn't tell him what had happened. They didn't offer reassurances or say that they didn't find anything like they usually did.

They just handed him his clothes and sent him on his way.

Like it hadn't meant anything.

But it had.

The silence—the missing explanations—caused something in him to snap.

For a while, before that visit, he thought he had been doing okay. He was managing his anxiety well, and everything had almost started feeling like he had everything under control. For once in his life, he felt what it must be like to string together a few wins.

But after that visit, that streak ended cold.

He walked out of that building not with relief, but with his old anxiety cranked up higher than it had ever been before—screaming in his chest, pressing on his lungs, and curling around every thought.

And once it was back, it dug in deep and refused to let go.

Now, sitting in Val's room, his pulse thundered in that same way.

This feeling wasn't just similar—it was identical. It was the same hum, the same pull, the same unshakable feeling that something was happening to him that he couldn't control.

He was just about to bail when she leaned in, casual and calm, like none of it was strange.

"So before we jump into everything," she said smoothly, as she settled closely next to him on the bed, "I thought it might be nice to relax first."

He exhaled as he forced his shoulders to drop slightly and leaned back against the bedpost. "Sure, I can relax. I guess."

He desperately needed answers, but the vibrations in his head clouded his thoughts, making it impossible to focus.

"How about some music?" Val suggested, placing one hand on his thigh while she reached for her phone with the other.

He immediately tensed when she touched him, but before he could say anything—

The speakers exploded without warning, and a violent blast of distortion tore through the room, shredding the air with face-melting guitar riffs and vocals that sounded like someone screaming through broken glass.

The aggressive sound hit him sideways, rattling his insides and throwing his heartbeat off rhythm.

She barely seemed to notice his discomfort at first, nodding along to the violent rhythm. Then—

"Oh, wait—no," she snapped, muting the song with a quick tap on her screen. "Not this. This isn't for you."

He tried to shake the noise from his skull.

"This is for another time," she replied, swiping to a new playlist with a flick of her thumb. "An occasion like this requires something a little more chill."

The speakers shifted to something new—something familiar.

A soft melody hummed through the room, and Nathan instinctively blew out a soft, easy breath as the suffocating wall of sound lifted.

He knew this song, but he couldn't place it.

Paranoia, paranoia, everybody's coming to get me...

He frowned as the first notes played.

He had known it for years, blasting through speakers, fast and sharp, full of defiance.

But this? This wasn't it.

The acoustic version was slower, softer, almost melancholy in a way that felt wrong at first. It was like hearing a familiar voice speak in a different language—everything was there, but it wasn't quite the same.

The sharp edges of the original version were gone, replaced by something raw, almost fragile.

He wasn't sure if he liked it—He wasn't sure if he hated it either.

"Wait, what is this?" he asked, turning to her. "I know this song, but—"

"Shhh."

She leaned in, her voice a whisper against his ear.

"Just listen."

He swallowed hard.

"Isn't this what it sounds like in your head?" she continued, swaying slowly in front of him. "Isn't this how it feels inside your soul?"

His body went rigid, and the hair on the back of his neck stood on end.

He didn't know what she was doing, or why she was looking at him like that—why she was being... sweet.

It made no sense, and worst of all, part of him liked it.

Part of him wanted to give in and let whatever was about to happen—happen.

The torment inside him was real, each side of his brain fighting to make sense of it all.

She traced a slow circle on his knee with her fingertip, her voice a gentle purr.

"Relax, Nathan. Let yourself sink into it. Don't fight it—just feel it. Doesn't it feel good to stop thinking, just for a second?"

She moved closer, her breath was warm against his skin.

Every instinct he had screamed at him to pull away.

This wasn't just flirting—this was something else entirely, and he knew it.

He could feel her trying to get into his head, like she had found the door to his mind and was trying to pry it open.

His body snapped into action before his brain caught up.

He shot to his feet, stumbling back as if her touch had burned him.

"No," he said, shooting his hands up to form a weak barrier between them. "What are you doing? This feels wrong—I need to go."

Val suddenly jerked back, rolling her eyes dramatically. The syrupy sweetness drained from her face in an instant, leaving only sharp frustration in its place.

"Oh, for fuck's sake," she snapped. "What does a girl need to do?"

Her eyes blazed red again, but it wasn't just a flicker this time. It was a full-on raging flame of hatred and frustration.

The intensity of her anger cut through the mask she'd worn, revealing the true force beneath.

Storm Val had arrived, and this time, she wasn't holding back.

He flinched, his eyes wide, seeing the Val he thought he knew—the one he feared—reappear right in front of him.

Her pupils darkened, swallowing the light, and for a brief, terrifying moment, he felt like prey trapped under a predator's stare.

A shadow stretched across her face. The tattoos twisting around her arms shifted under the dim red light. The inked vipers wound tighter around her skin as they prepared to strike.

Her voice—her entire presence—shifted.

"You really are a mess, Nathan Boone, aren't you?" she sneered.

Before he could react, she reached into her pocket and pulled out a card identical to his invitation to The Lighthouse.

In one sharp motion, she pressed it against his forehead.

The second it made contact, a violent jolt ripped through him like she had just poured ice water straight into his skull.

His vision blurred, a high-pitched whine filled his ears, and the edges of the room bled red.

For a split second, he wasn't in Val's room anymore—

He was somewhere else.

Suspended in static, weightless, and electric.

He reacted on instinct. With a strength he didn't know he had—stronger than a hundred Dantes—he shoved her away. She flew across the room, crashing into her dresser with a startled yelp.

She hit the floor but sprang up almost instantly as her laughter rang out like a spell, echoing off the walls.

"Don't fight it, Nathan," she cackled, her voice dripping with mischief. "You know you want this."

Panic surged through him. He bolted out the door, down the hall, and into the snowy night.

Behind him, her voice followed, sing-song and unshaken, slicing through the cold like a curse.

The world around him seemed to distort—the snow, the trees, even the night sky itself, stretched and warped, pulling him inward.

She was wrapped around his thoughts, threaded through the back corners of his mind like a fog that wouldn't clear. Her voice wasn't just behind him—it was *inside* him, echoing through every locked door in his head like a chant he couldn't shut out.

All he could do—was run.

39

RATIONAL FEAR

Nathan's breath tore out of him in ragged bursts, scraping his throat raw with every drag. Inhaling hurt like hell, and exhaling felt like he was giving up pieces of himself to the cold. The cold wasn't just a feeling anymore—it was alive. It was a force that crawled under his skin and curled around his spine before settling deep enough to freeze his soul.

It was clear — Mother Nature was pissed.

Every step came heavier than the last, but somehow, he kept moving. His body couldn't match the urgency of his thoughts, and terror had taken over long ago, forcing him into motion that felt more like instinct than intention.

His boots barely touched the snow-packed ground as he sprinted over it faster than he should have been able to move, as if the fear had personally reached in and rewired his legs to move faster than thought, to sprint without balance, to keep going even when the rest of him was ready to shut down. He wasn't running with control—he was flying forward in a blind, chaotic dash, faster than he'd ever moved in his entire life.

Val's voice sliced through the darkness as if carried by the storm.

"Come back, Nathan! You're mine!"

He turned to see if she was behind him, and all he saw was snow. It was swirling in thick bursts, whipping through the air, and swallowing the trail in both directions. It moved like it had weight, like it had purpose, screaming in every direction with a sound so violent it felt like the world was tearing open around him.

"There's no use running, Nathan. You already belong to me."

Her voice came from nowhere and everywhere at the same time, dripping with control, like it had been waiting for just the right moment to strike. It didn't ask for permission—it forced its way into his thoughts, and folded itself into the quiet places of his mind before locking the door behind it. It didn't beg—it demanded, leaving no room to argue.

"I can give you everything, Nathan. You already know that—you just need to stop fighting."

He looked back again, and what he saw nearly stopped his heart.

They were everywhere—hundreds of them. Not the stylized serpents etched in ink across her skin.

They were real—alive—and endless.

A full-blown swarm of vipers slashing through the snow with sharp, purposeful movement, their bodies flexing together like a monstrous tide. They poured out of the trees, crashing into the path like a flood as they hissed a chorus of whispers: *Surrender, Nathan.*

Then, through the white chaos, he saw it: the cabin.

It stood alone, and buried deep within the trees, exactly where he had seen it from his dorm window—too far to touch, but close enough to haunt him. Its dark wooden frame didn't glow or shimmer or break through the storm like some beacon of safety. It pulsed like the steady rhythm of a heartbeat, unwavering and strong. Each flicker of gold behind the windows felt like a promise—a place that could be his only hope.

His body screamed, nearly buckling beneath the weight of the cold as he forced himself forward, one breathless, trembling step at a time. His legs were on fire, and the more he moved, the more his body pushed back. His chest burned—not from the cold, not from exhaustion, but from something else entirely.

Val's snakes were gaining on him. Their slick forms pulsed with a sick shine, molting as they moved, leaving streaks of something dark and smoking in the snow behind them. They twisted through the night, their bodies merging and breaking apart, coiling in ways that were way too coordinated to be real.

He could hear the sound of their scales sliding across the ice and snow. And beneath it all, he understood them—not through exact words, but in a way that felt deeper, like the meaning had been wired straight into his brain and he knew exactly what they wanted.

They wanted her to have him.

The trees thinned, then split apart entirely as the path dropped away into open space. Just ahead, a narrow bridge stretched across the gap— barely wide enough for a single car, and so caked in ice and snow it looked like no one had crossed it since before the start of winter. There were no footprints—no tire marks. Just a blank stretch of white. It didn't just look old—it looked abandoned.

Beneath it, a river roared with a vicious current, half-frozen and fully alive. The metal railings, barely visible through the piled snow, shuddered in the wind like they knew what was coming.

Beyond it all, past the stretch of ice and storm and shadow, the cabin waited. It was the only path forward. If he could just get across—if he could just make it there—then he might have a chance.

The snakes began to swarm from every direction. They burst out from the snowy banks, shot up from the river below, and poured over the edges of the bridge like a flood with fangs. They surged in from the far end and headed straight for him with a speed that felt impossible. He was trapped.

Without thinking, he pulled himself up onto the icy railing. His arms flapped as he searched for footing on the narrow edge. The river screamed beneath him as the wind tearing at his back threatned to knock him off balance. His boots slipped more than they held, but he stayed up, perched high and exposed.

They grew closer. They didn't sneak or slither. They surged upward, dragging themselves up the bridge's spine with terrifying speed, scaling the steel supports as if they were made for it, as if gravity had no power over them.

Every one of them moved with purpose, like they knew exactly what they were doing. The ones wrapping around the railing that he was standing on stopped just as they reached his feet and coiled tightly, freezing in place, like they were waiting for some unspoken signal. He kicked at one, sending it tumbling from the railing, causing it to be swallowed up by the darkness below.

The rest didn't rush at him all at once. They took their time like they were savoring the fear, like they had all the time in the world, like they knew exactly what they were doing.

They wanted him to feel it. They wanted him to experience the fear crawling up his spine before they ever touched him. They weren't just hunting anymore. They were playing with him.

His legs buckled and burned and begged to stop, but he reached for something deeper, something buried beneath the panic and cold, and he kept moving because there was no other choice.

As the shaking in his hands reached his teeth and his heart slammed against his ribs like it was trying to escape, he felt a sharp sting at his ankle. Then another, biting deep into his thigh.

He screamed—his voice broke mid-shout, high and ragged as the pain tore through him. The first bite hit fast, slicing through him like a hot knife, but the second sank deeper, sending fire through his entire body.

They didn't stop. They came in waves, one after another. They wound around his legs, then climbed to his waist, and squeezed until it felt like his bones were seconds from snapping.

Another bite sank into his side. Then another, each one sent waves of heat crashing through him. The weight of them pressed in from every direction, and there was no room left to move. He couldn't breathe. He couldn't think. All he could do was feel the fire spreading through his body.

They climbed up his back, one after another, sliding up his spine. They locked around his chest and held him like a vice. He opened his mouth to scream, but nothing came out. The air had been forced out of him. His lungs buckled as they were crushed under their weight and flooded with venom.

Her voice sliced through the noise in his head. "I've got you now!"

He was finally hers. She had wrapped around him like a brand. She wasn't chasing him anymore. She was claiming him, owning every piece of him like he had always belonged to her.

She was now the only thing left holding him up. Her grip wasn't just physical. It was inside his head, inside his thoughts, winding itself through everything he had left.

He couldn't move—He couldn't escape.

One last snake coiled around his neck and then around his head, its scales sliding across his face, blocking his vision.

He couldn't breathe—He couldn't see.

And then—Everything stopped.

She let go, as if on purpose—like she wanted to feel him drop. His arm shot out toward the railing, fingers grazing the edge—close, but not enough.

An icy freefall took over as the world tilted and vanished, and he plummeted into the darkness.

The last thing he saw was the river—rushing toward him, black and frozen, the water alive with energy beneath its surface.

And then—nothing.

Just darkness.

40

THE AWAKENING

Mia was the first to wake.

After the initial waves of the reboot told them they'd be in for a long night, they decided to watch *The Goonies*. Not because it was sentimental, or some shared nod to nostalgia. It was just one of the few old films that still played without a signal—a rare bit of analog comfort in a world that didn't run without connection.

They didn't watch it because they felt safe. They watched it because they were terrified, and the sound helped cover the silence. It gave them something familiar to hold onto while the reset worked its way through the system.

Now, the projector was off, and the screen was blank. The only sound left was the low hum of the vents, making it feel like the building was breathing for them.

The shutdown had lasted hours. But now it was over. The network had rebooted. Everything was supposed to be back to normal.

She sat up slowly. Her back was stiff from hours folded into one of the velvet theater seats. Across the aisle, Dante and Wu were still out cold, draped across their rows like they'd passed up mid-conversation. Their legs hung over the seats in front of them. In the dim light, their faces looked calm. There was no panic, no sign that the reset had left a mark. At least, not one she could see.

She rubbed her eyes and stretched, trying to shake the weight that always followed a reboot. It wasn't painful—just disorienting. It felt like you were waking up from a dream you couldn't remember, but still carried in your chest. Her body was awake, but her head felt half a step behind.

She scanned the room, eyes catching on the dark projector and the frozen screen in front of her. The last thing she remembered was the octopus scene in the movie's final act. Had they really slept through the rest? Or had they slept through something worse?

She took a breath, held it for a beat, then let it go.

Then it came—

A full-throated and terrified scream sliced through the quiet with a force that made her stop in place. The sound echoing from the old bathrooms at the back of the theater was sharp enough to cut straight through the stillness they had been sitting in for what was probably hours.

"AHHHH! No! God, no! Why?!"

Her heart slammed against her ribs as she ran to the source, her feet slipping against the floor as she skidded to a stop in the open doorway.

"Oh my god…" she gasped.

Inside, Gabe stood frozen in front of a cracked, cloudy mirror, his breath coming in sharp, panicked gasps as his whole body trembled and his hands were locked around the edges of the sink so tight his knuckles had gone white.

The Gabe Kowalski staring in the mirror wasn't the one who'd fallen asleep in the theater before the reboot, not even close.

The weight he'd always carried—his broad frame, his thick build, the heaviness that had always made him easy to spot in a crowd—had vanished. His usual 6XL Hawaiian shirt hung loose around a physique that looked nothing like his, draped over sharp collarbones and shoulders that were suddenly defined.

He looked like someone had pulled him out of himself and put him in the wrong shape. His cargo shorts had slid down around his ankles, the waistband gaping wide, useless now, like everything else that used to fit.

He turned slowly toward Mia, his face twisted in what could only be described as pure horror.

"Oh god! This is terrible!" he exclaimed, his voice cracking under the weight of it, like just saying the words out loud made it more real.

The reflection blurred as his eyes filled with tears, burning at the edges and slipping down his cheeks before he could stop them. He reached up with shaking hands, feeling the curve of his heightened cheekbones, then lower, tracing the sharp line of a jaw he hadn't felt in years as if he was checking to see if it was real.

"Look at me," he whispered, the words barely making it past his throat. "I'm a goddamn hunk."

His hands moved across his chest, the lower, landing on the ridges of a six-pack that hadn't been there before. He stared at his own body like it had been swapped out in the night without his permission.

"Oh, this is awful," he said, his voice quivering. "I'm ruined."

Mia, still trying to figure out if he was in shock or fully losing it, stepped forward with caution. "Gabe, what happened—"

"I'll never get laughs looking like this!" he shouted. "After all that work—after years of cultivating the perfect look, this is what I get?"

He turned to Mia with desperation written all over his face, his eyes welling up. "Please don't look at me. I can't let anyone see me like this."

He scrambled backward, grabbing at the loose folds of his Hawaiian shirt and pulling it around his now lean body like it could somehow undo what had happened, like it could hide the parts that didn't make sense. "Oh god, this is my nightmare…"

Before Mia could respond, Dante and Wu, groggy from the reboot, stumbled toward the doorway and took in the scene.

"Well, look who decided to join us," Dante said, leaning against the wall. "Looks like *Killer Kowalski* is ready to get back on the team."

Gabe snapped his head toward him, glaring. "Shut up, dude! This isn't funny!" He gestured frantically at his body. "Look at me! Goddammit, I'm gorgeous!"

Observing him with mild amusement, Wu crossed his arms. "I fail to see the problem here."

Gabe groaned dramatically, burying his face in his hands. "Of course you don't."

Mia, still struggling to grasp what she was seeing, finally managed, "Wait, how did this happen?"

Dante tilted his head, one eyebrow lifting like he already knew the answer. "It's not exactly rocket science, Mia. The shutdown wiped a ton of third-party junk off the network. Maybe one of Gabe had a bootleg upgrade that didn't survive the reboot."

Gabe's eyes darted back to the mirror, a sinking feeling flooding him.

Everything he'd tried to hide was staring him back in the face.

"Great—this is just perfect," he muttered, the words cracking under the weight of disbelief.

His worst nightmare wasn't some wild-eyed villain; it was his own reflection that was nothing less than chiseled muscle and as far as he was concerned, symmetrical doom. It felt like a betrayal, like his body had been rewritten without permission.

Wu gave a slow, theatrical sigh and shook his head with exaggerated disappointment. Then, with the smug flair of a magician about to reveal a trick, he pulled out his phone. His grin stretched just wide enough to make the whole thing feel like a setup as he scanned the stream of data scrolling across the screen.

"Aha," he muttered, tone low and needlessly ominous. His eyes narrowed in that infuriatingly smug way that always made Gabe want to knock something over.

Gabe tensed, already regretting asking. "Aha, what?"

The sigh that followed was dramatic enough to qualify as performance art. "Aha, as in—you didn't listen to me."

His voice pitched higher than he intended. "What the hell does that mean?"

Wu looked up from the screen.

His face was unreadable, the kind of stillness that felt like it had been practiced in a mirror.

"It means that I set you up with everything you needed, and I did it right. The coding was flawless and stable enough to survive any reset without interference. I gave you the best possible enhancements for your system, and I told you specifically not to—"

Gabe's eyes widened. "Wait, No—No way!"

Wu nodded. "Oh—Yes, way."

Gabe grabbed him by the shoulders. "You're not telling me—"

"That's exactly what I am telling you," Wu replied, brushing Gabe's hands away with an air of controlled irritation. "It looks like someone chose to ignore everything I told them and went straight to, oh, I don't know, the most unregulated black market in existence."

He didn't speak right away. He just looked at Gabe with an almost pitying calm, like this was all playing out exactly as he'd expected. Then he shook his head like he'd just watched someone set fire to the Mona Lisa.

"You mixed my carefully engineered work with back-alley code from a sketchy developer, and now everything has been wiped clean. The shutdown didn't just clear junk—it cleared you. Think of it like a factory reset."

Gabe ran his hands through his hair, which now looked professionally styled without him ever stepping near a brush. His voice cracked as he tried to keep up with what Wu was saying.

"Okay—okay, but it wasn't like that," he insisted as the words tumbled out in a rush. "It was just a tiny add-on. Some guy in one of my performing arts classes sold it to me. I figured it would be safe. I mean, sure, it's off the grid, but everyone knows it's top-tier. It's not like I went behind a gas station and got it out of a vending machine or anything."

He started pacing in short, frantic bursts, arms gesturing like he was trying to draw the logic in the air.

"He told me it would help with stage fright. That's it—I tried it once, and honestly, I didn't like how it felt. I completely forgot that I even had it."

He stopped in front of Wu, trying to keep his voice steady even as panic pushed passed the edges. "Please tell me there's something you can do. I mean, can you fix it?"

Wu tilted his head, a hint of amusement flickering behind his eyes. "I don't know, maybe. It'll take some work. But Gabe—honestly, is this the biggest problem we have right now?"

Before he could come up with an answer, Mia cut in.

"It's not," she said, her tone even but tight. "We need to find Nathan."

Gabe groaned, glancing down at himself like his own reflection had just betrayed him. "Goddammit, I look like a friggin' Hemsworth. It's disgusting."

Mia crossed her arms and raised an eyebrow, giving him a slow once-over that she didn't even try to hide. "I'm not sure Eve would agree with that," she said, almost amused. "Come on, Gabe—it could be way worse."

He threw up his hands. "Are you kidding? She'd probably think I went full Enhanced chip-head. This is awful—I mean—like, worst-case scenario awful."

Wu adjusted his cuffs with meticulous care, as if the sharpness of his sleeves mattered more than whatever crisis Gabe was unraveling. "Tell you what." He paused, smoothing the fabric one more time. "We find Nathan." Another pause. "And if he's not in immediate danger..." He glanced up, just briefly. "I'll take a look at your—*situation*." A slight smirk ghosted across his face. "I'm sure we can do something to get you back into—*shape.*"

Gabe let out a long breath, rolling his shoulders like he was preparing to walk into something he didn't want to deal with.

"Alright. Fine. Let's go find our boy and fix this mess."

He turned on his heel and started toward the door, still adjusting his oversized shirt, tugging it tighter around his naturally athletic frame in a futile attempt to feel normal. His strides were quick and determined, like movement alone could fix the mess he was in.

Dante leaned against the doorframe, one brow raised. "Uh, Kowalski? Aren't you forgetting something?"

Gabe froze mid-stride. He looked back, slowly, already dreading what he'd see.

There they were—his cargo shorts, crumpled in the middle of the floor, looking like they'd been left behind by someone else entirely.

"SON OF A—"

With an exaggerated stomp, he stormed out of the bathroom, muttering a string of curses under his breath. His path was direct, with zero hesitation as he headed straight to the heavy curtains hanging near the movie screen. He grabbed a length of fabric and yanked it free with surprising precision, then wrapped it around his waist like he'd done it a hundred times before. A quick tug secured it in place, transforming the thick material into a makeshift kilt.

He turned to face the others, shoulders squared like he was about to take the stage.

Planting his hands on his hips, he puffed out his chest and raised his chin. "Well, lads," he declared, slipping into an exaggerated Scottish accent, "I always fancied myself as a kilt kinda guy."

Then, without missing a beat, he dropped into character and delivered the next line with heartbreaking precision.

"I eat because I'm not happy... and I'm not happy 'cause I eat," he said with sad eyes.

They all just stared at him.

"See? It doesn't work like this!" he gestured at his newly sculpted physique, his voice loaded with peak Gabe sarcasm,

"I look like a superhero, and I sound like a sidekick." He slumped against the wall and let his arms drop to his sides in total defeat.

Mia walked over and placed a hand gently on his shoulder.

"Hey," she said, her tone sincere. "I know this sucks. Really. But we don't have time for your existential comedy crisis right now. We need to find Nathan."

Gabe grumbled under his breath as he wrestled with the curtain, giving it one last frustrated tug. "Alright, alright," he muttered, more to himself than anyone else. "Let's track down Nathan before this night gets any worse."

Dante stepped forward, still shaky from waking up after the reboot. "Wait, guys, I need to tell you all something—"

He didn't have to say it—the look on his face said enough. Whatever he was about to say, it was serious.

The others turned toward him, pausing mid-motion, waiting.

Mia stepped closer, her eyes steady as they searched his face.

It wasn't something he could just say—it didn't feel normal or logical. But the feeling had stuck with him, stubborn and strange, ever since it happened.

"Last night," he said quietly, "while everyone was asleep, I felt him. I mean—I felt Nathan."

Gabe raised a brow. "What do you mean you felt him? Like, in a psychic way or a 'Hey kid, come see the puppies in my van' kind of way?"

Dante shot Gabe a look. "Neither, dumbass. I'm serious. It felt real."

Mia didn't flinch. "Dante, just tell us what happened. We're listening." She cast a sideways glance at Gabe.

He hesitated, searching for the right words. "I'm still trying to piece it together," he said. "At first, I thought it was a dream. Everything was hazy —but then it got clear. Way too clear to be a nightmare."

His hands balled into fists. "I didn't just feel him—I was there. In his body. He was running for his life. It was like he was being hunted."

Gabe frowned. "What do you mean, running? Who was after him?"

"I don't know. All I saw were snakes." He swallowed, and his voice dropped. "Hundreds of them. They were disgusting. Just thinking about them makes my skin crawl."

He stopped, voice catching. "I couldn't move. I couldn't help. It didn't feel like I was watching—it felt like I was actually in his body."

Mia's arms crossed, her stance stiff. "I'm sure it felt real. But it was just a dream. You were here the whole time. We all were."

He nodded slowly. "I know how it sounds. But it wasn't a dream. I could feel the snow, the wind, the cold tearing into my lungs. My chest was pounding, but it wasn't mine. It was his. He kept running. And then —there was this bridge."

Wu, silent until now, tilted his head. "What bridge?"

"I don't know. It was old. I think it might've been up in the woods behind the athletic fields."

Gabe's eyes widened. "So what happened?"

Dante's posture stiffened. "He tried to cross it," he said, the words slow and heavy. "He only got about halfway."

He ran a hand down his face, jaw tight. "Then he fell. That was it. I lost him."

His voice sank, brittle now. "After that, there was nothing."

Gabe blinked and shifted, a crease forming between his brows. "What do you mean, nothing?"

Dante put a hand to his chest. "I mean—nothing. One second, I felt everything—I was falling with him—and then..." He shook his head slowly. "He was just gone. Like someone flipped a switch and cut out the lights."

Mia's voice was barely a whisper. "If it went dark... does that mean he's—"

"I don't know—I mean, I don't think so." Dante rubbed his face. "Right after he fell, it was like... everything just cut out. Lights off, sound gone—just nothing. But now it's like... he's trying to come back online or something. All I'm getting is static. Like he's stuck in this glitchy in-between. I can't see him anymore, but I still feel him—sort of. It's hard to explain. The connection's still there, but it's weak. Like his battery's almost dead and he's trying to hang on."

He looked up. "I know none of this makes any sense. But whatever's messing with that signal? It's not just blocking him. It's trying to bury him."

Mia didn't hesitate. "Alright, then we need to move. Now."

Dante shook his head. "He's not close. If he's where I think he is, we're not getting there on foot."

Gabe rubbed his temples. "Awesome. That's just great. So unless Wu has some sort of magic teleportation upgrade in his bag of tricks, we're screwed."

Mia hesitated before saying, "Why can't we take your van, Gabe?"

"That wasn't my van," he said flatly. "It's Eve's."

Wu groaned. "Great. So we just have to convince the one person who probably wants to set us all on fire to drive us, sounds easy enough?"

Dante crossed his arms. "Guess you're right, Kowalski. We're screwed. That chick hates us. Probably you more than anyone."

"Shut up, man, she hates Val," Gabe corrected. "But she loves Nathan. Sure, she's super pissed right now, but if she knows he needs her? She'll come through." He cracked his knuckles. "It might take a bit of the old Kowalski charm, but I'll convince her."

Mia's jaw tightened, the thought of that conversation already settling like a weight in her chest. "No, Gabe. I think we need to put your 'charm' on the back burner for now. I think she blames me for all of this. I'll talk to her."

Wu raised an eyebrow. "And what exactly are you going to say?"

Mia stared at the floor for a beat, then lifted her eyes, steady and sure. "Whatever I have to."

Wu scoffed. "Right. Because that conversation is going to go well."

Mia ignored him, already pulling out her phone. Her fingers hovered over the screen before she locked it again with a frustrated sigh. "This isn't something you text."

Gabe clapped his hands together. "Alright, so what's the play? We just show up, knock on her door, and hope she doesn't slam it in our faces?"

"Pretty much," Mia said under her breath.

Dante scoffed. "Listen, I've known that girl longer than anyone, just as long as Nathan. She is not going to go for any of this. We need to find another way."

"There is no other way," Gabe said, already heading for the door. "Come on, kids. Cue the inspirational montage—it's road trip time."

Mia grabbed his sleeve before he could push it open. "Stop. Dante is right, if we all go storming up there, she won't listen to any of us."

Gabe sighed. "Okay, so what do you suggest, genius?"

Mia steadied herself. "I'll go. I'll talk to her alone."

Wu snorted. "Oh yeah, because she loves you right now."

"I know she doesn't," Mia admitted. "But she doesn't hate me like she does you three. If I can get her to listen—just for a second—I think I can make her understand."

Dante frowned. "And if you can't?"

Mia held his gaze, unmoving. "*Can't* isn't an option."

For a second, nobody spoke. Then Gabe threw an arm around her shoulders. "Alright, fearless leader. Go get our wheels."

Mia straightened, steadying herself. "Alright. Meet me in the lobby in fifteen minutes. Wish me luck."

She pushed through the door, stepping out into the cold. The wind cut through her jacket, biting at her skin, but she barely felt it. Her mind was already ahead of her, racing through every possible outcome.

She watched her breath cloud the air before it vanished into the dark. Then she squared her shoulders and started walking.

There was no backup plan, no alternative. Mia wasn't leaving without that van, and Eve was going to drive it—even if Mia had to drag her into the driver's seat herself.

41

MY CHAUFFEUR

Mia stood outside Eve's dorm room, trying to convince herself that she wasn't nervous. She'd stood up to Val and lived to tell the tale, stared down Dante, and made him listen. She had seen the network ripple through the Enhanced and bend reality itself. And yet, somehow, knocking on Eve's door felt harder than all of it.

Because Eve was different. She wasn't tall, elegant, or composed like Mia. She wasn't a powerhouse like Dante or a force of destruction like Val. She was small, all fire and passion, a wild thing held together by sheer defiance alone. She didn't need enhancements. She didn't need anyone, but they needed her because if anyone could bring Nathan back, it was Eve.

Mia exhaled, steady and resolved, and knocked.

No answer.

She knocked again, firmer this time. Still nothing.

Come on, Eve. Please, we need you, she whispered to herself.

Placing a hand flat against the door, she listened, feeling the weight of it, willing Eve to be inside, willing her to open up. She could feel it—Nathan was running out of time.

She raised her fist to knock again, just as the door flew open.

Eve stood there barefoot, her oversized sweater practically swallowing her frame, the strong scent of weed mingled with the dreamy echo of Jamiroquai drifting from somewhere behind her. Splashes of vibrant color peeked out from the doorway, but her arms stayed locked tight, her expression unreadable.

"No."

Mia barely blinked. "What?"

"I said no," she repeated, stepping forward to fill the doorway, small but unshakable. "Whatever you're about to ask, the answer is no."

Mia sighed, unsurprised. She knew that Eve wasn't going to make this easy. "Eve, listen—"

"No, Mia—" The word sliced the air.

"I did listen, Mia. I listened, I watched, and I walked away, because I refuse to be part of this insane little club you and your Enhanced buddies have going on."

Her voice was quick, like she had been holding it in too long, and now it was unraveling faster than she could stop it.

"I am done," she snapped.

Mia studied her, taking in the slight tremor in her hands. Eve was shaking. Mia wasn't.

"Eve, this isn't about me," she said, her voice calm, "Or them. It's about Nathan."

For the briefest moment, Eve hesitated. It was barely there, but Mia saw it. The worry, the crack in her armor.

She tried to slam the door, but Mia stopped it mid-swing, pressing her palm flat against the wood to hold it open.

Eve's eyes flashed with fury. "Get out!"

Mia didn't move.

"If you were done, you wouldn't have answered the door just to tell me no in the first place. You would have stayed inside with your comfort ritual, burying your head until all of this passed over. Well, I've got news for you, none of this is going to pass over."

Eve's whole body wound tight like she was bracing for an impact she couldn't see coming.

Mia stepped inside before Eve could try to shut the door again.

"You think I don't get it? That I don't understand what he means to you? That I don't know how it feels to lose someone piece by piece, to watch them slip away and know there's nothing you can do?"

Eve fought to keep her guard up, but the words spilled out in a wave of emotion.

"You think you're different, Mia? You think you're better than them?" she said, her voice rising. "You think just because you don't flaunt your power or use it to crush people that you're somehow less messed up than they are?" She shook her head, furious. "Well, I've got news for you: you're not. You still have it, Mia. That power—something I'll never believe in, something I'll never have."

Mia let her words settle before lowering her voice. "Eve, this isn't about me. It never was. And it's not about what we have or don't have."

She didn't push. She didn't defend herself. She just left the space open and let Eve decide what came next.

Eve swallowed hard, shaking her head like she was trying to keep the truth from sinking in.

"I'm just so tired of everyone acting like Nathan's defective. Do you have any clue how many hours I've spent with him in the hospital, watching doctors poke and prod and run test after test, only to find nothing? That does something to a kid. He feels broken because everyone —your buddy Dante included—convinced him he was. He's not sick, Mia. He's not broken. And he sure as hell doesn't need whatever cure you think he already has."

Mia's face softened, but her voice shook with an urgency that bordered on desperation.

"We're not trying to cure Nathan," she said, her eyes searching Eve's for a hint of trust. "I know that you think we're messing with his life, but this is about saving him before it's too late."

Eve's breath caught hard in her throat. Her entire body tensed, every muscle coiled like she was bracing for a hit she couldn't dodge. Her fingertips twitched by her sides, aching for something solid to cling to— some kind of anchor in all this chaos.

"You don't get it, Mia," she managed, her voice trembling despite the anger churning inside her. "You talk about 'saving' him like there's a neat fix, like a magic button you can push. But that's not how it works. He's been told his entire life that he's broken, and I've watched how that tears him up. What if your *'help'* just shreds him even more?"

The weight of it settled between them. Eve trembled, and Mia saw the moment she broke. She saw how, in an instant, her anger folded in on itself and was swallowed by something deeper, something harder to hold.

She didn't hesitate. She stepped forward and pulled Eve into her arms.

For a second, Eve stayed rigid, fighting to hold it together. Then she broke, and collapsed into Mia's arms as a deep sob escaped. She clutched Mia's shirt like it was the only thing keeping her steady.

Eve had always been the wildfire—the one who burned bright and out of control. But right now, she needed something solid to lean on.

"He needs you, Eve," Mia whispered. "We all do."

Eve pulled back like the moment stung. She looked up into Mia's eyes, letting her expression harden as she wiped away her tears.

She turned and grabbed her keys from the desk with the kind of certainty that left no room for second thoughts. Then she reached for her coat, slipping her arms into the sleeves slowly, like she was gearing up for something more than just a fight.

"This ends tonight."

She stepped past Mia, pausing only long enough to glance back. Her tone was quiet, almost casual—but it carried a promise that didn't need repeating.

"Time to burn this witch."

Mia didn't ask what she meant. She didn't need to.

She followed Eve out into the hall, her heart pounding like it already knew—

They weren't just going to get Nathan back.

They were going to war.

42

<hr>

EYE SPY

He wasn't dead.

That was the first thing Nathan knew for sure.

The second was that it wasn't Val who had pulled him from the snow.

His body wouldn't move. His arms and legs felt disconnected, as though they belonged to someone else. Even the slow rise and fall of his chest barely registered. But none of it mattered. Nothing mattered.

There was no fear. No panic. No pain.

He sat motionless on a deep leather couch, staring at the fire crackling just a few feet away. The flames danced and shifted, throwing soft golden light against the wooden walls. It should have warmed him, it should have reached through the numbness and touched something inside him. But it didn't. Not because the fire was weak, but because he felt nothing.

No heat on his skin. No lingering cold from the storm. No relief that he was, somehow, still breathing.

His vision drifted—not because anything caught them, but because sitting still felt impossible, and his eyes were the only part of him he could move. There was nothing else to focus on. The cabin was quiet and wide open, heavy with stillness. Exposed wooden beams arched overhead, leading into a high, vaulted ceiling that made the room feel way too big. It didn't feel like Val's world.

The walls weren't sterile. There were no screens flickering with coded

313

patterns, no glowing panels humming with power. There was no artificial light, no subtle vibration of machines built to watch, track, and control.

Instead, the space was filled with photographs—real ones.

Pictures of cities lit up at night, winding mountain roads, and wide-open landscapes untouched by concrete. Each frame looked carefully chosen and arranged with intention. They told the story of someone who had lived a life in motion. Someone who had run, maybe not from danger, but from everything.

He was sure of it, this place definitely didn't belong to Val.

Whoever lived here had stepped away from that world completely. There was no trace of technology stitched into the furniture. No sleek control hidden behind the walls.

But there was a guitar. Leaning against the far wall, its wood worn down from years of playing. Next to it, a small desk sat cluttered with notebooks. The pages were bent, the spines cracked, the paper full of ink. Words had been written here. Thoughts had been poured out and left behind. Whoever lived here wasn't trying to hide from the world—they had purposefully chosen to leave it behind.

Nathan let his eyes drift toward the front window of the cabin. The wall of glass rose from the floor to the ceiling, giving him an unobstructed view of the forest beyond. The trees stood still in the dark, their branches heavy under the weight of fresh snow. The mountain slope behind them was barely visible, its shape outlined by the faint glow of the moon. Light spilled across the clearing in front of the cabin, pale and cold, but not enough to chase away the shadows.

The snow had stopped, and the sky had cleared. On the surface, the scene should have felt peaceful. But the stillness felt wrong—too perfect, like the kind of quiet that follows just after something breaks.

It wasn't the view that made something stir in his chest. It was the silence. The kind that made you feel like the world was holding its breath.

Then he saw them.

Three telescopes, lined up behind the glass in a perfect row. Their frames gleamed under the moonlight, each one polished and perfectly aligned. Nothing about them looked casual. They stood like sentries, each one pointed in the same direction—down the mountainside, directly at Northern Connecticut State University.

From where he sat, motionless on the worn leather couch, it was obvious. The angle cut through the trees, past the clearing and the athletic fields, and landed right on campus.

But whoever lived here wasn't interested in the campus as a whole.

The scopes were fixed on a single building.

—Shaker Hall

—His window.

The same one he had looked out of for the last few nights, staring out into the woods, chasing questions he didn't have the words for. He had looked out, thinking he was alone. That he was the one observing. The one trying to make sense of what was hidden in the dark.

He had always believed he was the one watching.

But it had become clear—someone had been watching him first.

43

ROAD TRIP

The van rumbled down the frozen dirt road, its tires grinding over snow packed hard from the storm that had just torn through the region. The headlights strained against the dark, their glow swallowed by frost drifting through the trees like breath. The storm had passed—technically—but everything still felt stuck.

It felt like the world was bracing itself, waiting for the next bad thing to crawl out of the darkness and show them that things getting worse wasn't just possible—it was inevitable.

Eve leaned into the wheel as if she could force the van to move faster just by wanting it badly enough. She hadn't said much since they left campus. Maybe a few colorful curses when the tires slipped or when the windows fogged from the uneasy breath of her travel companions and the defroster couldn't keep up, but other than that, she didn't let out so much as a peep.

Mia sat quietly beside her, watching the road ahead, searching for any sign of Nathan. The headlights barely cut through the dark. The road looked abandoned, like no one had come this way in months. Her hands stayed on her thighs. She wanted to say something—to break the silence, to check in on Eve—but she didn't. She knew better. Whatever was going on in her head wasn't ready to come out.

Behind them, Dante and Wu hunched over a small screen. The last pin from Nathan had faded a while ago, but they kept checking anyway. Gabe sprawled across the back seat like he owned the place. He'd been quiet for too long, which meant something was coming.

"So," he said finally. "We're all just going to keep pretending this isn't the start of a horror movie, right?"

No one replied.

He draped his arms over the back of Wu's seat and leaned forward like he was settling in for storytime. "Oh, come on. We've got the perfect cast."

"Seriously? Tell me you guys can't see it— I mean, we've got the jock with a complicated past—obviously."

He pointed a thumb at Dante before smacking Wu on the shoulder hard enough to rock him, throwing in a shake for good measure. "Wu is our quiet tech guy with a secret identity. You know the type—the misunderstood genius just dying for someone to notice how brilliant he is."

Wu didn't flinch.

He threw a hand toward the front passenger seat. "And up there, we've got the strong, level-headed female lead. Smart as hell, gorgeous without trying, and the moral compass of the group."

And then, he shifted forward, lowered his voice just a little, as his smile turned sheepish, like he couldn't help himself.

"And my personal favorite..." He looked toward Eve. "Our unhinged yet adorable driver with a personal vendetta against technology."

He paused for a beat, then tacked on, "Maybe the one who's starting to realize that just because a guy gets rebooted with a jawline doesn't mean he's not still a softy on the inside. And hey—fingers crossed—he gets back to being one on the outside too, once this whole nightmare is over."

He tried to play it cool, but there was hope tucked under the joke, like he was throwing a line out to see if she'd take it.

She didn't.

She just glanced at the rearview mirror, met his eyes for barely a second, and then looked back to the road like no one had been talking at all.

After Mia had convinced her to lead their search party for Nathan, she came down from her room completely drained and barely holding it together. She was already running on fumes when she saw Gabe standing there. One look—that's all she gave him. A slow sweep, head to toe. She didn't say a word. Just climbed into the van like he didn't exist.

Realizing the joke hadn't landed—and that it was going to take a lot more than charm to win Eve back—Gabe cleared his throat and wrapped it up.

"And then there's me," he added. "The comic relief. I'm the guy who's supposed to stay behind but tags along anyway, because trauma-bonding is real, and apparently nobody else knows how to deliver one-liners."

Dante exhaled slowly. "I swear to God, Kowalski—"

"Oh, what?" Gabe replied, stretching his legs out like they belonged there. "Am I ruining your broody vibe? Or were you planning to drop a cryptic line about fate while staring out the window or something?"

Dante's jaw tightened. "Look, man, just pipe down, alright? I'm the only one who knows where we're going."

Gabe rolled his eyes. "Right. Because your directions have been super clear so far. Take the third left after the murder trees, hang a right at the River of the Damned, and go straight until we hit the frozen cemetery. Yeah, we're totally safe."

Mia sighed and rubbed her temples. "Will you *both* please just shut up?"

Eve didn't bother hiding her irritation. "No, let them fight. Maybe we'll get lucky and they'll kill each other—and we'll finally get some peace and quiet."

Wu finally chimed in, his voice the closest thing they had to reason. "Guys, seriously, we need to focus. We must be getting close." He glanced at Dante. "How far are we?"

Dante's eyes flicked back to the map. His brow pinched. "The signal's gone," he said. "It's dead, but I dropped a pin before it cut out, so we're headed there now. With any luck, we'll find footprints, a trail, something. Don't worry. We're almost there."

Eve's shoulders stiffened. "Define *almost.*"

"Almost means *almost,*" he snapped. "I've never been out here. Just keep driving. I think the bridge is just up past these trees."

For the sake of the greater good, she bit her tongue. Eve knew Dante was a big part of why they were all here, but she'd promised herself she'd push all that noise aside—for Nathan.

Mia looked over at her and could see the storm raging inside. She didn't say anything. There was no point. The silence between them wasn't empty—it carried too much.

Eve's anger wasn't loud, but it was there. It didn't need to boil over to make itself known. Mia could feel it in the way Eve shut down, in the way she didn't let herself speak. Whatever was going on inside her, it wasn't fading. It was sitting still, waiting for a place to unleash itself.

Dante looked up from his phone, squinting through the windshield as the trees began to thin.

"Hold on. Slow down," he said, leaning forward a little more. "The pin that I dropped looked further out, but—" he pointed ahead, "—the way the trees open up here, this has to be it. I think we're here."

The van stopped hard. The tires slipped on the frozen road and jolted them forward. Outside, the fog pressed in thick and close. The road was gone, swallowed by the mist. Shapes flickered past the windows, but nothing held. The world beyond the glass didn't look real—just shadows and outlines, broken up by the dark.

Eve threw the van into park, ripped the keys from the ignition, and was out of the driver's seat before anyone else had a chance to react.

Mia stepped out a second later. Cold tore through her clothes as her boots sank into the fresh powder. Ahead of her, Eve moved fast, eyes locked on Dante as he climbed out of the passenger side. Mia didn't need to hear a word to know how this was going to go.

"Alright!" Eve snapped, rounding on him. "Where is he?"

Dante sighed, waving his hands toward the trees, the fog, the nothingness around them.

"I told you. Here." He rubbed his hands together and breathed into them, trying to pull some warmth back into his fingers.

Eve let out a sharp, bitter laugh, her breath turning to frost in the air. "Wow. That's some brilliant detective work, Dante. Care to narrow that down a little? Because I sure as hell don't see him.—Do you?" She swung her arm impatiently toward the bridge. "You said that you knew where he was—that you 'felt him'—so how exactly do you just lose someone like that?"

She threw a frustrated hand toward the bridge, barely visible through the dense fog.

"You said you felt him here—but now, suddenly, he's just gone? How exactly does that happen?"

Dante's expression hardened, shadows crossing his face. "I don't know, Eve. I already told you—"

"No," she snapped, stepping forward, close enough for him to feel her breath clouding the air between them. "You said that you knew exactly where he was, like you had a direct line into his head. Now you've lost him? Explain to me how that makes sense."

Dante didn't budge. His voice stayed low and steady, though irritation flickered behind his eyes.

"I didn't say I knew exactly where he was. I said I thought I knew. You don't have an implant; you wouldn't understand—"

"You're right," Eve snapped, cutting him off sharply. "I don't understand. Do you know why? Because everything you've said so far is all complete bullshit."

Mia reached out cautiously, placing a gentle hand on Eve's arm, but Eve shrugged it away roughly.

"I should've never trusted you people," she hissed, spinning away from Dante and turning her anger onto the rest of them, eyes blazing and searching for another target.

"You," she spat, focusing on Gabe, her voice trembling with barely contained fury. "You're the worst one of all."

Gabe, who had been standing off to the side, kicking aimlessly at a crust of snow near the tree line, finally looked up. "Uh… what?"

Eve stalked toward him. "You lied to me. This entire time."

He shifted uneasily. "Eve, come on, don't say that—"

"No!" she barked. "Don't you dare joke your way out of this, Kowalski. You let me think you were normal—"

"I am normal," he shot back weakly.

Her voice exploded through the cold air. "No, you're not! You're exactly like them." She threw her hands up, the anger giving way to raw disbelief.

"I should have known better—shame on me. But you were smooth. You knew exactly what I liked, and you shapeshifted right into it." Her words cracked, jagged with humiliation. "God, I'm so embarrassed that I fell for it."

He swallowed the heavy lump forming in his throat. "Eve, I didn't tell you because I knew exactly how you'd react."

She stared at him, incredulous. "So now this is my fault?"

"No! I mean—well, maybe a little?" He sighed, running an anxious hand through his hair. "Look, I didn't want to keep it from you. But I saw how much you hated the Enhanced. How much you hated people like us —people like me."

"I trusted you," she said, her voice catching as tears welled in her eyes.

"I know," he replied softly, guilt woven through each word. "I'm sorry. I never meant to hurt you—honestly."

"Well, you did!" Her hands balled into tight fists at her sides. "You were supposed to be my friend. Someone who I thought understood me, understood who I really am. And you let me believe in a lie."

He met her stare, pleading quietly. "Eve. Every word I ever told you came from my heart. I never lied about how I felt about you. Not once."

She laughed bitterly, shaking her head in disbelief. "Really? Because it sure as hell *feels* like you did. Honestly, I don't even know what to believe anymore."

The sharpness in her voice hung between them, smothering whatever connection had once existed.

She drew in a ragged breath. "All this talk is a waste of time. We're here to find Nathan," she said, voice lower now but no less fierce. "He's the only reason I'm still standing here."

Without another glance, she turned and headed for the bridge, quickly swallowed by the mist.

Dante scoffed softly, shaking his head. "Chicks, man," he muttered under his breath. "That one's a real prize." He laughed quietly, eyes following her as she vanished into the mist. "You sure know how to pick 'em, Killer."

Gabe's head snapped up instantly, his eyes flashing dark and furious. "Fuck you, Dante."

Dante blinked, startled by the sudden venom in Gabe's voice. But Gabe didn't stop—he stormed toward him, shoving Dante hard toward the bridge, toward the darkness where she had vanished.

"You led us out here on some wild goose chase for my friend—for *her* friend," he shot back, voice quivering with barely contained anger. "And now you wanna crack jokes? Go ahead, make some more shithead comments like that, see what happens."

He let out a bitter laugh. "Classic Dante. Always hiding behind some bullshit remark instead of actually feeling something."

Dante's expression dropped. "Hey, man, I didn't mean it—"

"Oh, no, of course you didn't mean it," Gabe snapped back, mockingly mimicking his voice. *I didn't mean it, man.*" He kept his eyes locked on him. "That's your problem, dude. You never mean anything."

Dante squared up, standing toe to toe with his former friend, the space between them charged and shrinking by the second—but Gabe wasn't done.

When you were my roommate—when we were friends—we said we'd have each other's backs, no matter what. And when I couldn't take it anymore, when I realized my time on the field was done, I thought you'd understand. But you didn't. Instead, you turned your back on me like our friendship never mattered."

He moved closer, eyes burning, his voice low and rough as he looked down on him. "Then I find out about all the awful shit you put Nathan through—" his face flushed with rage. "You were a real piece of shit back then, Dante Edwards. And guess what? You always will be."

Dante's eyes narrowed, his posture tightening as he looked up, their faces inches apart. "Hey, man, don't make me do something I'll regret."

Wu stepped in fast, wedging himself between them and sliding an arm out to hold Dante back. "Alright, stop. We don't have time for any of this."

Gabe shoved Wu's arm aside, pushing him back with ease before getting nose-to-nose with Dante. They locked in, neither of them willing to back down.

"Something you'll regret?" Gabe snarled, his voice soaked in mockery. "And here I thought I was the only one trying to be a comedian. That, my friend, is the best joke I've heard all week."

He threw his head back in a sharp, theatrical laugh. "Dante Edwards— feeling regret—oh, man. That's gold!"

Dante's face tightened. "I'm warning you, Kowalski—back off. This isn't the time, and I have no problem closing your mouth for you."

Mia's voice cut through the fog. "Boys. Stop it." She didn't yell—she didn't have to.

Neither of them moved. The space between them pulsed with heat and history, years of resentment boiling over in the silence that followed.

After a beat, Dante let out a sharp breath and stepped back,

"Nah, man. Not today," he muttered, shaking his head. "You're not worth it." His mouth twisted into something colder. "Not even a little."

Before Gabe could fire back—verbal or otherwise—Eve's voice cut clean through the fog from just beyond the reach of the headlights.

"Hey!—I think I found something!"

The group stood in tense silence as they stared at the fresh tire tracks pressed into the snow, climbing partway up the hill before vanishing into the trees.

Eve stepped forward and motioned from the grooves carved through the snow toward the edge of the hill. Her hand swept toward a patch of trampled ground, where uneven footprints led up from the frozen riverbed below.

"Okay, so whoever was here— pulled in, got out of their vehicle, and walked down toward the river. That part's clear. But look at the way the prints come back up—there are two sets. Like they weren't alone anymore. It almost looks like one of them was being dragged along with them."

Gabe squinted down the hill. "So, are we just going to ignore how much this feels like a bad sequel to The Thing?"

Dante shot him a look. "Seriously, Kowalski. Would you please just shut the fuck up for once?"

Gabe didn't flinch. He just glared back, eyes burning, every muscle drawn tight like he was one wrong word away from snapping.

"Alright! That's enough!" Mia scolded. "There'll be plenty of time for you two to work out your issues—later."

She shifted her gaze to the tree line, her eyes tracing the narrow path that cut through the trunks. It twisted upward through the pines, almost hidden in the dark, but just visible enough to follow. At the top, tucked into the woods like it had been waiting for them all along, stood the cabin.

The structure looked out of place—too picture-perfect in its isolation. Warm light glowed through the frosted windows. Smoke drifted from the chimney, fading into the starry night sky. The house was warm and inviting.

Someone was definitely home.

And whoever it was, they had Nathan.

It wasn't a guess. It wasn't a hunch.

She *knew* it—

She could feel him in her heart. And he wasn't okay.

She turned to Dante. "Are you sure this is where you last felt him?"

Dante stepped closer to the edge of the bridge and looked down into the darkness. The memory of his shared connection with Nathan made him shudder. He stared down into the darkness below the bridge.

"Yeah, he was here. "I'm sure."

"Then he has to be up there," Mia said.

Eve surveyed the snowy driveway, pulled her keys from her pocket, and started toward the van before stopping short.

"She's not going to make it."

Mia frowned. "Who?"

"My van," Eve said, letting out a long breath. "The hill is way too steep. I love her to death, but I know the old gal's limits." She shoved the keys back into her jacket pocket. "Looks like we're gonna have to hoof it."

Gabe glanced at Dante with a smirk. "Hear that, Edwards? Guess it's time to test those upgrades of yours."

Dante scowled. "You never shut up, do you?"

Gabe shrugged. "No—Not really."

Dante muttered something under his breath but did not push it further.

Eve turned and started up the hill, her eyes fixed on the cabin at the top of the long, steep driveway.

One by one, the others followed. Their footsteps sank into the thick powder, which only deepened the higher they climbed. The wind pressed against them, cutting hard across the steep incline. With every step, the ground beneath them tilted more.

The hike wasn't impossible. But it wasn't easy either. Their legs ached. Their breath grew shorter. The only sound was the rhythm of boots in snow and the wind pushing through the trees like it wanted them gone.

No one complained. Not even Gabe.

He didn't crack a single joke on the way up. He'd started the climb with his usual bounce, but somewhere between the frozen trail and the silence still hanging from the fight with Dante, the weight of everything caught up to him.

The tension. The unknown. The fear of what they might find.

It pressed harder than the snow ever could, and he didn't have it in him to be funny anymore—not right now.

So he kept his head down and climbed. Step after step. Just like the rest of them.

By the time they reached the clearing, the cabin stood in full view. From a distance, it had looked quiet—almost peaceful—but up close, something felt off. Not exactly wrong, but not exactly right either.

It was the stillness. The hush that settled around it, like the place had been holding its breath, waiting for them. It pulled at them in a way none of them could name. Like they'd reached something important. Something that mattered.

It should have felt like safety.

But it didn't.

Mia stepped up first, quiet but determined. She raised her hand and gave the door a polite knock.

"Hello? Is anyone home?"

Completely out of patience, Eve flew up the steps, storming past her and slamming her fist against the door with every ounce of strength she had.

"Jesus, Eve—" Mia reached for her, but Eve didn't move. She stood rooted, both fists pounding.

"NATHAN BOONE!" she shouted, her breath exploding into the cold. "ARE YOU IN THERE?"

She didn't wait for an answer.

"Nathan! Nathan!"

A series of locks, old and heavy, clicked in sequence, one after the other. These weren't flimsy chains or a deadbolt slapped on for peace of mind. Whoever was on the other side had gone out of their way to keep the world out, and for a long time, it had worked. But tonight, for whatever reason, they were letting the outside world in.

The group froze, locked in place by anticipation.

No one breathed.

The heavy door groaned as it opened, creaking inch by inch.

When it opened, there was no towering figure. No evil presence lurking in the shadows. And to their collective relief, no sign of Val.

Only a man, framed by the warm light spilling from inside.

He wasn't what they expected. Not even close.

His face was lined like an old map. He looked as if each one of his wrinkles told a story, and every line on his face was a choice. Kindness lingered at the corners of his mouth.

He didn't speak right away. He just stood there, that small, quiet smile on his face—one that didn't quite fit the moment, but somehow made everything feel a little less scary.

"You're here for your friend," the man said, looking down at the group, each of them wide-eyed, searching for answers to the questions he already knew they were going to ask.

Mia swallowed. "Is he okay?"

The man studied her for a long moment, then let his eyes drift past her to the three boys standing stiffly at the bottom of the steps.

"He will be.—I'm glad you came," he said, his voice calm but sure. "He needs you."

There was no doubt in his tone. No urgency, no drama—just truth.

Eve studied him. There was something about the way he spoke, the way he held the moment so effortlessly, that made her uneasy.

Not because she felt threatened, but because she didn't.

Something shifted in her chest as she looked at him. It wasn't fear, but it carried the same weight. There was something in the way he stood, something about the stillness around him.

She couldn't place it. But it was there. He didn't look like anyone she remembered, but somehow, her body reacted like she should know who he was.

That's what threw her most.

He stepped back, swinging the door open wider.

"Come in," he said. "It's warm inside."

Quiet but certain, Mia stepped through the doorway first.

Eve followed close behind, but not without hesitation. Whatever had stirred in her when she first saw the man—whatever strange pull had crept in under her skin—she didn't trust it. The feeling had settled in too quickly, too easily, and with a warmth that didn't feel earned. It felt like some kind of trick, like black magic dressed up to look like comfort.

So she caught herself before it could take hold. She checked her instinct and snapped her guard back into place as she stepped through the doorway. If this was a trap, she was prepared to face it head-on. If there was even the smallest chance that Nathan was here, she'd find him—and she'd get him out of there. No matter what it took. No matter who she had to face.

She would bring him back.

Back to campus.

Back to where she could keep him safe, the way she always had.

The others followed. One by one, they crossed the threshold.

The door clicked shut behind them with a heavy, wooden slam that echoed into the silence. The world outside didn't just go quiet—it vanished, sealed behind them as if it had never been there at all.

44

THE WILDCAT'S DEN

Inside the cabin, the fire crackled low in the hearth, and the air was the warmest they'd felt since leaving campus. It *should've* felt safe. But the heat didn't reach them—not really. The cold was lodged deep, like something they'd swallowed whole. No flame could touch it. Whatever comfort the room promised, it stayed just out of reach.

The space was open, lived-in. The log walls glowed honey-gold in the firelight, and the ceiling beams vanished into shadow. A wide leather couch faced the fire, cushions still dented like someone had just gotten up. Across from it, a solid wooden desk was cluttered with hardcovers and notebooks. Titles like *Time and the Mind of God*, *Quantum Paradoxes*, and *The Problem of Evil* were stacked in uneven piles. Some pages were flagged with sticky notes, others scrawled over in a messy, slanted hand. A cracked leather journal lay open beside a mug of cold coffee, the ink still drying on a half-finished thought:

"Next time, it'll be different. But how many times have I said that?"

Mia stepped inside first, her arms wrapped tight across her chest, not for warmth, but like she was trying to hold something in. She scanned the space slowly, eyes catching on the half-burned candles, the stacks of marked-up papers, the kind of clutter only a person in hiding would allow.

Behind her, the others filtered in one by one. No one spoke. The truth still echoed in their heads.

They were safe for now, but it didn't feel like safety. It felt like the eye of the storm.

Eve didn't wait. She moved to the wall and planted herself there like she needed something solid at her back. Her eyes never left the man across the room.

"Alright," she said flatly. "Enough with the theater. What have you done with our friend?"

The man didn't blink. "He's resting," he replied. "He's safe. You have my word."

Mia stepped forward. Her voice was calm, but it held something firmer underneath. "Please just tell us that he's okay."

"He will be. He just needs a little time." The man motioned toward the couch. "Please. Sit."

She wasn't interested in waiting any longer, She'd had enough. "Oh, hell no. We're not playing your little mystery man game. You need to tell us everything right now, or I'll start tearing this place apart."

Gabe lowered himself onto the couch but didn't lean back. His hands rested on his knees, tension still threaded through his shoulders. "Eve," he said, voice steady, "I know you're frustrated right now, but maybe he's about to tell us what we need to know. Just give him a chance."

The man studied Gabe like he was trying to make sense of why someone would walk into a life-or-death situation wearing a skirt made from retired high school auditorium drapes—then, for some reason, his face softened.

"I can tell that you care about her," he said. "It's not hard to see."

He shifted his attention to Eve. Whatever was behind his expression wasn't creepy. It felt older, maybe even respectful.

"She reminds me of someone I knew a long time ago. She has the same fight in her— the same spark."

His voice dipped slightly, like the memory had caught him off guard. Whatever he saw in Eve—it had been a long time since he'd seen anything like it.

"It's obvious that there's something between you two. Don't let it go. That kind of fire—real fire—doesn't come around often."

Eve stepped away from the wall and turned. "Okay. That's it." She started toward the nearest door. "I'm done waiting."

"Be my guest," the man said, utterly unfazed. "But I don't think you'll find what you're looking for."

Gabe shot out a hand, catching Eve's wrist before she could storm off.

"Eve, please," he said, his voice quieter but firm. "He's going to tell us. Just relax."

Before she could yank free, he tugged her down beside him on the couch, his grip loosening but still holding her there. His voice dropped, steady but low. "I know you hate me right now, but for the sake of our friend, can you please just cool it?"

She didn't move for a second. Then, reluctantly, she sat beside him on the couch. Her arms crossed hard over her chest.

Eve glared at him. "Fine," she muttered, giving in and sitting next to him. She scooted away just enough to put space between them, arms crossed tightly.

"Just so we're clear, this doesn't mean we're cool."

Her voice was sharp, but when she turned to Gabe, her expression softened just a fraction.

"I'm only playing along just to get to Nathan."

Gabe nodded once. "Fair enough."

Eve turned to the man. "Alright. We're listening. How about you start by telling us who you are."

The man seemed to consider them for a moment. His shoulders eased slightly, like he'd made a decision.

"My name is Jeremy," he said. "Jeremy Anderson."

Wu was the first to react. "No way."

Mia felt a jolt of recognition—his name was familiar, but just out of reach.

"Wait—how do I know that name?" she asked, turning to Wu, searching his face for answers. "Who is he?"

Wu turned to her, looking paler than she'd ever seen him.

"That's Jeremy Anderson? As in—*the* Jeremy Anderson?"

He looked around, like someone needed to confirm it before he exploded. "Dude. I've watched every one of your old lectures on those grainy feeds on The Deep Network. And, I've read every archived forum post about your early work. You invented half the language we even use for neural tech. You're—holy shit—I mean, Sorry— Mr Anderson, you're a legend."

Jeremy raised a hand casually. "Please, just call me Jeremy."

Wu let out something between a nervous chuckle and a gasp, his usual composed self cracking apart, revealing something close to awe.

"Right. Sorry. It's just... you're the reason any of this is even possible. You're kind of my hero."

Jeremy gave him a small nod. "Sounds like you did your research."

Mia's eyes widened. "That's why I know you. One of my hybrid medicine journals had a whole spread on how some people think that you are responsible for the chip's original blueprint." She paused. "But they said you died."

Jeremy shrugged. "As far as anyone knows, I did."

Gabe leaned forward. "Wait, seriously? I thought the MIND chip was owned by some massive company in Texas."

Jeremy gave a quiet nod. "It is now."

"But way back when," Wu cut in, his energy still buzzing, "before the corporations got their hands on it, before anyone even called it enhancement—before people started using it to turn themselves into gods —it was his."

He looked around at the group. "I can't believe this. We're literally sitting in the cabin of Jeremy 'Freaking' Anderson."

Gabe leaned forward, elbows on his knees, staring at Jeremy like he was trying to make sense of a puzzle that refused to fit together. "So you're telling me the guy who basically reprogrammed human evolution is back from the dead and we're just sitting in his cabin right now?"

Wu gave a shaky laugh.

"Man, I have so many questions. How did you even come up with this tech? I've studied your entire career. I mean, in the early 2000s, we had just gotten the internet, and then out of nowhere, you showed up and single-handedly changed the entire definition of technology. We went from dial-up to broadband in an instant because of you. You didn't just speed up progress—you lit the fuse that detonated the digital revolution in a fraction of the time anyone thought possible. And you did it all before you even turned thirty."

Eve crossed her arms. "Alright, that's enough fangirling, Wu." Her tone didn't bother hiding the edge. "Forgive me if I'm not exactly in awe of the guy who made this whole mess possible."

She turned to Jeremy, eyes locked. "Enough of the history lesson. Where's Nathan?"

"She's right," Jeremy replied. "We don't have time for a full rundown of my career highlights."

He glanced at Wu. "Even if your buddy here is dying to hear all about it."

Wu clamped his mouth shut.

Jeremy stepped away from the table and walked to the wide window overlooking the dark campus. He didn't speak at first. The fire behind him snapped, casting uneven light across the floor.

"You want answers," he said. "And, I'll give them to you, but you need to understand something first."

He turned, his expression unreadable as he met their eyes one by one.

"Your friend Nathan isn't just another kid with an implant."

Mia's voice was quiet. "Yeah. We know."

Jeremy didn't look away. "No," he said. "You really don't."

Eve didn't flinch. "Then explain it. Spell it out. Stop wasting time."

Jeremy moved to the fireplace, standing near the flames like the heat might help him find the words.

"I can't explain how I know what I know—or why I've always been ahead of the curve, and there's no reasonable explanation for how I was able to design tech faster than anyone believed possible. Even if I tried, you wouldn't believe me."

He paused. "None of that matters. What does matter is why I did what I did—my purpose. And that purpose is the reason you're all here."

The firelight caught the edge of his profile as he stared into the flames. "I only ever wanted to save one person."

"I knew what was going to happen to her," he continued. "She always got sick. Every time."

He paused. Something tightened behind his eyes. When he spoke again, the words came slower, pulled back like he'd stopped himself from saying too much.

"I couldn't sit back and watch it happen—not again."

His voice dropped. "I thought I could fix it. I thought I was doing the right thing. But I got it wrong."

He let the silence hang.

"I always do—I'm still trying to figure out how to get it right. This time, it just got out of control."

Mia glanced at Dante. He stood still, arms crossed, listening in silence. Her mind moved quickly, processing Jeremy's words like symptoms without a diagnosis.

Wu stood frozen beside them, watching Jeremy like a moment from history had stepped off the page.

Jeremy's hands curled into loose fists. "So inspired by my purpose, I developed the prototype for the original neural device. I tested it, and it worked. Better than I imagined. The results were undeniable. Revolutionary. But the moment I proved what it could do, they took it."

His voice darkened. "And they didn't just steal it. They gutted it. Stripped it down, rewrote it, twisted it into something I never meant for it to become."

Gabe let out a breath. "That's messed up. You build something to save lives, and they turn it into a leash."

Eve shot to her feet. "We didn't come all this way for guilt trips. We came for Nathan."

She crossed the room in a blur before Gabe could stop her, yanking on the nearest door. Nothing. She moved to the next, then another. All of them were sealed shut.

She turned back, her voice sharp. "Why won't you tell us where he is?"

The silence dragged.

"Is he even—"

She stopped dead as soon as she saw it.

A photo hung above the fireplace. She hadn't noticed it until now—and now that she had, everything became clear.

She stepped closer and lifted it from its place. The frame felt heavier than expected. Her hands settled on it like they'd held it before.

In the picture, a couple stood outside a café, smiling at something just out of frame. The man had an acoustic guitar slung over his shoulder and an easy look in his eyes. It was Jeremy. Much younger, but it was definitely him.

But the woman next to him—

That was what stopped her.

The glass felt cold beneath her fingers. The fire behind her cracked, but it barely registered.

"In her mind, she saw Nathan's face—lit by afternoon sun, caught mid-laugh, turning his coffee mug in his hands like always—and for a moment, she forgot to breathe.

She saw the way he looked at people he loved, like they were the only ones in the world. That's how the woman in the photo was looking at Jeremy.

And it wasn't just the look.

It was the light in her eyes. Something honest and familiar.

Nathan had his mother's eyes.

—And his father's smile.

Her hands trembled around the frame as a single tear escaped, tracing a slow line down her cheek before falling soundlessly onto the glass.

When she finally spoke, she barely whispered.

"Okay.—I get it now."

Jeremy stepped toward her, his fingers brushing hers as he gently took the frame from her hands. He held her eyes, his expression soft, steady. Then, with care, he returned the photo to its place above the mantle, his hand lingering like he was closing a chapter only he wasn't done reading.

"I thought I could save her," he said quietly. "I thought if I worked fast enough—smart enough—I could outsmart death."

He stood there for a moment and let his hand rest on the mantle. His shoulders rose and fell with a slow breath as if weighing whether to say more.

He carefully composed himself and turned back to them, but something in his eyes made it clear—he was still figuring out what to say next.

"The thing is, when you create something that can truly help people— something that could do some real good for once—there will always be those who would rather own it than let it change the world."

Mia swallowed hard. She didn't doubt that for a second.

Jeremy's eyes shifted to Wu, studying him. "I'm sure you can imagine that better than most."

Wu shifted uncomfortably. "Yeah," he said, his voice tight under the weight of everything he had done. "I can. But I don't get it—why didn't you just do it on your own? You're brilliant. Couldn't you have pulled it off quietly, without anyone noticing?"

Jeremy didn't answer at first, but his gaze shifted toward the fire again, like he was watching a ghost. Then he spoke.

"The truth is, developing what I had in mind wasn't something I could do alone. I needed infrastructure, lab access, top-tier processors, and biological integration models—none of which I could afford or even get close to on my own. So, I met with a few big tech investors and I played the game."

Wu's expression darkened with regret. "That's exactly why I joined Val in the first place. She told me we were building something to help people —something that would bring people together. And I believed her. At least I wanted to believe her."

He paused, the weight of it sinking in.

"I see it now. We were chasing the same dream, just on opposite sides of the truth."

"Exactly, so you understand why I couldn't tell anyone what I was up to. I had to protect what I was truly working on. But to get them to buy into my vision, I had to give them a little taste of what I could do."

Wu tilted his head slightly. "So what'd you give them?"

His voice flattened. "Like you said, I took us from dial-up to broadband overnight. That was all they needed to believe in me."

He looked past them, like he was staring back at a version of himself that had made different choices.

"They didn't need much convincing. Once I proved what I could do, once they saw real results, they were hooked. They opened their checkbooks without hesitation and gave me everything I needed. For a while, I honestly believed that I could pull it off," he scoffed.

Mia leaned forward slightly, her brow furrowed. "You were playing both sides?"

Jeremy nodded once. "I had unlimited funding, full autonomy, and a perfect plan. I figured I'd deliver some flashy invention—maybe a dumbed-down version of the biotech I was working on—that they could flood to the masses. Something just impressive enough to keep them distracted while I worked in secret on what really mattered."

Wu glanced at the others, then back at Jeremy. "You really thought you could hide that kind of tech forever?"

"I did. I know it was foolish—and arrogant," he paused, feeling the weight of his mistake. "I figured I'd give them what they wanted and quietly do my secret work behind the scenes. The world would move forward with what I gave them, and they'd never know what I was truly doing."

Dante leaned forward, frowning. "Alright, I don't get it. I mean, I know I'm not some genius like Wu, but am I the only one who's completely lost here?"

Eve scoffed. "Oh, come on—you seriously can't see it?" She turned to the others, throwing up a hand. "It's obvious. Nathan was the first person to ever get a chip. And let me guess—you hid some kind of secret code in his head, and now Val wants it. Am I close?"

He didn't flinch. "Close enough— You've got the pieces. But you haven't put them in the right places—not yet."

His eyes drifted back to the mantle for a moment, landing on the photo like it was still trying to speak for him. He didn't say anything, but the pause was enough to make the weight of it land.

The way he looked at the woman in the picture was all Eve needed to see. Everything clicked at once—the secrecy, the guilt, the way Jeremy had looked at the photo like it held the answer to every unspoken question.

She stepped forward, pointing to the photo. "That's Nathan's mom," she said, turning to the others. "That chip—It wasn't meant for him. It was meant for her."

He nodded. "I knew what was going to happen to her, the same way I knew how to develop my tech. I built the chip for just her—to protect her from ever getting sick again. It was the only reason I ever created the damn thing in the first place."

He paused, the fire's glow catching the lines under his eyes. "She was the only one who ever knew what I was truly working on. And after a lot of convincing—and sharing things no one else would've believed—she agreed to be the first to get an implant. But it didn't take. Or at least not the way it was supposed to."

"And then we found out she was pregnant." He paused. "That wasn't supposed to happen—not yet, anyway." He hesitated, something tightened in his voice like he was one sentence away from unraveling a truth too big to explain. Then, with a subtle shift, he pulled himself back.

"Let's just say… even when you think you've accounted for everything, the universe has a way of rewriting the script."

He cleared his throat to compose himself and continue.

"Somehow, the chip didn't just implant—it fused with the developing neural tissue. But not in her, the baby." He shook his head. "I'd planned every angle, every safeguard. But the nano-sequencing adapted in ways I couldn't predict. It integrated with her system, then passed to the child growing inside her. It didn't just implant. It bonded and became part of him. The tech buried itself in Nathan before he ever opened his eyes."

Mia's breath caught. "So he's had it his whole life, and no one knew?"

Jeremy nodded. "I worked very hard to keep it that way."

He leaned forward slightly, voice low and steady. "There were a few early doctor appointments—when Nathan was just a baby. They'd run routine scans. Nothing unusual at first. But at his six-month checkup, they thought they found an *abnormality*. That's what started the whole wild goose chase. From that point on, they were convinced he had something."

His hands tightened slightly. "Once the red flags were raised, they came after me. They pressured me to hand over things they only assumed I had. The people who'd backed my research made our lives miserable before they even understood what I'd built."

"Once they figured out what I was hiding—once they realized the tech I'd created was more advanced, more dangerous than anything I'd shown them—they became obsessed with finding it."

"They demanded everything—my research, my notes, even my early prototypes. When I wouldn't give them the missing pieces, they threatened to kill me."

"What they didn't know was that the only fully functioning unit had already fused inside my child."

"They started to reverse-engineer their own version, trying to piece together what little they could from the scraps I left behind. But I knew it was only a matter of time before they uncovered the truth about what I had created and what I had done."

Jeremy's voice dropped lower, almost like he didn't want to hear himself say it.

"That's when I knew I had to vanish. There wasn't going to be a clean break or a soft exit. So I staged the crash. Burned the files. Cut every cord I could. Then I moved Nathan and his mother to a small town in Vermont, where I knew that they would never be found. I got them new names, new identities, and I made sure they blended in. I kept my distance, but I never stopped watching. It was the only way to keep them safe."

He let the words hang for a beat, then continued.

"But before I disappeared, I built something into Nathan. Call it an internal mask. Think of it as the network's first true mod. It was foolproof. I buried every trace of signal that might have pointed back to him, making it impossible for him to be found."

Wu pieced it together, the realization sinking in. "But they didn't give up, did they? They knew he had something."

Jeremy gave a grim nod before laying out the pieces. "They didn't know for sure, but they had their suspicions. Enough that they kept bringing him to hospitals, to see specialists who had no idea what they were looking for, much less how to find it. They told him it was for routine scans, regular checkups, and basic monitoring. But it wasn't. It was surveillance, dressed up as concern."

He paused, his voice tightening.

"They didn't know what they were looking for, not exactly. But they knew he was different. That something in him didn't add up. So they did what people like them always do—they pushed. They made every little thing feel like life or death. They filled his head with anxiety and made him doubt his own body. Hypochondria. Panic. Intrusive thoughts. They thought pressure might trigger a response. That the tech would somehow expose itself under stress to try and save him."

He looked down for a moment. "They didn't know for sure that he had the chip. But they believed enough to keep pushing him."

Wu's voice was quieter now. "But he has your version, doesn't he? The original. Not the corporate one. The one they never got their hands on. Couldn't you have done something, you know, to counterbalance everything they were doing to him?"

Jeremy nodded. "I did. I tried everything. But they kept closing in. The scans, the questions, the shadows that never went away. They were relentless, and I couldn't risk anyone finding out I was still alive."

He paused, a flicker of something old and hard flashing behind his eyes.

"But then Val pulled every string she had to bring him here—to this campus. And when that happened, I knew my time behind the curtain was over."

He looked around the room, the weight of it settling in his voice. "I've been close to Nathan his whole life, watching over him from the shadows. I knew this was the endgame. One way or another, it had to stop—here."

Silence wrapped around the room.

Then Gabe let out a breath. "Well, shit," he muttered. "I hate to say it, but I'm with Dante. I'm totally lost. What does all of this even mean?"

Jeremy exhaled slowly, choosing his words carefully. "It means that what's in Nathan's head isn't like anything else out there." His eyes swept over the group.

"The Mind Chip that exists today—the one corporations got their hands on, the one that's been modified and reprogrammed a thousand times over—isn't mine. Not anymore. What Nathan has—" He shook his head. "That's the original. The prototype. The one before all the backdoors, before all the monitoring, before all the enhancements they thought would make people better."

Mia's voice trembled. "You're saying... his chip is pure?"

Jeremy nodded. "Exactly. It's completely unfiltered. No modifications, no limitations. And because of that, it holds something the others don't."

Eve frowned. "And that is?"

Jeremy hesitated again, but Wu wasn't waiting. His mind was already racing ahead, filling in the blanks.

"The source code," Wu exclaimed, almost in disbelief. "Nathan has the original source code, doesn't he?"

"Bingo," Jeremy said, watching Wu's mind work. "You're a smart young man. I hope you find a way to put that brain of yours to good use someday."

Wu's mind spun with the implications, the sheer magnitude of what he had just uncovered.

"Yeah," he said, his voice quieter now. "Me too."

Jeremy's silence was confirmation enough.

Gabe let out a hollow laugh, shaking his head. "Okay, hold on. Just so I'm clear—our boy, Nathan Boone, the walking panic attack with glasses and all-around mess of a human, has the single most valuable piece of technology ever created locked in his head?"

His laughter faded almost as quickly as it came. He leaned back slightly, rubbing his palms on his jeans. The weight of it all started to register—his usual humor cracking under the pressure.

"Man, no wonder he never felt right. He was never just a normal kid."

Jeremy simply nodded.

Eve's expression hardened. "And Val knows about this—That's why she wants him?"

"She knows now," Jeremy said grimly.

"But she didn't always. She's been pulling strings and filtering candidates to campus on behalf of the corporation for years. I've been watching from up here. I thought I had hidden Nathan safely, but when he got here, she was too close. She knew she was finally going to get what she'd been looking for, and that made her even stronger."

"And what exactly did she want? What makes the source code so special?" Gabe asked, his brows pulling together in confusion.

Wu leaned in, his voice filled with urgency. "Val's goal was always finding new ways to modify chips—she was all about connecting people to each other. She invented the entire glitch network at NCSU. She spun it like some revolutionary breakthrough. She'd say it was the only way people like us could truly connect. To share emotions, thoughts, even memories. She sold it as progress. That's what we were supposed to be working on."

Jeremy remained still, his expression unreadable, but a shadow passed through his features as he listened.

Wu shook his head. "She told me we needed more people on the network—*her network*—to figure it out. That's why she was recruiting. That's why she wanted me involved. But now I see what she was doing." He exhaled sharply. "She wasn't trying to build anything. She was screening people. Searching for one person." He turned to Jeremy, realization solidifying like stone. "Someone with your original code."

Dante stepped forward, his expression darkening. "I used to think glitching was just another way to stay connected, like she said—something that could bring people closer, help them share experiences. I bought into it because I wanted to win. I didn't care what it really was, not back then. I thought it could give me an edge. I didn't ask questions—I didn't want to know." He paused, regret bleeding into his voice. "If I'd known what she was doing, I never would've gone near it."

He shook his head. "But now? Now I see what she was after. She wasn't trying to connect people. She was mapping them—tracking what they wanted, what they feared, what they craved the most. And once she had that? She was going to exploit it."

Gabe exhaled sharply. "Wow. The power someone could have if they could actually do that—sync into someone like that? The marketing alone would be priceless to those corporate bastards. And you're saying Nathan can? Or at least, the code in his head can?"

He shook his head, the weight of it settling in. "I can see why she'd stop at nothing to find him."

Eve scoffed. "Do you even hear how insane that sounds? Do you know how many people she would've had to go through to find that one person? That's impossible. There's no way Val had that kind of reach. No one does."

Jeremy's voice was quiet, but firm. "She had help. She had powerful people with unmatched resources—people who were just as desperate to control the future as she was."

Mia nodded slowly, the pieces falling into place. "The corporation. She wasn't doing this on her own. She had infrastructure, funding, and protection. That's how she got so far without being stopped."

She frowned, her mind piecing things together. Then—suddenly—her pulse quickened. A thought snapped into place like a puzzle piece she hadn't realized was missing.

"Wait," she breathed. "Val's from Texas, isn't she?"

Wu's brows drew together. "Yeah. So?"

Mia turned to Jeremy, her voice quieter now, but more certain. "She wasn't just recruiting. She came here—to NCSU—for a reason."

Jeremy met her eyes, steady and grim. "She did. Because Val isn't just some recruiter, and this isn't about finding the right candidates. She works for the corporation that stole my tech. The same people who steamrolled me, who forced me to disappear."

He exhaled, his voice lowering. "Their power is unmatched. I had to fake my death—and hide my family—just to keep us all safe."

He let that settle for a beat before continuing. "And now… they know where Nathan is, but we still have time to stop them."

He shook his head slowly, his face heavy with regret. "I thought I could stay ahead of them. That I could protect him from a distance."

His expression shifted. "But they're here now. And if we don't fight back—if we let them win, the world will never be the same."

He looked at each of them in turn, his voice steadying. "It's time to take the power back."

Without another word, Jeremy turned toward the bookcase lining the far wall. His fingers traced the spines until they landed on *In the Unlikely Event* by Judy Blume, before pulling it back—a title that felt like more than a coincidence. It was a reminder that everything in Nathan's life had hinged on improbable choices, narrow chances, and one man's refusal to let fate play out unchallenged.

With a soft click, the bookcase shifted, letting out a deep mechanical groan that broke the silence as it swung open, revealing a hidden room.

Inside, Nathan sat, motionless. His eyes were vacant. Shadows curled at the edges of the dimly lit space. The couch he was sitting on looked more like a holding cell than a resting place.

Jeremy crossed the room slowly and stopped in front of him. For a moment, he just stood there, looking down at him. Then he placed a hand on Nathan's shoulder, his fingers tightening slightly, like he was asking for forgiveness he didn't think he deserved.

"I've been watching over him his whole life," he said quietly. "All I wanted to do was keep him safe."

He stayed there a second longer, his hand still resting on Nathan's shoulder. Then he turned back to the group. His face was calmer now, but there was something tired in his eyes.

"But now I know I can't do this alone," he said. "I don't have what he needs."

The truth is, I haven't just been watching Nathan—I've been watching all of you. I know who you are. You're not here together by chance.

He turned to Wu first.

"You see the angles—the systems beneath the surface. You don't just understand how it works; you see how it fits. You solve problems the rest of us don't even know are there. Your brain is more powerful than you give it credit for. You're a lot smarter than you think—you just don't always see it yet."

Then he turned to Mia.

"You're a rare combination—technology and medicine, precision and compassion. But with Nathan, it's more than that. You don't just see what's wrong with him—you see him. You care about the person beneath the pain, beneath the silence. You acknowledge his fears, even the ones he can't bring himself to say out loud. The way you calm him, the way your presence cuts through the chaos—that's what makes the difference. That kind of goodness isn't taught. It's who you are. And when he's lost in the worst parts of himself, you remind him there's still something worth coming back to."

He met Dante's eyes next.

"You've lived the fallout. You've made choices you can't take back— and you carry that guilt with you everywhere. But the fact that it still breaks your heart, that it still matters to you—that's what makes you dangerous in the right way. You know exactly what this power can destroy, and you know you can't let it happen again. You're done living with any more regrets."

He looked at Gabe.

"You've been there for him. You've kept him laughing when everything else felt heavy. And in just a short time, you gave him something rare— your courage. You pushed him out of his comfort zone just by showing up. That makes you more valuable than you know."

And finally, to Eve.

"And you… You've always been by his side. When things were falling apart, you stayed. When he pulled away, you reached for him anyway. You were his first real friend—the only one who made him feel like he mattered. And now, more than ever, he needs that loyalty. He needs you to help him see who he can still become."

"No, I don't have what he needs," he said, voice low. "What he needs is you—every single one of you."

45

THE UNLIKELY EVENT

Nathan sat frozen on the deep leather couch in Jeremy's hidden room. His eyes were wide but vacant as he stared into nothing, oblivious to the fire's warmth and deaf to the sound of his friends closing in. He didn't blink, he didn't react, he didn't seem to be in the same world as them.

Eve rushed over to him, dropping to her knees beside him. Her hands closed around his—he was ice.

"Nathan!" Her voice shook as she gripped his fingers, trying to will warmth back into them. "Hey, it's me. I'm here. We're all here."

He didn't move.

"Say something, Nathan. Please—anything," she pleaded into the silence. Then she turned to Jeremy. "What's wrong with him?"

"She got into his head," he said. "Tried to hijack his chip and pull the code—his code—straight from his system. But the reboot I triggered cut her off before she got what she wanted. It stalled the connection and locked her out. Now that he's back online, she's trying to break in again."

He glanced at Nathan, then back at the others.

"He's safe. For now. He's working through it—flushing out everything she left behind. The fear. The doubt. The noise. He's almost there. But he can't do the last part alone. He needs someone to reach in and unlock what he is struggling to process."

Gabe gave Nathan's shoulder a shake. "Cheese, you in there? Snap out of it, buddy. You just got here… we've got so much more stupid stuff to do. Come on, man, say something."

Mia moved quietly across the room and lowered herself to the floor in front of him. "I know you're in there, Nathan. I can feel you, and I know that you can feel me too. I know it feels like everything's slipping—like you're stuck in something you can't get out of. But you're not alone. We found you. We're here. And no matter what she did, no matter what's pulling at you—we're not letting go."

She reached out and lightly touched his arm, her warmth meeting his cold skin. "Come back to us, Nathan. Please."

Her pleas fell short—only a whisper against nothing.

By the door, Dante took a slow breath, steadying himself against the weight of something unseen that was pressing into the space between them. He knew Nathan wasn't just in shock, he wasn't shutting down.

He knew he had to do something. He knew, with absolute clarity, that no one else was going to be able to pull Nathan back. It wasn't about guilt, or instinct, or even saving the day. It was about owning every awful thing he'd ever done to Nathan and finally making it right.

This wasn't a choice. It was a reckoning. And if someone had to step up, it had to be him.

He stepped forward and sat on the coffee table in front of Nathan, placing himself directly in his line of sight, eye to vacant eye. He leaned in, close enough to feel the weight of the silence pressing between them. Then, slowly and with purpose, he rested a steady hand on his shoulder.

The impact was immediate, sending Nathan's mind crashing into his like a tidal wave. It wasn't a stream of thoughts; it was a flood of static, a barrage of fractured voices overlapping with flashing images that moved too fast to hold. Each one flared behind his eyes—hot, then gone. It wasn't pain exactly, but it wasn't pleasant either. There was a pull to it, like gravity, like something alive. This wasn't just noise. It was presence.

Dante could feel it—Nathan was in there, somewhere.

He barely had time to brace before the second wave of memories slammed into him. They didn't come in flashes or fragments—they poured in all at once, overwhelming and relentless. Each one collided with the next, faster than he could process. There was no space for him to breathe, no way to shield himself. Everything was raw and unfiltered. He was being forced to relive every terrible thing he'd ever done, but this time through Nathan's eyes—and there was no looking away.

He saw everything. He felt everything.

The years of torment came rushing in—not as scenes, but as sensations. All the whispered taunts echoed in his skull. The sting of laughter that wasn't his. He felt the weight of every shove, every cruel nickname, as if they'd been carved into Nathan's skin and left to scar. He felt how small Nathan had to make himself, how hard he tried to be invisible.

And then came the cafeteria. Not a memory—an impact.

Dante reeled as it hit him. He saw Nathan's face, twisted in fury, but underneath it, disgust. Aimed at him. Pure rage. The kind that burned through skin and bone and screamed for something to break. Nathan had looked at him like he wanted to rip his face off—like violence was the only thing big enough to hold what he was feeling. And the worst part was that Dante understood. He agreed. If their places were reversed, he'd want the same thing. He deserved it.

Dante felt like the floor had dropped out from under him. The weight of it hit all at once. There was no warning, no way to soften the blow. Years of buried pain, regret, and guilt surged through him, collapsing over his shoulders like a storm front.

But beneath all of it—under the pain, beneath the fury—there was something else. It was faint, almost fragile, but it was real.

There was still a fight in Nathan. There was a quiet, desperate refusal to give in. Even after everything the universe had thrown at him, he still hadn't let go. But now, he was slipping. Too tired to keep pushing. Too worn down to pull himself back.

Dante could feel it—Nathan was barely holding onto the pieces of himself that still remained.

He knew that he had to reach him before Val crushed what was left.

Because this was on him.

He'd helped build the walls Nathan used to shut the world out. He'd stood by and watched as Nathan disappeared behind them. He'd been the reason for so much of the silence.

Even as the system stripped away years of pain, Nathan clung to what was familiar, and Dante could feel him trying to rebuild his old fortress of solitude, piece by piece. It was the only way he knew to survive. But now he stood at a crossroads—caught between standing up for himself, or vanishing into silence for good.

Dante couldn't let him disappear—Not again.

"Nathan, I know you can hear me. You have to. Focus on my voice. Follow it back."

Nathan didn't move. His breathing stayed shallow, and his hands sat limp in his lap. He looked more like a shadow than a person, caught in some space none of them could reach.

Dante took a breath and held it. Then, slowly, he let it go and tightened his grip on Nathan's shoulder.

"I want you to hear what I'm saying, Nathan. All of it," he paused, searching Nathan's empty eyes, his tone filled with deep regret. "I'm sorry for what I did to you. I'm sorry for everything. I had no idea how much pain I caused you... Not until now. I'm sorry. Really, truly sorry, man. I mean that.

His voice dropped, quieter now, but no less steady.

"I was so wrapped up in proving something to myself that I never once thought about what that meant for anyone else. I took every ounce of self-hate I was carrying and dumped it all out on you. I laughed at you. I pushed you down. I acted like you didn't matter because doing that was way easier than facing the fact that I was terrified of never being enough."

His breath faltered, but he pushed through.

"I turned you into a punchline so I would never have to feel like one."

He waited, watching for any sign that Nathan could hear him.

Still, nothing.

"I know I don't deserve your forgiveness. I probably don't even deserve this moment. But I'm not leaving you like this. You don't get to give up. Not now. Not after everything you've survived."

Dante leaned in slightly, close enough that his voice would be impossible to ignore.

"If you let this happen—if you let Val win—then everything you've fought through ends here. Is that what you want? For her to own you? For all of this to mean nothing?"

He saw it then—a shift in Nathan's expression. It was subtle, almost imperceptible. Just a twitch at the corner of his mouth followed by a flicker behind his eyes. Just a tiny crack that fractured in the stillness that had been holding him frozen since before they all arrived at the cabin.

It was small, but it was there.

And Dante grabbed it with everything he had, forcing it to open wider before it could close back up.

"I know what she did to you," Dante said, his voice steady. "I felt it back at the bridge—the way she tried to drag you under, how she tried to strip you down until there was nothing left but what she wanted."

He shifted closer, tightening his grip on Nathan's shoulder, grounding them both in the moment.

"But she's wrong, Nathan. She doesn't own you. She never did. And do you know how I know that?"

Dante leaned in as if he could reach through the silence and pull him out by sheer will.

"Because I was a total dick to you for years, and you never let it break you. You might think it did, but it didn't. I threw everything I had at you —all of my insecurity, all of my fear—and you took it. You took all of it. And you're still here."

He nodded to himself, letting the weight of his words land.

"You're stronger than you think, Nathan. But you've got to fight now. I need you with me. We all do. This isn't just about you anymore—it never was. It's about all of us, and we don't make it unless you come back."

Dante exhaled hard, the pressure building in his chest.

"Please, Nathan. Just snap out of it."

A single tear slipped from the corner of Nathan's eye.

"That's it, Boone," Dante encouraged. "I know you're in there."

He gave Nathan a short, rough shake.

"Come on, man. Fight. I'm right here. I'll fight with you."

Nathan gasped, like someone who'd just broken the surface after being under too long. His whole body jolted. One hand lunged forward, grabbing fistfuls of Dante's sleeve like it was the only solid thing left in the world. Then his head snapped up, and his eyes opened wide and wild, before locking on Dante's. They were unfocused at first, but alive.

He looked at Dante like he was climbing his way back from somewhere dark. His breath came sharp and uneven, but he was here. His fingers twitched, and his shoulders jerked back, like his body was trying to shield itself from a blow that had already landed.

He tried to speak, but the words caught in his throat, like his voice had forgotten how to form them.

"She's coming."

46

THE SHOWDOWN

The wind tore through the trees outside the cabin with the type of violence that felt personal, like it wasn't just moving branches—it was trying to break in. Every gust slammed into the windows so hard they shuddered in their frames, groaning loud enough to make you wonder if the next one would crack the glass wide open. Inside, the air felt too still. Like everything in the room had been caught mid-breath and was too scared to move or speak or even blink.

But Jeremy wasn't scared. He didn't think. He just moved—straight and fast—crossing the room in a few sure steps until he reached the window. He leaned in, the glass still rattling in its frame as he stared out into the dark.

"She found us faster than I expected."

Eve's eyes snapped to him.

"What do you mean faster than you expected? You knew she'd find us?"

Jeremy turned toward her, his voice already thinning with frustration.

"I tried to keep him hidden. This room—" he gestured to the shelves, the walls, the wood still humming from the storm outside—"it was masking the signal, dulling it just enough to keep her off his trail. She must have already been close. The second he synced with Dante, the signal spiked. That was all she needed. She must've locked onto it the instant it came through."

347

Nathan staggered where he stood, clutching the edge of the table to steady himself.

He could feel it again—that invisible thread tethered to something far too strong to sever. It pulled tighter now, coiled around the base of his skull, and tugged hard, like it was trying to drag his mind out through his spine. It didn't move him physically, but inside, he was already being pulled toward her. Not with force. With inevitability.

"She's almost here," he whispered, his voice fraying at the edges.

Mia moved fast, stepping to his side and bracing him with both hands, she wrapped her arm beneath his to keep him upright.

"Then we need to move."

He just shook his head once.

"No."

Eve stepped forward with disbelief etched across her face.

"You cannot be serious."

"There's nowhere to run," Jeremy replied. "Not anymore. He has to face her."

Dante scoffed, his breath a sharp break in the room.

"So that's the plan? We just sit here and let her walk in and just hope for the best?"

Jeremy didn't blink.

His voice was dead steady.

"No. Nathan has all the power he'll ever need. It's always been in him. He just has to believe it's real."

Gabe let out a dry, humorless laugh, shaking his head. "Oh great, so the fate of our entire existence lies in the hands of the terminally terrified kid? Sweet. Sounds like a foolproof plan."

Jeremy crouched in front of Nathan.

"Listen to me, son," he said, his voice low but certain. "I know you've got a thousand questions—about why this is happening, how you ended up here, who I am. I promise, all of that is going to make sense. Soon. But right now, none of that matters."

He paused, noticing the way Nathan's breathing slowly leveled out.

"I know it's hard. I know it feels impossible. But you've made it this far, and you're still standing. I believe in you, Nathan. I always have. It's time for you to believe in yourself."

A pulse ripped through Nathan's skull.

He felt her before he heard her—before she even arrived. Her presence slithered through him. She was close enough now that her thoughts bled into his mind, slipping under his skin as her emotions tangled with what little control he still had.

She knew he was awake.

She knew he was afraid.

—And she loved it.

He could feel her closing in; the invisible thread was twisting tighter around him with every passing second.

Outside, the turbo of a WRX whined as the engine cut off—a mechanical sigh swallowed by the night. The headlights disappeared, plunging the world back into darkness. A car door creaked open, then slammed shut, cracking through the silence like a gunshot.

Eve moved to the couch and dropped beside Nathan. She didn't speak. She didn't move. She just wrapped her arms around him and held on tightly, like it was the last way she knew how to protect him.

Mia stepped behind them, placing her hands gently on Nathan's shoulders. Her touch was steady, an attempt to ground him. She didn't say a word. She just stood there, letting him feel her presence, reminding him he wasn't alone.

Dante rolled his shoulders and cracked his knuckles, like he was stepping into a fight he'd been training for his whole life. Every part of him was lit up with adrenaline. He stood and turned to face the door, ready for whatever came through it.

Footsteps broke the silence.

They started quietly at first, just soft taps against wet wood. As they drew closer, the sound deepened. The boards on the porch creaked in rhythm, not with weight, but with certainty. Whoever was coming wasn't rushing.

They knew exactly where they were going.

They knew exactly what was waiting for them inside the cabin.

And they weren't the least bit worried about any of it.

The final step landed just outside the door.

A gentle, almost polite knock followed. It landed like a whisper as it pressed through the wood, but there was nothing friendly about it. It wasn't a request. It was a formality, a warning dressed up as courtesy.

"I know you're in there, Nathan. Just let me in so we can talk about this. Everything will be okay."

Val's voice slid through the space like silk. Every syllable landed with practiced ease, shaped by someone who understood exactly how much control she could wield by saying less. It almost felt like music. It almost felt—*nice.*

But something was engineered about it. The delivery was too clean, too balanced, like it had been practiced a hundred times in front of a mirror, spoken over and over again, and refined until it sounded human, even if it wasn't.

It was meant to sound like a lifeline, but they all knew it was a trap.

"Nathan." She sang again, her voice thick with that slow, artificial warmth he'd heard before. The tone hadn't changed. It still carried that same careful melody that was meant to draw him in and pull everything else away.

Another knock, firmer this time with a steady rhythm that carried a hint of impatience, her fingers drumming lightly against the wood like a heartbeat.

"We both know that you can't hide much longer. You're tired, You need to stop fighting. Just open the door, and I promise I'll fix everything. I can make all the pain disappear. You just have to let me."

Eve stood up fast, her hand brushing Nathan's shoulder—not to hold him, but to make sure he stayed close. Her focus never left the shelves.

"That's enough. This ends now. I'm not Enhanced—she can't do anything to me."

Nathan's breathing was weak as he stood up and slowly shook his head.

"No, Eve. This is *my* fight. I have to finish it."

A series of clicks echoed through the cabin, signaling that Val was somehow bypassing all the locks to the outer door.

They heard it creak open, followed by her heels tapping on the wood floor in a rhythm that felt almost seductive. Each step rolled into the next with practiced smoothness, like she wasn't walking so much as she was *drawing them in.* The sound moved through the room with quiet authority, claiming attention without asking for it.

"Come out, come out, wherever you are," she sang. Her voice carried through the space outside, wrapping around Nathan like a melody built to pull him in. It urged him to let everything go and give himself to her.

She scanned the room as she moved in a slow, controlled circle. Her eyes passed over every corner, taking in every detail without exception.

She stopped at Jeremy's desk and let her fingers glide across the surface until they reached a notebook half-covered by a scatter of maps.

She opened it with one hand, her lips moving slightly as she read, though no sound followed.

Then she tore out a page, folded it once, and slipped it into her pocket without looking at it again.

She paused beside the bookshelf and ran her hand across the spines, like she was choosing something to keep. She knocked one over, just to hear the sound it made. Then she tilted her head again and listened, as if she could hear someone thinking.

"I know you're in here—I know *all* of you are in here," she said, dragging out the words almost like she was playing. "You don't have to be scared. None of you do."

The way she said it felt soothing, almost reassuring, like there was nothing in the world to fear. Her words slipped between his thoughts like a quiet intruder, and for a moment, he couldn't remember why he was supposed to resist.

She moved through the great room with unhurried confidence, each step placed like she already knew where everyone would be. The way she moved—how she slowed at certain turns, how her head tilted before she stepped forward—made one thing clear.

She wasn't searching. She was closing in.

Her eyes moved from the fireplace to the windows, to the empty chairs still facing the hearth. She could feel them behind the walls. She could hear the tension bleeding into the stillness of the room she was in.

Her gaze locked back on the bookshelf, and she knew.

She glided toward it, her steps unnaturally silent, as if someone had flipped a switch inside her and shut off her ability to make sound completely. She moved with a kind of rhythm that made it hard to tell if she was walking or performing.

She stopped in front of the shelves and tilted her head, listening—not for movement, but for the soft, telltale hush of breath that was being held for too long.

She didn't touch it. Not yet.

She only stood there and let the quiet pull tighter around her, as if the room itself was leaning closer to hear what she'd do next.

"You really thought this would be enough to keep me out?" she whispered, her voice soft and full of contempt.

"I can feel you back there, Nathan. There's no use hiding anymore."

She stepped closer to the shelf and reached out, her fingers trailing along the spine of a book near the center. She moved with the kind of patience that didn't wonder *if* the way in would reveal itself—only *when*.

"You're doing that thing again," she said. "You're holding your breath like it makes you invisible—It doesn't."

No one moved.

No one breathed.

"You don't have to hide anymore, Nathan. I'm right here. Just let me in."

He started to stand—his body caught between resistance and surrender.

Eve saw it first. She stepped in front of him without hesitation, planting herself between him and the door like a living barricade.

"You stay right there, Nathan Boone. Do you hear me?"

He gripped the arm of the couch like it was the only thing keeping him upright. He wobbled slightly, caught between the instinct to give in and the will to hold his ground.

Her hand moved slowly across the bookshelf as if she were searching for something specific. She pressed gently against the wood, one spot at a time. Her touch was patient and methodical—like time bent to her will, and she had all the seconds in the world to find her way in.

Mia shot a glance at Jeremy, her voice barely above a breath. "What do we do?"

He didn't answer. He just kept his eyes locked on the back of the secret door.

Then Val spoke again, her voice sinking into a velvet-soft pout, every word pulled slow and sweet like it had been soaked in syrup. Each syllable was a promise disguised as a plea—something meant to draw him out, not push him away.

"Nathan," she said, almost like a sigh. "It's so lonely out here. Please let me in. I'm sorry if I scared you. I didn't mean to. It was the reset—it scrambled everything. That wasn't me. You have to know that."

The energy inside him shifted as her voice wrapped around his thoughts like it belonged there. Before he could stop himself, his body started to move forward—not from choice, but because something inside him whispered that he was supposed to.

Dante clamped his hand on Nathan's shoulder, holding him in place.

"Not happening, Boone," he said, his voice firm. "You're not going anywhere."

Nathan's head snapped toward him, his eyes unfocused, as if the world hadn't finished coming back into view.

Dante didn't flinch. "She's just trying to find her way back into your head, man. I can feel it too. Don't let her in. You need to fight."

Her voice slipped through the cracks in his mind again. Only it was softer now, shaped into something he wanted to believe.

Who are you going to trust, Nathan?

The question moved through him slowly. It wasn't a challenge—It was an invitation.

Dante Edwards? The person who broke you for years? The guy who made you afraid to breathe, afraid to speak, afraid to be you? Or me, the only one who sees all of you and doesn't look away.

Her voice leaned in harder.

I know everything he ever did to you. I know how it stayed with you. You don't have to hold onto it anymore. Just let me in. Let me take it from you. Let me show you what it feels like to stop having to pretend that you're fine.

A sharp pain stabbed through his temple. It twisted his vision, sending the room tilting as her presence clawed deeper.

"She's pushing harder," he rasped.

Jeremy's voice cut through like a warning shot. "It's time to end this."

Eve spun toward him as panic pressed into her chest.

"How?" Her voice cracked. "Just tell me what to do! I'll do anything!"

Jeremy lifted a hand—not to silence her, but to hold the moment still between them, just long enough to keep her grounded.

Then he turned to Wu.

"Do you have your glyph?"

Wu's hand was already in his pocket. He pulled out the device and placed it in Jeremy's outstretched palm before stepping back.

Jeremy turned to Nathan. "We need to snap her hold on you—just for a second. That's all you'll need. Just one breath. One chance to take everything back."

Nathan shook his head. "I don't know how to stand up to her. I don't think I can."

Jeremy didn't flinch. He stepped forward and pressed the glyph to Nathan's temple.

The second it touched his skin, a jolt surged through Nathan's skull that sent fire through his nerves. His vision shattered, bursting into a cascade of light and static, his body seized by something beyond pain, beyond control.

And then—

Val screamed.

Not from outside. Not from the other room. The sound came from inside *him*. It twisted through his mind, shrieking as if something vital was being ripped from him.

He clutched his head with both hands as he doubled over, struggling to adjust to the intensity that was crashing through him.

Jeremy's voice cut through the chaos. "Open the door!"

"What? No!" Mia's voice cracked with panic as her hands tightened on Nathan's shoulder, trying to hold him back.

"Do it!" Jeremy barked.

Dante locked his arms around Nathan's torso, muscles straining as he fought to keep him upright.

"He's not ready!"

Nathan bucked against him, caught in the split between the voice screaming in his head and the magnetic pull dragging him toward the door. He wasn't moving on his own. Something was moving *through* him.

"As soon as she steps inside, let him go," Jeremy commanded.

Nathan staggered as the last of her hold snapped. The pull was gone. The noise was gone.

He straightened, shoulders squaring as he braced himself. For the first time since waking up, his mind was clear.

Dante kept a hand on his back.

"Are you good, man?"

"Yeah," Nathan said. "I'm alright."

Dante didn't let go.

"You sure?"

Nathan nodded once.

"Yeah, man, I'm sure."

Dante met his eyes.

"Alright. I'm right here with you." He leaned in, voice low. "I'm not gonna let her touch you."

Jeremy gave the call with authority. "Let her in."

Gabe stepped into position and searched for the hidden handle cut into the side of the bookcase. He shifted forward and settled into the kind of stance that didn't come from training—it came from every bad idea that had ever worked. It was the kind that said: *You don't want to mess with Killer Kowalski.*

Just as he started to pull it open, the door exploded inward, like the house had been hit by a wrecking ball made of dynamite.

The blast threw him across the room and slammed him into the far wall with a brutal crash, before dropping him in a heap on the floor. His limbs folded under him as the air ripped from his chest before he could even scream. He gasped and clutched his side, like his body had to remember how to breathe as he fought to drag air back into his lungs.

Without a second thought, Eve rushed to him, dropping to her knees and cradling his head against her chest, her hands frantic as she pulled him close.

"Please, Gabe. Get up."

He groaned and blinked his eyes open. His limbs felt wrong, like they didn't fully belong to him.

"What the hell was that?"

His fingers scraped at the floor, desperate for something solid.

Then, through the smoke and over the wreckage, Val stepped inside like the space had always belonged to her.

Her movements were smooth. Every step she took was calculated and calm. She still carried that same air of control that she always did.

But something had changed.

There was heat behind her eyes now. It wasn't chaotic or frenzied. It was focused and controlled in a way that made her seem more dangerous. The rage she carried wasn't wild; it had been sharpened into a weapon, tempered into something precise and lethal.

She stepped into the room with fierce control. Her eyes moved over every face, like she already knew what each of them would do next.

Her lips parted, and a quiet sound slipped out—not a word, not a command, but a low hiss. She let it slide through the air like a quiet warning that told them all that the storm had officially arrived.

Mia crouched behind the couch, her hands gripping the leather as if it might hold her together. She couldn't breathe. She couldn't blink. She just kept her eyes on Val, unable to process what she was seeing.

Dante froze. He'd seen violence before. He knew what desperation looked like. But Val was something else. She was powerful in a way that felt more dangerous than anything he'd ever faced.

He knew it the moment he saw her that first day in West Hall. He thought she was intense, calculated, maybe even a little unhinged—but he never imagined it would ever come to this.

And now, staring at her in front of him the way she was, he didn't know how to stop it, but he knew that he needed to try.

He tightened his fists and tried to steady his breathing. Every instinct he had fired at once, screaming at him to move. This was his moment—the one where he would finally make up for every awful thing he had ever done, not just to Nathan, but to everyone.

He didn't wait for a signal. He just stepped forward and squared his stance, like he was standing on a field instead of the cabin floor. He filled his lungs the way he had before every snap—right before the handoff, right before he lowered his shoulder and drove straight into the line.

"Showtime," he said under his breath, as if he wasn't trying to convince himself that there was only one way this would go—and it wasn't going to be good.

Then he charged.

Val barely acknowledged him. With a single flick of her wrist, an unseen force slammed into his chest, sending him flying backward. His body crashed into a bookcase, the wooden shelves cracking under the impact before he crumpled to the floor.

She turned her focus back on Nathan, like she'd just squashed a bug with her overpriced Louboutins—and cared more about the mess on her sole than the damage she'd done to one of her pet projects.

"Oh, my sweet Nathan. When will you just let go?"

His name left her lips like a soft, affectionate sigh.

Eve tensed, kneeling beside Gabe, her hands trembling as she cradled him. Her voice broke as she turned to Jeremy with desperation threading through every word.

"Please, do something. You can't just stand there!"

Jeremy remained still. "Just let it happen," he said, his voice steady. "Nathan has this, I know he does."

Every instinct inside Nathan was screaming at him to run, but there was nowhere to run to. There was nowhere to hide.

"Nathan," she purred as she approached, her voice dipped in honey.

"You need to let go. You need to stop fighting it."

He stood rigid as the pull inside him twisted tighter. The invisible threads were no longer just wrapping around his mind. They were controlling his muscles, urging him forward like a tide trying to drag him out to sea.

She strolled over to him. Her hips swayed with quiet purpose. His body locked into place as she approached, stopping close enough that they were nearly eye to eye.

Her fingers drifted flirtatiously down his arm, like she was still trying to decide if he was worth keeping.

"This really is unnecessary, Nathan," she whispered. "All this running. All this hiding—It doesn't need to be like this."

She was close—too close. Her presence filled the air and pressed down on him, tightening around every ounce of his being.

"Stop fighting it, Nathan," she whispered, her voice weaving through the air like silk.

"Just let go. You don't have to be afraid. Not anymore."

Fear had buried itself in him, tangled with every doubt he'd ever carried.

His whole life, he'd wished he could just shake it off, but he never could. He always dreamed of a moment when he didn't have to feel small, fragile, and broken.

But now the weight of what was possible pressed in on him—the power he could hold, the change that was within reach. It wrapped around him, thick and intoxicating, like an offer he wasn't sure he could turn down.

Seeing the shift in Nathan's face, Jeremy moved toward him quietly, his eyes never leaving Val.

Nathan barely noticed. His world was shrinking. Val had a hold on his mind, and her pull was stronger than ever. He could feel her burning behind his eyes, digging into his chest. He knew what she was doing. She was trying to take control of him completely.

Jeremy stepped in behind him and gripped his shoulders.

"Listen to me," he said. His eyes stayed locked on her, but she barely acknowledged he existed. "You're not weak, Nathan. You're not broken. You never were."

Val's lips parted as her body shifted forward, her presence stretching toward Nathan, but Jeremy didn't let up. She shot him a fleeting glance, barely sparing him a second, as if his presence were nothing more than background noise interrupting a song she actually wanted to hear.

Nathan inhaled sharply as the tether between them began to unravel. The invisible grip that had bound him to her was weakening with every second.

Jeremy kept his focus on Nathan.

"You feel that?" he asked, his voice steady, pushing him to hold on to it.

Nathan gave the smallest nod, his body still trembling from the weight of it.

Jeremy exhaled, his hands firm on Nathan's shoulders.

"Good. Now fight."

For a second, doubt crept in.

But he moved anyway.

He forced his legs to shift, slow at first, like every step had to push through everything that had ever held him back.

He turned to face Val, who had already started to smile, like she was still in control.

Then, just for a second, her expression faltered.

"Nathan—don't."

Her voice was no longer a command. Her body began to tremble with a faint, involuntary shake that started in her fingertips and moved quickly through her core. It was as if something inside her was breaking apart, something she could no longer hold together.

When Nathan saw it, that was all he needed.

He took a step forward. Then another, causing her to step back.

His voice was calm, but there was no mercy in it.

"No more, Val. It's time for me to end this story."

The shift was sudden. Her body started to violently reject what was happening to her. For the first time, the confidence in her expression vanished. The perfect image she had so carefully constructed was evaporating.

In the space of a breath, she completely unraveled.

One moment, she was Val—the flawless and untouchable goddess, whose powerful perfection held the world in place like gravity wrapped in leather.

Next, the elegance she always wore like armor faded, peeling away in rough, uneven patches. The sharp lines of her face softened, and her smooth olive skin turned to a pale, blotchy, and sickly tone that drained the life from her features. The glow that had once made her seem untouchable was gone, leaving her exposed in a way that made it hard to look at her.

Her dark eyes, once full of control, shifted, like she couldn't hold on to who she was anymore. Whatever light had been there was fading fast, and struggling to stay alive.

The presence that had once filled the room in the heaviest and most suffocating ways had slipped away.

What was left was smaller, weaker, and desperate in a way none of them had ever seen before.

She stood before them, not as the force that had once dominated every room she walked into, but as something stripped bare. No enhancements. No perfection. No cold detachment.

Just a girl, trembling under the weight of her fears.

She wasn't some untouchable entity anymore. She was just a person who had built herself into what she thought was perfection, only to watch it all fall apart.

Her head dropped suddenly like her neck couldn't hold the weight anymore. Her shoulders twitched and spasmed, each one pulling at odds with the other. Her arms pressed tight to her ribs as her knees buckled beneath her. She was losing her fight to stay who she made herself into with every second.

"No," she breathed, shaking her head. "Please—don't—Nathan, stop. I'm scared." Her voice cracked, splintering between the remnants of command and the rawness of desperation.

Nathan stood firm, his breath steady now, his eyes locked onto her as she unraveled before him.

He had spent his whole life drowning in fear, questioning his strength, his worth, his place in the world, but not now.

Now, he knew.

Now, he understood.

This was his moment.

He was not weak.

He was not broken. And he would not be controlled. Not by anyone— ever again.

He reached out—not with his hands, not with force, but with certainty —and severed the last of the thread that tied her to him.

She gasped, and her body jerked violently as a strangled cry escaped her lips.

"Nathan! It could have been perfect!" Her voice wavered, breaking apart like her crumbling form.

"It still can! Nathan, please—stop!" she begged.

Jeremy's voice cut through the charged air.

"Now, Nathan! Do it now! Take it all out on her. Every bit of it. Let her have it."

Something inside Nathan cracked open.

He reached into the core of everything he had ever felt—every moment of anxiety, every fear that had gnawed at him since childhood, every doubt that had whispered he wasn't enough.

He let it rise. Let it build into something massive, something unstoppable.

And then—he unleashed it all onto her.

"No! Please!" she cried, panic fully spilling out of her. "It wasn't supposed to be this way!"

She struggled for breath as her body convulsed.

"Please, Nathan, stop. It hurts too much."

Her hands clawed at her arms until her fingers dug in hard enough to leave marks. She scratched without control and dragged raw lines across her skin.

"No—no, please! Stop! I can fix this! I can still make it right!"

Her voice cracked as the words broke apart, twisting into something guttural, something more animal than human. A scream ripped from her throat as the shift tore through her completely.

Nathan didn't hold back. He stepped forward into the blinding light that had started to consume her.

Every step he took closer sent a tremor through her failing form. Her body buckled as it struggled to hold onto the perfection she once effortlessly commanded.

Everything was breaking. The mask was gone. The truth she had buried deep was ripping its way through her, tearing her apart from the inside out.

Another violent shift.

Her scream echoed through the cabin, shaking the walls like thunder. Her body jerked and twisted in unnatural ways, like something inside her was giving up and unraveling at the seams.

The war between who she truly was and who she had pretended to be was coming to a brutal end, and there was no turning back.

She gasped as one last breath, like it was being ripped directly from her soul.

Her form collapsed inward, then exploded in a burst of searing light.

The air trembled. The room warped and bent, struggling to contain what was happening.

Her last sound was a shriek that wasn't fully human and wasn't fully machine either. It carried the sound of everything coming undone—of biology and technology being ripped apart at once. It tore through the room like a static-filled scream, and then vanished into the quiet.

In a final, dramatic act—true to Val's style—a bright light flared where she had just stood, and her form collapsed like a dying star.

A final pulse of energy surged outward, bending the air around it, then vanished.

She didn't fall.

She didn't crumble.

She simply ceased to exist.

Nathan had used his mind to will her out—not just from his thoughts, but from the world itself.

He had severed the last thread between them and cast Val into nothingness, along with all the bad memories he refused to carry anymore—

For the first time in his life, Nathan felt like he could breathe.

He couldn't believe it was all over.

Eve, still huddled on the floor beside Gabe, let out a breath she hadn't realized she was holding.

She wrapped her arms tightly around herself, like she was trying to keep from floating away.

"It's over," she whispered, her voice barely more than a breath. "It's really over."

Mia, still crouching behind the couch, looked around the room. When she realized that Val was truly gone, she let out a shaky breath and pushed herself to her feet. She moved straight to Nathan and wrapped him in a tight hug, like she could shield him from everything that had just happened.

"Thank God you're okay," she whispered, her voice thick with relief. She held him tight, like she didn't care who saw, like letting go wasn't an option. In that moment, she didn't have to say anything else. She just knew, and so did he.

Gabe groaned as he tried to sit up, one hand bracing against the floor like the ground might still be moving.

"Holy shit," he muttered. "Did all that really just happen?"

He looked down, saw his shredded shirt, and the kilt that was barely hanging on—despite its best efforts to betray who was wearing it.

"Well," he muttered, dragging in a breath, "remind me to never fight a digital witch queen in a kilt again."

Across the room, Wu hauled Dante upright with a grunt.

Dante winced and pressed a hand to his ribs.

"Yeah," he said. "It all totally happened."

He groaned again, lower this time. "Pretty sure I'm on the injured list for a while."

Wu nodded. "Don't worry, I've got you."

He stepped in without another word, slipping under Dante's arm and taking his weight across his shoulders.

Jeremy stood beside Nathan and placed a hand on him.

"You did it, son. It's over. I'm proud of you."

For the first time in his entire life, Nathan Boone was truly free. Not the kind of freedom that came from running or hiding, but the kind that came from standing tall, staring your worst fears in the eye, and being ready to face whatever came next.

And in that moment, he realized that he was no longer just Nathan Boone—he had become who he was always meant to be."

47

BECOMING BOONE

The old movie theater beneath Winston Hall had never looked so good.

The last time they had been down there, Nathan was convinced that he was going to die. Fear was all he had ever known. But now, for the first time in his life, he was relaxed—and he was happy.

The place felt alive. With everyone's help, Gabe had dragged in mismatched chairs from dorm lounges, strung lights across the crumbling balcony, and set up a makeshift concession stand stocked with snacks that he had pulled from his no-longer-secret stash. It seemed like half the campus had turned out for the show.

"I can't believe he's doing this," Mia whispered as they sat a few rows from the top of the theater. She nudged his knee lightly with hers. "I mean, this place looks great and all, but I'm always so worried that the roof will cave in."

Nathan gave a soft laugh. "Winston Hall will survive anything. Some buildings just weren't made to let go."

He wasn't sure what made him say it that way—only that it felt true, like the kind of thing you'd whisper in a place that had outlived its history.

He felt her eyes on him before he turned to look. He couldn't see her face in the low light, but he knew how she was looking at him—like she had ever since the night in the cabin, like she already knew what he was thinking before he did. That night—the one everyone in the group was now calling "The Digital Witch Trial"—had changed everything.

Since then, their time together had been filled with quiet moments, stolen glances, and a presence that never asked for attention.

"I'm glad you asked me to come with you to this," she said softly.

"Well, I'm glad you said yes," he replied as he turned to look at her.

The moment had already settled between them. He didn't have to say it out loud to know she felt it too.

This wasn't about comedy night—it was about everything that had come before. About what happened in that cabin. About how, after everything, the world had somehow, inexplicably, kept spinning.

There was no news story. No campus buzz. No suspicious rumblings in the caf over sushi night.

Val had been an undeniable force on campus, and yet her absence barely left a ripple. If anything, the silence made it worse. It made him feel like he had imagined all of it—like maybe she hadn't existed at all.

He could still feel the ghost of her inside him—the pull that wasn't there anymore, the space where something used to be.

And yet, after facing fear itself—standing at the edge of his mind—he had finally realized something. He had always believed that if he ever got a MIND chip, all his problems would be solved. He thought that having an implant would somehow save him. But the chip wasn't the solution he needed. He now knew that he never needed technology to fix something in him that had never really been broken in the first place.

What he needed was the confidence to stare down what scared him most—his insecurities, his doubts, the worst parts of himself—and meet them head-on. Once he did that, he was finally able to become the strong person who had been buried inside him all along.

As Mia rested her hand on his knee, he felt something he had never had before—certainty. She wasn't just grounding him; she was part of him now, woven into his life in a way that felt natural. He had spent years believing he needed a piece of technology implanted in his head to feel okay. But now that he had one, he knew—it had never been the chip that he truly needed.

What he needed was his people. The ones who had fought for him. The ones who had stayed. The ones who had pulled him back when he'd been seconds from slipping away.

And somehow, in the place he never wanted to go—college, he had found them.

She took her hand from his knee and locked her fingers with his, giving them a soft squeeze.

"You good?" She asked softly.

He looked at her and, for the first time, he didn't have to second-guess the answer. The fear, the uncertainty, the need to cling to something outside himself—it was gone.

"Yeah," he said. "I'm good—I really am."

Before she could say anything else, the theater dimmed and the crowd fell quiet. The makeshift stage lights—just old dorm room lamps that were held together with duct tape and hope—hung low over the stage and flickered to life as Gabe stepped into view.

He wasn't wearing anything ridiculous. No oversized Hawaiian shirt. No baggy cargo shorts. He had ditched the fat-guy gimmick and stepped onto the stage as his true self, wearing only a pair of faded jeans, a vintage t-shirt, and a pile of nerves.

"So apparently, if you ask to borrow a creepy underground theater with no ventilation and suspicious stains on the walls, people assume you're either filming an A24 horror movie or starting a cult. And honestly? Like... a really weird cult. Probably one where we worship discontinued sodas and meet weekly to rank our trauma. I'm not gonna lie—I think we're dangerously close to doing both."

A laugh rippled through the room.

"I mean, seriously, folks, let's be real—this is kind of terrifying. You're all down there, judging me, and I'm up here just praying no one throws a tomato at me. Let 'em rip now if you got 'em. Just save a few for the caf—we need 'em for pizza night."

He adjusted the mic with a dramatic sigh.

"I know, I know—I look like I was genetically engineered in a lab for the obnoxiously handsome. It's a burden. People think I roll out of bed, wink at myself in the mirror, and immediately get cast as the lead in the next big Netflix rom-com. I wish! You know how hard it is to live up to this face? I've been disappointing people with my personality for years."

He paused, flashing a crooked smile.

"But enough about my face—let's get honest with each other. You ready?"

He shot a quick nod at Nathan with a flash of gratitude.

Nathan smiled back, giving a look of approval that said it all.

As the crowd leaned in, Gabe found his groove. He riffed about how the caf's so-called chicken had to be some kind of science experiment gone wrong—because real poultry shouldn't bounce when you drop it. Then he moved on to how Professor Graham assigned extra essays based on vibes alone. One wrong answer, and suddenly you owed him a ten-page thesis on why you were unprepared for life.

The crowd loved him.

And Nathan felt something ease in his chest.

Because Gabe wasn't trying to be anyone but himself. He wasn't forcing the punchlines. He wasn't hiding behind recycled jokes that made him a copy of a copy. He was just him, and it was working.

Eve slipped into the seat beside Nathan, leaning in close so only he and Mia could hear.

"He's killing it," she whispered, offering Mia a soft, almost sheepish smile.

"He was so stressed about this show all week. He made me watch his act every night. I kept telling him he was good, but you know how he is. Seriously—this is some of his best stuff."

She leaned toward Nathan. "That mystery meat bit you wrote for him?" She nodded once, her voice steady. "That was pure gold. He totally nailed it."

"I wasn't sure he'd use that bit," Nathan said.

Mia gave his hand a soft squeeze. "I'm really happy you gave him something that you wrote. That's kind of a big deal for you. How does it feel?"

He looked over at her, more confident than shy. "It feels great. And I think it worked, didn't it?"

She smiled. "It really did."

For a second, they just sat there, watching Gabe work the room like it was the easiest thing in the world.

Nathan nudged Eve's shoulder, catching her watching him with that thoughtful look. "I'm glad you worked it out," he said, his voice quieter now, steady. "With Gabe, I mean. You two are kind of perfect for each other."

Eve held his stare for a moment before exhaling. Her shoulders dropped, like she was finally letting go of something she'd been holding too tight for way too long.

"Yeah," she said softly. "Me too."

She turned toward the stage again, her focus back on Gabe. "I know the big guy's still in there somewhere," she said. "Don't worry. I'll have him fattened back up in no time."

Nathan chuckled, settling deeper into his seat. For the first time in his life, everything was exactly where it should be.

Gabe wrapped up his set to a full standing ovation, the crowd erupting with applause as students rose from their seats, cheering like they'd just witnessed a legend in the making.

As he stepped off the stage, Eve was the first to meet him.

She smacked his shoulder lightly. "Not bad, big guy."

Gabe blinked. "Yeah? You really think so? I don't know, it felt kind of—off."

Eve sighed, shaking her head. "Yeah, I really do." She stepped onto her tiptoes and pressed a soft kiss to his lips.

"You were yourself. I could see it, and so could everyone else. You were really great."

They stood there for a second, her hand still resting lightly on his chest, like she wasn't quite ready to let go. Then she nudged him playfully as they all started walking toward the back of the theater.

"You know," she said, her voice quieter now, "I was so sure the chip turned people into soulless robots."

Gabe raised a brow, the corners of his mouth tugging up. "And now?"

Eve smiled at him sweetly. "Now I'm pretty sure you were a weirdo way before any implant."

He laughed, the sound easy, but then she caught his hand and held it, giving his fingers a squeeze that said everything she wasn't quite ready to put into words.

"Seriously, I was wrong about all of you," she said simply, looking back at Mia.

Gabe's smile softened as he squeezed her hand back. "Yeah, you were—but we won't hold it against you." He winked.

"You're such a jerk," Eve replied, rolling her eyes. "But lucky for you, I have a soft spot for jerks." She tugged him down for another kiss—this one slower.

Nathan watched the exchange carefully. He knew the weight of it—what had come before.

After everything that happened at the cabin, once the dust settled and they were all safe, Eve had unloaded on Gabe. For hours, she had screamed at him—about his choices, about having a chip, about every fear she had buried so deep she couldn't tell where her own beliefs ended and her anxieties began.

And, Gabe just stood there—and took it—all of it. He took every sharp word, every accusation, every unfiltered emotion she hurled at him.

And when it was all over—after the yelling and the tears and the silence that followed—long after anyone else would've had enough and walked away, he stayed.

That was when she had finally seen him. Not the MIND chip. Not the enhancements. Not the thing she had been fighting against for so long.

Just him. Just Gabe.

And in that moment, she realized something.

His eyes? They had never changed.

They were the same as they had always been—and she was okay with that.

The crowd slowly filed out, voices trailing behind them in bursts of laughter and leftover conversation.

A few people swarmed Gabe near the back of the theater. Some clapped him on the back. Others shouted praise, already repeating their favorite lines from his set.

Mia stayed close to Nathan, her arm linked naturally into his as they exchanged quiet smiles.

Dante approached with his hands in his pockets, his face hard to read, but the tension that used to live between them wasn't there anymore. He stopped in front of Nathan and held out a hand, then pulled him into a quick, one-armed hug.

"Hey, Boone," he said, stepping back. "We're heading over to Chubbie's as soon as Killer's done getting swarmed by his fan club. You coming with?"

The way he said it—*Boone*—there was no taunt, no tease. Just Boone.

Mia spoke up. "Well, we did have plans to go to the library, remember?" She looked over at Nathan, her eyes steady. "Don't you have to submit your final draft to Simmons before tomorrow?"

Nathan nodded. "Yeah, I do. It's done, though. I can submit it first thing in the morning. Whatever happens, happens."

No matter what life had in store for him next—the unknown—he was okay with it.

The future didn't make him nervous anymore. He wasn't afraid of the what-ifs.

He had accepted that uncertainty was part of living. And that was who he was now.

He wasn't the anxious kid who couldn't handle his own life.

He had people—ones who didn't judge him for his flaws but loved him because of them.

And for the first time, he didn't feel like he had to be more than that.

Nathan Boone had become who he was always meant to be—himself.

And somewhere, someone was watching over him.

Still trying to figure out how to get it right.

To my favorites—

Casey and Lauren, forever my two leading ladies. Thank you for helping me build enough confidence to put my voice into the world, and for listening to me talk about my ideas ad nauseam. Hopefully, this time wasn't as bad as the last. I love you both tremendously.

Natalie, I am as much a fan of you as you are of my stories. I can't wait to see the story you will tell. Thank you for reading.

Chad, you truly are one of the greats. Thank you for always being in my corner—and for being there when liftoff doesn't go as planned.

Kensworth and Dincy, it's rare to make such great friends at this stage in life—never mind ones who support my weirdness so well. Thank you both for reading, for showing up, and for being the kind of people who make it easier to be myself.

Chris Regan, you have no idea how helpful that one hang was at the two-minute warning before final edits went in. Your artist's perspective helped me push myself over the finish line.

And to my Editor-in-Law, Heather—thank you. You helped me cross every T, dot every I, and remove those nonsense question marks. Thank you for giving my stories the polish they deserve.

Finally, to everyone who has ever taken the time to read my work— Whether you've been with me from the start or found your way here unexpectedly, your time, attention, and willingness to dive into my words mean more than I can ever fully express. Every page you've turned, every sentence you've sat with, has helped make this real. For a guy who clearly likes to use words, your support has left me with none. So instead, I'll leave you with the only two that matter:

Thank You.

Copyright © 2025 by Andy LaPlante

All rights reserved.